Warwickshire County Council

Ken 12/22		
LIC 10/23		

DISCARDED

This item is to be returned or renewed before the latest date above. It may be borrowed for a further period if not in demand. **To renew your books:**

- **Phone the 24/7 Renewal Line 01926 499273 or**
- **Visit www.warwickshire.gov.uk/libraries**

  Discover ● Imagine

D1470901

014458123 7

Also by Louisa George

The Princess's Christmas Baby
Nurse's One-Night Baby Surprise
ER Doc to Mistletoe Bride
Cornish Reunion with the Heart Doctor

Also by Amy Ruttan

Falling for His Runaway Nurse
The Doctor She Should Resist

Caribbean Island Hospital miniseries

Reunited with Her Surgeon Boss
A Ring for His Pregnant Midwife

Discover more at millsandboon.co.uk.

RESISTING THE SINGLE DAD NEXT DOOR

LOUISA GEORGE

PARAMEDIC'S ONE-NIGHT BABY BOMBSHELL

AMY RUTTAN

MILLS & BOON

All rights reserved including the right of reproduction
in whole or in part in any form. This edition is published
by arrangement with Harlequin Enterprises ULC.

This is a work of fiction. Names, characters, places, locations
and incidents are purely fictional and bear no relationship to
any real life individuals, living or dead, or to any actual places,
business establishments, locations, events or incidents.
Any resemblance is entirely coincidental.

This book is sold subject to the condition that it
shall not, by way of trade or otherwise, be lent, resold, hired out
or otherwise circulated without the prior consent of the publisher
in any form of binding or cover other than that in which it is published
and without a similar condition including this condition
being imposed on the subsequent purchaser.

® and TM are trademarks owned and used by the trademark owner
and/or its licensee. Trademarks marked with ® are registered with the
United Kingdom Patent Office and/or the Office for Harmonisation
in the Internal Market and in other countries.

First published in Great Britain 2022
by Mills & Boon, an imprint of HarperCollins*Publishers* Ltd,
1 London Bridge Street, London, SE1 9GF

www.harpercollins.co.uk

HarperCollins*Publishers*
1st Floor, Watermarque Building,
Ringsend Road, Dublin 4, Ireland

Resisting the Single Dad Next Door © 2022 Louisa George

Paramedic's One-Night Baby Bombshell © 2022 Amy Ruttan

ISBN: 978-0-263-30145-8

11/22

MIX
Paper | Supporting
responsible forestry
FSC™ C007454

This book is produced from independently certified FSC™ paper
to ensure responsible forest management.
For more information visit: www.harpercollins.co.uk/green.

Printed and Bound in Spain using 100% Renewable Electricity
at CPI Black Print, Barcelona

RESISTING THE SINGLE DAD NEXT DOOR

LOUISA GEORGE

MILLS & BOON

CHAPTER ONE

TAP. TAP. TAP.

Owen Cooper opened an eye. Someone was tapping out a Morse code message in his bedroom.

Or was it a dream?

Tap. Tap. Tap-tap-tap.

He opened the other eye. A faint orange light from the rising sun partially lit the room, leaving corners still shrouded in darkness.

Dawn. Great. Add curtains to the shopping list.

Tap. Tap.

Not a dream.

Someone or something was in here with him. 'Mason?' he whispered. 'Mason, it's still night time. Go back to bed.'

Tap. Tap. Tap.

Not his son Mason—a dream. Which was a surprise, given he'd barely had any sleep.

The ferry had been late docking last night and there'd been no welcoming party for them on Rāwhiti Island's main pier. But he'd found an old, battered, red Jeep-style four-wheel drive at the end of the deserted pier with an envelope with his name on it stuck to the windscreen. It had contained an apology from the practice nurse, saying that they'd been busy, so hadn't been able to meet them, a set of keys and a hand-drawn map to his new house.

'New' meaning 'acquired for the first time', rather than

'recently built and unused'. Because this little house was well used—so used, in fact, that it needed bowling and completely rebuilding. And so not what he'd been led to expect when the island doctor job had been advertised as coming with accommodation.

There'd been no mention of Morse code messaging from his bedroom either.

He turned over, releasing a cloud of dust, and came face to face with two beady red eyes staring at him and a long grey beak.

He shot up and waved his hand. 'Hey! Get out!'

There was a flurry of feathers and a loud squawk. He managed to get a glimpse of caramel-brown feathers, something around the size of a hen, before it disappeared into the corridor.

A weka. One of New Zealand's flightless but feisty native birds. How the hell had that managed to get in? He lay back down on the old iron bed again, releasing another puff of dust, and mentally ran through his to-do list.

Secure the doors.

Clean the house.

Air his bed. Get a new bed.

Bird-proof his bedroom.

Reconsider his choices all over again, *ad infinitum*.

Had coming to this island twenty-two kilometres off the Auckland coast been a mistake? Uprooting his boy from everything familiar just so Owen could be the father he should have been all along? Everything familiar in the guise of Mason's mother had already left them and, he had to admit, left *him* floundering somewhat.

It was time to step up. It was long overdue.

But first…more sleep. He closed his eyes.

'Daddy?'

Okay, maybe not more sleep. He imbued his voice with a cheer he did not feel. 'Mason! Good morning.'

'Want Mummy.'

Owen's gut clenched like a tight fist. 'I know you do, buddy. How about we try to talk to her later on my tablet?' If she could fit her son into her busy schedule.

Mason's bottom lip wobbled and he nodded, blinking back tears. It sucked, just how brave his four-year-old was trying to be. 'There's a good boy. How did you sleep?'

His son scrambled up onto the bed and put his cheek against Owen's. 'The bed's all lumpy.'

He looked at his son in navy and white stripy pyjamas and his heart squeezed. 'I know, kid. I'm sorry. Mine is too. But it's only for a little while until your racing car bed arrives on the big boat. Did you see the weka?'

Mason's eyes grew huge as he nodded. 'He's my friend.'

The poor kid's world had been ripped apart by divorcing parents and a mother who'd decided she'd had enough of parenting, and generally being adult, and had left them so she could forge an acting career in the States. And now he was finding friends in the local fauna. Was that a sign of emotional damage, or resilience and resourcefulness? 'He's a bit skitty for a friend. When you start kindy on Monday, there'll be loads of other children to play with.'

A nod. 'Can we go fishing now?'

'Later. We've got so many jobs to do first.'

There came a pout reminiscent of his mother's dramatic talent. 'Fishing first? Please.'

'No, Mason. We've got too much to do.'

The pout hardened into a sulk. 'You said fishing.'

He had. Last night, as they'd hauled their suitcases across the dirt from car to house, they'd passed a little tinny boat moored off the end of the property's jetty and Owen had promised Mason that fishing would be high on the agenda of their *Boy's Own* adventures.

What was the harm if they ignored all the chores and started the adventures ASAP? There was no one to tell him not to. No one they had to report progress to. No one else to take into account. It was just Mason, him and two whole days before the job started.

He could either clean the house now or later. The dust wasn't going anywhere. So why not spend some time with his boy before diving into chores?

The harm was that it had been fifteen years since he'd taken a boat out onto the water and he wasn't prepared. But, after a bit of detective work, he found some dusty fishing rods propped up in the shed. And, luckily, the newest things provided in his accommodation were life jackets in assorted adult's and children's sizes hanging up in the porch.

After securing one on himself and one on his son, he gathered up the ancient fishing rods and lures and then pushed the little four-and-a-half-metre aluminium boat out into the calm water and they hopped in. There was even petrol in the outboard motor. 'Hey, we're in business, Mason! Whoever lived here before us clearly paid far more attention to boating than the living quarters.'

Having cranked up the motor, he steered the tin boat out from their cove and turned right. There was probably a proper name for the direction they were heading in, but he couldn't remember. From this vantage point, he could see the contours of the island stretching out ahead and above. Undulating hills were covered in dense, natural bush of kanuka, manuka, beech trees and assorted ferns. He pointed out tui birds and fantails. 'The Te Reo Maori name for those little fantails is *piwakawaka*.'

'Piwaka…?' His mini-me echoed and grinned.

'Almost. Good effort.' Owen looked at the bush and sighed, hoping he'd made the right decision to come here. It was a far cry from their modern suburban house on the edge of the city and close to the motorway.

Here, housing was sparse, but a range of old villas, crumbling holiday homes and new architecturally sophisticated buildings dotted the hillsides, each with its own private path down to the golden beaches and coves. Numerous jetties jutted out into the calm turquoise water.

Owen tried to remember the things his grandfather had taught him about fishing, quieted the engine, attached the lures to the line and cast them into the sea. But soon all fishing was forgotten as Owen made out shapes scudding through the water towards them.

'See the dolphins, Mason? Look!' He lifted the boy onto his lap and pointed to the silvery shapes jumping out of the water. 'Wow. Look at that. They're doing acrobatics.'

Mason's hesitant smile grew as he watched the beautiful creatures splash ahead of them, tumbling and turning. Then his boy started to laugh, a full, gurgling, belly laugh that Owen couldn't remember having heard for a very long time. He took a huge, deep breath and let it out slowly. Okay, so despite the early-morning bird alarm clock, the fact his accommodation was falling apart and that his son still wasn't convinced he was going to survive without his mama, moving here had been a good decision after all.

The dolphins swam faster and faster ahead of them, and Owen quickly pulled in the fishing lines, cranked up the outboard motor and followed them, struggling to juggle the steering, but managing his son's safety and laughing along for the first time in far too long.

Over on shore he saw a woman in a cove frantically waving her arms at him. He waved back, then realised she was beckoning to him, so he slowed the boat down and steered towards the property's little jetty.

As he closed in, he could see she was around medium height. Young…at least, a few years younger than his thirty-two, maybe. He wasn't the best judge of women's ages these days. Or women in general, it seemed, given his failed marriage.

She was wearing a zipped-up navy wetsuit top and short black shorts. Bare feet. Tanned. Bloody great legs. Strawberry-blonde hair scraped back into a tight ponytail. Behind her and nestled into the bush was a small collection of wooden buildings, and to her right was a large playground complete with swings and slides. To her left, a huge boat shed housed a lot of bright orange kayaks and little Optimist boats and, maybe a hundred feet beyond the boat shed, was a cute cream-coloured cottage that looked in a lot better repair than his.

Attached to the small jetty he noticed a sign.

Camp Rāwhiti
Outdoor education specialists
For Sale

Ah, he'd been told in his interview that part of his remit would be to offer medical advice and assistance to a school camp place. Maybe this was it. Or wouldn't be for much longer, given it was for sale. He cut the engine and moored the boat onto a cleat.

Then he tried to find his best smile for the scowling woman in front of him.

Carly Edwards was sick of the careless weekend island visitors' total disregard for safety and serenity. But she was surprised the man in the boat, who seemed older than she'd first assumed—mid-thirties—had a small child with him. Certainly, he should have been setting a better example.

When he stepped off his little boat, she dashed over to the jetty and couldn't help railing at him. 'Just exactly what the hell do you think you're doing? Can't you see there are children here?'

He frowned as he looked over at her stand-up paddle-board class in the shallow water. 'I wasn't anywhere near them.'

'Not yet, but I had no way of knowing if you had control of your vessel. And you were going far too quickly.'

'I can assure you, I wasn't.' Dark eyes glittered in anger. 'I was in full control.'

'The wash is enough to make them feel seasick. We're on island time here. Slow down.'

He glanced down at his son and then back at her, clearly not wanting to argue in front of the boy. His eyes were a deep, dark brown, like his hair, which was slicked back with a clipped fade at the sides—very 'city'. His skin was smooth, clean-shaven and pale, as if he spent a lot of time indoors. His clothes were typical weekender. Pale blue polo shirt and sand-coloured cotton shorts. He filled them very nicely. She could be objective about that. He had strong-looking arms, she'd noticed as he'd tied the rope, and a body that looked used to exercise. But there was one thing that surprised her—he wore jandals on his feet rather than boat shoes. A mistake in her assumptions there—usually, the city people wore new boating shoes.

'We'll just have to agree to disagree.' He bristled, his jaw set. 'I'll make sure to keep an eye on my speed in future.'

If it was meant as an apology, it lacked the basics, such as the words *I'm sorry*. But she guessed it was all she was going to get. 'Thank you.'

'Mason hasn't seen dolphins before, and we were following them.'

As excuses went, she had to admit it was a good one. The dolphins out here were so enchanting and friendly, and they liked to show off their tumbling skills. She knew how spellbinding they were. Even so, shaking her head and trying to control her frustration, she turned and walked to the edge of the water, scanning to count her class in. All present and correct.

'Okay, everyone. Come in. Time's up,' she shouted. 'Bring the SUPs out of the water and load them back on the racks, please. You know the drill.'

Behind her the little boy asked, 'Daddy, can I play on the swings?'

'I don't think so. The scary lady might tell us off. Again. We should go.'

Scary lady. Was that what she was now? She really hoped not. But there was humour in his tone and it was infectious. She pressed her lips together to stop a smile escaping. Speeding was no laughing matter.

'But, Daddy...*pleeease.*'

Despite the longest 'please' she'd ever heard, the little guy's voice was tentative, almost resigned to a negative response.

And it came. 'I'm sorry, son. I promise we'll fix up the garden and I'll build you a playground as soon as we can get the supplies sent over.'

So, he was a new resident of the island. He could have bought any one of the houses for sale recently.

It was none of her business. Her business was here, these children in the lesson. This camp. But not for much longer. Someone would come and buy the place and she wouldn't be the warden of the cove—tempering visitors' enthusiasm and speed and protecting the sanctity of the place. She'd be off exploring the world beyond Rāwhiti Island, trying to forget the heartache and shake off the sting of bittersweet memories.

'Today?' Hope resonated in the little boy's tone.

'No, buddy. It's going to take a bit longer to build a playground.'

'Okay, Dad.'

Scary lady. She turned and watched the boy's eyes look

greedily at her playground as they started to climb back into the boat. Poor kid. 'Hey, bud. What's your name?'

He looked up at her with eyes as dark as his father's. 'Mason.'

'Well, Mason, you can play in my playground if you want, as long as Daddy promises to enrol in a day skipper class.'

The boy's head whipped round to look up at his father. 'Daddy?'

The man shot her a look that was filled with shock, and possibly anger. He held her gaze for a moment and she steeled herself for whatever he was about to throw at her—that he was a skilled boatsman and how dared she suggest such a thing?

But his shoulders dropped, as if he was consciously making himself stay calm, and he gave her a sharp nod. 'Okay. Yes, Mason, go and play. Five minutes. Then we have to go back to do the list of jobs we're avoiding.'

She could relate to that at least. 'Excellent. They run the courses at the Coastguard offices in Auckland, or if you're here for any length of time you can do them at the yacht club. Or online.' How to ask if someone lived here without asking if they lived here? But he just gave another nod. 'I'll look into it.'

'Tell them Carly sent you. Should get a discount.'

'Thanks…um…Carly.' He looked down at his feet then back at her. 'Your accent is English, is that right?'

'Sure is.' She didn't have to explain anything.

The man nodded as if he understood her reluctance to have a conversation. 'Well, thanks again. It's been a difficult time. He'll love just being able to play.'

His eyes were deep and soulful. For a beat she was spellbound by the flecks of gold in his irises, and simultaneously her heart crushed to hear of the boy's struggles. Which was a heady combination—she knew exactly how it was to deal with difficult things and she certainly didn't wish that on a little one.

But she could not want to know why things had been difficult or why they were here. She could not want to know anything more about them, no matter how curious she was. Or how good-looking this man was. She was drawing a line under this place, finally, after her own very difficult time.

'Talking of jobs...' She returned his nod with one of her own, then turned and walked away back to her class and her home...for now.

Above all, she didn't have time to stand around looking into any man's eyes. Especially one who'd put her class's lives at risk. She wasn't going to give him a chance to risk her heart too.

CHAPTER TWO

'THE ISLAND POPULATION is around five hundred and sixty now—we've had a huge growth spurt with the new development round at South Cove. But that number easily quadruples, and more, in the summer with holidaymakers, day-trippers and boat races swelling the numbers.' Mia, the nurse practitioner, put a tray of steaming mugs of tea down on the white plastic table in the surgery staff's lunch-cum-meeting room. 'Although, we have such a great microclimate here, we have visitors all year round. Have you been to the island before?'

Owen shook his head. 'I tried to get over a couple of times, but the trips were cancelled because of lockdowns. I even interviewed online.'

'Thank goodness those lockdowns are well and truly in the past. So, it's your first time here.' She clapped her hands. 'Oh, you'll love it. Everyone's so friendly. It's such a happy community.'

Apart from the scary lady, clearly.

It had taken the best part of their boat journey home for Owen to get over the grumpy way she'd spoken to them. Although, she had let Mason play on the swings—her one redeeming feature. Not counting the amazing legs and pretty face, obviously. Hopefully, their paths wouldn't cross again.

He realised Mia was staring at him, waiting for a response. Not wanting to let her know he hadn't been listening, he cleared his throat and put the grumpy woman out of his head. 'It's definitely different to the city practice. We were rushed off our feet all day, every day.'

'Then you'll soon start to enjoy this slower pace of life.' Mia nodded.

'I already am.' It had been a busy morning, trying to get Mason ready for kindergarten and then getting himself into work on time, so Owen was relieved they'd closed his appointment template for the day so he could orientate to the computer booking system and get to know the staff and routine. Now it was lunchtime already, and the time had flown by.

'We have appointment slots every morning. Monday to Friday.' Anahera, the elderly receptionist, put a large plate of raspberry lamingtons on the table, then sat down across from him. 'Then you're free to do paperwork and home visits if necessary.'

'Home visits? Not something we did in the city.'

'We have a very different approach here. Much more of a community feel. We help each other out.' Anahera picked up the plate and offered it to him. 'Please, take one. Take two. You'll be doing my waistline a favour. And you'll be on call every alternate day, just for emergencies. Mia's on call the other days. You'll get the hang of it all.'

And that was the team. Him, a nurse practitioner and a receptionist. No handy X-ray machine. Blood tests were sent by the last ferry every day. But at least the results came back via email, and there was a small pharmacy on the island that doubled up as a souvenir shop. It seemed every business here did double duty. The yacht club was also the postal service, and the tiny supermarket did take-away hot food.

He took a bite of the bright pink cake covered in coconut and sighed at the pillowy softness and sweet fruity flavour. 'I could get used to lunch like this every day.'

'Only for special occasions. But we like to think most days on Rāwhiti are special, eh, Mia?' Anahera winked at the nurse.

'I'm all for that.' Owen laughed and kept his thoughts about healthy eating to himself. 'At the interview I was told I'd have babysitting back-up if I needed it.'

Anahera grinned. 'That'll be me. I can come over any time at all. I've had six of my own and have three grand-babies. That's why I wasn't here on Friday to welcome you. I had to go to the mainland to see my newest. A wee preemie. Wasn't due for another six weeks and took us all by surprise. We had a mad dash to get my daughter over to hospital before little Aroha made her dramatic entrance.'

'Congratulations.'

'And I was dealing with an asthmatic who needed an urgent evac to City hospital,' Mia added. 'We've had a run on evacs recently. Sometimes we can go for weeks without anything, then we get a rush on.' She smiled apologetically. 'I'm sorry no one was there for the big welcome. I hope we're making up for it now?'

'It was fine—' He was interrupted mid-speech as the door was flung open.

'Anahera! Mia! Anyone home…? Yoo-hoo! Oh.'

Oh, indeed.

The scary lady from the school camp was standing in the doorway, breathless, her pony-tailed hair dishevelled. She had a faded yellow T-shirt on today and a pair of denim cut-off shorts above those gorgeous, toned legs. He drew his gaze up to her eyes. She glared intense brown back at him.

'What's up?' Mia jumped up. 'Got a problem?'

'Not until now.' Carly's fixed stare on Owen grew into a smile the moment she looked at the younger woman. 'I was just grabbing some things from the shop and remembered I need some extra supplies of EpiPens and Steri-strips until my order comes through from the wholesalers.'

Anahera stood up. 'Sure thing, honey.' Then the receptionist turned to Owen before going into the back supply room. 'Dr Owen Cooper, this is Carly from the island outdoor camp. Our designated first responder in the event of any major incident. We all take orders from her then.'

He imagined she'd be very good at bossing people around in the event of an emergency and, from his experience, just for breathing or enjoying the outdoors on a boat.

'*Dr* Cooper?' Carly pressed her lips together as her eyebrows rose. He sensed her surprise wasn't exactly positive. 'Signed up for the class yet?'

'You're going to do paddle-board lessons?' Mia laughed. 'That was quick work.'

Carly just frowned. 'Day skipper lessons. Crucial for round here, don't you think?'

Mia's gaze slid from Carly to Owen. Her eyes narrowed. 'What's going on? What am I missing?'

Carly shrugged. 'Just trying to keep everyone safe.'

'Okay.' The nurse frowned suspiciously at them both and then hauled a large bag onto her shoulder. 'I'll leave you two to whatever it is that you're not telling me. I've got to pop over to kindy and drop off Harper's lunch. Silly me left it in my bag. Then I'm popping over to do Winnie's dressings and to check in with Nicky Clarke. She's not due for another couple of months, but after last week's preemie adventures I'm not taking any chances.'

Call him a coward, but Owen nearly yelled at Mia to take him with her. Instead, he stood up and put his hand out to the camp woman. 'Hello. We should probably have done this on Saturday, but hi, I'm Owen. New doctor.'

She fitted her hand into his and shook tightly. Her eyes sparked and glittered. He got the feeling she was irritated and amused by him, or by the situation, and he had no idea why. 'Carly Edwards. Although, I think you probably gathered that the other day.'

No 'pleased to meet you' or other niceties.

He let his hand drop from hers but not before noticing her warm, soft skin and assured grip. 'So, we're going to be working together.'

'Only in an emergency.' Her gaze caught his and held.

He got the message loud and clear. *Back off. We're not as friendly as we say we are here on Rāwhiti Island.*

'And the camp's up for sale?'

'Yes.'

'So, will it still be a school camp when it's sold?'

'That depends on the new owner.' A frown settled again across her forehead. 'Why?'

'Just interested in what my new neighbours are likely to be doing.'

'A lot of the bush on the property is covenanted so they won't be able to change that. But I suppose they'll have free rein to do what they like with the buildings. Develop the whole place, probably, but we're trying to find a buyer who'll keep it as a camp first and foremost.'

'We?'

'Me and Mia.' Carly nodded towards the spot where Mia had stood moments before. He detected a frisson of pride tinged with something else. Her demeanour softened and she smiled, almost sadly. There was clearly a lot more to this story. 'We own the camp.'

Oh. Not what he'd expected, although he wasn't sure what he'd expected…a husband-and-wife team perhaps? Plus, Mia was a New Zealander, and Carly very definitely had an English accent. 'Right. Okay. So, are you two married or something?'

Carly's eyes nearly bugged out of her head and she spluttered on a chuckle. 'Something, yes. We're sisters-in-law.'

But so far no husbands mentioned or seen... 'And Mia lives at the camp too?'

'No. She and her little one have their own place just round the corner, near the marina. A few houses along from the yacht club.'

'I haven't ventured along there yet.'

'You should. Wiremu does a good pint.' She gave him a stiff smile that he chose to decipher as polite friendliness. Then, 'But, anyway, I doubt that whatever the new owners do will make much difference to you. There's a hill between us.'

There's a lot more than that.

He was trying to work out the jigsaw puzzle of her life. Although, why, he didn't know. First, it was none of his business. Second, he knew from his own experience just how complicated families could be. Third, he had a sneaky suspicion that his interest had a lot to do with her spark and bite. And he could not pursue that. 'What will do when you sell up?'

'Travel.' A curt nod. She was forthright but not gushy. 'There's a lot of world to see beyond Rāwhiti Island.'

'And your husbands...?'

The door swung open again and a portly old man staggered in. 'Carly!' he managed. 'Thank God.'

His words were slurred and his movements sluggish. Then he clutched the doorframe, his knuckles white with the effort. His lips worked but no more words came out. His face drooped like molten wax on one side, then he slumped forward.

Everything else forgotten, Owen jumped up and caught the man before he slid to the floor. 'Let's get him onto the examination couch. My room's closer.'

'Sure.' Carly took the other side, ducking under the man's underarm and holding him up with her shoulder. Together, they manoeuvred him out and across the small waiting room and into Owen's consultation room, where they propped him up against the couch. He slumped heavily to one side, as if he couldn't hold that part of himself upright.

Carly swung the man's legs up and they laid him back on the couch, a pillow under his back and head. 'Wiremu,' she said gently but with authority. 'Wiremu, can you tell me what's happening to you? Do you have any pain?'

Wiremu. She'd mentioned that name only a moment ago. Owen slipped a pulse oximeter onto Wiremu's finger then grabbed the sphygmomanometer and started to take the man's blood pressure.

Anahera bustled into the room, arms full of packages. She stopped short as she recognised the man on the couch. 'I wasn't sure where you'd got to, but I heard voices. Wiremu? Oh, Wiremu.' She glanced worriedly from Owen to Carly and dropped the packages onto the desk. 'What's happening? What is it?'

'Looks like a stroke, but we can't be sure. His oxygen levels are okay, but his blood pressure is very high.' Owen fitted his fingers into Wiremu's clenched fist. 'Wiremu, can you squeeze my hand?'

The man blinked up at them but said nothing. He squeezed Owen's fingers well with his left hand, but didn't seem to register that he had a right side at all.

Anahera fluttered next to them. The capable, calm woman of before had gone and been replaced with worry. 'What do we do? Can't you give him something? A blood thinner?'

'I don't know if it's a clot or a bleed, Anahera. If I give him the wrong treatment, we could make him worse. We need to get him to hospital as soon as we can and get some scans done of his brain.' It occurred to him then that everyone knew each other here. Perhaps this man was a relative. 'Do you have details of his next of kin? Family?'

Anahera's eyes filled with tears. 'He's my brother.' She patted Wiremu's hand. '*Ae*, boy? My little brother. And we're going to sort you out.'

Carly had the satellite phone in her hand. She was calm, clear and concise, showing no emotion at all and anticipating exactly what Owen had been about to ask her to do. 'I'm through to ambulance control. They're dispatching a helicopter immediately and need some more medical information.'

She passed the phone to Owen for medical details. 'Suspected CVA. Right hemiplegia. Dysphasia. Hypertensive at two hundred and four over one hundred. Needs urgent admission.'

A crackle and then, 'On our way, Doc. Over and out.'

'How long?'

'Twenty minutes, usually.' Carly took the phone from him and hung up. 'There's a helicopter landing pad behind the yacht club. Three minutes away.'

Owen did another round of observations on Wiremu, and tried to engage him in conversation so he could assess his mental and consciousness state, but it was clear he was deteriorating fast.

'Anahera, go tell Lissy what's happening. She's going to need support, especially with those grand-babies staying with her too. Someone's going to have to go to the hospital.' Carly wrapped her arms around the older woman and hugged her tightly. 'I'll let Mia know what's happened. Go be with your family.'

'It's okay. I'll call her.' The older lady's eyes slid to Owen with regret and sadness. 'I don't want to leave the new doctor on his first day.'

Amazed at the dedication of his little team, Owen shook his head. 'Hey, I can absolutely manage. Go. Please.'

He wasn't sure exactly how he would answer the phones

and simultaneously tend to the patients on his own if Mia was going to be out on calls, but he'd do it.

'Thank you.' Carly managed a soft smile as she glanced at him, and for a moment he felt wildly happy that he'd made her smile, as if he'd achieved some small victory and put a crack in her armour.

She walked Anahera to the door. 'Yes, go now. You have to prioritise yourself and your family. I'll put something on the *whanau* chat group. There'll be food in your freezers by this evening. Anything else you need?'

Anahera shrugged. 'I don't know.'

'When you've had a chance to think, let me know.'

'I can't believe this is happening on the heels of Friday's hospital dash.' The receptionist put her hand on Carly's arm. 'Thanks, love.'

'Hey. You did so much for me. You do it for everyone else.' Carly watched her go and exhaled. 'She's always the first to help others but can't accept it for herself.'

The *whanau* chat group—'family' chat group? 'She's your family? Wiremu's your relative? You should have said.'

'Not blood family. But we're all close. You can't not be, living in a place like this. Mia's my family. She grew up here and they all adopted me when I arrived. Didn't you, Wiremu?' She stroked their patient's hand, picking it up and examining it, and he could see her eyes glittered with tears.

You did so much for me. Carly had said that to Anahera.

More questions stacked up in his head. What was her story? She was calm and controlled, guarded and forthright. And yet when she'd held Anahera, and now with Wiremu, there was a gentleness and caring he hadn't expected.

And now, close up, he could see things he hadn't noticed before too. There was no wedding ring on her slender fingers. No rings at all, in fact. No jewellery, apart from silver studs in her ears. Her hair had strands of red and gold running through it. She had more freckles than he could count running across her nose and kissing her cheeks.

Kissing...

His eyes darted to her sensuous mouth and he dragged them away. It was so inappropriate to think like that.

What the hell was wrong with him?

She lifted her head and caught him looking at her. But, instead of berating him as he expected, she nodded. The smile she gave him was almost friendly. 'Thanks for the help, Doc.'

She was thanking him? And yet hadn't he been told she held higher ranking in an emergency? 'Carly, do you mind if I ask...are you medically trained?'

'I've got advanced first aid training and fire training, plus logistics and civil defence. Which means that if anything happens on this island, be it medical, fire, tsunami or other emergency, I have to deal with it, then send for help. We've got emergency response jet-skis to get to any emergency faster, be it on land or sea. The roads here don't go to every house, and they're gravel and winding, so sometimes travelling by sea is quicker. I attend first, assess and then get help. It works for most things. Although, we're grateful to have a doctor here now. First permanent one we've ever had.'

'Why now and not before?'

'We couldn't get anyone to fund a doctor, so we raised money for the medical centre, which has always been nurse-led. But with the population growing we needed more. Poor Mia can't be on call twenty-four-seven, especially with a toddler. We put a case to the health board and they finally agreed to partially funding a GP role. The other funds come from us, the users, just like on the mainland. So here you are.'

Here he was. Wondering how he was going to fit in to such a close-knit community. Would they have room for him in their hearts too and, more importantly, space for his son?

He realised Carly was looking at him with a puzzled expression.

She tugged at his arm and walked him a little away from their patient. 'Is he going to be okay?'

He made sure they were out of Wiremu's earshot. 'With a stroke patient it's imperative to get them help immediately, before too much damage has been done, and I'm hoping we're doing that. You did well to stay so calm, given you know him. A lot of people would have panicked.'

She exhaled deeply, sticking her hands into her denim shorts pockets. 'I deal with hundreds of kids in my job. They provide enough drama and hysterics, closely followed by the parent helpers. I've learnt not to get emotionally involved.'

He wondered, briefly, whether she meant just in her job or in her private life too. And it occurred to him that she hadn't answered his question about husbands living at the camp. But now wasn't the time to go back to that conversation. He hadn't come here to get involved with another woman. He was here for his son and that was all.

And then the sound of chopper blades rent the air and the only person in his head was Wiremu.

CHAPTER THREE

CARLY HID HER face from the sandblasting caused by the updraft of the helicopter as it rose above the bay into the clear summer sky. Then she turned and walked back towards the medical centre to collect her supplies.

The new doctor strode purposefully ahead of her, in a hurry to get back to the surgery. She had to admit he was impressive. Not just in looks, but in his demeanour too. In the aftermath of an emergency, people often crumbled, but he seemed just as level-headed now as before. But then, he hadn't known Wiremu for years, the way she and Anahera had.

Or maybe he was always like that...calm and considered. Except on Saturday when she'd growled at him and he'd clearly fought to keep his temper at bay. Which meant there was more to him than he liked to portray...hidden depths. *Stop it.*

She did not want to know what was going on behind his professional exterior.

The emergency bleeper on her shorts belt started to vibrate against her waist. Now what? There was still so much she had to do to get ready for the influx of children tomorrow morning. She looked at the message coming through.

Emergency. Bream Bay. Fallen tree. Simon injured his leg.

Okay. Everything else had to wait.

Taking a deep breath, she called out, 'Hey, Doc! Owen?'

He stopped short and turned to her, his dark eyes roaming her face. *God*, he was lovely to look at. 'Yes?'

'Don't get too comfortable, we're needed out at Bream Bay.'

He gave a slight frown, more curiosity than irritation. 'Do you have any details?'

'There's been an accident. Not quite sure what we're going to find, but apparently a tree has fallen on someone.'

His eyebrows rose. 'Wow. Okay. We'd better get going. Good job I don't have any patients booked in.'

He must have been feeling overwhelmed, especially with his receptionist gone now. 'It gets like this sometimes, but people do understand if you run late. They realise if it's an emergency then it's likely to be someone they know, and usually want to help out too.' She pulled out her phone and sent a text to Mia. 'I've just let Mia know what's happening. The surgery phone has an answer-machine, so don't worry about missing anything. You can follow up when we get back.'

He nodded. 'Of course. Do you have everything, or do I need to grab emergency supplies?'

'I've got a full first aid bag down at the marina.'

'Okay.' He unlocked the surgery door. 'I'll just grab my work bag, put the closed sign up and lock everything up.'

She stood in the open doorway. 'Have you got any swimwear with you?'

'No. Why?'

'It's jet-ski time.' Her gaze slid over his body...purely for sizing purposes. At least, that was what she told herself. She was not checking out the man's body. She was not noticing the broad shoulders or the nice backside. She was not thinking about what was under his neat white shirt and grey chinos. 'We'll grab some togs from the pharmacy. They sell stuff like that for the tourists.'

He nodded. 'I'll remember to bring some to work in future. I just expected I'd be in the clinic all day.'

'You usually will be, but best to have a bag of swim stuff close by for emergencies. I'll meet you down at the marina. Just along that road.' She pointed out of the surgery window. 'Orange jet-ski on the floating dock. I'll get it ready to go and grab the first aid kit from the locker while you get changed.'

'Give me two minutes.' He dashed into the pharmacy while she ran to the quay.

He was by her side in no time, wearing a black rash vest that hugged his toned body, navy-and-white-striped swim shorts and jandals. A pair of trainers was slung over his shoulders, hanging by the laces. His dark hair was mussed-up, presumably from pulling his clothes over his head. He looked, quite simply, gorgeous.

Then she gave herself a good talking to. Just because a man was gorgeous didn't mean anything. Just because, despite her first impressions, he was actually quite nice, calm and controlled in an emergency, had a cute, dimpled smile and showed compassion to his co-workers, didn't mean a single thing.

Not. A. Thing.

But she did quietly thank her lucky stars that the new doctor wasn't averse to adventure. Although, she'd realised that when she'd watched him zoom across the cove in pursuit of dolphins with his little boy.

And, far too quickly, questions began to crowd her head. Where was the mother of his child? Why were just father and son here? What had made him come to the island when, by all accounts—background info from Mia, mainly—he'd had a perfectly successful city practice?

She brushed those thoughts away and gunned the jet-ski

engine, then threw a life jacket to him. 'Put this on. Hop on. And hold on.'

'Got you.' He slid the jacket on, pulling it tight across his chest, and then slipped his messenger-style work bag across his body.

She was aware of the slide of his legs against hers as he straddled the jet-ski. She was aware of the warm stretch of his hands at her waist and his scent of anti-perspirant—something minty and very definitely male.

Acutely aware…as if someone had flicked a switch inside her. A switch that hadn't been working for three long years. Hell, she hadn't wanted it to work ever again, but now, with his hands round her waist, she felt jittery and off-balance.

How long since she'd been held? Kissed? Cared for? Her chest hurt at the thought of what she'd lost. So much. So many plans, hopes and dreams with the man she'd loved had been cruelly snatched away from her in a freak accident. It hit her that what she missed most was human contact. The little, everyday affections. Someone to ask how her day had gone. Someone to hold. Someone to hold her.

And why was she having these thoughts right now? And around Dr Owen Cooper? A few weeks before she was leaving?

She lifted her chin, felt the spray refresh her cheeks and wipe away the sadness she'd thought she'd come to terms with. Had come to live with. But, she realised, it was an unwanted talisman she carried everywhere, tainting everything, every thought, every plan.

Which was why she needed to leave this place to create some new memories and find out who she was, now she no longer fitted the description of wife or daughter-in-law.

Soon enough they were at Bream Cove, where Simon's wife, Michaela, was frantically waving. After securing the jet-ski to the jetty, Carly waited for the woman to fill her in.

'Carly, thank God. He's out the back of the house. He was supposed to be trimming the lower branches, but the old idiot got carried away without thinking it through.'

They raced up the jetty, along the gravel path and out into the paddock behind the old cottage where tall, thick podocarp trees provided a natural barrier between workable land and bush. Carly scanned as she ran and eventually made out a figure pinned underneath a large branch that must have spanned almost half a metre wide.

'There! Quick.' She turned, expecting Owen to be somewhere behind her, but he was at her side, now overtaking her, covering the distance in no time. Somehow, he'd managed to put his trainers on—a good move, given the thistles and clumps of sedge grasses that scratched her ankles and feet.

'Crush injury. We need another helicopter. Quick.' Without even having to assess too closely, Owen clearly knew this was urgent as he knelt next to the man's head. 'Hey, Simon. I'm Owen, the new doctor. We're going to get this branch off your leg and see how much damage you've done.'

'Hurts.' Simon grimaced and tried to sit up.

'I know. Try to keep still, mate.' Owen put his hand on the man's chest and gently encouraged him to lie back down. 'We'll sort you out. I just need to make sure you haven't done any damage to your back or neck before we move either you or the tree.' After assessing for any other injuries, Owen turned to Michaela, calm and totally in control. 'When did this happen?'

She shrugged, her face pale, her fingers knotted in the hem of her T-shirt. 'To be honest, I don't know. Could be half an hour. Could be two hours. I was out on the boat for a while, then pottering in the kitchen.'

He turned to Carly and nodded. 'We need to be careful when we get the pressure off his leg.'

'Crush syndrome?'

'Yes, although it's his leg that's trapped, not his torso, so I'm not expecting it. But we don't know how long he's been here, or how much toxin build-up there could be, so we need to be careful and watch for signs.' He slipped a pulse oximeter onto Simon's finger. 'I'm just going to see what your oxygen levels are, and I'll give you some pain relief. Then we'll get that log off your leg.'

Simon groaned. 'Thanks...Doc.'

Carly dialled up the satellite phone, got through to ambulance control, and gave all the details of the injury and the location of the nearest helicopter landing pad, which, luckily, was at a neighbouring property only a few minutes away.

Owen pulled the small portable oxygen cylinder from the first aid kit, fitted it to a mask then slid it over Simon's head. Then he pulled out some ampoules, drew liquid into a syringe and jabbed Simon's arm. 'Right. That will hopefully take the edge off while we work out how to do some heavy lifting.'

Carly almost didn't want to see what was going on under the branch but somehow, with the help of Michaela, some thick rope and some clever physics Owen came up with, they managed to roll it off Simon's leg, exposing a bone-deep wound across his shin.

As the branch shifted, he moaned and screamed, but now he was eerily quiet and pale. Carly kept a close eye on his blood pressure and breathing while Michaela was sent next door to meet the chopper crew.

Owen pressed two fingers at various points over the man's ankle and foot. Then he did it again, methodically touching and pressing. 'No medial pedal pulses. We need him air-lifted as soon as possible. In the meantime, we need to keep monitoring him and stabilise that fracture.'

The leg was clearly broken, oddly flattened, with deep

bleeding cuts and the start of some impressive bruising
and swelling. While Owen applied dressings to the gashes,
Carly took out her inflatable splint and together they slid
it under Simon's leg and inflated it to provide stability and
keep him safe until the helicopter arrived.

They were doing another round of vital signs when
Simon began to shake uncontrollably.

'Blood pressure is dropping. Ninety over fifty.' Carly
watched the electronic machine inflate the cuff around
Simon's arm again. 'Pulse is getting faster. One hundred
and two.'

Owen put his hand on the man's shoulder. 'Looks like
you're in a bit of shock, mate. How about I put in a line and
give you some fluids? That should help.'

Carly opened the silver emergency blanket. 'I'll go see
if I can find some more blankets in the house.'

'Mind reader.' Owen smiled and took the crinkly
blanket, wrapping it around their patient.

She watched as he knelt on the ground, completely
unaffected by the thistles and gravel, his focus purely on
his patient, and she wondered what it would feel like to
have Owen's gaze on her, his focus only on her. Those
strong hands around her waist again, the way they'd been
on the jet-ski. Pulling her close against his toned body.
Holding her.

What the heck? She barely knew the man. Why would
she want him to hold her? Why was she thinking about his
hands? His body? About the way her body had responded
when those hands had spanned her waist?

Because, she realised with a shock, she was attracted
to him. Properly attracted, as in intrigued, endeared,
interested. Very interested. It felt as if her body was
springing to life after years of hibernation, prickling with
goosebumps, heating low in her belly. She liked Owen
Cooper enough to think about holding him.

Panic radiated through her, making her heart thud against her rib cage. She couldn't. She just couldn't. She couldn't hold anyone, not after everything she'd been through. It was too much of a risk to her heart, which had only just started to heal. She couldn't let herself fall into anything meaningful again. So she forced herself to follow his lead and focus on the needs of the patient.

Mind reader...

'I sincerely hope not,' she quipped back, then dashed to the house to get some more blankets and hopefully find some perspective.

For the second time that day, Owen watched a helicopter rise into the sky.

Carly stood next to him on the jetty, her hand shielding her eyes. The wind whipped strands of her dark hair out of her ponytail, framing her face in wispy waves. Her nose was peeling. Her skin was tanned. She looked vibrant and healthy, like an advert for outdoor exercise. Loose-limbed and free.

She was so different from Miranda, who refused to go anywhere near the sun in case it damaged her skin. And, no, he wouldn't let his bad marriage intrude on his new life...unless it was to facilitate Mason seeing his mother.

Carly bent and riffled through her bag. Thinking she was fishing out the jet-ski keys, he asked her, 'Back to the surgery, then?'

Although, if he was honest, spending a few more moments in this beautiful cove with a beautiful woman was very enticing.

'In a minute or two.' She took out a flask and poured hot liquid into two battered white tin cups with *Rāwhiti Camp* printed on the side in forest-green ink. 'Refreshments first.'

'That's like Mary Poppins's bag.' He pretended to peer inside it. 'Is it bottomless?'

She laughed and followed his eyes to her large rucksack. 'I'm an efficient packer. I teach rucksack packing to the kids before we set off into the bush on our overnight camps. You wouldn't believe the kind of things they like to sneak in there that add so much weight, they complain all the way in and all the way out again.'

'Like what?'

'Books. More food than they could eat for a week— sweets, mainly. All sorts of devices to entertain them. They don't realise they won't have the energy for anything but holding a cup of hot chocolate after I've had them bush whack, build a shelter and then cook their dinner over an open fire.'

'Sounds fun.'

'It is. The kids love it. Some of them have never even seen the sea, can you imagine—living in the city or in a farm in the middle of nowhere and not ever going to the coast? You should see their faces.' She suddenly looked wistful and he remembered she was selling up. Did she want to? Was she being forced to?

He made sure to catch her eye. 'Are you okay, Carly?'

'Sure. I'm fine.' She flashed him a confused look and offered him a cup of hot brown liquid before sitting down at the end of the jetty, her legs hanging over the side. 'Why?'

'You seem...' He wanted to say 'emotional' but knew that wouldn't go down well. 'It's been a stressful afternoon.'

'Simon's leg wound was pretty gruesome, but I've seen worse. But, if you're asking why I need a hot drink and a rest, it's because it's important to stay hydrated, especially when going from one emergency to another. It's easy to forget about eating and drinking in all the hustle and bustle. But even superheroes need a cup of tea every now and then.'

He laughed, sat down next to her, took the cup and sipped the sweet hot tea. Interesting that she'd assumed he was asking her about the accident and not about the sudden change in her demeanour when she'd talked about her job. He wanted to ask so many questions but didn't think it right to pry. He'd hate it if anyone wanted to know all about his business. 'Well, that was certainly an interesting introduction to island life.'

'It's not usually like this.' She turned to look at him at the same moment he turned to look at her. Her eyes sparkled like water in sunlight, like diamonds glittering. 'Don't get too excited, Dr Cooper.'

Interesting choice of words. Especially as the word 'excited' falling from her lips seemed to set off an echoing thrum inside him. But he didn't want to misinterpret anything, and certainly didn't want to imbue the conversation with his wayward thoughts, so he changed direction. 'Look, about the other day…'

'Yes?' She gave a coy sideways glance, eyebrows raised in a question. Her dark eyes played and a smile hovered on her lips.

'Was I really going too fast? Because, if so, I need to get a handle on that boat, especially when I have Mason to look after too. From where I was, it didn't feel too fast.'

There was a long pause, during which Carly sighed and nodded, her smile gone. She slid her foot along the decking. The kind of hedging mannerism that his son did when he didn't want to admit to a wrongdoing. 'Okay, I guess not, if I'm honest. Only, I'm very protective of my little cove and my students.'

'It's good to be safety conscious.'

'Yes.' Her voice was soft. 'But I can be over-the-top protective.'

He wondered why, but that thought dissolved the moment he glanced at his watch. 'Damn, I was supposed to collect Mason ten minutes ago. It's my first pick-up from kindergarten and they'll probably shout me down.'

'No, they won't. They'll be very polite and understanding.

Not everyone's as brutally honest as me around here.' She laughed as she bundled the empty cups and flask back into her bag and jumped up. 'Come on, then, jump on.'

He settled behind her on the jet-ski and slid his hands around her waist, feeling her heat against his skin. Her back was ramrod-straight. Sea spray covered the fine hairs on her arms. Her scent—flowers and fresh air—mingled with the salty air and made him want to inhale deeply.

He inched away from her. This was getting ridiculous. He couldn't be attracted to a woman's scent. Or notice the warmth of her skin or her toned legs and, more than anything, the sad smile she had when she thought no one was looking at her.

When they arrived back at the marina, Mia was sitting on the sand with both her own little girl and Mason, building sandcastles. Owen jumped off the jet-ski, helped Carly secure it on the floating dock then ran towards the nurse and his son.

Carly jogged alongside. 'Hey, Mia,' she said with the huge grin she seemed to save for her sister-in-law. 'Bless you for bringing Mason down to meet us. Owen was starting to stress.'

He had been. And it was getting worse. 'Don't they have a policy for not allowing children out without a named guardian?'

Immediately he'd said it, he wanted to take it back. Mason was safe and sound, playing contentedly in the sand as if he was on holiday. He certainly didn't look as stressed as Owen felt about the delayed pick-up.

The happy smiles on both women's faces fell. Mia was quick to say, 'Jackie would have been happy to keep him until you arrived, but she had to dash off, and there was no one else. I couldn't leave him there all alone.'

'Of course. Yes.' He wrapped his boy in a hug, but Mason brushed him off with, 'Stop it, Daddy. Build a castle.'

Owen turned back to Mia, to find her frowning at him. 'Jackie knows me. We grew up here together. She knows I'm not about to abduct your son. She also left a couple of messages on your phone, but there was no reply from you. We waited as long as we could but, in the end, she had to close up.'

And all the while he'd been having tea and inappropriate thoughts about Carly. He shrugged apologetically. 'No phone service out there.'

'It happens.' Mia nodded. 'We islanders understand. There's a different pace of life here and we help each other out. We have to, because we're isolated, and there are limited services.'

'What the doctor means is thank you.' Carly smiled, pulling Mia's daughter, Harper, onto her lap and blowing a raspberry onto the toddler's belly, making her giggle and squirm.

It was such a happy scene, and he'd ruined it with his own over-protectiveness and city-borne suspicion. 'Yes, yes, I'm so sorry, Mia. I do mean thank you. Thank you very much. I'm sorry if I came across as rude. I'd been worrying about my boy and, being the only parent here, I need to put him first. I'd hate to think of him left there all alone.'

'It's okay. I'm a single parent too. I totally understand. Any time you need me to pick him up, just let me know. It's no hardship at all, and the kids seem to play well together.' But Mia shot Carly a look Owen couldn't read.

'Can I come to your playground again?' Mason asked Carly, completely out of the blue.

'Mason, where are your manners?' Owen reminded his son, then turned back to Carly. 'I'm so sorry. Just say no. It's fine.'

She looked a little uncomfortable at the suggestion, but glanced down at Harper, and her body language immediately softened. 'Yes, of course, Mason, come and play. That would be lovely. I've got a wonderful playground, and I know your place needs sprucing up. I have school children here every Tuesday to Friday, but they go back home on the one o'clock ferry. Why don't you come over one Friday afternoon?'

'Thank you.' Owen knew he didn't deserve such a kindness, but his son did.

'Not a problem.' She looked up at him and grinned, as if she'd won some battle they'd been waging. And...wow... Her eyes shone, and the sun framed her face, and...she really was beautiful. He didn't know what to say, because telling her she was beautiful was the only thing he could think of, and he really, really couldn't do that.

And yet she was still looking at him and he couldn't drag his eyes from her. The world seemed to shrink to just him and her. What was she thinking? Did she get this weird vibe too?

After a beat or two, she nodded and looked at her watch. 'Shoot. Now I really have to dash. These emergencies have derailed my whole day. See you all later.'

Owen watched her jump up from the sand and then trip lightly away, bag in hand. But he refused to turn to watch her go, even though another glimpse of her would be good for...

'So, Dr Cooper. Had a good afternoon with our Carly?'

He turned and saw Mia looking at him with a quizzical expression. He dragged his thoughts away from Carly. 'Eventful, shall we say?'

'Sounds like you handled everything well. A good team?' She glanced in the direction Carly had headed.

Owen followed her gaze with a little pang in his heart to see no sign of the woman he'd spent the afternoon with. 'We worked well together. It's great that she knows everyone and has the whole routine down pat. It makes my life easier.'

'Underneath all that armour, she's actually lovely.'

'Is she?' He laughed, just to show he was joking, but in truth he wasn't sure where this was going. 'She's definitely capable.'

'Aha. That's what we call it, right?' Mia smiled and raised her eyebrows, as if she was in on some private joke. A joke he hadn't been let in on.

'She handles the jet-ski well and anticipates danger and the right kind of response needed.' And that was as far as he was going to go with this conversation.

'Just…look, Owen…' Mia grimaced. 'Carly's had a hard time. We both have, if I'm going to be honest.'

'I'm sorry to hear that.' Seeing the nurse's eyes fill with tears, he sensed this conversation straying into difficult territory. 'Hey, please. You don't have to tell me anything personal.'

'No doubt you'll hear all about it anyway from one of the locals. It's not a secret.' Carly shook her head and gave Owen a wobbly smile, wiping her cheek with the heel of her hand. 'But I guess it is her story to tell and, if I blab it all, it will sound like gossip, which she'd hate. But…well… she doesn't like to let people close.' Mia swallowed and Owen could see how hard it was for her to be telling him this. 'She has good reasons, Owen. She's been through a lot. Just…be gentle.'

'Are you warning me or…what?' What kind of impression had he given Mia? Or Carly? He'd stuck to being professional, but maybe something had given away his… interest…attraction to Carly? 'Because, I can assure you, we're purely work colleagues.'

Who exactly was he trying to convince here—Mia or himself?

'Sure you are.' Mia jumped up, gathered her bag and the buckets and spades and called to her daughter. 'Harper, come on, missy. Time for tea. See you tomorrow, Owen. Bye, Mason.'

Then she gave him a quick wave and left him there with his son and a whole lot of emotions he couldn't put a name to.

CHAPTER FOUR

IT WASN'T A DATE. Well, it was a *play* date, but that was all. *For Mason*. This outing was just to make his son happy.

So, why Owen felt strangely excited and simultaneously nervous he couldn't say. But his gut tightened just a little when he saw her strolling down the jetty as he tied the rope round the cleat.

In some ways he wished Mia hadn't hinted about Carly's past because he knew it would affect the way he reacted to her. He liked the sparky banter, he was comfortable with that kind of casual interaction and wasn't sure it was a good idea to take things deeper, especially after Miranda and their complicated relationship. He was intrigued by Carly and had to admit to, well, caring about her. If you could care about someone after knowing them for five minutes. But there it was. They had a connection, and he wasn't sure what to do about it.

'Hi, Owen. And Mason!' Carly put out her hand to haul Mason out of the boat onto the jetty. 'Hey, buddy. Seriously? Have you grown since I saw you on Monday?'

'Yes.' The boy nodded solemnly and puffed out his chest.

'His appetite's increased, that's for sure.' Owen climbed out of the boat, carrying a bag of spare clothes and snacks for Mason. 'He's eating me out of house and home.'

'All this fresh air does them a world of good.' Her hair was loose today, soft titian waves framing her face and skimming her shoulders. Her skin glowed. She was wearing a teal-blue gypsy-style top with beads sewn around the V-neck, a long tiered white skirt, beaded sandals and, unexpectedly, bright red nail varnish on her toe nails. Which made him curious. It was so feminine and fun. There were clearly other sides to Carly's personality than supremely efficient first responder and over-all superhero.

She looked like something from a magazine advertising healthy living as she nodded at him and smiled. 'So, how was the rest of your first week on Rāwhiti?'

'Not as exciting as the first day. Luckily, we've been quiet, because it's only been Mia and myself, what with Anahera being with her family. But now I'm proficient in answering the phones and making appointments and attending to any queries as well as seeing patients.'

Her eyebrows rose as she grinned. 'You have to be a Jack of all trades here. I'm glad you've managed.'

'Oh, it's nothing compared to the eighteen-thousand-patient practice I had before. The mornings have been calm, with no call-outs and need for babysitters in the evenings, which I'm grateful for. We needed to get into a proper routine, and being AWOL for pick-up was not a good start.'

'Seriously, no one minds if you turn up late, or even early. We're all very flexible here. Right, come on, Mason! The playground's been waiting all afternoon to see you.' She jogged along the jetty towards the little playground area with Mason skipping by her side, giggling with excitement.

Owen's chest contracted as he watched the way his son looked up at her with abject adoration.

Don't get too close, boy. She's leaving.

Was this a mistake? Should he have insisted they stay away? The poor kid had already been abandoned by his mother. Was Owen setting him up for more heartbreak? Panic rattled through him but he breathed it out. They were here now. He'd let him play today and then gently discourage him from coming back.

By the time he got to the playground, Mason had skipped off to climb the ladder at the back of the slide, leaving Owen and Carly alone. They stood under the shade of a flowering *pohutukawa* tree, its fallen red stamens carpeting the ground like a scarlet blanket. Native flax and clivia bordered the sides of the little play area that gave onto a large grassy area leading down to the shoreline.

'Watch me, Daddy!' Mason sat at the top of the slide then inched forward and down. 'Whee!'

Seeing the happiness on his son's face convinced him that this had been a good idea. He'd just have to wean him off the camp and the camp owner. Although, she'd be gone soon enough. Which was enough of a reminder that he could admire the woman from a distance, but that was all it could ever be for him.

She smiled up at him. 'So, how's the old Nelson place treating you?'

'Nelson place? Where's that?' Had he missed something?

'The previous owner of your house was called Horatio, so his nickname had to be Nelson, right? When he died last year, he bequeathed the house to the Rāwhiti Island Community Trust and we voted on it being used as the doctor's house as a lure to bring a medic over here. But I realise it needs work.'

He laughed as he thought about his feathered friend alarm clock and the holes in the walls that needed blocking. 'It needs bowling, to be honest. I'm waiting on an order from the hardware store over in Auckland, but I'm not entirely sure when it'll arrive.'

'These things take time. I've got some old bits of timber out the back if you need them.' She pointed over to the little cottage on the edge of the shore. 'Happy for you to take a look. Once this place is sold, I'll have to get rid of everything like that anyway, so you might as well have it.'

She's leaving. She's leaving.

'Great. Thanks. I'll take a look. I could drive over and collect what doesn't fit in my boat.'

'I don't think you'll fit much in that.' She laughed, her brown eyes shining. 'I can get the ferry to bring the big stuff round, don't worry.'

'They do that?'

She gave him a questioning look. 'Has no one explained that to you? We charter barges to bring big items in, but the ferry brings small things over for us, and there's the mail run boat three times a week. Which means I get to do as much online shopping as anyone in the city.'

'I bet you don't do as much as my wife does. In fact, I doubt anyone shops as much as Miranda.'

'Wife?' Carly blinked, and her demeanour changed from soft and light to something more guarded. He immediately regretted bringing his past into the conversation.

'*Ex*-wife.'

'Mason's mum? Where is she?'

'In the States. She's an actress, and that's the best place to be for her career.'

An eyebrow rose, and with it all the judgement he'd felt from everyone he explained their situation to. 'She had a job opportunity she couldn't turn down,' he quickly explained.

'And you couldn't go with her? She couldn't take her son?' Carly looked over at Mason, her expression one of affection mixed with concern. 'He must miss her.'

'Let's just say there wasn't an invitation for me and my boy.'

She looked back at Owen and frowned. 'I see.'

'Actually, I'm not sure you do.'

She held up her hand and shook her head. 'Hey, it's none of my business—'

'No, but it makes her sound callous, and she isn't, just...'
He searched for the right word to describe Miranda without casting too dark a light on his ex. 'Self-absorbed and career-focused. She never wanted kids, and I knew that going into the marriage. When she accidentally fell pregnant, I hoped her attitude might change, but it didn't. She gave it a go, for my sake really, I think, although I didn't pressurise her either way. But she found family life suffocating and difficult. She stuck it out for just over three years and, believe me, I tried hard to be the husband and father we needed me to be—to be present and give them what they both needed—but I also had to work to pay the bills and was growing the business too. So I spent the week working all hours at the practice and then tried to make up for it at weekends.'

Why was he telling her all this?

Carly blew out a breath. 'Sounds like a lot of pressure.'

'Yes, and Miranda couldn't cope. She genuinely tried. But it wasn't the life she wanted. And, sadly, we weren't the people she wanted around her in Los Angeles.'

She gave a curious frown. 'I meant a lot of pressure for you, Owen.'

He looked over at his son, screaming with pleasure as he slid down the slide again. 'Mason's no pressure at all, apart from fuelling my determination to be two parents instead of one. In that, I can honestly say, I'm failing. At least, I was. It became very clear very quickly that I couldn't work full-time and only see him asleep. Which I did for a few months after Miranda left, because I was trying to maintain Mason's routine with the help of a nanny, but he suffered. We both did. I barely saw him, and when we did spend time together it was like two strangers not knowing how to react or reconnect. So I took this job, which is half the hours I was working in the city. And now I get to be a rubbish parent for more hours each day.' He huffed at the irony. 'Lucky kid.'

'You're not a rubbish parent. I've seen you in action, and I've seen you go all growly protective over him.'

'Not my finest moment.' He grimaced, wishing she'd forgotten about his *faux pas* on the beach with Mia.

'Look, you've seen me growly protective over kids that aren't even mine. I get it.' There was a pause, then her tone turned tentative. 'How can you not be angry at her for leaving?'

'I was. I am. I mean, look at him—how could you not want to be here and see him grow? But I knew she didn't want kids. I can't blame her for being the person I always knew she was. And she does try to stay in touch, although time zones and filming schedules don't always work in our favour.'

Carly's eyes widened and she smiled. 'You're a better person than me, Owen Cooper. I'd be furious.'

'I'm angry that she left Mason, of course, because he's too young to understand her reasons, and he's acted out and grieved. He misses her.'

The boy in question was now chasing a weka across the grass. Carly laughed as she watched him. 'He's a good kid.'

'He is. Although not quite mature enough to realise that no weka is ever going to let him catch them. They're fast.'

'They also eat the baby ducklings and steal the kids' food if they're not watching out.' She started to follow Mason. 'They're a pain. Funny, but a pain.'

'I know. I have one as an alarm clock.' He fell into step with her, but she came to a halt and turned to him.

'A what?'

He laughed, although he'd stopped thinking it was funny by Wednesday, the fifth morning he'd been woken by the tapping. 'There's a hole in the kitchen wall and a very clever weka manages to squeeze through it and into the house.

I've tried to cover it over with what bits of wood I can find and a makeshift hammer—aka my shoe heel—and some nails I found in an old, dusty jam jar in the shed, and I've stuffed the hole with newspaper, but the damned bird always manages to work its way in.'

'You definitely need my timber and tools. I can come and help, if you like. It's no trouble. I like getting my hands dirty. I built the barbecue area last year and it hasn't fallen down...yet.' She pointed over to the very impressive barbecue area on a flat concrete standing, with a wooden arbour overhead.

'Looks great. You built that?'

'What? Don't you think a woman could build something like that?' She growled but her eyes sparked humour. Her hands hit her waist. It was a gauntlet.

He held up his palms in surrender. 'Whoa. No assumptions here. I'm impressed that anyone who isn't a qualified builder could make that.' The struts of the arbour were interlaced and there was a trellis at the back with a mandevilla plant climbing up it. 'It looks like a professional job.'

'I like to think so.' She pursed her lips. 'It's just me here. I can't wait around for someone to help me do stuff. I just have to get stuck in.'

'If you can do that, then I'll definitely take you up on the offer.'

She grinned. 'Excellent. I'll drop some stuff round tomorrow and we'll take it from there.'

'Great.' He imagined her, all grubby in her short shorts, and his body prickled in response. Every cell felt awake and alive and tugged towards her. And, inconveniently, he realised it wasn't just a physical attraction. He wanted to find out more about her. To uncover the story Mia had hinted at. To uncover Carly Edwards.

Whoa. He hadn't expected to feel anything like this

again. Not for a long time, anyway. But then, he hadn't expected meeting the whirlwind that was this woman. His focus had to be on Mason. He should have been building barriers, not thinking of her building barbecues and getting all dirty…

In an effort to douse the ripple of need thrumming through him he asked, 'Give us a tour of the camp?'

She glanced at the row of buildings behind them. 'Oh, yes. Of course. Hey, Mason, come and see what else we've got around here.'

Camp Rāwhiti was a fully equipped educational facility with a huge kitchen and dining room, bunk rooms, bathroom facilities, the barbecue area Carly had built, a laundry and drying room. Deeper into the bush was a ropes course designed to build confidence, strength and endurance, evidence of bivouac-building by previous students and, at the top of a steep incline, an observatory for viewing the stars. On the shore side was a quaint white cottage where Carly lived, neat and pristine with a plentiful vegetable garden bursting with produce. Next to that was the boat shed.

'What's in there?' Mason pointed to the shed.

Carly rolled back the door to show him. 'We've got paddle boards, little optimist sailing boats and kayaks.'

Mason frowned as he peered in. 'What's a kayak?'

Owen cringed. The boy had grown up in Auckland, the self-proclaimed City of Sails, but they'd barely been to the beach, never mind on the water. It had been busy enough doing the chores every weekend, setting them up with food for the week and doing the laundry. He'd barely had the energy, never mind the time, to do day trips.

His eyes met Carly's and he wanted to tell her he wasn't a bad parent, just a busy one, but she just smiled. 'It's like a little boat that you sit right in and paddle out on the water.

It's great fun. We've had dolphins and whales visit us in this bay and they like to show off to the kayakers.'

'Can I try kayak, Daddy? With Carly too?'

Uh-uh. Mason was wheedling his way into this woman's life. He ruffled the boy's hair. 'Not today, buddy. Carly's busy.'

She beamed at the boy. 'Actually, it's getting a bit late, and it takes a lot of time to paddle out and back. How about next Friday after kindy? We'll go out straight away.'

Mason nodded, his big, dark eyes pleading and irresistible. 'Yes, please.'

'Good. Mr Mason, do we have a date?' She put her hand out to shake.

Mason turned and looked up at Owen, his eyes wide, his little body trembling with excitement. 'Kayak, Daddy! Kayak! Kayak!'

Oh, God. What was he doing letting Mason spend more time here? But seeing him so excited made Owen's heart squeeze. He couldn't remember the last time Mason had shown such enthusiasm for something. What they both needed was distance from Carly, not more time with her. On the other hand, he wanted to protect his son from more heartache, but surely learning to kayak would be a great life skill?

They were both looking at him expectantly. He reluctantly nodded at his son. 'Shake Carly's hand like a gentleman. Firm, but not tight. Seal the deal.'

After they made their solemn agreement, Owen turned towards the playground, but Carly said from behind him, 'Right. You two head over to the outside tables and I'll bring the picnic over.'

'Picnic? You didn't have to cook anything.'

She shrugged it off with a smile. 'It's a lovely evening, and I know kids like to eat early. It's not much, but I'm sure it'll fill him up.'

How could he refuse? 'Can I help?'

'No, it's all ready. You stay and watch him. I won't be long.'

So, even though he'd have much preferred to watch her languidly stride across the grass, he took his son to the swings and pushed him.

'Higher and higher, Daddy!'

Afterwards they sat on a wooden picnic table and ate home-made sausage rolls, which Mason exclaimed were the best he'd ever had, with salad and chopped vegetables, and fresh home-grown strawberries for dessert, and chatted about life on the island and Mason's week in kindy.

Which, it transpired, had been lots of fun and, even though Mason hadn't really opened up to his father, he was very chatty with Carly now. Apparently, his son had made a collage, played with bricks, been to the beach on an outing and done some art. Which was all news to Owen, because the most he ever got out of his son at pick-up time was, 'Good, thanks,' in answer to, 'How was your day?'

When would that change?

When Mason went back for a final play on the playground, Carly wandered over and sat on a nearby wooden bench, keeping her eye on the boy.

Owen slid in next to her, out of touching distance, but next to her.

A gold plaque on the back of the bench caught his eyes.

In loving memory of Wendy, Malcolm and Rafferty Edwards
They loved this place
Sit a while and remember all the good things
They'd want you to be as happy here as they were

Edwards. Carly's surname. Who were these people? He sensed her watching him so he turned his gaze to the kitchen block behind them. 'This is a big place. How many kids do you have at a time?'

'Depends on the school. We can take up to a hundred.'

'I can't believe you run the place by yourself. Does Mia work here as well as being a nurse?'

'She helps with the admin, that's all. She doesn't have time for anything else. I have a couple of employees who help me out when things get busy. But mainly it's just me, the teachers from the school and the parent helpers.'

'How do you manage it all?'

'It's a well-oiled machine. Most of the schools have been using this place for years, they know how it all works. They bring all their own food and bedding, and the parent helpers cook and are allocated to small groups of students. The kids clean up. It's a lot of fun for them all.'

'It sounds like it. So, did you buy it?'

'God, no. I couldn't afford to buy a property like this, it's worth millions.' Her forehead crinkled with a frown. 'Mia and I inherited half each when her parents died.'

'Okay.' Which didn't explain much to him.

But her hands tightened into fists on her lap. She pressed her lips together, as if trying to hold in a scream or a cry, then eventually said, 'Along with my husband. They all died together. In an accident.'

Wendy and Malcolm and Rafferty. The corners of the gold plaque jutted into his back. He sat forward, wanting to cover her hand with his. Wanting to pull her close and just hold her, anything to wipe away the haunted grief on her face, to take away some of the pain she must have been carrying.

He turned to face her properly. 'Oh, Carly. I'm so sorry. But please, you don't have to go over it all. You don't have to tell me.'

She shook her head, her eyes filled with tears. 'You'll hear about it soon enough. In fact, I'm surprised you don't know already. I thought Mia might have told you. They were out on the boat. A freak wave, we think, during a storm. You know what it's like here, we have four seasons in one day. It's beautiful in the morning and by lunchtime there's a deluge. It's predictably unpredictable. All we know is that one day the three of them went out on the water and never came back. Their boat was eventually found in pieces at the far end of the island. And Malcolm's—Mia and Raff's dad—body washed up on Kawau island, a few miles west of here. No one else was ever found.'

He didn't know what to say. Nothing could make this better. 'I'm so sorry, Carly.'

She shrugged, the corner of her mouth turning into a sort of resigned half-smile. 'It's okay.'

'No, it's not. It's tragic. It's awful. No wonder you're so concerned about safety on the water.'

'I always was, because it's stupid not to be, but I'm pretty intense about it now. I'm sorry I blasted you on your first day here. You must have thought I was horrible.'

'Scary.' He wiggled his eyebrows.

She laughed. 'Good. It means you took notice.'

'Oh, I noticed all right.' He probably shouldn't have said that—actually, he *definitely* shouldn't have said it—but it was too late.

She looked up at him, surprise softening her features. But she didn't look shocked, disgusted or angry. Her smile grew sad, yet hopeful. 'Yes. Me too.'

Something inside him felt as if it was cracking open, as if they'd made a breakthrough. As if this moment was significant. He didn't know why or how, just that it meant something. Carly Edwards was important and special.

And yet how could she be? She was leaving, he was staying and they were both protecting their hearts. And he was protecting Mason's too.

But they were talking about her losses and he wasn't

going to detract from that. 'Tell me about him. About Rafferty?' He guessed that was her husband.

The smile she gave him now was filled with gratitude and he wondered if she'd been wanting to talk about this but hadn't known how to start.

'I met him on a holiday in Nepal. We were both into the same things: the outdoors, fitness, nature. We just clicked immediately and, even though I'd planned to see much more of the world on my gap year, it was his last stop before heading home. But it just felt natural and right for me to come with him. I met his family and, well, you know Mia, they're so loving and inclusive, and I felt as if I'd finally found my "for ever" place.'

His gut knotted into a tight ball. Sitting on this bench with the plaque rubbing against his back, he was well aware the ending wasn't happy. 'And then…?'

'We got married and were planning to live and work here and bring up our family, like his parents had. When he died, I didn't have anywhere else to go, so I stayed.'

'How so? No family? You're English, right?'

'Yes. But no family.' At his frown, she rushed on. 'Apart from Mia and Harper. But now I think it's time to spread my wings, see what I want to do with the rest of my life. They would hate that I was so torn up over it and they'd encourage me to find out who I am again. Me. Not a wife. Not a daughter-in-law.'

A beautiful, competent, smart woman who deserved the very best in life. 'You have plans?'

'Not really. Probably back to Nepal to pick up where I left off and to pay a sort of homage to Raff. Where it all started, you know?'

She had obviously adored her husband. 'Sounds like a great starting point. And then you can have an adventure.'

'Exactly. I've been here for five years, having been absorbed into this place without really thinking everything through. I just need some headspace away from here to work out what I want and who I am.' She sat up straighter and her eyes sparkled.

He had to admit that his admiration for her grew deeper. 'What if you decided you wanted to come back here? Can't you find temporary managers?'

'I've tried, believe me. But it takes a special kind of person to run this place and we just haven't found the right fit. So we made the decision to sell it.' She inhaled deeply and he could see she was torn by the decision. It would be hard, giving up this connection with the man she'd loved.

'What does Mia think about you wanting to sell up?'

At the mention of her sister-in-law's name, she beamed. 'She's sad, of course, because she grew up at the camp, but she's realistic enough to know she can't expect me to keep it going. She always wanted to be a nurse, so running this place has never been on her agenda. And now she has little Harper too, she said she can use the cash from the sale as a nest egg and it'll give her options in the future.'

Here was an opportunity to clear another question up. 'I don't mean to be nosy, but she said she was a single parent too...?'

'Oh, she's a secretive one, is our Mia. Even I don't know who Harper's dad is. Mia's been very tight-lipped on that, all through the pregnancy and the last eighteen months since the birth. She's never said a word about him.'

'Oh, I do like a mystery.'

Carly laughed. 'Trust me, if she hasn't told me, she's not going to tell you.'

'You never know. I might have special charms.'

'I think you probably do.' Laughing, she looked up at him and gave him a very pretty smile. The air around them seemed to still. She was caught in a sunbeam of light, her hair firing red and gold, her eyes a soulful brown. He didn't think he'd ever seen anyone look more beautiful.

For a moment he was transfixed and couldn't take his eyes off her.

He held her gaze for just long enough to know she'd meant it exactly the way he'd thought she had and it was both a shock and a thrill to realise she might have the same weird feelings he had.

He thought about the connotations of her words. God knew what was going on inside her head, but she was looking at him with the same expression he felt. That this was…something.

His gaze slid from her eyes to her mouth. Her lips were blush-pink, full and lush. Perfect for kissing.

What would she taste like? Fresh strawberries?

She'd just told him about her tragic past and he wanted to comfort her, but more too. He shouldn't think about kissing her. But, damn, he really wanted to.

And still she was looking at him, her gaze heated and misted, as if she was wondering how he would taste. Before he knew what he was doing, he slid his hand over hers.

She blinked but didn't pull her hand away.

Thoughts crowded his head. *Too fast. Too soon. Too stupid. Too rash. Too beautiful. Too…everything.*

He tugged his fingers from hers and jumped back as reality seeped into his muddled brain. What the actual hell was he doing? He stood and shoved his hands into his pockets. 'Shoot. I'm sorry. I don't know what just happened.'

She shook her head, eyes startled, as if working through the ramifications too. 'It's…okay.'

'No, it isn't.' For so many reasons—not least because they were so close to where Mason was playing. How would he explain that to a four-year-old?

His son was still chattering away on the far side of the

slide. Owen walked across the playground, trying to control his rattling heart and raging libido. 'Mason? Are you done? It's time to go.'

CHAPTER FIVE

WHY WAS SHE offering to help him? Why was she allowing herself to fall deeper and deeper under this little family of two's spell? She had no business getting to know them more. Owen was a good man, underneath the gruffness. Mason was a cutie who just needed coaxing out of his shell.

But she was not the one to do the coaxing. She was heading off on an adventure.

And now…? Well, now she was just being neighbourly, the way she'd helped Horatio towards the end, and the way she baked cupcakes for Mia and Harper. Or the way she… Carly hit the steering wheel of her old truck. 'Who am I trying to kid?'

She wasn't being neighbourly—she was getting involved. She'd wanted to kiss him last night, so badly. Only the thought of Mason catching them had stopped her.

But what if the boy hadn't been there? Would she have kissed him?

She would have. Unlike other men she'd met since Raff's death, and the few boyfriends before she'd met her husband, Owen seemed to get her. There was an unspoken understanding. Something deepening. She couldn't explain it. The only other person she'd ever felt such a connection with had been her husband.

Was that a bad sign?

Truth was, it was all a bad sign, given that she was leaving.

The driveway to the old Nelson one-storey cottage was winding and gravelled and by the time she arrived she felt as if she was covered in a sheen of dust. As she stepped out of her truck, Mason ran out of the door. 'Carly! Carly!'

Her heart tripped at the grinning boy. 'Hey, Mason. How's it going?'

'Good.' He ran back to the front door. 'Daddy! Carly's here.'

'Great. Thanks, Mason. Now, go finish your call.' Owen stepped out of the front door and her heart didn't just trip, it stumbled. He was dressed in a faded grey T-shirt and battered jeans. His hair looked damp, as if it had just been washed, and it curled cutely up at the edges. His city skin was sun-kissed now, his toned arms tanned. He was gorgeous as he smiled. 'Hey, Carly. How's it going?'

Her mouth was dry. Words were lost somewhere in the mix of attraction and heat, but she managed a husky, 'Great, thanks. I've brought some wood and tools over. Thought we could have a look at fixing the weka version of a cat flap.'

His smile broadened. 'I never thought of it like that.'

She looked past him for Mason, who'd disappeared back inside. There was safety in having the child around. There'd be no hand-holding in front of Owen's son. 'Does Mason want to help too?'

Owen shook his head. 'He's on a call with his mum.'

'Oh.' Her stomach knotted. Why, she didn't know. It was none of her business. 'Bad timing?'

'No, it's fine. They're just finishing up.' He grimaced. 'They don't need me around for that.'

Silly woman, giving him up. 'Well, anyway. I'll just drop this stuff and head back home.'

'Let me get it.' He strode across to the truck's open flat-bed tray and reached into it for the planks of wood. As he stretched, the hem of his T-shirt lifted, giving her a bird's eye view of rippling abs.

Stop looking. Her mouth wasn't just watering, it was positively drooling now. She dragged her gaze back to the planks of wood and gave herself a good talking to. *Just being neighbourly. You're leaving.*

Grabbing her tool bag, she followed him back to the house. 'Right. Where's the hole the weka gets through?'

He leaned the planks against the wall, then crouched down, brushed some low bushes away from the side of the house and showed her the ragged weka-sized hole. 'Don't know if it's wear and tear, or whether it's been hit by something.'

She crouched down next to him and leaned forward to examine the hole at the same time he did. He must have sensed they were going to touch the broken wood at the same time she did, because he jerked away. As they both reeled backwards, she caught a hint of his scent: shampoo and soap and something distinctly masculine that made her insides buzz with need.

This was getting ridiculous. How could the way a man smelt make her tummy tumble?

She focused on the rip in the side of the house. 'It looks like a hit to me. Nelson had Parkinson's and couldn't manage at all without help at the end. I wouldn't be surprised if he reversed his car into it or something at some point, and possibly didn't even notice. With the bushes growing so tall here, we didn't notice either when we came to stock the place up for you. You want me to fix it for you?'

'Thanks, Carly.' Owen gave her a savvy smile and shook his head. 'I know I'm a city slicker, but I can manage this.'

'Go right ahead.' She stood up and crossed her arms, happy to watch him work. But she'd only said she'd drop the things off, not leer at his muscles. 'Oh. Right. Yes. I'll get going—'

'Carly!'

She turned to see Mason running towards her, arms outstretched as he chased a weka. 'Carly, this is my friend.'

'Also known as my alarm clock.' Owen straightened and laughed as he watched his son. God, they were both irresistible. 'Although, there are a few around here, and I can't tell them apart. So it could be a different bird each time.'

'No, Daddy. This one is my friend. He's got sticky-up feathers on his head.' Mason stopped chasing and came over to her. 'His name is Wallace. Like *Wallace and Gromit.*'

Carly laughed. 'I love those films.'

'Me too.'

'*The Wrong Trousers* is the funniest thing I've ever seen.' She watched the weka escape across the dusty path towards the undergrowth and laughed to herself. She was going to have to have a word with Owen about little Wallace.

Owen hammered the last nail into a piece of timber covering the hole. 'I defy the little blighter to get through that. Right. Thirsty work. You want a glass of something cold?'

'Err, I think I should go.'

'Okay. But don't blame me if you miss out on the best lemonade this side of the island.' His eyebrows rose, as if in a dare.

'Oh? Fighting talk. You've obviously never tried mine.' And she could never turn down a dare, so she followed man and boy into the kitchen. The cupboards and floor had been scrubbed and the place looked spotless—tired and old, but spotless. 'Wow. This looks a lot cleaner than when Nelson lived here.'

'We try our best, don't we, Mason? Looks like Carly's impressed with our work, buddy.' He held up his hand and his son gave him a high-five. 'Good job, son.'

Owen's mini-me looked up at him as if he was the sun, moon and stars all rolled into one. 'Good job, Dad!'

Carly's chest heated. She'd never had a connection with a blood relative, so didn't know how it felt to be praised by a parent, but she understood the look in Mason's eyes. Despite their difficult times, she knew that these two would grow closer and closer. It would have been nice to watch it all unfold.

Owen washed his hands in the big white butler's sink, poured them all a glass of lemonade and they clinked their glasses together, as if they were a team. She had to admit, 'This is really good lemonade.'

The corners of Owen's mouth turned up into a beautiful smile. Praise looked good on him. 'The trick is to use the peel too, not just the juice.'

'I'll give it a go.' The scent of tomatoes and garlic filled the air. She turned to the old cooker and saw a pan bubbling with sauce. 'And, hmm…something smells good.'

'We having 'getti Bolo-nose. I stirred it.' Mason's chest puffed out. 'You want some?'

'Spaghetti Bolognaise,' Owen clarified. 'And, trust me, you might like my lemonade, but you don't want to eat my cooking.'

This was the kind of family she craved, like the one she'd lost. She craved real food, a real connection. A willingness to do better, be better. But she had too many reasons not to stay. 'No, I'm okay. I mean… I'm not saying I don't want to eat your food. I just…should probably go.'

Owen's eyebrows peaked, as if he was rethinking his earlier statement. 'There's plenty. It's fine, really. It won't poison you.'

The heat in her chest thickened into an ache. Was she trying to run away because she was scared of caring about these people? Rafferty would have laughed at her. So would his mother, who was a stickler for manners and gratitude. *Feeding people is a sign of respect and friendship here on the island. We don't have much but, what we do have, we share.*

So what kind of an example would she be if she turned them down? Plus, she hadn't got round to preparing her own dinner today, and it did smell delicious. 'Okay. Thank you. But I can't stay late, I have a ton of things to do. I've got a viewer coming to see the camp tomorrow.'

'A buyer?'

'Prospective.' She held up her crossed fingers. 'Wish me luck.'

'So it's happening.' He smiled, but there was something else there too. She tried not to read too much into it. Was it…sadness? Regret? And she noticed that he didn't wish her luck, as she'd asked.

She felt like butterflies were fluttering in her stomach when she thought about selling up. Kind of the way she felt every time she looked at Owen. And there it was: confusion, excitement, apprehension and fear, all mixed up. 'It might be. This is the third viewer we've had come to look the place over, but the estate agent says this one is super-keen.'

'How do you feel?'

'Sad about leaving, but excited too.'

'Yeah. I know that feeling. I had it when we got on the ferry with our suitcases to come here. Leaving what we knew for something completely new. Wish I'd had the foresight to bring some paint and tools, though.' He looked round the room and grimaced. 'Anyway, this is ready. Mason, can you please set the table?'

They sat round the wooden kitchen table and ate the rustic dinner. Conversation was easy, especially with Mason there too, entertaining them by pulling silly faces, which they all joined in with. It was roundly agreed that Carly could pull the funniest one.

Then, after clearing up, Owen scraped back his chair. 'It's a clear night. Let's go outside and light the fire pit.'

Even though it was way past time for her to leave, Carly just couldn't bring herself to. *Ten more minutes.* 'Do you have marshmallows? We could cook them on sticks.'

'Strangely, I do. There were a few things in the cupboards when we arrived. Coffee, tea—that kind of stuff—and some marshmallows.'

'That was my idea.' She grinned. 'We thought you'd need some basics to help settle in.'

'Marshmallows are basics?' He reached into the cupboard and brought out a bright pink packet.

'For fire pits, yes. Come on, Mason. Let's go find some sticks for the marshmallows…'

After eating melted, delicious gooeyness, Mason fell asleep on his dad's knee, head lolling over to the side. Owen hauled the boy and himself to standing and spoke quietly. 'I'll just pop him into bed.'

She forced herself to grab the opportunity to leave. 'I'll get going, then.'

But Owen frowned. 'Really? It won't take long. To be honest, I could do with some adult company after spending all day talking with a four-year-old. I mean, I love him to bits, but there's only so much kiddie talk I can take.' He batted his eyelashes. 'Please? Ten minutes?'

She sighed. Did the man know just how gorgeous he was, and how hard it was for her to keep her distance? One little request and she was putty in his hands. 'Okay. Ten minutes. I'll make some hot chocolate while you put him to bed.'

'You certainly know about home comforts.'

She followed him back into the house, whispering, 'I run a school camp, Owen. I know what kids need to help them get over homesickness. And, funnily enough, adults love the comfort too.'

He was back in no time and sat down next to her in

front of the fire pit on a rickety wooden chair. The sun was setting and dark orange and red filled the sky, illuminated by flashes of sparks rising from the fire. When Owen smiled, it felt as if the flames flickering between them were in her belly.

He took the cup of hot chocolate and sipped. 'Now, that is delicious. Thanks for all the help, Carly. I really appreciate it.'

'Just being neighbourly.' She forced herself to shrug nonchalantly, even though she felt anything but.

He raised his eyebrows. They both knew there was a lot more to it than that. 'Well, thanks anyway.'

A bird's cry disturbed the silence and she remembered why she'd been smiling earlier on. 'Oh. Yes. Owen, I'm sorry to have to tell you this, but Wallace is actually Wilma.'

'Sorry?'

'He's not a boy weka. He's a girl.' She couldn't help but laugh at the distraught look on his face as her words sank in.

'Ah.' He guffawed. 'Call myself a doctor? I should know the difference.'

'I would hope you do.'

'Believe me, I do when it matters.'

She almost choked on her drink. The thought of the good doctor knowing exactly how to act when it mattered made her hot all over. She managed a coughed-out, 'Thank God for that.'

When she glanced over at him, she realised he was watching her, his eyes alight as he laughed too. What was he thinking? That this was too cosy? Too sweet? Too hot?

Or that she was truly just a neighbour?

He shrugged. 'Oh well, Mason will never know if I don't tell him.'

'Owen Cooper, are you going to lie to your son?' She laughed some more, feeling more relaxed than she had for a very long time.

'Hey, I already do. Who's the Tooth Fairy and Father Christmas? The Easter Bunny? None of them exist. It's all make-believe.'

'I guess. He's a lucky kid. I don't remember having those kinds of fairy-tales when I was growing up.'

He shuffled closer and frowned as his gaze searched her face. 'Really? No Father Christmas? No Easter Bunny?'

'They're not so big on the bunny in England. Or maybe they are these days, but not when I was growing up. I was lucky if there was a present under the Christmas tree with my name on it. And I'm not saying that for you to feel sorry for me. It's just what it was.'

'Why? Didn't your family believe in Christmas? Or was it something else…?' The fun in his eyes died and they turned sad—for her, even though he had no idea what her story was.

His innate compassion reverberated through her and she felt embarrassed that she'd snapped at him at their first meeting, assuming the worst. But that kind of suspicion had been programmed into her from an early age.

'I was taken away from my mum when I was eight months old and placed in foster care. Then spent many years being shunted from foster home to foster home, being moved on for a host of different reasons. The family I'd been placed with were moving, or pregnant with their first child and didn't have space for me, or a divorce… It never seemed fair to me that I was the one who had to go. But, well, there it was. So, if I was with a good family there could be a present, but I learnt not to expect anything in case I was taken away.'

'God, Carly, that's awful.' He really did look as if he meant it too.

'It is what it is. The children's home did the present thing, but we all knew it was the staff who bought them. There was always some older kid willing to tell you the truth about where the presents came from, to show you they were so much more clever and so much older.

'One year, I was in a foster home right up until the week before Christmas. There was a present under the tree with my name on and I was so excited about opening it. Then stuff happened and I was uplifted and moved on.' She could still remember the wrapping paper design after all these years. The reindeer with the bright red nose and the jolly Santa. 'So, I'd never really known what it meant to be fully part of a loving family, where you were loved unconditionally, until I came here and met the Edwards family.'

Here she was telling him things she'd never told anyone and yet it felt natural to confide in him. Was it because he was a doctor and he knew about confidentiality? That she trusted him to keep her secrets? Or was it because he was a genuinely good guy?

She trusted him...or was beginning to. That was a revelation, especially after such a short time knowing him.

He drained his cup and placed it on the ground. 'And your birth mum?'

'I don't know much about my birth parents. I have a birth certificate with my mum's name on it and just an empty space where my dad's name should have been. My mother was very young, apparently. Clearly, she couldn't cope with having a baby. Maybe I was a mistake she didn't want.'

It occurred to her that that was exactly what Mason was to his own mother. And it made her like Owen even more that he was so determined to care for his son.

'You are absolutely not a mistake.' He slid his hand over hers and gripped it, all the while his gaze fixed on hers. She could see the flash of censure in his eyes at her words and felt the power of it flicker through her. He wanted her to believe in herself. She liked very much that he was so passionate about it—liked it too much. Liked *him* too much.

A warning thud in her heart almost made her slip her hand out from under his, but it felt right to be talking about her life with someone who wanted to listen, who *saw* her, wanted to hold her hand and give her comfort. It had been so long since she'd felt this close to anyone.

She had to be honest and admit she was lonely here… even with the hundreds of kids who came through every week, and with her sister-in-law down the road and the lovely community on the island. Everyone had been so supportive since the accident, but she was lonely and pining for physical contact, for affection and caring. And to give all that too. But, as always, she put on a brave face. 'Well, my inauspicious beginnings don't matter, really. Here I am. Doing okay.'

'Better than okay. You're amazing, if a little scary.' Smiling, he squeezed her hand. 'You don't want to find her, your mum?'

'No. I don't want to look back any more. I'm so tired of living in the past—although I don't ever want to forget Raff and his parents,' she added hurriedly, as if they were all looking down on her and listening. Maybe they were. And, *if* they were, they'd know how hard she'd hurt and for how long. How much she still missed them. Every day.

Owen smiled gently. 'Of course not.'

'But I'm all about looking forward now.'

'Ah. Your adventure.' The light in his eyes dimmed a little, or maybe it was just the flames in front of them dying down. She couldn't tell.

'My adventure.' And there it was. The reminder of why she shouldn't be sitting so close to him. She tugged her hand away and wedged it under her thigh in case it had any ideas about fitting itself back into his hand again. 'Anyway. What about you?'

'Boring, really.' A shoulder rose and then fell. 'My parents split up when I was eight and I lived with my dad.'

'Unusual.'

He looked over to the house where his sleeping son was. 'Not so much, it seems.'

Indeed. 'What happened to your mum?'

'They split up because she had an affair with someone she worked with and then moved in with the guy. Dad said he wanted me to stay in the family home, and she agreed. So, my dad brought me up...after a fashion. Let's just say he didn't read the rule book on parenting, so I'm learning a whole lot of new things. Like the importance of routine and boundaries. It's been a steep learning curve.'

Which explained why he'd been so irritated to have missed kindy pick-up the other day. He was just trying to get it right. 'Do you see much of your mum?'

'Not really. She has another life and another family now. She moved to Christchurch for her new man's job. We lived in Auckland, so I saw her in the holidays. Sometimes.'

That last word was tinged with sadness. 'Not often?'

'It got difficult. We'd plan things and then she'd cancel. My dad didn't handle it well and there were arguments. That was worse than her not showing up.'

'That's why you're keen to keep Mason's mum in the picture.'

'It's important to me that he stays in contact with her. I really didn't want it to be like this, but what can you do?' He shrugged, palms up, as if he was okay with this, but his eyes told a different story. He clearly hurt, just reliving it. 'In the end, I gave up making plans with my mum. It was easier that way. And I think she was relieved, to be honest. It's not easy to start a new life with a kid hanging round.'

He paused and sighed. 'I always felt like the spare part at her house, like I didn't fit in and that the new guy only tolerated me being there for five minutes then got irritated with me. I'd hate that to happen to Mason.'

So many parallels with his own life. 'I don't know. There

are plenty of women happy to have a relationship with a single dad.'

'It's okay. You don't have to be kind.' He laughed. 'I'm not looking for anything. I don't want to get involved in a relationship and have that kind of thing happen again. I'd always be waiting for the ball to drop, right? I'm here to settle my boy and give him a good life. Anything else would be a distraction.'

'But in time?' Why she was asking this and holding her breath waiting for his answer, she didn't know. It wasn't as if she would even be here.

'I haven't really thought about it. But she'd have to be someone very special and someone who was committed to sticking around. The last thing he needs is another person flitting in and out of his life.'

'Of course.' It was suddenly chilly, but strangely there was no breeze. She shivered and stood up. 'It's getting dark. I should go.'

'Okay.' He stood. 'I'll walk you to your truck.'

'You don't have to. I'm perfectly capable of walking a few metres.'

'I know. You're capable of so many things. You're a very impressive woman. But I want to.'

And she wanted him to. Despite everything he was saying about no distractions and not wanting to get involved, and despite her own plans and dreams to leave the island, she didn't want to leave this fireside with the fresh night air, the smoke, the stars and this wonderful, caring man who listened and didn't judge. Whose touch set her alight.

But it was what she had to do, for all their sakes. She pulled herself upright and dug her keys from her shorts pocket. 'Right.'

He walked with her in silence to the truck. Only the sound of their footsteps on gravel and the wekas' night calls rent the air. And yet there was a feeling, a stirring anticipation that seemed to shiver in the atmosphere and shimmer deep inside her, that this wasn't the end, but a beginning. Of a friendship? Yes. She wanted that.

More…? Impossible. He'd just said anything else would be a distraction. And yet…

She pressed the key fob and the truck's lights flashed. She pulled the door open but jumped at the feel of his palm on her hand.

'Carly.'

She turned to face him, her belly dancing with lightness. 'Yes?'

'Thanks again.' He leaned in and pressed a friendly kiss to her cheek.

She closed her eyes as the touch of his skin sent thrills of desire rippling through her. She pulled back, looked at him and caught the heat in his gaze, the need.

She should have turned then and climbed into her truck. She should have driven away into the darkness. But she was transfixed by the way he was looking at her, as if she was…everything.

His previous words about not being distracted seemed to melt from her brain and all she could focus on was his face, his heated eyes, his delicious mouth. So tantalisingly close.

Later, when she thought back to this moment—and she thought back to this moment *a lot*—she wasn't sure how it had happened. One minute they were looking at each other, the next moment they were kissing. Hot, hard and greedy. Desperate. Frantic. Out of control.

The heat of his mouth made her moan and stoked the burning in her belly. She spiked her fingers into his hair and pressed her lips against his, her body hard against his. The outline of his muscled chest pressed against her and, lower, she could feel just how much he was enjoying this. How much he wanted her.

'God, Carly...' His hands cupped her face and held her in place as he captured her bottom lip in his teeth, then took her mouth fully again and kissed her, kissed her and kissed her.

He tasted of hot chocolate and a warm, delicious spice that she couldn't get enough of. He smelt of the smoky fire. He tasted of coming home and of somewhere new, exotic and enticing. Exciting.

It was too much and not enough all at the same time. She didn't want it to end, this night, this kiss lasting for...

Someone committed to staying around.

His words came back to her in a hard jolt of reality. She had an interested buyer visiting tomorrow. A plan to be gone as soon as feasibly possible. So kissing Owen was an impossible and ridiculous idea and a sure-fire way of ruining the fledgling friendship they'd grown.

What on earth was she doing?

'Sorry. I've got to...' She took two shaky steps away from him, jumped into her car and got the hell away.

CHAPTER SIX

'WHO THINKS THIS would be a good spot for a shelter? Let's have a look. There's a good amount of shade from the sun, but also lots of light filtering through the trees, and the ground is nice and flat to lie on. But, before we start to build anything, we have to check to make sure the area is safe. That means looking on the ground and clearing away any wet or rotting debris for a nice, dry sleeping area.'

Carly looked at each of the six Year Eight students in turn, making sure they were listening and engaged. Two of the boys were already on their knees clearing away soggy leaf matter. Two girls were gathering sticks. The other two were staring at her, nodding intently, just as she liked it.

What she didn't like was that her thoughts kept winging back to the other night, to Owen and the kiss. And, even though it had been wonderful, sensual and delicious, she needed to keep her distance from him and rebuild her defences.

'Miss?' One of the boys was staring at her and she realised she'd lost her train of thought. Or, rather, had found a more pressing one instead of teaching…as she was being paid to do.

'Oh, yes. Right. Keep hold of any long sticks and branches we can use to build the shelter walls. And check overhead to make sure nothing can fall on us in the night.' Six heads turned to look skywards. 'Excellent. Then we have to find a long log we can use as the main shelter strut. Bonus points for finding one with a V-shaped notch in it where we can rest branches and sticks to create a perfect angle for an A-frame shelter.'

A crack of dry wood had her turning to see Wayne, one of the more experienced teachers, running down the hill towards her. His face was pale and he looked shocked. 'Carly, come quickly.'

'What's happened?' She kept her voice and manner calm so the children wouldn't detect any panic. Not that she was panicking. She'd learnt long ago to expect anything and everything by way of incidents on this island. 'What's the matter?'

'There's been an accident.' Wayne's eyebrows rose and his eyes narrowed in a gesture she took to mean *hurry!*

'You can't bring them to me here?' In an emergency situation, she preferred to be closer to the camp if possible, which meant walking wounded should be brought down. That way she could co-ordinate everything, keep an eye on the camp and be on hand for anything else.

'Yes, she's okay to hobble down here. But, no.'

Which sounded like a lot of confusion to Carly. 'Okay. Kids, I need you to go back to the lecture room and wait for me there. There's a folder with photos of the kind of shelters we're going to build. I'd like you to have a look at them and plan your design for when I get back.' Grabbing the first aid bag she carried with her everywhere, Carly turned to the teacher. 'Okay. Tell me as we walk.'

She followed him at a trot through the bush and up the steep hill behind the bunk rooms, listening to the man's words. 'Tegan and her friends were exploring up by the old mines and she fell onto an old, rusted metal spike. She's got a big gash in her shin that looks quite deep. She's very upset and wouldn't move because she was freaked out by the blood.'

'Right.' Carly stole herself for what she was going to have to deal with. 'There's a lot of it?'

'Not enough to make her weak or need a transfusion, but enough to freak a thirteen-year-old out.'

'Okay. Noted. Don't freak out at the blood.' They turned off the main track and walked towards the Keep Out sign. She pushed the wire fencing down for him to clamber over. 'But why were they here? This place is strictly out of bounds.'

The teacher turned and held the wire for her. 'They were doing the orienteering challenge and got distracted by an adventure.'

She held back her irritation, keeping the lesson about following signs until later, once she'd assessed the patient's mental state.

Which proved to be a good idea, as it turned out, because Tegan was sobbing as they approached. She was propped up against the base of a huge kauri tree trunk, her left leg extended out in front of her, covered in a waterproof jacket. 'I'm… I'm sorry…miss.'

Carly's heart squeezed at the girl's distress. She knelt down to get a good look at the leg injury. 'Hey. Right now, I'm more concerned about your leg than where you are. We'll talk about that later. Can I have a look at the damage?'

The girl's face crumpled again as she sobbed. 'It's nasty. And it hurts.'

'I know, honey. Look away.' Carly glanced up at one of Carly's friends and beckoned her over. 'Pop your arm round Tegan and give her a hug while I have a look.' She peeled back the coat and, sure enough, the wound was wide and deep, and far beyond her skill set. It was still oozing blood, which had also carpeted the ground. 'It looks like you need stitches, and we need to find out if your tetanus injection is up to date. I can manage small wounds, but this is a bit too tricky for me to deal with.'

'Do I have to go…?' There came a stuttering inhaled sob. 'To…hospital?'

'I'm going to let the doctor decide. We'll have to take you over to the island medical centre, unless I can get him to come here. I'll radio in and see if he's free.'

Wayne stepped forward. 'That's a big call. We can take her over there.'

'He has clinic in the morning and then does visits in the afternoons. He could be anywhere on the island right now. But he only lives in the next cove over so he might be closer than we think. I just need to find his whereabouts.'

If I can get over my embarrassment about the kiss. Her cheeks heated as she pulled out the satellite phone and called him.

'Hey, Carly.' His voice was thick with warmth and her body reacted to it with a full-on blush. And heat. So much heat and need. It didn't seem to matter that her head had decided the kiss had been a bad idea, her body wanted more.

It was the first time she'd spoken to him since she'd dashed away on Saturday night. Since the kiss that had been ever-present in her head. She relived his taste, the exquisite press of him in her arms. The way he'd made her feel. All giddy and turned on and discombobulated and yet safe at the same time.

Had made her feel like that. But giving in to their desires had been stupid. She cleared her throat and imbued her tone with as much professionalism and urgency as she could muster. 'Owen, I'm up at the old copper mine site with a young woman. She's got a nasty shin wound from a rusting metal spike and it'll need stitches.'

'Right.' The honey seeped away and his tone relayed a sharp alertness. 'I can be there in twenty. Tetanus status known?'

'No. Can you check, please?' Carly relayed the girl's

personal information for him to check on the national vaccination system.

'Okay.' He came back to her. 'I'll have a look. See you *very* soon.'

The way he emphasised 'very' made her heart trip with excitement. 'Sure. We'll get her down to base before you arrive. See you there. Over and out.'

They had to convince Tegan to walk first. And somehow between now and then Carly needed to get her body into line with her head.

After taping some gauze and wadding as a rudimentary compression dressing over the gash, she explained, 'Tegan, I know it's going to be hard for you, and that your leg hurts, but we do need to get you down to the camp.'

'I...don't want...'

'I know. But the sooner we get you there, the sooner we can give you the right pain killers and get you comfortable. Plus, I'll make you some hot chocolate. That makes everything better.' Hot chocolate was always the answer to every woe, as far as Carly was concerned.

The girl gave a sniff, a sob and then a shaky, 'Okay.'

Between them they managed to help Tegan down to the little medical room and wait for Owen's arrival. Carly tried not to watch out for him, instead busying herself with instructions to the little group she'd had to leave earlier, and then double-checking on Tegan and making her a jug of hot chocolate for when Owen had assessed the wound.

And then there he was, striding across the jetty with his medical bag slung over his shoulder. Her heart jolted and jigged and she told herself to stop being silly. They were both professionals. They could deal with an emergency without letting the kiss get in the way.

Couldn't they?

But she wasn't sure how to act around him now. Before... before the kiss...she'd been able to put him into a 'friend' box and a 'colleague' box, but now the edges had all been mussed up and she didn't know how to feel or how to be. Which explained her shaky hands as she pulled back the temporary dressing to reveal the nasty gash on Tegan's leg.

To his credit, Owen showed little emotional reaction to the wound or the blood as he examined Tegan. 'I'm going to have to do some fancy needlework to get this sorted. But don't worry, I'll try to make it look as good as new.'

'Needlework?' The girl stared up at him.

'Stitches. I'll give you some pain relief first, then I can clean it all up without causing you too much pain.' He drew up some anaesthetic into a syringe and said in a soothing voice, 'Tegan, this is a local anaesthetic. I'm sorry to say it might sting a bit, but then when it starts to work you won't feel a thing.'

He injected the tissue around the wound, explaining everything he did.

'Ow!' Tegan's eyes snapped closed and her face crumpled.

'I know. I'm sorry. You're doing so well, Tegan. This anaesthetic is like magic. Just wait and see.' He waited for her to open her eyes, then held the girl's gaze and smiled, which made her smile back, and made Carly smile too. He was so good with Tegan. He'd been so good with Wiremu and Simon. He was a world-class good guy. And he was still chatting brightly.

He washed his hands and opened a sterile suture pack. Then he slid on some gloves and got Carly to pour saline into a pot before he syringed it over the wound, giving it a thorough clean.

Carly assisted, trying not to catch his eye and willing her trembling hands to settle. Since when had she had shaking hands in response to a man?

Since the man in question was so close, smelt so good

and kissed like a god. Too bad the minutes she'd spent trying to align her head and body had come to nothing.

As Owen expertly sewed up the wound, he distracted Tegan with conversation. 'You're going to have an interesting story to tell everyone back home. Talking of... I'll need to have a chat with your parents in a minute. Just to let them know that you've had a little fall and that I'm sorting you out.'

Tegan grimaced. 'My mum will go mad. They'll want to come over and take me home.'

Carly stroked the girl's hand. 'Do you want to go home?'

'No. I want to stay here with my friends.'

Owen's eyebrows rose. 'Are you sure? You won't be able to swim for a few days because of the stitches, and I'm going to have to give you an injection, because your tetanus wasn't up to date. And some antibiotics, in case there were any nasty bugs up there. It's not going to be so fun just sitting around. Won't home be more comfortable?'

'I don't want to miss out. Can I just sit and watch the others?'

'FOMO. I totally get it,' Carly chipped in. 'But I've got some books you can read if you get bored.'

'I brought some with me. I'm reading the *CHERUB* books again.'

'Brilliant.' Owen grinned and he looked so boyishly handsome and delighted that Carly's heart did a little flip. 'There's nothing like spy stories to take your mind off your leg. So, it's decided then. If your parents are okay with it, I'll check the dressing every day until you go home with the rest of your group.'

'Thank you.' The girl beamed up at him.

'No problem. Just don't go off-piste next time. Stick to the path.' His tone became just a tad more assertive. 'Stick to the rules.'

'I'm sorry.' Tegan looked at Owen and then at Carly. 'I'm so sorry, Carly.'

'I know you are.' Carly didn't feel much like telling the girl off now, especially given that Owen had handled it so well. 'Off-piste' was the perfect way to describe the side trip to the mine. 'Here's your hot chocolate. Sit here for a while and drink it. Dr Cooper will chat to your parents.'

Carly took the opportunity to leave them to the call. It had been an easier interaction with Owen than she'd expected but she definitely needed to get away from him.

She was just finishing up outside the lecture room with the shelter group when she saw him striding across the grass towards her. Her heart hammered against her ribcage. What was he going to say? How did he feel about the kiss? What did he want from her?

What did she want from him?

The answer to every question was simple and difficult at the same time. She just didn't know. Apart from the jittery heart and excitement rolling in her tummy, of course…she knew about that. And the desire to kiss him again. And the many, many reasons why she shouldn't.

She clapped her hands to get her students' attention. 'Okay, everyone. We're finished here. Well done for some great ideas. Go wash up for lunch.'

'Carly.' Owen's tone was friendly, but his manner was… she couldn't describe it…apprehensive?

'Hey. Thanks for coming over so quickly.' Her mouth suddenly felt dry. Everything felt stuttered and difficult compared to the other night, with marshmallows, hot chocolate, the glowing fire and the magic of his mouth. 'Apparently Tegan was upset by all the blood but you put her at ease. You've got a friend for life there, Dr Cooper.'

'I'll make sure to come and check her dressings tomorrow.' He frowned. 'How come there's bits of rusting metal around the island?'

Oh…that was what he wanted to talk about. She almost sagged in relief. She knew they had to address the kiss, but she wasn't sure she was brave enough to do it right now. 'It's from old mining machinery and it's impossible to move, I'm afraid. A lot of it has been absorbed into the landscape. Nature has almost subsumed it and few people even know it's there. But I'll make sure I put up a bigger sign and more barbed-wire fencing. There's always something.'

'Good.' There was a pause. He shoved his hand deep into his pocket then looked right at her. 'Look, Carly, I think we need to have a quick chat.'

And she knew exactly what it would be about. But he was right; they needed to sort out their boundaries whether she was brave enough or not. 'Okay. You'd better come over to the house.'

He hadn't even known he was going to say those words until they'd tumbled from his mouth. It had been easy to talk to her with the buffer of an emergency between them, and he could have just waved goodbye and got back into his boat, but that would have been the coward's way out. They'd stepped over a line and they needed to deal with it. Even if he felt tongue-tied and off-balance.

He was not sure about going over to her house, being surrounded by her things and her scent, being alone with Carly. Every minute spent away from her was a torture of needing to see her again, railing against his decision not to. Every second spent with her made that decision fade into nothing.

Truth was, he was smitten, and he didn't know how to cope with that. His relationship with Miranda must have started with a little smitten-ness, but he couldn't remember it. 'Don't you need to get back to your students?'

'No. It's fine. I'm finished for the day now. Like you, I tend to have structured stuff in the mornings then wing the afternoons.' A little frown hovered over her eyes as they strolled to her house, and he wondered what she was really thinking behind all this small talk. 'This afternoon the teachers and kids are going for a hike over to the Mansion House for a history lesson, so I'm going to do paperwork.'

'I've never managed to get to the Mansion House.'

'Oh, you should.' The frown lines smoothed out a little. 'It's a beautiful old colonial building and used regularly as a wedding venue. There are lots of photos of the island over the years charting its history.'

'I should take Mason.'

'He'd love it. You can either walk over the hill or take the boat round—there's plenty of mooring, and a little cafe with home baking and the best ice-cream on the island. And a lovely beach to cool off with a swim, if it's a hot day. All quite safe.'

Safe. That was what this conversation was. Polite, well-mannered and avoiding the very thing they should be talking about.

The inside of her cottage was cosy and homely, with well-worn furniture and what looked like hand-made knitted throws in rich blues and subtle reds. It was a home, unlike the place he was living in. Mason needed a home. Owen made a mental note to add soft furnishings to his next online shopping list. Not something he'd ever thought he'd give a damn about, but he could see how they added softness and comfort. Mason needed that.

Carly led him into the kitchen and put the kettle on. He watched as she gracefully moved around her space. She was dressed in the short shorts for teaching, hiking and water sports, which he now knew to be her work outfit, along with a blue T-shirt with the bright yellow Camp Rāwhiti logo above her heart. The sunlight streaming through the big bay window caught the red in her hair, making him transfixed. She turned and gave him a hesitant smile as she dropped tea bags into two cups.

His gaze landed on her lips and, even though he knew their conversation had to be about not kissing, it was the only thing he wanted to do right now. So, he avoided the subject altogether. 'How did it go with the buyer?'

Her smile wavered and she shrugged. 'I don't think she was interested. She certainly hasn't put an offer in or anything.'

'Is that good or bad?'

'It's frustrating, to be honest. I feel like I'm in limbo.'

So did he—caught somewhere between his warring heart and head. If he'd been free and not a father, he might have gone with his heart and suggested a fling before she left. But he wasn't free, he had a child to think about. The spectre of the kiss hung over them and if he didn't say anything it'd always be there.

He took a deep breath and exhaled slowly. 'Look, Carly. I'm so sorry, after what I said about not wanting a distraction. I shouldn't have kissed you.'

Her cheeks pinked and she gave him a hurried nod. 'No. Well, yes. I mean, I kissed you first, I think. And I'm sorry too. I was out of order.'

'I think we both got carried away with the lovely night sky and the marshmallows and the fire.'

'Yes.' She poured hot water into the mugs and didn't give him any more eye contact, but she said, 'It's something, isn't it? This thing we've got going.'

'This thing we're not going to act on.'

'Yes. That thing.' She finally lifted her head and looked at him, and he could see the same struggle he was experiencing mirrored in her eyes. He could see lightness and some darkness, need and affection, confusion, hope and regret… But nothing had really happened between them apart from the kiss. And yet, it felt as if something was happening.

Her eyebrows rose. 'It's weird. I haven't wanted to kiss another man since Raff died, and yet here I am, wanting to do it again, even though I'm leaving and I won't be back for a long time. If ever. Well, I will come back, obviously, because Mia and Harper are here, but you know what I mean... I'm going. You're staying. You've got Mason. I've got plans.'

Wow. He hadn't expected all that. It was a revelation and a responsibility. A revelation, because he hadn't expected her to say something so honest. And a responsibility, because the first kiss after something so traumatic as losing your husband had to be perfect. Symbolic or something, he imagined. Was that why she'd run off—because it hadn't been perfect? Because he wasn't Raff? Because it was too soon, too much?

He wasn't sure how to react, because she'd just admitted she wanted to do it again and they really shouldn't. 'It's just a physical thing, I think. Two people on their own and all that. I know I sometimes feel kind of lonely.' Now he just sounded like a loser. 'Well, not lonely. Alone. You know how it is.'

But she smiled again. 'Yes. *Alone.* That's exactly right. Which is fine, until it isn't. Some days you don't even notice the silence, and some days it's deafening and you just want someone to talk to, right? Like this.'

'Like this.' Except, he was probably making a mess of it all. 'Okay. So we're both agreed—it can't happen again.'

'Agreed. Let's drink to it. No kissing.' She handed him a mug of steaming tea and they clinked cups together. 'You have my permission to stop me if I make a move.'

He laughed, grateful they could both see the funny side of this—even though it did nothing to erase the torment and deep ache to spend more time with her. He was relieved, too, that it was a mutual thing and he wasn't dreaming it. 'Back at you, Carly. I mean, I can control myself. It's just hard around you.'

'I'm not sure we should even say things like that.' She pressed her lips together, but the smile spread across her face. Heat and need hit her eyes. 'But I'm glad you did. And I'm glad I'm not the only one feeling it.'

'We'll just have to stick to a hands-off, mutual appreciation society.'

'A mutual appreciation society.' She giggled. 'Yes. That's what it is. At least we can laugh about it. In another life, we might have made something of it, right?'

He ached to make something of it right now. To touch her again, to kiss her. To make love to her right here in this kitchen. The only thing he could do was keep his distance until she left. 'I'd say so. Yes.'

'Bad timing, then.' She shrugged, looking up at him through impossibly long eyelashes. 'You're a good guy, Owen Cooper.'

'Which goes to show how little you know me.' He took a sip of tea to stop himself from saying any more, or something he might regret.

Because in another life, where Carly was concerned, he'd have preferred to be very bad indeed.

CHAPTER SEVEN

'MIA! YOO-HOO!' WITHOUT KNOCKING, as always, Carly rushed into her sister-in-law's house and found her in the kitchen, sudsy hands in the deep, battered sink, baby Harper in her high chair, her cherub face smudged with something that looked like yoghurt. Carly slicked a kiss on her niece's head and then caught Mia's gaze. 'We need to talk.'

'And good morning to you too.' Mia wiped her hands on a tea towel. 'Sure. What about?'

About the camp. About my crazy, mixed-up feelings for your boss. About a mind-warping kiss...

'The estate agent just called me. The woman that viewed last weekend has more questions. I think…' Carly's tummy fluttered with nerves, excitement and a smattering of anxiety. 'I think she's going to put an offer in.'

'Wow.' Mia's eyes grew large and sparkly. 'I thought she wasn't interested.'

'Me too. When she was here, she played disinterested, but she's keen. Apparently, she was asking about resource consent for multiple dwellings.'

'Multiple?'

'Apartments, probably.' Carly imagined towering blocks and a busy resort-style feel to the haven she'd come to love. Her heart contracted.

Mia frowned. 'Oh. I see. Well, we can't do much about

that. But I guess it's good news if she's asking questions like that.'

'Is it good news, though?' They'd come to the truth of the matter now. 'Apartments. Holiday lets. I imagine there'll be a swimming pool and a bar. It's not exactly the legacy your parents wanted.'

'We can't dictate how someone's going to use the land once we've sold it.'

'I know. I wish we could. At least some of it is covenanted, so a decent acreage will remain bush.'

'Oh, honey.' Mia wrapped her arms round Carly's shoulder and gave her a tight hug. 'Do not beat yourself up about this. Things move on. Change is the only constant. I grew up at the camp, and I don't feel bad about selling it, so you shouldn't.'

'Are you sure?' Because, even though Mia was saying the words, there was something in her eyes that gave Carly pause. She just hoped her friend wasn't saying all the right things just to make her feel better about leaving. 'It's your family home.'

Mia shrugged. 'I know and, to be honest, it does feel strange to know it's not going to be there any more. But I'm a single mum, and on a nurse's salary I don't get to save much. I need to be able to set Harper up with a college fund and selling the camp will do that.'

'College? She's not even two years old. If she's got any sense she'll be a builder…there's so much development going on here, she'll have a job for life.' Carly jokily pumped her pecs but then saw the anxiety in Mia's expression. Then she glanced round the kitchen, noticing that the unit doors were cracked and the walls needed a coat of paint…in fact, the cute cottage needed an overhaul, something that would cost time and money Mia didn't have. She needed this sale to go through. 'But I totally understand. It must be hard being Mum and Dad and the only breadwinner.'

Carly had grown up used to being on her own, but losing her whole family in one accident must have changed Mia's outlook for ever. Change might be the only constant, but it was clear the woman needed to feel secure and to provide enough for her daughter, just in case anything should happen.

And now Carly felt torn apart. Should she stay here for Mia and Harper—be their constant?

But Mia squeezed her tightly again before letting her go and focusing back on the sudsy water. 'I may be a child of the camp, but I'm also a parent, and I would never, ever expect Harper to do anything just because I wanted her to do it, or because of my legacy—whatever that means. Please don't spend your life doing things just because they'd make my parents happy.'

'And Raff.' Carly's chest hurt at the thought of her late husband. She wanted always to make him proud.

'Of course. Yes. And Raff.' Mia smiled sadly. 'My brother would want, more than anything, for you to be happy. To have a future and a family. And to travel, just like you both planned to do. He wouldn't want you to be sad for ever.'

'I'm not.' Carly dug deep for a smile and thought about the last few days of confusion, attraction and excitement. 'At least, not all the time.'

'Particularly not when you're with the good doctor?' Mia's eyes twinkled and she pretended to swoon.

'Who? Owen?' Just thinking about him brought heat to Carly's cheeks, and other places that had no business getting heated. 'There's nothing happening there.'

'Hmm.' Mia's gaze focused on Carly's face. 'I mean, what's not to like? The man's a great doctor. And very resourceful. He's not complained once about having no receptionist while Anahera's away, and he's dealt with all the messages coming through to the surgery every day, even the mundane stuff. And I saw him doing DIY the other day when I went to drop Mason off at home. That man looks good in a sweat.' She wafted her hand in front of her face, as if suddenly hot.

Carly wished she'd seen him in a sweat, but wasn't going to admit that to her sister-in-law. 'Still nothing happening. If he's that perfect, why don't you make a play for him?' Then she winced, wishing she hadn't said that. She didn't like the idea of Owen being with another woman.

But Mia shook her head. 'Not my type.'

'Oh?' Good. And also interesting… Mia had never spoken about the kind of guy she might be attracted to. 'Which is?'

'I don't have one. And this isn't about me.' Mia eyed Carly with suspicion. 'Do you know what parents are really, really good at?'

'What?'

'Knowing when someone is lying to them. There's something with the doctor…right?' She pierced Carly with a steely stare that almost had her spitting out the truth.

We kissed. It was good. I want more kisses…maybe more other things. But everything's confusing. 'He's a nice guy.'

'He is. So, tell me, is the wobble about the sale only because of my parents' legacy or is there more to it? Because you don't have to sell. You don't have to go travelling. You could stay a while, see how things develop.'

'I really, really do need to go. I need to get my head straightened out, and I can't do it with the memories of the camp and now Owen blurring everything. I have to have some space.'

'So he's in the picture?' Mia looked hopeful.

'No. But he's stopping me looking at things with a clear head.'

'Okay. I get that. Men, huh?'

'And what do you know about that? You haven't dated

for years.' It was gentle ribbing, although Carly thought it was high time Mia started to date again. Did she feel alone sometimes too?

'Because of men. Huh?' Mia laughed and rolled her eyes. 'Seriously, though, talk to me any time. I'm here for you.' She grabbed a washcloth, ran it under the sink, squeezed it out and then handed it to Carly. 'Now, would you please wipe Harper's face while I finish the washing up? I'm taking Harper and Mason to the beach for a play date and I'm late already. There's some apple and feijoa pie in the fridge, if you're hungry. You're getting too thin. Eat, woman.'

'Sounds lovely, but I'm fine. Thanks.'

She wasn't, though. She wasn't fine at all. She was all muddled up and desperately wanted someone to talk things through with all over again.

It was no use. Keeping his distance from Carly was impossible on this small island when their lives and those of the people around them were so intertwined. He saw her when she called in to see Mia at the medical centre, while lunching at the yacht club and bumped into her in the tiny supermarket. They waved as their boats zipped past each other across the glittering bay. Everywhere he turned, she was there. And alongside that came the crushing craving to get to know her better, despite everything they'd said.

It had been almost a week since their 'mutual appreciation society' agreement and the ache hadn't dimmed. In fact, if anything, it had grown stronger.

But right now the only thing he needed to do was put her out of his head and write up his notes from this morning's surgery. Then review the messages on the answer-machine, chase up blood results and go on his afternoon visits... Who had said coming to a tiny island would be easier doctoring? Not to mention fixing up the cottage, which he tried to do in the little spare time he had when not looking after Mason.

But he couldn't concentrate today. His last conversation with Carly kept coming back to him, resonating deep inside.

Alone.

He hadn't realised he felt like that.

When Miranda had left, he'd felt lost and totally out of his depth, but in some ways it had been a relief to end the struggle between them and accept things weren't working. He'd been thrown into sole care of their son, and he'd floundered, asking for advice from anyone and everyone about how to deal with a devastated child. His focus had been only on Mason.

Sure, he'd chatted about the failure of his marriage to his friends, but he hadn't looked for anyone else to fill the gap Miranda had left. Certainly, he hadn't had the headspace for someone else in his life. But, now things were settling, he noticed the space more.

It would be even larger when Carly left.

The door to his consultation room flew open and a woman's voice made him jump. 'Doc? Are you in here? Ah, yes. *Kia Ora*, Owen.'

'Anahera? You're back?' He jumped up and gave her a quick hug. 'Am I pleased to see you.'

'I'm pleased to be here.' She grinned. 'But I've heard you've been coping just fine without me.'

'Barely.' He pointed to the piles of paperwork he'd been wading through and the filing he'd put off because he didn't know the system well enough yet. 'I'm drowning under bits of paper. How's Wiremu?'

She shrugged but smiled. 'He's okay. A bit wobbly, but getting there. Try telling that man to slow down. He doesn't know the meaning of the word.'

The ringing of the reception phone interrupted her and

her eyebrows rose. 'Not even in the office for five minutes and it starts.'

Owen laughed. 'The island gossip machine knows you're here already.'

'Honey, I *am* the island gossip machine!' she bellowed as she disappeared down the corridor.

Laughing and relieved that he now had an extra pair of hands to run the surgery, he went back to reviewing his notes. But the door swung open again. Anahera. 'We've got a boat versus jet-ski accident in the harbour. There's a head injury and some minor scrapes, by all accounts.'

'Just as I thought things would start to quieten down. There's no rest for the wicked.' He just wished he'd a chance to be wicked…with Carly. He slid his chair back and grabbed his bag. 'Tell them I'm on my way.'

She nodded. 'I'll try to find Carly and get her to join you at the harbour.'

'Great. Thanks.' *I think*. But working with her would be no different from passing her in the street, with a quick nod of the head and focus elsewhere, right?

Wrong.

The head injury victim was lying prone on the harbour causeway, apparently having collapsed after jumping off his boat. He had a nasty cut on his forehead and a lumpy bruise blooming around his eye socket. The jet-ski rider was nursing what looked like a dislocated shoulder and a grudge against the boat owner, given the stream of curse words coming out of his mouth, but Owen had assessed priority and was attending to the semi-conscious head injury patient first. If jet-ski man was shouting and cursing, he was at least conscious.

He was stabilising the collapsed man's neck and head when Carly came bounding along the jetty. The moment she swung into view, his heart stumbled over itself. He tried to convince himself that he was just relieved to have someone else's help to deal with the incident, but he knew it was more than that. 'Hey, Carly.'

'Hey. What have we got here?' She knelt next to their injured man, across from Owen, and her scent swirled around him, sending his memory spiralling to their kiss. The fire. The moment of true connection.

It was good she was leaving. It was. Then he'd be able to focus wholly on the things he needed to focus on. Like on the job in hand, and not on how great she smelt. 'Head injury. He's slipping in and out of consciousness. Glasgow coma score of twelve but fluctuating.'

'Okay.' She pulled out her satellite phone from her backpack. 'Have you radioed in for an evacuation?'

'Not yet. I've only just got here.'

'What about the other guy?' She crooked her neck towards the jet-ski rider who was propped up against the wooden fencing that edged the top of the causeway. He'd stopped cursing and now looked shocked and hunched in pain as he held his left arm tight against his side.

'Could you assess him? Looks like a dislocated shoulder. If it is, he'll need a sling to immobilise it. If he's in too much pain for you to touch it, we can swap jobs and I'll give him some inhaled anaesthetic while you keep this neck stable.'

'Sure thing. I'll just radio for an evac. One or two passengers?' She frowned and he saw then that her eyes were puffy and her cheeks blotchy, as if she'd been crying.

He glanced over to the jet-ski rider then back to Carly. 'Two. Are you okay?'

Her reddened eyes widened in surprise. 'Sure. Why?'

'You look upset.'

She blinked and shook her head quickly, as if to tell him, *not here*. 'I'm radioing in. Then I can stabilise this man's neck if you want to administer pain relief to the other guy.'

'Later, then.'

She looked as if she was going to say no, but her

shoulders sagged and she nodded. 'Actually, I could do with a chat.'

It gave him a sharp punch of pride to his chest that she trusted him enough not to pretend she was okay and considered him someone she could talk to. He had to be that person—her person. The friend she needed.

He nodded and caught her gaze—and there it was again...the invisible but tangible connection that seemed to pull them closer and closer. For the tiniest moment, she smiled.

He smiled back.

Then he focused on their patients.

The next hour was a blur of activity, stabilising the injuries, handing over to the paramedics, clearing up the debris from the flurry of open sterile packs and oxygen tubing. Then a quick debrief in the yacht club that he'd tried to turn down but had been unable to, because Wiremu's son, Nikau, had come out and wrapped them both in a bear hug, thanking them for saving his father's life and insisting on buying them a drink.

And now it was just the two of them, standing outside the yacht club on the deck overlooking the moorings, finally alone, the chaos subsiding...apart from the chaos in his chest whenever he was close to Carly. 'So, how are you doing now?'

She turned to look at him, clearly understanding what he was alluding to. 'Okay, thanks. I was just having a wobble.'

'About?'

'Life in general.' She laughed ruefully.

'You want to chat now?'

She looked at a group of locals walking towards them and shook her head. 'Not here. Can we go somewhere else?'

'Absolutely.' He put his hand on her arm then took it away. Where did the boundaries between friends who were attracted to each other, but who'd also sworn off anything physical, start and end? Could he touch her?

He forced himself to shove his hands into his pockets and looked up the road to the start of a trail that disappeared into the bush. 'I haven't explored that track. You want to go for a walk?'

She looked towards the trail head and then back to him again. 'Yes. Actually, I do.'

She set off walking hard and fast, as if she was trying to get away from something. He hoped it wasn't him, but she stopped every now and then to make sure he was there. She didn't say anything, and he took her lead. When she was ready, she'd talk.

Whatever was eating her fuelled her pace as they wound deeper and higher through the bush. When he reached the top of the hill, he found her bent double, red-cheeked and breathing raggedly.

'You're hard on yourself. That's one heck of a climb,' he managed as he hauled a lungful of fresh air into his lungs.

'I like the way I feel after… I've got to…the top.' She panted and plopped onto a wooden bench—this one had no engraved plaque on it. 'Not during it.'

'Have you exorcised your demons yet?'

'Is that what it looked like? I was just seeing if you could keep up with me.' She giggled, the bubbly sound a salve to his ears. He hated seeing her anything but happy.

'And clearly I can. Any time.'

'Oh, yeah?' Her eyes sparked. The puffiness was starting to subside but there were traces left. 'You want me to show you how fast I can move through the bush?'

The roots…the branches…he wasn't as familiar as her with this terrain. He was bound to lose. He put his hands up and winced. 'Maybe another time.'

'Coward.'

'Yes.' He grinned and sat next to her, then raised his head and looked through a gap in the huge kauri trees. 'Wow.'

Below them was a beautiful bay of glittering turquoise water and white sand beaches. At one end of the bay was a huge white colonial villa that dominated the promontory. 'The Mansion House?'

'Yes. Isn't it lovely? They don't build houses like that any more.'

'Probably no double glazing. It'd be freezing in the winter.'

'Ah, come on. Where's the romance, Owen? It's beautiful, with its sweeping verandas and all that dainty filigree carving.'

'How is keeping warm unromantic? If it's too cold, you're not going to want to take your clothes off.'

'Oh, trust me. You would with the right person.' She started to laugh, and he was mesmerised by the sound that made his body heat and his chest warm.

He also didn't miss the way she'd looked at him as she'd said those words, as if he just might have been the right person once upon a time, in a different life. It was a joke and a dare and, not for the first time, he wondered how she would look naked. Under him. Straddling him.

A crackle of dry leaves and snapping branches had him on alert and turning his head, although the adrenalin of desire still rippled through him. There, a few feet away from them, was… He blinked. *Really?* 'What the hell is that? A kangaroo? Tell me I'm dreaming, or did we just go through some weird travel portal and end up in Australia?'

She laughed softly and bent towards the animal, her hand outstretched, whispering, 'It's a wallaby. There are a few wild ones in the bush.'

'How come? They're not indigenous to New Zealand.'

They both watched as it hopped away into the dense bushes. 'By all accounts, years ago an old governor general imported all sorts of exotic animals and plants to see which would thrive and what flora and fauna the land would be useful for. Most things didn't survive, but the wallabies thrived. Unfortunately, they destroy the wildlife and vegetation, so we've got trappers to catch them and re-home them in a more suitable environment. But I have to admit, they're cute and add a quirkiness to the place. The kids love them if they get a glimpse. We only have a few left now.'

'Is there anywhere more wonderful than Rāwhiti Island?' As soon as he said it, he wished he could take the words back, because her face had grown sad again.

'I hope there are lots more wonderful places all over the world, and I intend to visit them all.'

'Oh, there are many, Carly, and you'll have an amazing time.' His chest hurt to say this and to be positive about her leaving, but he really hoped she did have the best adventure. 'Someone once gave me a *One Hundred Places to Visit Before You Die* book. I think I've still got it somewhere in one of the boxes that finally arrived last week. You can borrow it, if you like.'

'Are you trying to get rid of me?' Smiling, she raised her knees up, anchoring her feet on the bench and wrapping her arms round her shins.

'Just helping you fulfil your dream. And yet…you don't look too excited about it all.'

'Well, it's rushing at me now.' She inhaled deeply and let out slowly. 'We've had an offer on the camp.'

'Oh?'

'She wants to turn it into apartments. I'm not sure how I feel about it not being a camp any more.' She gave a shrug. 'Mia says I need to get over myself.'

'What will the schools do if they can't come here?'

'We're not unique. There are plenty of camp options across the country for them to choose from.'

'So that's not what's got you rethinking? What aren't you happy about the sale?'

'Well, I am happy, of course. It was the plan. And there again, no. I'm wobbling.' She chuckled but it was tinged with something else. Anxiety? Regret? 'Sorry, I'm not making any sense.'

'Far from it. When Miranda and I split up, I didn't know if it was the right thing for any of us. It was a relief to end the arguing and struggles, but I had no idea how I was going to manage or how Mason would react to his mum leaving. And, when I sold up to come here, I didn't know if it was the most ridiculous idea in the world. Giving up everything for the unknown is not just exciting but unsettling too.'

'I'm so glad you understand. Everyone else is all about the "live your best life while you have the chance" and they don't understand why I'm apprehensive. Of course I'm excited. But the excitement's all tangled up with other emotions too. I'm not sad about leaving, so much as drawing a line under everything. I guess I feel a bit overwhelmed that it's finally happening.'

'You don't have to go anywhere, right? You could stay.' Was that the wrong thing to say?

It was a *selfish* thing to say. Life on the island would be just a little bit less bright without her here, but he couldn't ask her stay for him. What was he even thinking? No one ever stayed around for him.

'Mia said that too. And I know it sounds stupid, and I'm not making any sense, but I feel like I owe it to myself to go.' She jumped up from the bench and waited for him to follow, then they started to wind their way back down the path. 'Plus, Mia won't say anything, but she needs the money. The sale will set her and Harper up for life.'

Owen frowned. 'I didn't know she was in financial trouble.'

'It's not that exactly. She's getting by. But after everything she's been through—losing all her family—she deserves a bit more than just getting by, right?'

'I'll see if I can do more to help her. She's babysitting Mason right now. Maybe I should pay her?'

'God, no. Don't do that.' Carly put her palm up. 'She'd be mortified. She's happy for Harper to have a friend. Just return the favour every now and then and have Harper over to play—give Mia some space to have some me time.'

He wondered what exactly that was, because he hadn't had any for a very long time. 'We've barely had time to breathe since Anahera was called away, but I'll make sure I help her more.'

She slowed and looked up at him, a smile on her lips. 'I knew you would. Look after her for me.'

It sounded so final. 'You haven't gone yet.'

'But soon. Selling the camp is good for her, but that's the end of that part of my life. I keep telling myself that everything that happened to me before Raff was preparing me for his death.'

'Living in foster care must have given you a lot of resilience, but even so, no one should go through what you did, moving from place to place.' And yet here she was, planning to do it again.

Her walking pace picked up. 'I don't know about resilience. Being uplifted time after time hurts. I mean, really hurts. You try to settle in, watch to see how everyone in the family acts, what roles they have…what kind of dynamic is in the house. You mould yourself to fit into it, you take on a role…the clever one, the funny one, the quiet one. Mainly, I was the quiet one, observing, trying not to trip up and do something stupid and be moved on. But I was always moved on eventually, for one reason or another.'

His heart squeezed at the thought of a little Carly, someone Mason's age, trying to fit herself into a new space, then another, then another. 'That must have been so hard for you.'

'You learn to become self-reliant, in the end. To block off the feelings. To not get emotionally involved in case you lose it all again. Because it's exhausting, trying to rebuild and to survive. But then I met Raff and came here and I settled in straight away. There was no role to take, other than to be myself, even though I didn't know who that was. Who that *is*. I belonged here, I was part of something...and I didn't get moved on, but the family did. And I was left all alone again. I mean, sure I have Mia and Harper. But I wake up alone every morning and go to bed alone every night. I make the decisions here. I'm the boss of a place I never asked for, in a job I never applied for. And now... I don't know what I want.'

'You'll work it out.'

'I hope so.' She smiled, raising her eyebrows.

'You're pretty special. You don't need to go anywhere to see that.'

'Thank you. Wow, that's kind.'

He stopped walking and turned to face her. 'It's not kind, Carly. It's honest. You're stunning. Beautiful. Strong.'

'Not strong, just bloody minded. Trust me, it's taken a long time for me to be able to talk about Raff and his parents in the past tense.'

'You must have felt as if your whole world was ripped apart.'

She nodded. 'But I have to move on, and I think that means I have to leave. To be honest, I'm so confused, but I think I can only find out who I am if I'm not here. I'm excited and a bit daunted to find out.'

'I can't wait to see who Carly Edwards is when she comes back, because I'm not sure she can get any better than who she is right now.'

If she came back at all. Which should have been a shrill

warning alarm, yet made part of him want to deep-dive into getting to know her while he had the chance.

He took in her bright eyes that always reflected her emotions. She was honest, deep to her core. The beautiful mouth tasted so fine. But it wasn't her physicality that appealed as much as the person she was. Deep-down good. A fighter. Endearing. Funny. Beautiful. And mixed-up, too. And that made her even more perfect. She wasn't trying to be someone else, or to put on a brave face, she was living through uncertainty and admitting she felt lost sometimes.

Didn't everyone? But not everyone was open enough to say it out loud.

Her gaze snagged his and for a few beats they just looked at each other. So much passed between them. Understanding. Compassion. Need. Heat.

He couldn't take his eyes off her. He didn't want her to leave. He wanted to get to know her better. Wanted to make love to her, to share parts of his life with her. Explore something new together.

This was crazy mixed-up. He was crazy mixed-up.

But she still held his gaze.

He took a step closer to her and she closed the gap, reaching for him and wrapping her arms around his waist, leaning her head against his chest and holding on.

He stroked her hair, closed his eyes and fought every instinct to kiss her. This was what she needed, just the hug, nothing more.

But when she pulled away she was breathing heavily, her eyes misted. He put his palm to her cheek and she curled into his touch.

'Thanks, Owen. You're a good listener. And a fine hugger.'

He dropped his hand from her face, wondering how wise it was to be honest. Probably not wise at all, but he did it anyway. 'I want to kiss you. I want to make you feel better about everything.'

'We can't. It'll make everything too complicated.' She curled her fingers into his. 'But I already feel better. Thank you. Just having someone to listen really helps.'

'Sure. Any time.' He squeezed her hand then let go.

It always seemed to be like this with her—an opening of their hearts, an acceptance of each other's desires and all the reasons not to act on them. It helped that it was so honest and yet it didn't help at all. Because what was the point in telling someone your deepest desires if you couldn't act on them? Might as well keep them locked inside.

And then there was Mason, who was as soft on her as Owen was. Who didn't need any more confusion.

This was crazy. This wasn't about Mason. This was about himself. His concern for Mason getting too close to Carly was a deflection or, indeed, a reflection of getting too close to her himself. He knew all about women leaving; his mother had done it and his wife too.

Carly had good reasons. Hell, they'd all had good reasons to pursue the life they wanted and deserved. He was just tired of being the fall guy. He needed to focus on the kind of life he wanted. Like Carly, he wasn't sure what that was yet, except creating security for Mason.

He quickly stepped back. 'I have to go.'

Carly blinked, shocked. 'Did I say something wrong?'

'No. It's me. I have a habit of wanting things I can't have and all that leads to is a headache and a lot of stress.'

'So you're running away.' She laughed, but it was gentle and sad. The words stung but he couldn't deny the truth.

'Yes. Actually, I am. I'm going to pop by Mia's and pick up my boy, then take him on an adventure, the way we planned when we decided to come here.'

Then he pivoted away from her and started to jog down the hill, in exactly the opposite direction from Carly.

CHAPTER EIGHT

SHE SHOULD HAVE cancelled the kayaking, but then what would that have taught little Mason—that adults made promises and didn't keep them? That wasn't a lesson he needed to learn at four years old.

Hell, she'd had enough life lessons growing up to make her protective of any child, but for some reason her heart had made space for this little boy.

She found a smile for Mason, who was standing in front of her in a cute short wetsuit with a shark on the front, and a huge, excited grin. 'Right then, buddy. First off, we need to lift the kayak down to the water.'

'I'll take one end…you take the other.' Owen stepped in and picked up one end of the bright orange kayak, his manner clipped and assertive.

He'd been right, of course, when he'd said he needed to focus on having a wonderful life filled with adventures with his son, but watching him jog away from her the other day had made her chest contract with hurt and confusion. He hadn't even pretended he was running for any other reason.

I have a habit of wanting things I can't have.

He wanted her, despite everything. And he had been willing to say it. And she wanted him too, which threw everything about her plans into upheaval. Should she stay, just in case something came of this attraction?

No. She couldn't put all her hopes and dreams into this man. She needed to grow and explore the world.

And was it her imagination, or was he being standoffish today? His gaze wasn't quite so intense as usual, his smile not as full.

He was closing himself off.

She couldn't blame him. She was struggling with her emotions too. Spending time with him just made her want more of him…more time, more kisses. She'd do well to take a leaf from his book and keep her distance…as far as she could, when giving them a personal kayak lesson.

'Thanks. Mason, you bring the oars.' She showed him how to carry them, hoping that focusing on the child would keep her from focusing too much on the man.

Of course, it didn't work. Even with them in a separate kayak she was too aware of Owen's strong hands, his powerful stroke, the tightening and relaxing of his muscles. Which were far too prevalent, given that the man was bare-chested save for the life jacket she'd insisted they all wear.

She took them across the bay to explore the mangroves, pointing to the little shoals of jumping fish and the stingrays swimming languidly in the shallows.

Mason's face broke into a huge smile as he watched the large flat shapes moving beneath the water. 'What are they doing?'

'They're feeding on the little sea worms, insects and shrimps.'

'They eat insects?' His eyes widened.

'Sea insects, yes.'

Mason pulled a face. 'Yukky!'

'You don't want to eat insects?'

'No way. I like ice-cream and marshmallows.'

'Good choice.' As she watched the little boy's amusement grow as large as his eyes, she realised she was falling for him too.

What on earth was she doing, spending more time with them? It was like an addiction. Instead of putting distance between herself and this little family, she gave herself excuses and reasons to see them. She just craved more and more.

She smiled over at them both and realised Mason was starting to shiver. 'Right, we should probably get back. The wind's picking up and it's getting cold. Last one back to camp makes the hot chocolate.'

'Hey, not fair, you're a fantastic kayaker.' Owen put his oar in and splashed cold water over her. It was the first time today that his face had broken a smile.

'Hey!' She splashed back. 'There's two of you against one of me. That's an unfair advantage right there.' Not just for kayaking but for an arrow of longing straight to her chest.

'It helps if the two of us both row at the same time and in the same direction,' Owen yelled and then started some seriously frenzied rowing.

By the time she reached the shore, men and boat were back up in the boathouse. Owen sauntered back and took the end of her kayak to carry it up. 'Mason's hooked. It looks like I'm going to have to add a kayak to my list of things to buy.'

'Look no further. We have to sell off everything here.'

'Good call. I expect mates' rates.' He turned to look at her and she couldn't read his expression.

But she felt a tight twist in her gut. It was like being on a roller coaster...fun, laughter and the looming end. The push and pull of attraction and the struggle. And the excitement. Oh, the excitement of it all. 'I'll talk to Mia and see if we can come to a deal.'

Mason was still shivering as he helped them stack the kayaks and hose them down. She stroked his head. 'Hey, buddy. You look cold. Go up to the house and have a nice warm shower.'

But Owen frowned, back to standoffishness after that glimpse of warmth. 'We can just use the one in the bunk house.'

'Ah, I'd prefer it if you didn't. I've just cleaned it in preparation for the next group.'

'We'll just have one at home.'

Why was he stalling about going into her house? 'The boy's cold, Owen. Use mine.'

He caught her gaze, his eyes boring into her soul. 'Okay. And then we'll be on our way.'

Owen hoisted Mason into his arms and sped through the house, trying not to linger. It felt intensely personal here, surrounded by Carly's things. There was no evidence of any other person, apart from the photo of her wedding day in the hallway. She looked so happy, a certain sort of sparkle in eyes he'd yet to see—true joy.

God, he wished that for her more than anything. But not at the cost of losing his heart. Again. Hadn't he already learnt that, when it came to women, he had absolutely no clue?

He grabbed some towels and took Mason into the shower.

Then it was her turn to shower while he poured the hot chocolate into mugs in the kitchen. He heard the water rushing through the pipes, heard her singing and tried hard not to imagine her in there. He honestly did. But, having seen her in her tight-fitting rash vest and shorts, he knew far too much about her shapely body for his thoughts to keep straying there.

She appeared a few minutes later, her hair wet and curling in waves around her shoulders. Her face was shiny from what he imagined was from one of those face creams in the bathroom. She was wearing a white crop top and white tiered skirt that reached her toes.

He didn't think he'd ever seen anyone so beautiful. It actually hurt his chest. He'd been trying to keep his distance, but he couldn't stop himself from liking her. From wanting her. And he didn't think that he'd feel any different even if she was halfway across the world.

Which didn't bode well for her impending departure.

'Feeling a bit warmer?' she asked as she ambled across the cottage garden to the picnic table and benches where Owen and Mason sat.

'Yes, thanks.' He pushed back from the table and stood, reminding himself of his promise to keep his distance. 'It's probably time we headed off.'

But she frowned, looking at Mason's chocolate moustache, and then at Owen's still half-full cup. 'What's the hurry? Drink up your hot chocolate.'

He gave her a faltering smile, trying to keep the barriers up but failing. 'We need to make a move soon. I've got to get sleepyhead to bed.'

She peered at him, as if looking deep into his soul. He hoped she couldn't see how confused he was. 'Owen, are you okay?'

No. 'Fine, thanks. Why?'

'You seem...off today.'

He pressed his lips together, wondering just how much to say. It wasn't exactly good form for him to admit that he'd been trying to keep his barriers up when she was being so hospitable. He sighed and sat back down. 'Yeah. I'm fine. Honestly. I've just got things on my mind.'

'Such as?'

Luckily his mini-me diverted their attention to two large tents that had been erected on the grass. Mason pointed to them and asked, 'Why have you got tents?'

Carly grinned at his son. 'For the school children to sleep in.'

'Don't they sleep in the house?'

'Not always. The children come to stay for three nights, and for one of them they sleep inside, one of them they have to build their own shelter called a bivouac and for one night they have to set up camp. These two are here for them to learn how to put up a tent. I was going to take them down, but they got very wet in the storm the other night so I'm drying them out.'

Mason looked thoughtful. 'Can I have a look inside?'

'Sure thing.'

Both Owen and Carly said it at the same time.

Great minds.

Mason ran across the grass, disappeared inside the tent and then came back out again, his mouth split in a wide grin. 'It's like a little house. Daddy, can we have a tent?'

Owen glanced over to Carly and gave her a 'kids, hey?' shrug. But she just grinned and mouthed, 'Pushover.'

And here was the thing—he was trying so hard to keep his distance but one smile from her, one word, one look had his heart and, if he was honest, his soul too, barrelling straight towards her again.

He turned his attention to his son. 'Sure thing, buddy. We could go camping—cook sausages on the fire too.'

'And marshmallows?' His son looked at him hopefully.

'Of course. Our own adventure.'

'I like this adventure, Daddy.'

'Me too.' Owen turned and caught Carly looking at him. He smiled and the words tumbled out of his mouth, 'I like this adventure very much.'

Her cheeks bloomed bright red at his words, clearly understanding that they weren't referring to the kayaking. 'Like I said, I'll most likely be selling the kayaks, and I'll offer you a competitive price. In the meantime, feel free to borrow them any time. Same goes for tents. We have a few here and we'll have to sell them off too. Unless the new owner decides to keep the camp as it is. But I can't see that happening.'

'Well, if it makes things easier, I'll definitely buy some stuff from you. Right, Mason? A tent and a kayak?'

'Yes, please.' Then the little boy grabbed his backpack and shuffled back inside the tent.

Which left just the two of them sitting there. Her cheeks still bore glimmers of her blush.

There was so much he wanted to say to her, questions he wanted the answers to... *When will you come back? Is it worth waiting? Are you interested in me, in us? If you came back would you leave again? Do you keep your promises?*

But they all broke his cardinal rule of backing off.

He glanced across the table and caught her gaze.

She smiled.

His body prickled.

He ached to say something important. But instead he turned away from her and looked to the tent. *Coward.*

'Mason? You okay in there?'

'Playing hide and seek with teddy.'

He laughed. There was nothing in the tent to hide behind or under. 'You need anything, just shout.'

'Yes, Dad.'

Carly leaned back in her chair and smiled as she too looked over at the tent. 'He's going to remember this special time you spent with him. You're a great dad, you know that?'

'I wish. But I want to be, so I guess that's half the battle, right?'

Now her laser focus retrained on Owen. 'Must have been hard when his mum left.'

'I was lost, to be honest. We'd tried hard and we'd failed. I watched her pack her things and then leave, and wondered just how long it would be before Mason saw her again. He didn't cope well. We had endless sleepless nights and wails of wanting Mummy. Which made me feel totally inadequate, because there's something about a mother's love, right?'

'I wouldn't know. Although Wendy was lovely.' Carly shrugged sadly.

Damn. How utterly careless of him. 'You'll be a mother one day, and you'll get to lavish those babies with everything you didn't have.'

'Oh, don't worry. I'm going to be the worst kind of mother.' She laughed. 'Helicopter parenting. Spoiling them completely. So much love.'

She really did have so much love to give to the right person. Whoever that might be. Whoever she met on her travels.

She pierced him with her gaze. 'You loved Miranda, right? Once?'

'Of course. She's a remarkable woman and a very talented actress. But she needed to follow her own path.' He paused and looked down at his feet. A sudden sadness filled his chest. 'Just like my mother.'

And now Carly was planning to go too. He needed a way out of this conversation.

He sat up and walked over to the tent. When he crawled in, he found his beautiful boy fast asleep with his teddy bear tucked safely in his arms.

Now what to do? He turned to walk back to Carly but, when he turned round, she was there behind him, so close, in touching distance. Like a worried mother hen. A worried mother. The thought slid into his head, and he banished it immediately. 'He's fast asleep. Completely out for the count. Shame to wake him up, but I really should get him home.'

Her eyes fixed softly on Mason as she whispered, 'Bless. I'll go to the cottage and grab some blankets.'

'Or I should probably wake him up and take him home.'

'Or...don't wake him. You could stay.'

He wasn't sure he understood the subtext of her comment. 'Here?'

'Why not? I've got all the gear. Won't take a minute to grab some sleeping bags and mats.'

He blinked, trying to make sense of her words. 'You'll stay too?'

But she laughed, frowned and kind of blushed all at the same time. 'No! I have a perfectly good bed in the cottage.'

'What if we get scared or attacked by bears?'

She shook her head, eyes full of tease. 'You'll be fine, you big burly man. There are no bears on this island.'

He played along. 'But there are wallabies. Maybe that old guy brought over bears too. Bears you know nothing about.'

'I know every nook and cranny of this island, and I can promise you, there are no bears.'

'That's a shame.'

'Too bad.' She tutted and rolled her eyes. 'Looks like you're staying the night. It's time for that *Boy's Own* adventure you've been promising. I'll bring you both some blankets.'

'And more hot chocolate?'

She gave another eye-roll. 'Okay, and hot chocolate. What an intrepid adventurer you are.'

He laughed, words slipping freely from his lips before he could stop them. 'Hey, I have plenty of ideas to make it more exciting.'

She spluttered, laughed and her eyes twinkled. They were back to being friends, being friendly, and a step closer to that line they'd promised not to cross. 'Okay. I'll bring it all over. Back in a minute.'

In the meantime, he probably needed another dip in the ocean to cool off.

* * *

By the time Carly got back to the camping area, the sun had well and truly set. They covered Mason with the blankets and zipped up his tent.

As Owen straightened, something glinting in the water caught his eye. No, not glinting—sparkling. The waves rolling onto the shore were bright with light. 'Look, the water's sparkling. Wow. That's awesome.'

'Bioluminescence. Yes, it happens sometimes. Come and look.' She started to walk towards the shoreline.

But Owen glanced back at the tent and concern rattled his chest. 'What about Mason? What if he wakes up?'

'Seriously, he'll be fine. Hundreds—no, thousands—of children have camped here and been completely safe. We'll only be there...' She pointed to a spot about a hundred metres away.

Reassured, he followed her down to the beach and put a blanket on the sand. They sat down on it, close but not touching.

He stared at the silvery white lights in the ocean wash. 'It's like stars dancing on the waves.'

She looked up at him and smiled. 'Yes. It's exactly that. That's a perfect description.'

And there she was, smiling and perfect herself. 'I've never seen anything so amazing.'

He meant her, of course, but he directed his gaze back to the sea. 'It's beautiful.'

Then he remembered not to remind her about all the fabulous things Rāwhiti Island had going for it. She was clearly finding it hard to leave without remembering all the reasons to stay. Which, he had to admit, was crazy when his whole body was screaming for her touch, for her to stay just long enough for him to kiss her again. But he had to support her plan. That was what friends did. 'How's the sale going?'

'Okay. It's conditional on a builder's report, and a few other things, but all being well we'll be heading off to Auckland in a couple of weeks to sign the paperwork.'

'A couple of weeks? That's quick.' He'd hoped for months. 'When I sold up in Mount Eden it took about twelve weeks for everything to be processed.'

'We're not in a chain, neither is the buyer. Should be smooth running.'

'Do you have to go into the city? You can't sign from here?'

She shook her head. 'Not when lawyers are involved. We have to sign it all in person. Mia and I have decided to have a couple of days' R and R in the city. Then, once the contract is signed, I'm heading off.'

'I'll offer to have Harper, so you can have some child-free fun before you go.' He couldn't believe he was making it so easy for her to leave.

She turned and blinked, surprise filling her expression. 'That's so kind.'

'I know.' He shrugged, feeling so many emotions other than kind. 'I'm selfless to a fault.'

He laughed and lay back on the blanket, looking up at the cloudless night sky, the myriad stars and purple slick of Milky Way.

She lay down next to him. Silence stretched between them. Comfortable, in that he didn't feel a need to fill the gap in conversation. Uncomfortable, because he was painfully aware of her breathing, the rise and fall of her chest and breasts. Her scent.

The fact she was so close, in touching distance but not touching. Painfully not touching.

A couple of weeks? That was all they had left. No chance for anything to develop even if they both wanted it to.

He closed his eyes and breathed deeply. He was fooling himself by pretending he didn't want to. And the way she looked at him, the way she looked at his son—with such affection and care—made him believe she wanted something too. But maybe they were destined to be just good friends.

Suddenly, he felt the soft brush of her hand against his. For a beat he thought he'd imagined it, or she'd done it by accident, but when her fingers stroked the back of his hand again he knew he'd misjudged.

Just that light touch set his body aflame.

He swallowed, unsure how to outwardly react when internally he was jittery and hot. Jeez, it was the first time he'd been unsure about his next move with a woman. Carly's precarious past, her present vulnerability and the fact she was leaving all gave him pause.

But, man, he ached for her.

He turned on to his side to look at her. To see if what she was doing was intentional. She drew her hand away and turned on her side to face him, her eyes hidden by a floppy lock of hair.

He was so turned on by the simple touch of her skin against his, he could barely form words. *I want you. I want to kiss you. I want to be inside you. Here. Right now. On this magical beach.*

'Hey, Carly,'

'Hey.' She smiled.

He slid a finger under her chin and tilted her head so he could see her face.

And—*oh God, yes*—her moves were intentional. Her eyes were as sparkling as the water. Her mouth was slightly open, her body inching closer.

And, just like the last time, it took just one look... one desperate, sexy, hungry look...and they were in each other's arms.

CHAPTER NINE

LIKE A SPARK to dry tinder, heat crackled through her, searing her nerve endings.

This kiss was as out of control as the first one.

She couldn't stop. Just couldn't stop putting her arms around his neck and drawing him closer. Couldn't stop pressing her lips against his. Tasting him. Feeling the solid weight of him—real, hard, honest. Here.

His throaty groan as her tongue slid against his stoked any remaining embers inside her that hadn't already caught fire.

She pressed against him, fitting herself against his hard body, running her palms over strong shoulders and across his back. She wanted to touch him everywhere.

He laid her back on the blanket and propped himself up on his elbow, his other hand stroking her cheek. 'Carly, we shouldn't be doing this. We agreed.'

She closed her eyes, not ready for a conversation. 'If we dissect it, we'll stop, and I don't want to stop. I don't want to talk. I want to kiss you. I want to touch you. I want to feel. God, I want to just feel, Owen. I want you inside me. So badly.'

His Adam's apple dipped as he swallowed, the expression in his eyes telling her he didn't want this to stop either. 'I want that more than anything, but are you sure?'

She'd been broken before. Completely. Utterly. Wretchedly torn apart. The death of her husband had had her numb one day and then awash with cruel, painful, roiling emotions the next. Rinse and repeat for two whole years. Another year on and she was starting to recover now, a welcome relief from such intense grief.

She'd vowed never to give her heart again, but this...? Surely, this was safe? There was an expiry date. She simply couldn't get emotionally involved, because she was leaving. It would end. They both knew it. So why not enjoy it while it lasted?

'Yes, Owen. I'm sure. We both know the score, right?'

'We do.' His tone was pained but he bent to kiss her again and she closed her eyes, losing herself in the sensations she'd been denying herself from the first moment she'd seen him.

His fingers stroked across her ribs, below her breasts, and she was almost driven crazy with the need for him to slide his hands over her nipples.

She pressed against him, stifling her own groans as her thigh connected with his erection. One slight shift in position and her core pressed against the hard ridge in his shorts. She wanted to rock against him, desperate to feel his hard length inside her.

He kissed a trail from her breasts back to her mouth. 'Carly, you have no idea how much I want this.'

'I think I do.' She moved against his erection teasingly, and giggled.

He inhaled sharply, eyes widening, and groaned. 'You're amazing. I want to see you. All of you.'

He slowly, almost reverently, removed her top. Then he slid the straps of her bra down, kissing trails along each arm. Undid the clasp and dropped her bra to the ground. Then he dipped his head and sucked a nipple in. As she watched the slow, deep suck, she wanted to scream with pleasure but controlled herself so much, her body shook. Or was it trembling out of pure sexual need?

His mouth was hot and his kisses greedy. She felt alive, reckless, wild.

Free.

Yes. Free to be herself. To follow her desires. To take what she wanted. To put away her past...all the good and the bad. To revel in the now. In this man. Every touch was more fuel to the fire burning inside her. She wanted to beg him to hurry, but also tell him to slow down, so she could revel in every second.

He worked his way up her body, back to her mouth, and she melted into another of his searing kisses until her thoughts were nothing except his taste, his touch, his scent.

Owen Cooper—a surprise and a gift. Her going-away present.

A loud bleeping sound had her pulling away.

What the hell?

Damn. It had been so long since she'd done anything like this. Couldn't she just have had one precious moment with this hot man? Okay...a few precious moments. 'Shoot. What now?'

She peered down at the neon message.

Bush fire. North Bay.

And her heart rattled. 'Oh, hell. Owen, I'm so sorry. I need to go.'

His breathing was rapid, eyes suddenly alert. 'What is it?'

'Bush fire. North Bay. No other details.' Suddenly cold, she sat up, slid her bra straps up her arms, pulled on her top and settled her clothes back in place. Her need for him did not wane. Would she ever stop wanting him? Would ten minutes, ten hours, ten months, ten years away from him douse this burning?

Would a thousand miles? Ten thousand?

He jumped up and ran his palms down his shorts. '*We* need to go. It's a fire…there could be casualties.'

'Okay. Yes. We need to get there ASAP. Everything's so dry, the whole island could go up. What about Mason?' Her heart stalled at the thought of the little boy fast asleep in the tent. A few moments ago, he could have caught them behaving like teenagers. But she was aware he was like most other youngsters and slept heavily.

They'd been safe.

And she felt bereft to have to stop, to peel her hands away from Owen. To have his kisses abruptly terminated.

'I'll see if Mia can have him. I'll call her on the way.' He gave her a sharp nod, all business. 'I'll just go wake him up. What about more help?'

'We've got it covered…unless it gets too big. Then we radio for help from the mainland. The coastguard brings the other volunteer firefighters round from other parts of the island, and I have my gear and the jet-ski, so I'll head straight over now. There's a depot down at the yacht club with emergency equipment. Wiremu's son, Nikau, will bring over the smoke chaser. I'll meet you there. North Bay.'

'And then?' His hand snaked around her waist, drawing her closer to that toned chest.

She inhaled his scent, pressed a kiss to his throat then stepped away. 'I think the universe is telling us this is not going to happen.'

He nodded again and she couldn't read him. Was he relieved they'd been interrupted or as frustrated as she was? Every time they moved forward, they took more than a few steps back.

And he was all closed down again, seemingly in agreement that it wasn't going to happen again.

No matter how much she ached for it.

Having quickly dropped Mason off at Mia's, Owen steered into the bay and secured his own boat up against the jetty, then ran towards the smoke and flames. Judging by the number of boats anchored in North Bay, the whole island had come to fight the fire. Two locals had fire hoses attached to their jet-skis, pointing plumes of water towards the bushes on the west side of the bay. A helicopter hovered overhead, dumping a huge bucket of water over the trees towards the east.

His heart had barely recovered from the intensity of their passion, then the dousing of it. Now, trying to find Carly in the chaos of the scene, he wondered at the wisdom of snatching kisses like that when she was not going to be around in a couple of weeks.

He shoved those thoughts to the back of his mind.

We both know the score.

He did. They hadn't committed to anything serious, just a few kisses. He could walk away any time and still keep his heart intact.

Smoke filled the air, flames flickered high in the bush and the smell of burning tinged every inhale. But the sounds surprised him more than anything. He hadn't expected fire crackle to be so loud.

He dashed over to a familiar face who was pulling out a hose reel attached to a high-pressure pump on a quad bike. The Rāwhiti Island smoke chaser. 'Nikau, are you okay?'

The young man nodded. 'Sure.'

'Any injured?'

'Not so far.'

'Thank God.' But Owen knew that it was probably only a matter of time before his skills would be needed. He didn't want to think about the kind of injuries people could sustain in a bush fire, but was as prepared as he could be. He dropped his doctor's bag and helped unroll the hose reel. 'Have you seen Carly?'

'She was over there, last time I looked.' Nikau pointed towards a group of firefighters in helmets and mustard-yellow gear heaving a pulsing water hose in the direction of the thickest smoke. 'Thanks for the help, Doc. I'm good to go.'

Owen ran to the huddle of firefighters and there... in the middle of the line of these valiant, volunteer first responders...was the woman he'd had so much respect for. And now it skyrocketed.

'Carly!'

She turned at the sound of her name, her eyes seeking him out, her posture softening as she found him. She gave him a small smile. 'You made it.'

'Yes. Any one hurt? What's on fire? Just bush or houses too?'

'It's closing in on Anahera's home. If we can get this water closer, we can hopefully stop it before it spreads further.'

'On three,' one of the firefighters at the front of the line called out. 'One. Two. Three!'

As they started to run towards the fire, Owen's heart lurched. 'Be careful.'

Please, be careful.

Carly turned back to look at him. For one tiny second their eyes locked and he tried to convey to her, in that briefest of looks, all the jumble of things in his chest. He wished her to be safe. He wished... *Hell*, he just wished she'd come back to him.

Then she was gone, disappearing into the trees, the darkness and the swirl of smoke that felt as if it had curled into his chest and wrapped tightly around his heart.

'Help! Help us, please!' Over on his left, two people staggered out of the smoking bush, their faces covered in black streaks, hands covering their mouths as they coughed and struggled for air.

Pushing his fears for Carly's safety away, he ran to help the casualties—Anahera and her husband—and hooked them up to the portable oxygen, assessing for smoke inhalation, burns and shock. When they were able to answer, he asked, 'How close is the fire to your home?'

Anahera shook her head and sighed. 'It was closing in on the barn when we left. We hosed everything down and, luckily, we'd just finished pruning and thinning the bigger trees. We just have to hope they can stop it in time.'

Owen Cooper wasn't a praying man but right then and there he sent up a message to whoever would listen that Anahera's house would be saved, and that Carly would come out of this unhurt.

His receptionist put a warm hand over his. 'Are you thinking twice about having moved here, Doc?'

'Well, there's certainly never a dull moment on Rāwhiti, is there?' He peered towards the bush, looking for Carly.

Anahera gave a sad, throaty huff as she followed his gaze. 'That's why we love it.'

Two firefighters staggered out of the bush and he ran to assist them, dressing their minor burns and giving them water.

No Carly.

Where was she?

How was she?

Two more people were brought to him, people with smoke inhalation, cuts and grazes. Then more—a potentially torn retina from a falling branch, a panic attack, more burns...

And through it all he kept half an eye out for Carly. His heart wouldn't stop pounding against his ribcage, as his attention was continually being pulled back to that little path into the dense trees, desperately searching for her to walk out.

And he realised the agony she must have endured, waiting for her husband to come home. The torment and pain she'd lived through, the slow realisation he wasn't coming back. The final acceptance that he was dead. How had she lived through that to become the amazing woman she was now? How had she not let that taint everything?

And why had she chosen him, Owen Cooper, to be the one she now bestowed with sexy-sweet kisses? The one to bring her back to life after her years in grief?

He didn't have any answers, just a heart full of panic, pain and hope.

It was two hours before she returned, covered in soot and sweating from the heat and the restricting uniform. She bent forward to catch her breath and he stroked her back as she coughed and cleared her throat. He was beyond glad to see her and yet…he couldn't name the emotion that sat heavily in his chest. Frustration? Helplessness? Anger? He wanted to shake her for scaring him so much. He wanted to wrap her in his arms and kiss her. He wanted to hold her and not let her go.

Then, finally, yes…he admitted to himself that he wanted her to stay. But that was a futile dream.

The other firefighters were close, a team working and resting together. Even if he knew what he was feeling, he wasn't going to express it in front of these people.

He handed her a water bottle. 'Drink.'

She took it and gulped down half its contents. Then she hauled in a deep breath, a frown forming as she looked at him, searching his face. 'You okay?'

He chose not to answer, not trusting himself to be able to hold every emotion in. 'How's Anahera's house?'

'We got to it just in time. It's okay. The barn's gone. The trees around her property are badly singed. It was a very close call.'

'You could have been killed in there.'

It was only now that he recognised the emotion: desperation. The same root as the frantic need to kiss her, and now, the panic about her safety. He'd never felt this—not when his mother had left, not when Miranda had filed for divorce—a desperate ache for another person.

But it was a two-sided coin. An insatiable need and an absolute threat to his equilibrium.

She glanced at him, still frowning. 'But I wasn't killed, Owen. I'm fine. I know my limitations. I know when to go in and when to stand down. I stick to all the health and safety rules.'

'I... I...' He paced back and forth, trying to douse the other emotions rushing through him—fear, anger, want, need—and failing. When it came to Carly, it was all or nothing.

All.

He lowered his voice. 'I thought I was going to lose you.'

'You can't get rid of me that easily.' She grinned and winked. The wink was for fun, for the observers and volunteers all watching this interaction. But the smile was for him. 'But thank you for caring.'

'Carly?' Nikau called over, giving her the thumbs-up. 'Just had confirmation from the helicopter that it's all out. They'll do some regular flyovers overnight to check and the Blue Team will stay on and keep watch. You get off home.'

'Thank God.' She sighed and smiled, exhaustion bruising below her eyes. Then she turned back to Owen. 'You go get some sleep too.'

'Sure.' He nodded, fighting the urge to pick her up and take her back to his place.

Thank you for caring?

His heart had almost hammered its way out of his chest, which should have been a warning that he was getting too involved, but he didn't want to listen. He knew he was getting involved...but he was on a collision course he couldn't stop. The rush was addictive. The *utter desperation* of their kisses, the frantic energy, made him feel the most alive he'd ever been. He couldn't walk away. He had a matter of weeks to sink into it. The rest of his life to remember it.

He didn't want to sleep. He wanted to sear her image on his brain. Her beautiful face streaked with soot, her eyes alive with adrenalin. And her kisses. Her taste.

Why would a man sleep when he could relive that over and over?

CHAPTER TEN

JUST HOW FAR would they have gone if the fire alarm hadn't gone off? A question Carly pondered all night, and again the next morning, as she hosed down the kayaks after her last lesson.

All the way? Some of the way?

She had to tried to forget it, but she couldn't. He was all she could think about. The way he'd looked at her with such desire on the beach, the kiss, then the panic she'd felt resonate off him at the fire. Panic about her safety. Care for her.

Such intensity made her giddy. And she craved it, relished it.

Her last retort about him caring had been offhand and probably rude, but it was the only way she'd been able to shake the need to slide into his arms again, especially in front of all the people who knew her and had known her husband and in-laws.

After Raff, was it wrong of her to want another man? She didn't think so. Not after all this time. She didn't feel guilty about being attracted to Owen. Raff was gone and she'd grieved him—so much. Of course, she still missed him. His loss was a piece of her heart that would never be filled. He'd given her roots she'd so badly needed and a home she'd never had before. A place to be. A family.

But that was all gone now, and she knew he'd want her

to be happy. She just wasn't sure what steps she needed to take to make it happen.

She'd thought that travel would help her find her way, but now there was Owen. He wasn't a Raff replacement. No one could ever be that. Raff had been amazing. But there were other men, amazing in different ways to her husband.

Owen.

His expression as she'd come out of the bush was seared onto her brain. He cared. Really cared.

And she liked him too.

But, what now?

Confused, exhausted from the late night and overly emotional, she took photos of each of the kayaks and the optimist boats and then went inside to her laptop to upload them to the marketplace website. This bit was hard—selling off the camp things, drawing that line under her old life—but it was necessary. As necessary as following through on her promise to see the world and give herself some well-needed space from this island, from the pain that reared every now and then. Less intense, and less frequent, but it was still there. And space, too, from Owen. Every moment spent with him was fuzzing her head. She needed fresh perspective and she wouldn't get that by staying here.

So she did what she'd been planning to do for a long time but had kept putting off. After she'd clicked 'enter', she inhaled deeply and blew out slowly. It was actually happening.

Chase it, girl. You only have one life.

Raff used to say that to her about so many opportunities she'd almost turned down because she hadn't felt good enough, or worthy or had felt that she might fail: Coming from the background she did, she'd developed an outward veneer of capability and independence, but inside she was a mass of insecurity and self-doubt. What if she wasn't good enough? What if she failed? What if she didn't fit in?

Basically, what if she was rejected or abandoned all over again?

Knowing this about herself, though, didn't mean she could always rise above it. It just meant she'd learnt to cover her self-doubts well. But Raff had been a good teacher and had been amazing for her self-esteem. Hell, the man had chosen her, had married her. If his death had taught her anything, it was that she needed to grab every opportunity with both hands.

The sound of a boat engine had her glancing out of the window.

Owen.

Her heart jittered as she thought of him last night, grimy and smoky, giving first aid to all those people. She'd put out a fire, but he'd made sure everyone had stayed safe. They were a great team.

And now he was running down the jetty.

Her heart rate doubled. What the hell had happened? The fire...had it flared into life again? No. She'd have been alerted. And where was his mini-me shadow? Where was his son?

Panic gripped her chest as she ran across the grass and met him at the playground. 'What's the matter? What's happened? Is everything okay?'

'Yes. And no. Everything's not okay. Not for me. I just wanted...' His breath was ragged and jumpy, his eyes telling her that the only emergency was his need to be here with her. 'I just wanted you, Carly.'

He wanted her, still.

'God, Owen.' She put her hand on his chest and felt the rapid fire of his heart. The solid muscle. His heat. Relief shimmied through her, along with excitement at his words. 'I thought there was a crisis.'

'There is. I can't sleep. I can't do anything. I just want this...' He pulled her to him the way he had last night at the beach, his arms strong and steady as they circled her waist. His fresh shower scent filled the air. 'I want you, Carly.'

Her body instantly responded to his touch the way it had last night. The embers deep inside her burst back into flames. She curled into his embrace. 'Yes.'

It was the only answer.

Then there were no more words as he tilted his mouth to hers and kissed her so achingly slowly, and with such need and care, that her insides felt as if they were melting into liquid. This kiss was so different from the others. It was a gift so beautiful, so wonderful, she felt herself drifting in sensation after sensation. His mouth, his tongue. His touch.

Finally, he released her, smiling as she stepped back to catch her breath, and what she saw in his eyes made her blush. 'Um…where's Mason?'

His smile grew more sexy. 'Still at Mia's. They had a broken night, so she's hoping they'll sleep late. We've got a few hours.'

Carly swallowed, her mouth suddenly wet and dry at the same time as she anticipated their next move. 'So, no interruptions?'

'Nothing but you and me and this…' He slipped his hands under her knees and swung her up into his arms.

Whoa. He was playful too. Could she like him any more? She giggled, crying out, 'What the hell do you think you're doing, Dr Cooper?'

He took a step forward. 'What I wanted to do last night. What I've wanted to do since the moment I set eyes on you, fifty metres from here. Your hair was a tangle and your face all screwed up in anger as you shouted at me. I wanted you that very second.'

Oh, God. She was lost.

He made short work of the distance to the house and up the stairs to her bedroom. He laid her down on the coverlet and kissed her again, mussing her thoughts and awakening every cell in her body.

As she shifted underneath him, she put her hand on his arm. Time to be honest, even if it meant putting an end to this right now. 'Listen, Owen. I need you to know that I've bought a plane ticket. One way to London, with stopovers all the way. I'm actually doing it. In two weeks' time.'

'Okay.' The light in his eyes dimmed for a second as he took in her words before it flickered back to life again. He pressed his lips to her throat, making her squirm. 'All the more reason for us to make the most of this time, then.'

She sighed against him. 'I hoped you'd say that.'

He stripped her top off and unclipped her bra. Then he paused, looking at her with something akin to greedy adoration. His fingers stroked around her nipple, teasing. 'I know this is probably crazy, and stupid, and might mess everything up. But I don't care. I can't stop thinking about you. I can't stop wanting you.' His mouth captured hers again.

Breathless, she panted out, 'All I want…is this moment.'

'I'm hoping it'll last longer than a moment.' He guffawed as he lowered his head and took her nipple into his mouth. Hot shivers of lust rippled through her, making her writhe against him. She pulled his head up and kissed him again, dragging off his T-shirt and smoothing her hands across his chest.

As she did so, she glanced across the room, catching a glimpse of the engraved kauri wood jewellery box Raff had made for her as a wedding gift. The box in which she kept her wedding ring. Her heart gave an involuntary shudder. She closed her eyes.

Owen must have sensed her hesitation. He pulled back to look at her and stroked her cheek. 'Hey. Are you okay?'

She blinked and looked up into his handsome face. Was she okay? She was in bed with a man who wasn't her husband. With a man who made her feel the most sexy she'd felt for years. Who lifted her heart. Who made her laugh. Who made her believe in herself and what she could achieve. Who listened. Who she trusted with her heart—totally. She wanted this. She wanted him.

'Yes, Owen. I am very okay.'

'You know we can stop any time. We can just talk. We can do whatever you want.'

Her heart flooded with warmth and she smiled, because how could she not? He was so caring and considerate, and an amazing kisser. She only hoped he was as good at sex. Because that was where she was heading right now. 'Is that a promise?'

He nuzzled against her. 'Absolutely.'

'Good. I want you to kiss me.'

He leaned in and kissed her again. It started as a repeat of the slow-build kiss from earlier, but before long it was frantic and so damned hot, every nerve ending was crying out for his touch. She arched against him, trying to fit her body tight against his. To feel all of him along all of her.

He grabbed her butt cheek and squeezed playfully. 'These short shorts drive me absolutely crazy. Every time you wear them I imagine what's underneath.'

'This is my work wear.' She chuckled as she ran her fingers suggestively around the waistband of her shorts. 'You like a woman in uniform?'

His eyes widened as he watched her play with the denim. 'To be honest, I think I'm going to prefer you with no uniform. No clothes at all.'

'Be my guest.' She raised her hips and wriggled as he unzipped her shorts and drew them down her legs, then her panties. He sucked in a breath as he looked at her. 'Jeez, Carly, you are so damned beautiful.'

And she felt it. She felt beautiful for the first time in years. Felt wanted, needed. Felt important to someone. To

Owen. This fine, sexy man. The heat in his eyes almost seared her skin. She would have blushed had she not felt deep-down sexy too. Instead, she felt emboldened. Renewed. Alive again.

She slid her hand down his chest, skimming over his flat belly to that delicious line of dark hair arrowing to his erection. She palmed his hardness and laughed as he groaned into her ear. Then she unzipped his fly and took him in her hand. He was so hard. So big.

She stroked him. He groaned again and arched against her. 'God, that feels good.'

'I want you inside me,' she whispered against his throat. He smelt so good, tasted so fine. Her body pulsed with desire. She didn't think she could wait...

'In time. Too soon.' He pulled away, put his hand over hers and stopped her stroking.

She growled and pretended to pout. 'You said you'd do whatever I wanted. I want you inside me.'

'Oh? Demanding now, hey?' He kissed down her breasts, across her belly and then lower. 'I will do exactly what you want. But *when* I want.'

His eyes fired tease, fun and heat, and then he parted her thighs and dipped his head to her core.

When his mouth made contact with the little bundle of nerve-endings, she laid her head back on the pillow, unable to stop the whimper coming from her throat.

She lost herself in the dizzying magic of his tongue, arching against him as he slid a finger inside her, then another. She felt herself clench around him, her thoughts and emotions spiralling into a blur of touch and sensation... his mouth...his tongue...his fingers giving her so much pleasure, her body pulsed and shook.

How long had it been since she'd been touched like this?

Then she didn't think at all. She rocked against him as

her orgasm broke, racking her body in ripple after ripple of mind-warping sensations.

He kissed back up her body and she sat up, reaching for him. 'Wow. That was something else.'

'No, you are.' He cupped her face, pushing her hair back. 'You look sublime, Carly. Like something I've dreamed up. Shimmering. Bloody magical.'

Her chest contracted at his words. She'd wanted sex but hadn't expected the flood of emotions that came with it, emotions for this man. She'd never imagined this could happen again, that she'd feel these things—not just sexy, but wanted and frantic with desire.

One orgasm wasn't enough. She wrapped her legs around his thighs, drawing him closer and closer, wiggling underneath him so his erection was at her entrance, almost wild with desire. 'I need you, Owen. I need you inside me.'

'No hurry.' His gaze caught onto hers and held, serious yet fun, reverential yet playful. He leaned over the side of the bed, produced a condom from his shorts pocket and was sheathed and back in position in no time.

'So much hurry.' She rubbed the heart of her against his erection. 'Please.'

'Well, I suppose so. I did say I'd do anything you want.' He shrugged and laughed, as if sex with her would be no big deal. But his eyes told her a completely different story; he was alight with need for her.

'Don't you dare stop.' She licked up his neck and he gasped, 'I wouldn't dare.'

Then he moved his hips and entered her on a thick, slick thrust. He gasped again. 'Oh. Wow. You're so ready for me.'

She breathed through the pleasure-pain point—it had been a few years, after all—then sighed as her body relaxed to let him in.

'I… I don't even know what to say. That feels so good. *You* feel so good.' She found his mouth and kissed him again.

'You are amazing.' He thrust again, then withdrew almost wholly, then slid inside her again.

'Oh, God. Please, never stop. Never…stop.' There was heat everywhere, low down in her core, in her belly and bright white heat in her chest. She was all aglow for him.

She lifted her face to watch him and their eyes locked. Gone was the playfulness and the fun, replaced by someone intent, driven and so damned sexy.

And suddenly it wasn't enough. She wanted harder and faster. She wanted all of him. She clawed at his hair and his skin, fingers raking down his back.

He groaned and changed his rhythm, and she matched it, forcing him to thrust deeper and faster and harder. To fill her completely. And, as she finally lost all control, his name was on her lips over and over and over.

But when he growled her name on a loud sigh she completely broke open, torn apart with need and want and an earth-shattering release. She clung to him, pressing against him, skin to skin, body to body, chest to chest as she rode their climax. Gripping him.

Would she ever have enough of him?

Two weeks. The plans were made. The ticket was bought. There were just signatures to be given. She would be free. Mia and Harper would be financially secure.

But what of Carly? What of her plans? Would she be able to relax completely into her new adventure, meeting new people, visiting new places, experiencing the world and growing? Or would she be forever looking back at Rāwhiti Island for the man she'd lost and the man she'd just found?

Oh, Owen. Why did I find you now?

It was the worst timing ever. She'd spent her life craving a family—her family—stumbling from one to another, being rejected or neglected. Then the one time she'd finally come home, the foundations had been ripped away.

And now...now another little unit was pulling her closer. But what if...? What if she allowed herself to fall into it and it was all ripped away again?

What then of Carly Edwards? She wouldn't be able to cope if she lost them too.

It was better for her to leave. Not to forge bonds.

But it was so hard.

Why did it have to be so hard?

In the silence that followed Owen closed his eyes and took some deep, steadying breaths. His heart hammered at the exertion, but more...it hammered because of the emotions swirling through him. Emotions he didn't want to name. Hell, he didn't know if there was a single name for *adoration, yearning desperation, delight, release...*

All quickly followed by alarm that gripped his chest like a vice. Because it didn't matter how much he told himself this was just sex, that this was just temporary, this was just a moment...her moment. He couldn't imagine not wanting it again, on repeat for ever.

He held her tight against him as her body relaxed after her orgasm. Her fingers stroked down his back and her head nestled against his throat.

Two weeks.

Two weeks and then nothing. No more of this. No more snatched kisses. No more pretending this wasn't something when it was plain to him now that it was...everything.

He'd promised himself he could deal with it. But how could he deal with losing Carly?

How had he let himself fall so hard for her when she was yet another woman leaving his life?

How could he be so cavalier with his heart?

He suddenly couldn't get his breath. He needed air. He

gently slid out and away from her, trying to make some space, but realising it didn't matter how far away from her he was. The attachment wasn't geographical, it was inside him.

She smiled lazily and stroked his thigh. 'You rushing off?'

Her expression told him she didn't want him to.

'Not at all. Just getting comfortable,' he lied. Well, he hadn't been about to leave, just give himself some breathing space.

The exact words she'd used about her upcoming trip. And he got it now. The emotions rolling through him threatened his sense and his equilibrium. If every thought was tinged with her, then how could he be objective about anything? If every thought she had was connected to this island and to her past, then how could she be objective about her future?

She had to leave to make sense of everything.

And he had to stay to give his son the stable home and security he deserved.

He probably should have been honest and explained. He should have admitted he needed space to breathe. But, instead, Owen leaned up on his elbow and breathed her in, grasping every moment they had left. Selfish. Greedy. Reckless.

The afternoon sun caught the gold and red strands of her hair splayed out on the white pillow. She was breathtakingly gorgeous as her expression turned from concern to satisfaction.

She blinked up at him, her eyes searching his face, and he wondered if he imagined something sad there for a moment. But then she smiled and rubbed her head against his arm. 'That was amazing, Owen.'

'It was.' He ran a finger down her cheek, wondering if she could feel the panic in his touch.

But she just kept on smiling. 'Thank you.'

'For what?'

'For showing me that I can be me again. That I'm not just a widow. That I'm capable of feeling.' Her eyes filled with tears and his throat closed over. He pulled her into his arms and hugged her close.

'You are so much more. You're...a miracle.' And, as she'd gone there, he followed. 'I wasn't sure if you were going to be okay with it—you know, after Raff.'

Her chest rose as she inhaled. Then she swallowed. 'I... um... I didn't know either. But I was okay with it. I am.'

'He sounds like he was a great guy.'

'He was.' She put her hand on his chest and edged backwards, more to look at him, he thought, than to make space between them. 'But we shouldn't be talking about him.'

'Why not?'

She frowned. 'I thought it might upset you.'

'God, Carly, no. Not at all. You have a past, so do I. We all have... I don't want to call it baggage, because your life with Raff is not something that dragged you down, it clearly gave you joy...' He dug deep for the right words, because he didn't want Mason to be thought of as baggage either. 'We all have *experiences* that we've had to live through. But I want to know you better, and that means we have to be open. I don't want you to edit what you say or think just to make me feel better about something. Raff was the most important person in your life. Please don't censor your thoughts or words about him.'

Her eyebrows rose as she looked at him and the tears welled again as she cupped his cheek. 'You're a remarkable man, Owen.'

'Not really. I lived with a woman who tried to be something she wasn't. And that just ended in disaster. I don't want you to feel you can't say what you think or feel around me.' He shrugged. 'Maybe I'm just being selfish and lazy, because I don't want to have to guess where your head is at.'

'You're a single dad who wants the best for his kid and a doctor who serves the island, Owen. There is nothing selfish or lazy about you.'

'I'm just greedy to know more about you, really. If ever you want to talk about Raff, or what happened or anything at all, I'm here.'

She slid out of his arms and propped herself up against the pillows. She sat for a few moments, staring into space, deep in thought, and he didn't want to push her, so he sat in the silence and waited.

Eventually she turned to him and he sensed she didn't want to be touched as she said, 'I waited for him. And waited. And prayed. I don't even know who to. The skies? The water? Anyone who'd listen…yes, God, if there is one. Anyone. Prayed for him to come back to me. I'd wake up thinking it was all a dream, and then the cold, black reality would come crashing in. And that's how it was for over a week until they finally gave up looking.'

A thick weight pressed on his chest. 'I thought I hurt when my mum left, and I prayed for her to come home, but this is on another level altogether. I can't imagine the pain you lived through.'

She shook her head. 'You don't live. You barely survive. Thank God for the island people, they were so lovely. They sent out search parties, held vigils, filled my freezer with food I couldn't stomach. I couldn't eat. Didn't sleep. We were in a sort of limbo for days. I couldn't make sense of any of it. Their disappearance made no sense to me. Raff's family lived on the water. They knew it so well.'

Her expression crumpled into anguish. 'Then they found Raff's dad's body off one of the neighbouring islands. So we knew then, for sure. Not what had happened, but that they weren't coming back. I was numb. I was raging. I was desperate. I was scared. I was…so many things.' She wrapped her arms round her knees and hugged them close to her chest. 'I was alone. Again.'

He put his hand on her shoulder and she shuffled close and leant her head on his arm. He wanted to tell her that she didn't have to feel alone again. Ever. But he sensed it wasn't the right time, or maybe even the right thing to say, because she was choosing to travel solo. She needed her alone adventure.

But he imagined her broken and raging, and then stumbling numbly through each day. How hard she must have prayed and searched. How hard she'd worked to recover. And he had nothing but admiration for the woman she'd become, despite everything she'd been through.

Maybe it was more than admiration. More than sexual attraction. More than care…so much more.

Maybe… The pressing weight on his chest intensified. The panic returned. He couldn't love her. No, that wasn't where he was with this. But he held her in…high esteem. Because love would be too devastating, too much to feel for someone who was leaving.

He would not allow that emotion to creep in. He just wouldn't. He'd loved and lost too many times now to willingly walk right into that again.

After a few minutes, she took a deep breath and sighed, then blinked up at him and smiled. 'So, what are your plans for the rest of the day?'

What he wanted was to stay here and make love to her again, but if he was going to keep his heart intact he needed to leave, and soon. 'I'll go collect Mason, then we've got a day of decorating. We've moved on to the outside now. God, it all sounds so small and mundane compared to your big adventure.' But he wouldn't change it for the world. Mason was where his focus needed to be.

'Not at all. You're making a life for you and your son. It's beautiful.' She slid her palms down the crisp white sheets. 'I've got to list a load of things for sale.'

'Ugh. I've been there when we downsized our house in the city. Do you need a hand?' And, yes, it appeared he was looking for excuses to stay just a little longer. Like an addict craving the one thing he shouldn't have.

She smiled, oblivious to the turmoil in his chest. 'Thanks, but no. Mia's going to come over later with Harper for a sleepover. We're going to go through everything that needs to be sold, donated or thrown away.'

'You missed out *kept*. If you have anything you want stored, I can look after it for you. The shed is now clean and tidy.'

'It's fine. Thank you. When it comes down to it, I don't have much. Raff and I met when we were travelling and only had the bags on our backs. We weren't married long enough to accumulate too many things. Mia's going to look after my precious stuff.' Her eyes darted towards a small wooden box on the dressing table. It was a beautiful hand-carved thing with inlaid paua shell on the lid. He guessed either the box or the contents were important to her.

'Because you don't know when you'll be back to collect it.'

She pressed her lips together then nodded slowly. 'Exactly that.'

And there, right there, was the moment he should have left. But instead he pulled her to him, nuzzling her hair, on a trajectory he seemingly had no control over. 'So... I have maybe ten more minutes before I have to collect Mason. You want a hand sorting anything out?'

She laughed and straddled his lap, her beautiful breasts

pressing against his chest. 'You can definitely sort me out, Owen Cooper.'

Then she kissed him again and, with that one single act, all his promises to keep his heart intact fell away.

CHAPTER ELEVEN

THEY WERE PAINTING the front of the house when Carly arrived the next afternoon. As she drove down the gravel driveway, she watched them work, man and boy side by side. Owen was dressed in an old paint-splattered T-shirt and denim cut-offs. Mason wore a white *Mr Happy* T-shirt and yellow shorts.

Owen said something to his son that she couldn't hear, but the boy looked up, beamed at his dad and chuckled. Then Owen put down his paint brush, picked Mason up and threw him over his shoulder. He jogged in a circle, with the child screaming, giggling and waving his paint brush in the air, then put him down.

Most people would have been worried about the splashes of white paint on the ground. But not Owen. He just cared about making his son happy.

Her heart constricted. Yesterday had been intense and wonderful, a surprise and a gift. But they hadn't discussed what happened now. Were they neighbours with benefits? Friends? Temporary lovers?

What, exactly?

Feeling a little unsure about it all, she climbed out of the truck and pasted on a smile. 'Hi, guys!'

'Hi, Carly.' Grinning, Mason waved his paint brush again while Owen's slow grin was almost too lazy and sexy for words. She took in the muscled arms that had held her tight as he'd entered her, the mouth that had given her so much pleasure, and her body hummed for more. So, part of her question was answered. They were two single people who'd had consensual sex and they both wanted to do it again. Why put more of a label on it than that?

'Where do you want me to put this?' Trying to rein in her libido, she pointed to the bright orange double kayak strapped to the flat bed of her truck. 'I saved the best one for you two. The rest are up on the marketplace website. Four have sold already.'

'It's a beauty.' Owen sauntered over, looking simply delicious as he wiped his hands on a towel. 'Let's put it in the shed. Mason, are you okay waiting here for a few minutes while I help Carly?'

The boy nodded, serious again and concentrating on his work. 'Sure, Dad.'

'Don't go anywhere. Just paint that corner. You're doing a great job, mate.'

Carly's heart jittered. It was all well and good for her to want sex again, but did he? Had he had second thoughts? Did he regret what they'd done?

But as soon as they'd put the kayak on the ground he was in front of her, toying with a curl of her hair, running it through his fingers, his eyes searching her face. 'Hey, you.'

'Hey, you.' Her heart hammered and her body tugged towards him as she played with the hem of his T-shirt.

'Come here.' He wrapped an arm round her waist and dragged her closer, kissing her deeply, and she felt exactly how much he wanted her.

But she reluctantly pulled away, her hand on his chest. His heart beat hard and fast like hers. 'What about Mason?'

'True.' Owen grimaced and turned to look at the open doorway. 'He's very quiet.'

'Is that a good thing? Or bad?'

'You can never tell with kids. But usually bad.' Smiling,

he slipped his hand into hers and squeezed. Then he let go and strode out into the sunshine. Mason was still in the same place, painting the corner, his tongue jutting out in concentration just like his father's had.

Her heart swooped. 'Good job, Mason. You're an expert painter.'

'Thank you, Carly.' He beamed up at her. 'Can we go kayaking now?'

She caught Owen's eye and raised her eyebrows in question. He shook his head. 'Not today, champ. It's getting late, and it's dinner time soon.'

A cue to leave. But her feet seemed reluctant to turn her round and walk her back to the truck. She forced out a lame, 'I'll leave you to it, then.'

Owen met her eyes and smiled secretively. 'You want to stay for dinner? It's nothing special, just sausages and a bit of salad and bread.'

'Man food,' Mason said, and showed her his arm muscles.

'Is that what Daddy calls sausages? Well, I like them too. So, it's also girl food.' She showed him her guns and Mason ran over to squeeze them. 'Wow. You're strong.'

She wished she was, she really did. Was she strong enough to go on her trip? To leave this new friendship, leave everything she knew? She sighed. 'Okay, I'll stay for dinner. But only because you're serving my favourite girl food, and only on the condition that I do the washing up.'

It was almost a rerun of the first time she'd stayed for dinner…partly because Mason insisted on marshmallows by the fire again, and partly because they were both so welcoming. Mason tripped off tales about kindy and his friends and more about Wallace the weka.

Carly laughed at the bird's apparent antics. 'And is she still waking you up every morning?'

'*He* hasn't been able to break down our hardy defences so

far.' Owen's expression was a mixture of humour, surprise and censure. Clearly, he hadn't confessed the bird gender confusion to his son.

'It's only a matter of time before she…er…he does.' She giggled at their shared joke.

Shared. Her throat felt scratchy at the thought of leaving these people she'd become so fond of.

'Right. I'll go clear up.' She washed the dishes in the newly decorated kitchen while Owen put Mason to bed. He'd done a great job of sprucing up the place and had even added some soft furnishings that made the house more homely. That was surprising for a guy. She could hear him reading a bedtime story as she flicked the switch for the kettle.

This was all feeling very cosy. He'd called it mundane and small, but wasn't giving a child a secure and stable upbringing one of the most amazing things a parent could do? Even though Mason's mum wasn't around, he had the safety and love of his father. It was home. It was a family—something she'd had a brief taste of and had loved.

But now… No, she couldn't move into this heart space. She had to create something for herself.

There was no denying she ached to stay here just a little longer, but was that just because she was wobbling about her plans? About stepping into the unknown?

She was reaching to put the plates in a high cupboard when she felt a kiss on her neck, arms circling her waist. A hard erection pressed against her bottom. She whirled round and caught Owen's mouth in a searing kiss.

'You smell so good,' she managed as she pulled away, her body straining for his touch all over.

He laughed. 'Mason's bath bubbles?'

'No. Something else. Something that makes me…'

He held her arms by her sides as he looked at her, his eyes misted and heat shimmering there. 'Horny?'

She giggled. 'Yes.'

'You could stay.'

What? A pause. Maybe he read the confusion on her face because he followed it up with a quick, 'The night, I mean.'

'Oh. No. I shouldn't.' For a moment she'd thought he was asking something else. But...no. He knew her plans.

His fingers tiptoed to the back of her neck and he stroked the sensitive skin there. 'Do you have to be back at the camp tonight?'

'Well...no.' She inhaled a stuttering breath as his fingers trailed down her back. *God*, that felt good. 'The school teachers are very capable and experienced, and they know how to contact me in an emergency. I have my bleeper.'

'Which I hope remains silent.' He lifted her hair and kissed her neck, making her shudder in delight.

Her determination to leave melted away. Just one touch and she was his. 'I can stay a while, but perhaps it'll be better if I don't sleep over.'

'Stay, Carly.' He kissed down her spine and across her shoulder. 'I want to wake up with you.'

Oh, what a lovely idea. What a wonderfully amazing idea. But no. She turned and captured his mouth in a kiss. She would stay a while. She would leave in the middle of the night. No need for any concerns. No need for questions. No damage to anyone. Just a lot of fun...while it lasted.

Tap. Tap. Tap.

   Tap. Tap. Tap.

   Tap. Tap. Tap.

What the hell...?

Someone was doing Morse Code in Carly's bedroom. She opened an eye and took in the dark drapes, the fingers of yellow light streaming through the gaps. Took in the sleeping body next to her with his arm slung casually over her hip. The unfamiliar shapes of furniture she hadn't chosen.

No. Not *her* bedroom.

She jerked upright. *Hell.* After an amazing night of love-making, she'd fallen asleep in his arms and now it was morning.

'Shoo. Get out. Get out!' she whispered at the weka that was tapping the wooden floor.

'Again? How the hell did he get in?' A bleary-eyed Owen rose up next to her. 'What time is it?'

Carly glanced at the clock over on Owen's bedside table. *Oh, no. Oh, no. Oh, no.* 'It's seven-seventeen.'

A string of curse words rose inside her and she put her hand to her mouth to hold them back.

'What?' Owen bounded out of bed. 'Damn it. I am so late.'

Suddenly aware of her nakedness, and also suddenly shy, she grabbed the top sheet and wrapped it round her—as if he hadn't just spent hours caressing and kissing every inch of her—while she scrambled from the bed to find her clothes, keeping her voice a hoarse whisper. 'I have never slept in in my life. I wake at six every morning. I don't need an alarm clock.'

'Me neither, I usually have Mason to wake me at way too early o'clock and, well, I'd thought I'd got rid of Wallace.' He quietly shooed the bird out of the door she'd sworn they'd closed last night, just in case Mason felt like wandering in while they were…

'Mason.' Her gut tied in a knot as she wrestled with her underwear. Someone seriously needed to invent bras that were easy to put on in hurry. 'What if he sees me?'

Owen came over and crouched on his haunches in front of her. He put his hand on her knee, warm and steady. His eyes were soft and kind, although she detected some panic there too. 'Calm down, sweetheart. I'm sure he won't.'

Sweetheart. Her heart squeezed at the endearment. Meanwhile, her head was full of panic and images of facing that poor little boy and trying to explain...what? That it was all only temporary. That she was leaving, just like his mum had. Her gut roiled at how that would make him feel. 'What if he does?'

'Then we'll...' Owen scraped his hand through his hair as he thought. 'Tell him you slept in the spare room.'

'Okay. Right. Great idea, Owen. The spare room that doesn't have a bed in it.' She dragged on her T-shirt and tucked it into her shorts.

But Owen just shook his head. 'We just play it cool, okay? If we don't make a big deal out of it, he won't.'

'Are you sure?'

'Honestly? No. But what's done is done. We'll deal with it.'

He sounded certain but he looked a little shaken. She was not doing this again. She wasn't going to compromise Owen's position as a father or Mason's little heart. Or sneak around like some sort of scarlet woman. She hadn't done anything wrong, but it wasn't fair on any of them.

She hurriedly finished dressing and tiptoed across the bedroom, hopping on each foot as she slipped her sneakers on one at a time. But she overstepped and landed heavily with a thud.

'Easy does it.' Owen was quickly by her side, helping her up. 'I've never seen you like this before.'

'I've never slept in before.'

What she actually meant was, *I've never had to navigate this and I don't know what to do. Because half of me wants to wake up in this house with this man every morning. And half of me is filled with very real panic about disturbing a sleeping child...about giving everyone including myself false hope. About falling more deeply. And falling and falling...*

'I hope I didn't wake him.'

They both stood stock-still and held their breath for a beat. Two. Owen whispered against her throat, 'See? He's fast asleep. You can make your escape.' Then he grabbed her backside and squeezed. 'Man, I love your short shorts.'

'Stop it!' she hissed, whacking away his hand as laughter bubbled from her throat, because surely she was overreacting? She gingerly pulled the door open and crept out.

But the laughter died in her throat as a tired little boy in stripy pyjamas wandered along the corridor, rubbing his eyes. He was suddenly alert the moment he recognised Carly and he ran towards her. 'Carly!'

Damn.

She shoved her hands into her pockets and tried to act as if she hadn't just had a lot of fabulous sex with his father. 'Hey, Mason.'

'Did you have a sleepover, like I did at Mia's?'

Heart rattling, she glanced over at Owen. He nodded. 'Sure she did. It's great fun, isn't it?'

She bugged her eyes at him, but then remembered they weren't making a big deal out of it. 'But now I have to go.'

'Stay for breakfast, Carly?' Mason frowned. 'Can we have pancakes, Daddy?'

'It'll take too much time, buddy. We're running a bit late today and I need to grab a shower and have a shave before work.'

The little boy's face crumpled. 'Can I show Carly my trains?'

'Another day, bud.' Owen ruffled his son's hair, but Mason slumped down on the floor in a sulk. Owen crouched down and jollied him along. 'Maybe later? Or tomorrow? Or something. We've got to a get a wriggle on this morning. How about you get dressed? Then I'll fix some toast.'

'No.' Mason folded his arms.

'Come on, mate. We've got to get a move on.' A note of frustration had slid into Owen's voice. 'It's getting late.'

Carly watched this all play out and her gut tightened. She'd seen first-hand with Mia and Harper how hard it was to be a solo parent, especially when time was limited. She also knew, from dealing with hundreds of kids herself, that getting all het up with them was unlikely to smooth things over.

Since this was all her fault, she needed to give him a hand. 'Can I do anything to help?'

Owen huffed out a breath of relief and smiled at her. 'Thanks, that would be great. Would you mind giving him a hand to get dressed while I get breakfast on?'

'Sure thing.' She offered her hand to Mason. 'Come on, champ. Let's get you ready for the day.'

The little boy's bedroom was bright and airy. Fresh pale blue paint covered the walls. He had a red racing car bed, a set of drawers and a little desk, shelves loaded with books and two large wooden chests she imagined were filled with toys. Owen had done a fine job of creating the perfect little boy's bedroom.

She pulled open a drawer, looking for clothes. 'What are you going to wear today, Mason?'

He sauntered over and picked out a blue T-shirt and grey shorts.

After he took off his PJs she helped him into the T-shirt and then bent down and held the shorts so he could step into them.

He put his hand on her shoulder as he put one foot in and then the other. 'Are you going to sleep over tonight too?'

'No, honey. I don't think I'll be sleeping over again.' She definitely wouldn't.

'Aww. Please.'

She scanned the room to find something to distract him. Over on the desk was a drawing pad and some crayons.

From a distance she could see a picture on one of the pieces of paper. She wandered over. 'Hey, what's this?'

He grinned his mischievous grin. 'I drawed you a picture.'

'Oh? That's kind. When did you do this?'

He shrugged. 'Don't know. After kindy.'

'What is it?' She could make out some rudimentary round shapes making up a number of people with circle arms and legs and tufty lines for hair.

He pointed to two small circle figures. 'My family. That's me and daddy.'

Ah. A stabbing pain lanced her chest.

'Who's that?' In the top corner, far from the little family of two, was another circle figure.

He ran his finger over it. 'Mummy. She's holding a tablet and talking to me from 'Merica.'

Poor, poor kid. Her heart stung at his words. But at least Miranda had been included in the picture, and at least Mason still spoke to her, even if he didn't get regular Mum hugs.

She looked closer at the picture and saw another figure next to the little boy wearing a crudely coloured-in blue top, very similar to that of her work uniform. She thought she might know exactly who it was, but didn't want him to say the words. She turned away, her throat suddenly tight and raw.

But he grabbed her hand and tugged her round. His stubby finger traced over the unnamed figure. 'That's you.'

She stared at the picture, trying to make sense of it and trying to work out the scramble of emotions clogging her chest. *My family.* What the hell? How could something so innocent hurt her heart so much? She cleared her throat and nodded. *Do not cry. Do not cry.* 'That's nice.'

'Will you be my mummy too?' He looked up at her with huge, pleading eyes.

She straightened and started to make his bed just for something to do, so she wouldn't have to look at him. 'You have a mummy already, Mason.'

'My friend Tane has two mummies. I want two mummies. I want you.'

She squeezed her eyes shut and counted slowly to five, trying to gain some composure. She hadn't wanted this.

Or, rather, hadn't *known* she wanted this deep down. Hell, she'd been him once—a child with no mother at home. She knew how desperate he might be feeling. But, even so, she couldn't be this little fella's mother. Hell, she didn't know anything about parenthood. Sure, she was a good teacher, she knew how to interest and excite kids about being in nature. But real stuff…day-to-day stuff? Routine and boundaries…?

And a mother? How could she be a mother when she was exploring Vietnam? When she was hiking the Camino in Spain?

When she opened her eyes, she saw Owen standing in the doorway. His face was ashen, his expression one she couldn't read.

She swallowed and turned back to Mason, caught between the two and not knowing what to say to either of them. 'Um. You have a mummy who loves you very much. One is good. I mean, two is fine, but I can't be your mummy, Mason…' Nerves were making her babble. She had to get out of here before anything else happened. Such as breaking down in tears or her heart breaking. 'I…um… I have to go now.'

'Take it.' Mason held the picture out to her.

She glanced at Owen, then at his son. Then she took the picture in trembling hands. 'Thank you.'

She reckoned she could be in her truck in about three seconds, if she ran. Which was what she felt like doing. But she couldn't. Owen was staring at her. Mason was looking at her as if waiting for more, wanting more. Wanting what she couldn't give him.

'Bye!' Panic got the better of her and she dashed outside, where she gulped in fresh air, hoping it would calm her down.

It didn't. She was rattled. Panicked. What confusion had she caused in that poor little boy by her selfish behaviour? She'd wanted to make love with Owen. She'd wanted to bask in his attention, to fill her need. But at what cost to Mason? To her own heart?

She ran to her truck and dragged the door open. As she was climbing in, she heard Owen's voice behind her. 'God, Carly. I'm so sorry. I didn't know he was going to draw that.'

She looked up and saw his hair all ruffled from their lovemaking—and no doubt from a good deal of scrubbing his hand through it, trying to explain things to Mason.

She put her hand to her chest, more to calm her racing heart than anything. 'What did we expect, though? All this time spent together, camping, kayaking. Being friends. Being close. He must have seen you being…happy.' Because, yes, they'd both fed a need. Last night was the closest she'd been to happy in a long time.

She put her head on the steering wheel. 'I'm sorry. I'm so sorry.'

CHAPTER TWELVE

OWEN WATCHED THE flash of emotions rushing behind Carly's eyes just before she dropped her head onto the steering wheel, and his heart just about stalled in his chest. She was hurting and Mason was confused.

Hell, he was confused.

It had all gone too far. They'd been grasping something for themselves, but the ramifications rippled out like a stone thrown into the ocean, causing who knew what damage to each of them? A friendship. Sex. More. Reaching. Hoping. And now Mason was starting to hope for the impossible too.

At all costs, he had to protect his little boy.

Yet he looked at Carly, hurting too, and his heart pumped again, hard and fast. She was...everything. This woman was the closest thing to perfect he'd ever met. His head buzzed. His chest felt as if the world were pressing in on it.

He probably should let her drive away, but he couldn't leave it like this.

'Carly.' He gripped the open window frame. 'Look at me.'

'You're late for work.' She groaned into the steering wheel. 'And I have to go.'

'Not yet. We need to talk.'

'Yeah.' She raised her head and looked at him, eyes bruised with worry. 'So, what do we do now?'

'I don't know.' He was paralysed by anguish, because

what he wanted and what they had to do were completely at odds. There was no way out of this.

'What do you want from me, Owen? What do you want?'

What the hell? Wasn't that obvious now? He wanted to wake up with her every day. He wanted a woman who wanted to be in his life.

But he couldn't put that kind of pressure on her. 'I want you to be happy.'

Her eyes blazed as she shook her head. 'Wrong answer. What do *you* want? From me? From us?'

'What does it matter what I *want*?' What was the use in explaining it all? Each time he thought he knew where he stood, the rug was pulled from under him. Women didn't stay. 'Will what I want make a difference? You're going, Carly, and I totally respect that, but we have to be honest about it. We're kidding ourselves that we can share our lives in the short term without getting hurt. I care about you. Too much.' He couldn't watch someone walk away again and allow his heart to be shattered for the third time. Hell, he'd only just recovered from the emotional whiplash Miranda had caused. 'There isn't any "us". There can't be.'

She pressed her lips together. Her bottom lip trembled. 'What was last night, then? The "I want you"... The running down the jetty desperate for me... All of this...' She waved her hand between them.

Good question. He shook his head as he tried to control his breathing and his thoughts and failed on both accounts. 'It's reckless. It's...dangerous. To me and to my boy. It's false hope.'

'What do you mean?'

'Hell, Carly. Isn't it obvious? I want to ask you to stay. To give up your dreams and be here with me and Mason. But that's not fair on you. You have a dream and a plan, and you have to be true to yourself.'

Her eyebrows rose. 'You want me to stay?'

'No. I want to be...' He'd come to the truth of it now. Pain lanced his chest. '*Enough* that you'd stay.' His gaze connected with hers and he saw the torment running through her mind. She hadn't planned to get involved. She hadn't planned any of this. They should have been more careful. 'I know you have to leave.'

She kept on looking at him. Silence stretched.

Then her eyes lit up briefly, as if she'd found the answer. 'You could...wait for me?'

'How long do I wait? How long do Mason and I put our lives on hold?' He knew how long. He knew what it was like to hope and then have those hopes smashed. He wasn't going to give up his agency this time, hand over the dregs of his power to someone else. 'Even you don't know how long you're going to be away. You have no plans to come back permanently, you said so yourself. So, no, I really couldn't wait. I've played that game before, Carly. I'm tired of waiting, of putting my own plans on hold.'

Her eyes fluttered closed and she inhaled, her chest stuttering, then exhaled slowly. 'I understand.'

'I don't think you do. Hell, I know you've been through so much pain, and I know how much you want to grab some happiness. I know how much you deserve all of it too. Everything. You deserve a life that is created by you, to be cherished and loved, and you deserve a cheerleader to support you through it all. Someone who's free, who could maybe come along with you and watch you blossom.

'Hell, I'd love to be that person. I really would. But I can't. You know that. Mason's had too much upheaval, and now we're just getting settled.' He couldn't throw it all away, uproot the foundations he'd so carefully laid... not for someone who might not stay around. Because they never did in the end.

'Oh, Owen.' She blinked, her eyes swimming in tears. 'I could...maybe I could stay.'

'What? No.' He knew what it must have taken for her to say that. To reach out and try, to offer to put her hopes on hold for him. He closed his eyes as possibility swam in front of him, and he wanted so much to grab hold of it. But how could he do that again? How could he put Mason at such a risk?

'When I was a kid, I watched my mother leave and there was nothing I could do to stop her. My whole life was blown apart, my safety net in tatters. I didn't understand that it was something she needed to do, I just thought I'd done something wrong. That I wasn't good enough and that was why she was leaving me. And then I had to watch it happen to my kid. Have you any idea how that feels? To watch someone break your child's heart and be able to do nothing? I couldn't make her stay…couldn't make either of them stay. I can't let him go through that again. Hell… I can't do it to myself.'

'I'm not Miranda.' She was shaking now, and he hated that he made her be like this. But he had to break this off. It was the right thing to do, even if it hurt like hell now.

'I know you're not, and I know you have every good intention, Carly. She did too, she's not a monster. But I can't take that risk and ask you to give up your dreams and stay just a little longer. Hope you'll settle with me, with us. Hope you'll forget your plans, and that you'll change and fit into our life. All it does is put off the inevitable. I'll just end up waiting for the end.'

She slid her hand over his. 'There doesn't have to be an end.'

'Really? Not when you start to get itchy feet again? When you realise this small family life isn't the kind of wild adventure you'd been planning?'

'No.' She shook her head quickly. 'It doesn't have to end like that.'

'But it will. I won't tell myself lies and I certainly won't tell them to my son. It's best if we finish it all now. That way you're free to leave and we can…' *Recover.*

He'd seen the *Under Offer* banner slapped across the Camp Rāwhiti sign. If the camp, all her island history and Mia and Harper weren't enough to keep her here, how could he be?

Or…maybe he was tarnishing her with the same brush as his ex-wife and his mother. Maybe he was being unfair. Perhaps she would stick to her word. Perhaps she would come back to them. Maybe they could reach some sort of deal.

But she pressed her lips together, as if holding in something she didn't want to escape in front of him. Then she managed, 'Are you saying you don't want to try to reach a compromise? That you don't care about me? Because I care about you, Owen.'

'Of course, I care about you, Carly. You're amazing. Beautiful. Funny. Sexy. Bright. So damned bright. I lo—' He slammed his mouth shut as he realised what he was about to say.

Love.

Now, that was a wild notion. But, hell, the only thing that could cause this amount of hurt, confusion and chaos stemmed from love. He'd tried to protect himself, had tried to put up walls, but she'd broken them down with her smile, her touch and her kisses.

He loved her.

And it was the worst possible thing he could ever do. It made him desperate, it blurred his logic. It derailed him. Look at him now, trying to make a deal with himself. Trying to think of ways he could have it all when, deep down, he knew he just couldn't.

Because he'd loved before and he'd been left behind, trying to mop up the mess. 'I have to care for myself and my son.'

'You're hiding behind Mason. Making excuses not to jump in.' She shook her head and snatched her hand back, her eyes wild. 'You say you care about me, but you don't want to wait or make promises. And now you're saying you won't let me stay either. You're pushing me away. What the hell kind of care is that?'

'I'm not going to make promises that will clip your wings, Carly. Promises that will turn into regret, or a bind you want to shrug off. We really don't know each other.' If he told himself that enough, he might start to believe it. He knew her enough to lose his heart to her. Knew her enough that he wanted the best for her. He loved her.

Hell.

'I know what I feel.' She put her hand to her heart, and he suddenly wanted to hear what more she had to say about that.

'Which is what?'

'I like you. A lot. I really do care about you and about Mason. We could at least try. We could do video calling.' But even as she said it her hopeful expression dissolved and her shoulders slumped, telling him she realised what she was suggesting. 'Like Miranda.'

'Daddy! Daddy! Mummy's calling.' As if on cue, and with the worst possible timing in the world, Mason ran out of the house waving his digital tablet, his eyes dancing with excitement as the screen lit up with light and sound.

Mason. He shouldn't be watching this. And Miranda most definitely shouldn't be.

Owen closed his eyes and tried to control the rush of panic, of pain and, yes, of love. The joy of seeing his son so animated mingled with the loss of Carly.

Once again, his gaze connected with hers and he saw, with that one plaintive statement from Mason, that she knew he was right. He wasn't about to make a deal that could hurt him or his boy. He would always put Mason before his own needs, wants or desires. Always.

He dragged his eyes away, but not before committing her beautiful face to memory. The eyes that bore into him as if she was reaching into his soul and making him question everything he believed to be true. The mouth that made him laugh with her jokes and that broke him open with her kisses. The wild red-gold hair.

Love. It sure as hell made you crazy.

Then he turned to Mason and dragged up a smile and jolly tone he wasn't sure he could maintain for long. 'Hey, bud. Just chatting.' The screen had gone dark. 'Sorry, she's hung up. Give me the tablet and we can dial in. But we'll have to be quick or we'll be very late for kindy.'

That was what was important. He needed to keep the lines of communication open between Mason and his mother and a solid routine. Nothing else.

He took a step towards his son, who raised his chubby fist and waved happily at Carly, showing her his tablet. 'It's Mummy!'

But Owen didn't wave, he didn't look back to see Carly's reaction, not when he heard her sharp intake of breath, the soft sob in her throat, the roar of the truck's engine and the tyres on gravel.

He didn't look even when he was desperate for one last glance. Because he was an idiot, not a masochist.

Walking those few steps was one of the hardest things he'd ever done, because she'd wanted him to make a promise and it would have been so easy to agree. To put off the pain for another day just to save himself from it today.

Sure, we'll wait a few weeks. Months. A year. We'll sit on the sidelines until you're ready to come back to us, a different person with different ideas and expectations.

He wasn't going to do that to Mason.

And he certainly wasn't going to do it to himself.

* * *

Carly fisted away the tears that blurred her vision. It wasn't such a great idea to drive when she was crying this hard, but she'd had no choice. She'd had to leave.

Bloody man.

Bloody beautiful, amazing man. Who loved so hard, he'd protect his son from anything.

Protect himself too, because he'd been hurt in the past. His mother had left, his wife had gone and he couldn't take that risk again.

Love.

Had she imagined it? Had it been on the tip of his tongue? Her heart had squeezed in hope, and then crumpled, because who loves you and then pushes you away?

Don't go.

She'd watched each step he'd taken away from her and had willed him to turn round. Just once. Just one time, so she could look at his face. But he hadn't. She'd watched his rigid back and taut shoulders retreat from her, had watched him bend to pick up Mason and hold him close, and every part of her had craved his hug, had wanted those arms around her waist, those lips on her cheek. She'd wanted to run to him, hammer her fists on his back and make him promise to wait for her. Hell, she wasn't going for ever.

But she was going long enough that he'd forget her.

It looked almost as if Mason had forgotten his second mummy request already. She hadn't missed the excitement in his eyes at the thought of his mother. Who knew, if she stayed, Mason's and Miranda's contact might fade...and she knew first-hand how important it was to keep those ties sacrosanct.

But now? Her heart had been blown into tiny pieces all over again. Her chest hurt. Her throat hurt. She'd tried to keep her heart out of it, had tried to convince herself she could leave unscathed and untouched by them. She didn't want to care for them this much. Didn't want to imagine the next few weeks without them. But Owen had made it clear that, whatever she said, he was going to reject her.

She pulled up behind her cottage and saw Mia waiting for her, her hair whipping around in the breeze. Summer was turning to autumn and, as usual around the equinox, with big sea swells and squally storms. Everything was unsettled. Tumultuous. The way she felt right now.

No, please. Not now. Not this.

Carly's heart sank at the sight of Mia because she knew she'd be forced to talk to her when she just wanted to hide away and cry. But time was running out, so she swallowed down her pain, wiped her eyes and found her sister-in-law a smile as she jumped down from the truck. 'Hey.'

Mia frowned. 'What's the matter, hun?'

It was plain she couldn't keep anything from her. 'It's nothing. I'm fine. Why are you here? Is everything okay?'

'Look at you, always worrying over everything.' Mia grinned and cupped Carly's cheek, peering closer at her face. 'Are you sure you're okay? You don't look fine to me.'

Please don't ask. I'll cry all over again.

'Oh, you know.' Carly sniffed and wiped her nose on her sleeve because she'd just used up the box of tissues she kept in her glove compartment.

'Oh, honey, I do. I do. Grief hits us in weird ways. I still get overwhelmed by it sometimes.' Clearly Mia thought Carly's tears were for Raff and his parents. 'Um…we arranged for me to come collect some of your things this morning.'

'Oh. Yes. I forgot.' But it was Owen, not Raff, who had made her forget her grief, her history and even her plans. Or, rather, she'd been desperate enough to put them on hold for him. She'd almost bargained herself out of her trip. Tried to make rash promises she knew neither of them could or should keep. Tried to get one more family to accept her and love her. And for one mad moment she'd been prepared to give everything up for them.

It really did look as though she was destined to be on her own. Alone.

But she'd been there before and she could do it again. If only her heart would ever stop hurting.

Mia was still chattering. 'Countdown to the big day's started, so it's only natural you'll feel a bit wobbly. Don't forget, this is your big adventure. You've been planning it for so long, dreaming about it ever since you cut it short to come here with Raff.'

'Everything's in here.' Carly opened the door to her cosy lounge and gestured to the piles of things she'd been supposed to pack last night. But, instead, she'd spent that time with Owen.

Together they put her treasures into boxes and secured the lids with sticky tape. They were just filling the last one when Mia picked up the kauri jewellery box. 'Oh. Isn't this the box Raff made for your wedding present?'

'Yes.' Carly inhaled deeply and steadied her ragged breaths. 'I want you to keep it for me.'

Mia opened the lid and gasped. 'Oh. Your wedding ring.'

'Yes.' Was this the right thing to do? Yes, it was. She had to put a line under everything. Raff, this house, Owen. She had to take her place in the world. Carly Edwards…whoever she was…was waiting to blossom. 'I don't… Please don't take this the wrong way. I will never forget your brother. But I have to step out into the world as me. Not as a widow.'

'I understand. I really do. I get it.' Mia wrapped her into a tight hug. 'Please promise me you'll have lots of fun. I want you to message me daily with updates. We can video call. You can show me and Harper all the amazing places you visit.'

Video call…like Mason and his mum. Like countless others who found a way to connect with people they loved and cared for despite the miles keeping them apart. Like she'd offered Owen.

She sighed. 'I will. Will you be okay without me?'

Mia grinned. 'We're two amazing, strong women. We've got this.'

'Yes, we have.' Carly found Mia a smile. She was right; they'd both faced impossible sadness and survived it. They had a future to look forward to. Happiness waited for them.

But whatever else happened, and despite herself, Carly knew she would carry her losses with her wherever she went. The memories of Raff and his family, and now of Owen too.

Because the man she'd thought might heal her heart had broken it instead.

CHAPTER THIRTEEN

OWEN STOOD AT the harbour and watched the ferry depart, taking with it Mia and Carly, and any hope that things could be fixed between them.

She hadn't seen him there. Hadn't come out on deck. Hadn't said goodbye—not a single word. Hadn't even come in with Mia to drop Harper off at the surgery.

They'd managed to avoid each other over the last few days. He'd even stayed away from her leaving party, telling everyone that Mason was under the weather. Truth was, he hadn't been able to say goodbye. He'd done that too many times in his life already and this time, he knew, would be the worst.

And yet here he was today, unable to let her go.

But he had to.

The wind picked up, sending an old brown paper bag scuttling across the ground. The clouds threatened rain. He put his hands on Mason's and Harper's shoulders and caught their attention away from feeding the baby ducks that hung around on the water. 'Come on, kids. Let's get back inside. There's a storm on its way.'

'From what I hear, it's a big one too.' Anahera slipped her arm into his and walked with them back to the surgery. But his focus was on the boat. 'I hope the ferry's going to be okay.'

Anahera squeezed his arm and smiled softly. 'You mean, you hope Carly's going to be okay.'

Busted. 'Yes. Mia too. Obviously.'

'Of course, Mia. But Carly mainly.' She raised her eyebrows, letting him know she'd guessed and understood. She shivered as a cold wind whipped round their heads, dragging strands of grey hair from her clip. 'It's an easterly storm, unusual for here, but they always bring a good dousing and even cyclones. We need to batten down the hatches. And my hair.'

'Cyclones and ferries aren't a good mix.' Owen craned his head to catch a final glimpse of the boat disappearing into rough-looking seas.

'It'll hit us first. Hopefully they'll be on the mainland by the time it reaches the city.' Anahera pushed open the surgery door and they all clambered in. The pressure of the wind made him lean hard against the door to close it. Anahera bent and opened the children's play box in the reception waiting room. 'How do you feel about being the island's first responder now?'

'Good. I think. Everyone knows what they're doing, right? It's just following protocols. We'll be fine.' His heart fluttered with pride at having been asked, but also with a little trepidation. People were depending on him. 'If the storm gets worse, or there's likely to be a threat to life from flooding, we evacuate to the camp.'

His receptionist nodded. 'For the next three months. After the new owner moves in, we'll have to rethink that emergency plan.'

'I've called a meeting for next week to discuss it all.'

She looked up from pulling out some building blocks for Harper. 'You'll make a great leader here, Owen. You've got good ideas and great intentions. I'd say you've made it your home.'

'I hope so. I love it here.'

She pierced him with one of those stares only wise women could get away with. 'But you'll miss having Carly here to help.'

I miss her, full stop. I love her.

He couldn't deny that any longer. Although, he'd yet to say it fully out loud. But now he'd watched her leave and there was no chance for them.

'You're soft on her.' It was a statement, not a question. His receptionist was astute.

Or... had he actually said it out loud? 'She's a great woman, Anahera.'

She gave a nod in agreement. 'She'll be back.'

In two years or something.

'I hope she has an amazing time.'

'You hope she changes her mind.' Anahera winked then patted his shoulder. 'What will be, will be, Doc. These things have a habit of sorting themselves out.'

Yes, but not always in my favour. In fact, never.

He was about to reply when a loud howling noise ripped through the air, making Harper jump in surprise. Her little face crumpled and she started to sob.

Owen pushed his thoughts about Carly back and focused on the little girl. 'Hey. It's just the wind. It's okay. It's okay.'

He sat down and pulled her onto his lap, cradling her and rocking her the way he'd always done with Mason. Meanwhile, his big boy son played happily with some trains. Anahera stood up and busied herself at the reception desk.

There was a strange feeling in the atmosphere. Owen felt as if he was in some weird kind of limbo. He felt unsettled, unsure, as if he was holding his breath, waiting...

Maybe it was the static from the encroaching storm. Maybe it was his heart, not quite believing that she'd gone.

The phone rang.

Carly? His chest hurt.

Anahera answered.

Owen looked up expectantly. But why was he hoping? He'd just watched her sail away.

Anahera shook her head, as if reading his mind. 'That's your last patient cancelling their appointment. No one wants to come out today and I don't blame them. I've just seen on the online news that there's a cyclone likely.'

Not surprising, given that the walls felt as though they were trembling, the windows rattling in their frames. 'You should go home.'

'This building's safer than my house in a storm. I'll go put the kettle on.' The lights flickered, then went out. Anahera sighed. 'Power cut. Great. We need a generator here, Doc.'

'Add it to the list.' Still holding Harper, Owen shuffled to standing and dashed to the window. The yachts in the marina were being tossed about like toy boats in a kid's bath. Every building was dark. The flag on the flagpole whirled in a brutal, jagged dance. More debris tumbled down the street.

All he could see, far out on the water, were huge waves—white-topped and violent—and a sky as black as night. It was three-thirty. It shouldn't be this dark.

What if something happened to them in the storm? What if...? No. He wasn't going there. He turned to Anahera, 'We'd know if there was a problem with the ferry, right? We'd hear about it.'

Anahera stretched her arms out to take Harper from him and cooed as she rocked the girl back to sleep. 'We'd be first to find out. They'd radio in.'

It couldn't happen twice, not to the same family—two boating disasters. No, they'd be fine. The women would be drinking cocktails in an hour, celebrating signing the papers that set them free.

While here he was, hostage to his heart.

'Daddy, can I have a snack?'

Thank God for kids. They kept you sane and gave you a reason to focus. He wandered through to the lunchroom and grabbed some fruit, cut it into pieces and gave it to them. Then he played trains for what felt like an interminable amount of time.

The clock ticked. The wind howled. The frames rattled. Then the rain started, thick, greasy drops on the corrugated iron roof. It felt as if someone was hammering into his skull.

What if something happened to her?

He wouldn't be able to endure what she'd been through when she'd lost her husband. She was stronger than he was. She'd loved Raff and lost him. Had prayed he'd come back to her. Had waited. And waited.

Was this a little of how she'd felt? No. He couldn't imagine the horrors she'd been through. And yet...he couldn't think straight or be rational. He wanted to rip open the door, dive into the turbulent water and go find her.

He wanted to hold her and kiss her.

What if something happened to her?

He'd go out of his mind. All their missed chances— all that love, days of laughter, sexy sleepless nights. Her warmth, her skin. Her optimism. Her strength. He'd let her go. No, he'd made her go.

He couldn't live like this. He couldn't...

These things have a habit of sorting themselves out.

How, when she was following her own path and it certainly wasn't converging with his any time soon?

But maybe he could forge a way.

How? He didn't have any answers.

But he knew he wanted to try.

He'd pushed her away without giving her the time and space to talk things through. He'd knee-jerk reacted to panic that his son was getting too close to her. All that protectiveness had made him wary.

He'd been an idiot. Why hadn't he listened? Why hadn't he talked?

Because he'd been too scared to take a risk.

Like the risk she was taking by leaving this island. Like the risk he'd taken coming here. Like the risk he was taking, agreeing to be the island's first responder. Hell, he was happy to carry the weight of everyone here on his shoulders, but too cowardly to allow one person into his heart, into his life…

How was that even living, being scared, being closed off? He'd already taken a lot of risks. What was one more if it brought her back to him?

His chest flickered with hope. Maybe if he just talked to her, one last time. Maybe if he said yes to the video calls. Maybe if he was just brave enough to take a step.

He turned his back to the window. 'Anahera, do you think you'd be able to look after the kids tomorrow?'

'Sure, thing. Why?'

'I need to make a trip into the city.'

I need to get her back. Somehow.

'Of course—' She was interrupted by both their bleepers sounding shrilly at the same time.

Ferry run aground North Bay.

He looked up and saw Anahera's ashen face. And his heart stopped.

'Sign here and here.' The officious lawyer pointed a perfectly polished nail at the yellow stickies on the forms, indicating where they had to sign away the camp.

'Here we go.' Mia grinned as she scribbled her name. 'This is a good thing, Carly.'

'I know. I just…have a funny feeling.' Carly looked out of the window on the top floor of the tower block, over the city buildings and out to the Hauraki Gulf. She'd hoped it would be glittering today, but it was rough and foreboding. Thank goodness she didn't get seasick, because their crossing had been dire.

Mia followed her gaze. 'About what?'

'I don't know. Everything.' She shivered. 'And I'm not used to air conditioning. I'm freezing.'

'It's actually really warm in here.' Mia stroked Carly's back. 'It's probably just nerves. Try and look at it as excitement. We're going to go and drink cocktails, get drunk and silly and dance and then tomorrow night you're off on an adventure.'

She didn't feel adventurous. She felt…weird. Lost. Alone. Her head and heart kept slanting back to Owen and Mason.

'Sure, must be that.' Carly signed her name in the numerous places the lawyer indicated then shook her hand.

'Congratulations, ladies. The sale is now unconditional. Contracts are signed. If all goes to plan—and I don't see why it won't—you'll settle in a month.'

Mia squealed. 'So that's it? It's sold?'

'It is.' The lawyer nodded and grinned.

Mia's eyes grew huge. 'I'm so going kitchen shopping. Right now. Come with me! Help me choose something very swanky for my little cottage.'

So, they did. And, even though it felt endlessly domestic, Carly enjoyed it. More, she enjoyed seeing her sister-in-law happy and excited for the first time in too long.

'Let's celebrate.' As the sun started to set over Auckland, Mia hooked her arm into Carly's and pulled her into a bar that overlooked the waterfront. Out on the horizon the darkening clouds dumped fat fingers of rain into the unsettled ocean. Carly's stomach felt as choppy as the sea.

Was this all such a good idea?

When their champagne arrived, Mia picked up her glass and held it to Carly's. 'I never thought I'd be in this situation, doing this. Saying goodbye to the house I grew up in, to the camp that grounded me, that taught me to love and respect nature...even though she can be an evil mistress sometimes.' Her eyes darted towards the tumbling waves and they both knew she was talking about the accident that had ripped their family away. 'But I'm glad I have you by my side, Carly. Even when you're overseas, I know you'll be there for me. I'm glad I have you.'

Carly's throat felt ragged and sore. 'I'm glad I have you too. Thank you for being there for me through everything.'

'You were a gift my brother brought home, and I couldn't thank him for a better present than you. You were there for me in the worst time of my life and the best. You're the best godparent for Harper. And a total all-round wonder woman.'

'Aww, shucks.' Carly clinked her glass, hoping she looked better than she felt. Maybe she did get seasick after all. Maybe it just took a little while to settle. 'To us. The Edwards girls.'

'Sisters by family, friends by choice.' Mia took a sip of her champagne and laughed. 'I could get used to this. It's a good feeling when you know you can splash out every now and then on something frivolous like bubbles.'

'Wait...isn't champagne an essential food group?' Carly couldn't help but laugh too. 'Sorry, I know I need to start focusing on the positives. I've got financial stability. I've got independence. I'm very resilient...hell, I could face just about anything now. Not that I want to.' But her heart ached for what she'd left behind. 'I want to be happy. I want to be part of something.'

'You have your whole life in front of you. I envy you

a bit.' Mia sighed and twiddled with her flute stem. 'All that opportunity. Doing new things, meeting new people.'

'Oh? This isn't like you. I thought you loved Rāwhiti, and you adore Harper.'

'Oh yes, of course, and I wouldn't change that at all. But there's something missing.'

Carly frowned. How had she missed the fact that her sister-in-law was feeling like this? Because she'd been too absorbed in her own woes. 'You're a woman of means now. You can travel, do things. What do you want, Mia, right now?'

Her friend looked straight at Carly and sighed. 'Oh, man. I want good sex. And a lot of it.'

Carly spluttered her champagne and had to wipe her mouth with a napkin. 'Wow. I wasn't expecting that. You never talk about it. Never talk about Mia's dad or that night.'

'Which was the last time I had sex. Not that I'm counting.' Mia bugged her eyes. 'There's simply no point in talking about him. I tried to find him and I couldn't. He's gone. I've accepted that.'

'There are other men.'

'On Rāwhiti? I doubt it. You've snagged the only decent single guy there. Or, rather, had snagged.'

Another choke on the bubbles and Carly snorted. 'No snagging happened.'

'Just good sex, then? I'm so jealous.' Mia giggled. 'Lucky duck. You never know, you might meet the next man of your dreams in Greece. Or Spain. Or...'

Carly's thoughts immediately jumped to Owen. Again. No matter how hard she tried, she couldn't forget him. She'd always measured every man against Raff, and none had ever compared. But he was gone. Owen was now the yardstick by which she'd compare every subsequent lover.

And she'd left him behind. A sharp pain lanced her chest. She missed him so much.

'Talking of my daughter's father, I really should check in.' Mia pulled out her phone and scanned the screen. 'No messages. I'll give Owen a call, just to make sure they're okay.'

'Give him my love.' Carly closed her mouth quickly.

Mia blinked and then peered at her, her eyes searching, guessing and then realising. She gave Carly a soft, sad kind of smile, then she started to scroll and pressed call.

Carly imagined him sitting round the fire about now, toasting marshmallows for Harper and Mason. Reading them books before bed. She thought about him pottering around the kitchen, kayaking, painting, tending to the injured with soot streaked across his face. She thought about the rhythmic rise and fall of his chest after very good sex. She wouldn't tell Mia about that.

She imagined his neat spruced-up cottage. His special scent. The touch of his fingertips. His laugh. The care for Mason. The intention only ever to put his son first.

She thought about the way he'd looked at her as he'd slid inside her as if she was everything. Thought about the gentle touch of his fingers in her hair.

Did his heart hurt like hers did?

She'd wanted to reach for him, but he'd closed himself off. She wanted... Oh, she didn't know what she wanted. She was so confused. And, anyway, it didn't matter what she wanted. He'd made up his mind. He'd set her free.

Stupid thing was, she didn't want to be.

Give him my love.

It hit her then, deep in her heart, that she did love him. Loved them both. But he was pushing her away and she was wilfully going. How could she walk away from love, the one thing she'd craved her whole life?

How long would it take for her to forget his smile?

Never.

How long would it take for her heart to heal?

Mia put her phone down and frowned. 'That's strange. He's not answering.'

'He's probably busy. You know what it's like with two small kids. He won't have his phone with him all the time.'

'Yes. Probably right.' Mia slid her phone back into her bag and glanced up at the TV screen in the corner.

Her eyebrows rose. 'Oh. You see that? The storm over Rāwhiti has knocked out the power. That's why he's not answering. Apparently, there's a cyclone on the way.'

Heart hammering, Carly whipped round to look. 'I hope they're okay. I hope they're coping without us.'

'You wrote the emergency plan. You know how good it is. If they follow the rule book, they'll be fine.'

'Yes. Yes, you're right. I can't spend my whole life looking back and panicking at the slightest thing. But what if...?' Carly knew her grip on Mia's arm was tight but she couldn't stop herself. What if he wasn't okay, as Raff hadn't been? How could she lose him too?

She felt as if she was going to be sick as pain roiled through her, piercing her heart. But he didn't want her. He'd sent her on her adventure. He hadn't looked back at her.

The cosy fireside image died, and she imagined him now battling the storm with the kids, securing the windows and doors... Was Wallace-Wilma okay too? Maybe he was taking them all to the camp, just as the rule book said. Hunkering down in safety with her friends, her family.

Then she imagined him taking so much care with any injured people. Keeping them safe. Walking forward into risk, danger and adventure. She thought of the islanders relying on him, the way they'd relied on her. She thought of all that going on without her. All that love, care and community. Her home.

And Owen. The kingpin of it all. A beacon of hope.

A sexy beacon of hope. She smiled, even though

she was concerned for him and for the islanders in this weather bomb.

She envied him, admired him and loved him.

She loved him.

Oh, God. She loved him. The man who thought his life was too small for her when what he was doing was the most amazing thing of all...building a life, a real, happy life, that nurtured his son and helped him thrive. What could be better than that?

And suddenly her own adventure felt small and unnecessary. She didn't have to fly halfway around the world to find out who she was. She knew who she was. She was Carly Edwards, first responder of Rāwhiti Island. Carly Edwards, lover of Owen Cooper. Carly Edwards, a woman capable of many, many things, including loving this man and receiving that love back tenfold. She didn't just want to look back...she wanted to go back.

'I think I've made a mistake,' she whispered to Mia's back. 'I think I love him.'

But her friend was standing completely still, staring at a red banner running across the bottom of the screen.

Breaking news... Ferry runs aground at Rāwhiti Island. Storm hampers rescue efforts.

Carly's heart jolted.

Then she grabbed her bag and shook her friend gently. 'We have to go back, Mia. Now. We have to get back to Rāwhiti.'

She had to get back to the man she loved and wanted to spend the rest of her life with.

If it wasn't too late.

CHAPTER FOURTEEN

CARLY STOOD NEXT to Mia at the edge of the helipad on top of the ambulance control building. Rain lashed their faces as wind whipped around them, biting their skin. She wrapped her raincoat more tightly around her, but it didn't make any difference. Rain found a way of getting in, made worse by the chopper's rotors turning each drop into a barb pricking her skin.

Mia shivered next to her and swiped her hand across her eyes. 'We're never going to get there in this weather.'

'We just have to pray for a decent weather window. That's all we need. Thirty minutes to get there. But we have to be ready to go.' Carly shifted her weight, her rucksack straps digging into her back.

'Thank goodness you're well enough connected to grab us a lift with these guys.'

'As soon as I heard they were trying to rescue some of the ferry passengers, I knew they'd dispatch a chopper.'

'Right.' Mia nodded towards two paramedics stomping across the tarmac. 'Here goes nothing.'

Bent almost double against the downdraft and the wind, they followed the two men and huddled next to each other until it was their turn to climb in.

Carly went first, hauling herself up into the helicopter's main body. The two paramedics were already seated, not talking. The only sound was the roar of the engine. And was it her imagination, or was the helicopter actually rocking in the wild wind?

Stomping on her nerves, she found two empty seats across from them, buckled in, put on her headphones and listened to the pilot talking them through the plan. 'There's been some casualties over there. Sounds bad. As soon as I get a chance to go, we'll go. Be ready. It's going to be a bumpy ride.'

Mia climbed in and sat down next to Carly, her face ashen. She made a weird sort of sound.

Carly glanced at her. Was she scared of what they were going to find on their beloved island?

Of course she was. Carly was too. Scared of what she might find and what she might have already lost.

She slid her hand over Mia's and squeezed, summoning up an optimism she hadn't known she had. 'Hey, it's going to be okay.'

But her friend's eyes were fixed on one of the paramedics in the seat opposite—a tall guy with cropped hair. Good-looking. 'I don't think so.'

The weird thing was, he looked spooked too. Then he blinked and turned away, one hand pressing on the headphones as the pilot began to speak again.

Their panic was infectious. Carly's heart rate ramped up, her palms starting to sweat. Now it wasn't just a case of, would Owen have her back? It was more a question of, were they going to get there alive?

Owen stood in the pitching fishing boat, shivering in the cold and rain as he helped lift his patient onto the Rāwhiti Camp jetty, being careful not to jolt her in any way. The wood was slippery and slick with water. The noise from the wind was almost deafening but its ferocity had definitely lessened over the last few minutes. The rain blurred his vision but it didn't stop him seeing the flotilla of boats bringing back the wounded from the ferry. The storm might be dying down, but his work was far from over.

'Careful!' he shouted, so the wind didn't steal his words, and the greeting party of island helpers heard his instructions. 'I've given her some pain relief and stabilised the fractures. Get her up to the camp and keep her warm until I get back. She's going to need an evacuation.'

One of the helpers shouted back, 'The chopper's just landed, Doc. Paramedics are on their way down.'

'Thank God. The ferry's listing badly and there's more injured to come.' But the sense of relief of not being alone almost made his legs give way. It was one thing to be a first responder, but another to be the only medic on the island. He couldn't go back out on the boat to help rescue the victims and stay here to tend to the injured all at the same time.

He needed more experienced helpers. He needed Mia.

No, he needed Carly. For her strength and clear head. For her kisses. For her warm open-heartedness.

God, he missed her.

'Okay, Doc. We've got her. You're free to go.'

Free? He was tied to Carly for ever. His heart was hers. And, as soon as this nightmare was over, he was going to find her and tell her. Promise that he'd wait for her, no matter how long, or that he'd give everything up, and Mason and him would go with her. Anything to be with her. Whatever she wanted. Because a love like this didn't come round twice in a lifetime.

He turned back to the boat, wishing he didn't have to go back out there to the swollen, dark sea and the screams for help. But he pushed against the jetty and let the boat glide deeper into the sea.

'Owen! Owen!'

He looked up and blinked and for a moment his heart almost exploded. The rain was definitely blurring his vision, or exhaustion was making him see mirages of hope, if he thought Carly was running towards him in a bright yellow raincoat, her hair flying behind her, like some kind of superhero.

No. It was not Carly, just wishful thinking. He blinked again and watched the chasm of water between the jetty and the boat grow.

'Owen! Wait!'

It was her voice. His body went into some kind of shutdown. At least that must have been why he couldn't move, not one muscle.

It was Carly, and she was haring down the jetty. In one smooth motion, she jumped into the boat. He couldn't read her expression. 'Owen.'

'Carly.' His heart was the first thing that came back to life. Hope was a flower opening in his chest. 'What the hell?'

She gripped the side of the rocking boat. 'Where are the kids? Harper and Mason. Where's your boy?'

Her first thought was for his son. 'At the camp with Anahera.'

She put her hand onto her heart and nodded, sighing. 'Good. Right. What do you need?'

You.

He wasn't sure what she meant. Why was she here and not in the city? Why had she come back? 'Um. We've got to get back to the ferry before it sinks. There might be some people who need immediate life support.'

Like me.

She grabbed the steering wheel. 'Okay. Let's go. Tell me where to head.'

She'd come to help. Of course she had. She'd come back to the island when it needed her. She hadn't come back for him.

After a stomach-churning trip, he pointed to the ferry as it started to lurch sideways. 'Don't get any closer. Stay here.'

'What about the passengers? We've got to get them. Save them.' Her hand was over her mouth as they watched the boat's white hull slip deeper under the water. She edged the boat closer, but he made her stop. 'No, Carly. No closer.'

'We've got to help them, Owen. Please. Please.'

'No.' The white paint was subsumed now. 'It's not safe for us to be there. If we get any closer, we could be dragged under too. This time, you don't put your life on the line. I'm not going to lose you.'

'No. No...' Her body crumpled and she swayed with their pitching boat. Ugly waves thrashed the sides, spilling over and soaking their feet.

He held her arms and held her steady until she broke and sobbed against him. 'It's not fair. It's not fair.'

And his heart broke along with hers. He wrapped his arms around her and stroked her hair. He thought about the way her husband had died, the emotions all wrapped up in that and how witnessing this would be unbearable. 'I know, darling, it isn't fair. It just isn't. But we've done what we can.'

'It's not enough.' But she gripped his shoulders, trembling, tears streaming down her face. And he let her cry and cry until all that was left were dry sobs.

A smaller boat with a bright white light slowly made its way towards them. The coastguard. Owen reluctantly let go of Carly, leaned over the side and shouted to the people on board, 'What's the score? How many people are left on there?'

'All evacuated. Captain here says he was the last person on board.' He pointed to a forlorn-looking man in uniform shivering in the hull. 'It's going down, so keep away.'

'No one's left on there? Really?' Carly's voice was cracked but hopeful.

'All rescued, thanks to this man and his team.' The coastguard pointed at Owen and then waved. 'See you back at base.'

'Thank God.' Carly closed her eyes and gripped the side of the boat.

'Let's go back to help the survivors.' Noticing she was shaking, he gently peeled her hands from the metal and brought her into the cab. 'You sit down. I've got this.'

'No. Thanks.' But she leaned against him. Or had that just been caused by the sudden lurch of the boat? 'You okay, Carly?'

She pressed her lips together and nodded. 'I think so. I'm sorry. I just lost the plot there.'

'I told you, don't ever apologise for being you. I know how much you lost, Carly. I just wish I could help.'

'You do.' She smiled sadly and closed her eyes.

I love you so much. Even more now, and more each day.

He brushed wet tendrils of hair from her face and looked at her. He was so glad to see her but worried too. 'You cut your trip short.'

'Yes. I had to come back.' She looked at her hands. He didn't want to hear her say that she'd only come back to make sure everyone was safe.

And he realised that, if he didn't want to watch her leave again, it was time to take that risk. 'Listen, I've got something to say. I need you to hear it.'

She looked up at him and frowned. 'What is it?'

He swallowed. *Jump, man. Do it.*

'I made a mistake. A huge one. I was scared about you leaving, so I did the most stupid thing and made you leave. Just to take some control and protect myself. I didn't want you to go. I thought I wasn't enough to keep you here.'

'Oh, Owen.' She cupped his face. 'You are more than enough for me.'

Was he, though? Dared he ask? He covered her hand

with his. 'Truth is, I do want you to stay here, Carly. With me and Mason. But I know that's a big ask, so I'm not going to say that.'

'What?' She shook her head, no doubt confused by his rambling.

'I'm going to take Mason out of kindy, put the job here on hold and we'll come with you on your adventure. If you'll have us. Plenty of families travel. We could just do it slowly, visit all the places you wanted to explore. It'll be great learning for Mason.'

'Oh, no.' She shook her head vehemently.

His chest tightened like a vice. 'No, we can't come? No, you don't want us?'

'No, I'm not taking my boy out of kindy. He needs stability—he's only just settled in. And we both know what a rough ride he had before that.'

His heart swelled. '"My boy"?'

'Our boy.' She swallowed. 'I shouldn't have left you when I saw how much you wanted me. But then you told me to go, and I felt rejected again.'

He'd done that? Done what all those families had done to her in the past? 'God, no. I am so sorry. I want you more than anything. I just didn't have the guts to admit it to you or myself. Until it was too late. I didn't want you to put off your plans for me.'

'I should have insisted that I stayed and made you see sense, but I was confused about how I felt. So I ran. Being alone has been my default. Sure, I had Raff for a few years, but essentially I've been on my own my whole life. I lost so much when Raff and his parents went, but I lost myself too. And I thought that if I was on my own I'd come back to me. But I know who I am, and I have to believe in myself. I have to listen to my instincts.'

'Which are…?'

'I don't need to go off on an adventure when the

adventure is right here. Falling in love, growing close, building a future, building a life. The biggest risk we can take is to open our hearts, right?'

'It's been a hard lesson, but yes.' He stroked the back of his knuckles down her beautiful cheek. 'But what will you do here, if you've sold the camp?'

She shrugged. 'I'm going to take some time to work that out. I've got a few ideas around conservation and regeneration, and I love teaching, so I might start a sustainability and nature business. Take people on tours of the island and teach them about the bush and growing native plants. We have enough visitors here now that I think I'll be busy enough. I need to do some research and get together a business plan, but the money from the camp will give me some breathing space to work out what I really want…other than being here with you and Mason. If that's okay?'

'Okay? It would make me the happiest guy alive.' He pulled her to him, just about managing to stay upright as the boat lurched from side to side.

She gripped onto his arms and looked up at him. Then he pressed his mouth to hers and kissed her, long and slowly.

When she pulled back, she was smiling, and even in the dim light he could see it: that certain sparkle he'd wanted to see. He couldn't quantify the pride he felt at putting it there. He barely had words, but he found enough. 'I love you, Carly Edwards.'

She smiled. 'I love you too. Now, let's start this adventure. Together.'

EPILOGUE

Six months later...

CARLY LOCKED THE front door of their lovely refurbished cottage and pocketed the key. Excitement rippled through her. It was really happening. 'Right, then, who has the passports?'

Owen pulled them out of his rucksack and waved them at her. 'Me. And the guidebook.'

'Excellent. I've got the money and the games for the plane.' She helped Mason put on his little carry-on backpack. 'Okay, bud. Where are we going first?'

He grinned up at her, all big, brown eyes like his dad. ''Merica, to see Mummy.'

Now, that was going to be an adventure all of its own. But Miranda had been nothing but supportive about Carly's presence in her son's life. Carly suspected that Mason having a stepmum lessened the emotional turmoil for the successful actress who still spoke to her son very regularly. Carly and Owen had made sure of it. And now Tane wasn't the only child at kindy with two mummies. They were all keen to meet up and share their love for the little boy. She ruffled his hair. 'Yup. Then where?'

'Rocky mountain.'

She giggled. 'Yes. The Rocky Mountains. For a camp out in the park. And horse riding.'

'And bears!' He pulled a face and growled.

'Hopefully not close up.' She winked at Owen. 'Lucky us. Our own adventure.'

Sure, it wasn't exactly the one she'd been planning, and it was only for the kindy holidays, but it meant more to her than any other trip she'd ever planned.

Owen pulled her close for a quick kiss. 'Did I ever tell you how much I love you for doing this? We are so lucky to have you.'

She leaned against him. She'd created a good life with the man she adored and the boy she grew to love more and more each day. 'Hey, I get to do all the things I want to do, and have you guys come along for the ride. I'm the lucky one.'

Then they jumped into the little tin boat and sped round to the harbour. To their adventure and their future. The three of them.

A family at last.

* * * * *

PARAMEDIC'S ONE-NIGHT BABY BOMBSHELL

AMY RUTTAN

MILLS & BOON

For my Aunt Margaret.

You were a true lover of all books.

You were a great storyteller
and I'll miss you tremendously.

Fly free.

CHAPTER ONE

Fogo Island, Newfoundland

WHAT AM I doing here?

Dr. Josephine York—Jo—looked around the dark little pub that was filled with locals of Nubbin's Harbor, which was going to be her new home for the next year.

It seemed friendly enough. It just wasn't her scene. If there were pubs like this in Toronto, it wasn't her usual place to go.

Not that she went anywhere.

You're here now. This is the first step out of your comfort zone.

If there was going to be any kind of change in her life, then she had to do things out of the ordinary. She had to rip the bandage off and live again. She'd been living in grief and loneliness for far too long.

This was an adventure.

Or at least, that's what she kept telling herself.

This little inn was not her first choice. She'd rather stay in the new hotel, which wasn't far from here, but they had been full up since the prime season for icebergs was coming. It would mean, according to the owner of the place she was staying at, that Nubbin's Harbor and indeed all of Fogo would be full of tourists from all over the world.

People came to watch the big hunks of ice make their way south from the Arctic.

Jo had seen pictures and was looking forward to seeing it firsthand.

Still, it meant lodgings were sparse so she should be thankful for what she'd got, even if she was a bit anxious at the moment.

At least the little hotel above a pub had rave reviews. It was a good-enough place to stay until her apartment became available in a couple of weeks. Gary was lending her his place, and until he left, the hotel would have to be her home. At least she'd had the sense to think ahead, when Gary had asked her to take over his practice, to buying a small car here online so it was ready for her when she'd landed in the capital city, St. John's.

She needed a vehicle to get around Newfoundland with ease.

Not that she'd seen much of the island driving four hours through the rain and then taking an hour-long ferry ride to get to the island and then another hour to wind her way up toward Nubbin's Harbor where Gary's practice was located.

It was bitterly cold for a spring day this late in April, but then the weather had been nasty all day since she'd left St. John's, and headed northeast toward Fogo Island, which was an island off another island. Yesterday, when she'd landed in St. John's after her flight from Toronto, she had felt such hope.

The sun was shining.

It was a beautiful spring day.

It was mild, the Atlantic was blue. And on that sunny first day in the capital, the brightly colored houses and the blue sky had given Jo hope that she'd made the right decision to change her life completely and move to the eastern coast of Canada, leaving everything she knew behind.

It had put Jo in such an optimistic mood. It made her

think, for a nanosecond, that leaving her life in Toronto was definitely the right thing to do. That even at thirty-eight, with a settled surgical practice, a house, and a great salary in the best city in the world, she wasn't too old for an adventure or for an abrupt change.

There had been a time in her life when she'd been more carefree. Once.

As she glanced around the small pub on the edge of what people thought was one of the four corners of a flat earth, she suddenly wasn't so sure about her decisions.

Come on, Jo. Where is your sense of adventure?

And she smiled to herself thinking of her late husband's voice. Usually she tried not to think about him at all. She would throw herself into her work instead, so she could ignore the pain.

Only, right now, she was glad to remember his voice. David had always wanted to live life to the fullest. He'd been an adventure seeker to the max. He was such an avid adventurer that he'd even had to depart this mortal coil well before she did.

A lump formed in her throat as that sweet memory faded to pain, like it always did. It wasn't as sharp as it had been, but it was still there, nonetheless. Gnawing at her and relentless at times.

He'd been gone for three years.

And it hadn't been his choice to leave her.

An aneurysm had decided that course of their life.

Don't think about it.

David had been dead for three years, and she needed to live again.

She wanted to feel again, she told herself.

Experience life.

She'd always love him. Losing him would always hurt, but this was a fresh start, and she needed to grasp it with both hands.

She straightened her spine and got up, alone in a pub full of locals.

What she needed right now was a drink.

Jo made her way to the bar and sat down on an empty stool at the far end. She was completely out of place in a room of flannel-clad, bearded men.

The live music from the house band didn't help her clear her head.

And as she sat there, she was trying to remember why she had agreed to this change.

Because David completely haunts your life in Toronto, and you need to move on, a small voice reminded her.

It was true.

David was everywhere back home.

Even at work in the hospital. That's where she'd met him, where they'd worked together and where he'd ended up after she'd frantically called an ambulance finding him unresponsive one morning.

She had come to the farthest corner of Canada, and yet, he was still here. Still around her. His memory was still reminding her of all the hopes and dreams they had planned.

A family.

Happiness.

Adventure and love.

Dreams that were long gone now.

Except, she needed a change. An escape. She wanted to feel alive again, even though that prospect was scary indeed.

So a change of scenery was just what the doctor ordered. Another province, the other side of the country, was as different as she'd dared to go at the moment.

David would've totally been up for an adventure like this, and this time so was she.

Jo was nervous, but she needed to get out of this rut she had been stuck in.

Maybe she could rediscover the woman who'd loved life.

"What'll you be having, miss?" the barkeep asked, smiling and his eyes twinkling behind his bushy eyebrows.

"Some white wine?" she said.

He nodded. "Coming right up."

Jo relaxed a little and took a glance around the pub. It might've seemed dark and kind of off-putting at first, but as she had a glance around it, she relaxed. It was actually pretty homey, and the more she looked at the patrons, the more she realized that they seemed genuinely happy.

It had to be the weather that was off-putting.

That was it. And miserable weather couldn't last forever. At least, she hoped it couldn't.

Her friend Gary loved his life on Fogo, and the only reason he was leaving his work here was because he'd been offered the amazing chance to teach at a prestigious medical school in Munich. Gary hadn't wanted to leave his practice to just anyone, and so he'd reached out to her.

She and Gary had met in college. They'd gone to medical school together and become fast friends.

"Take over my practice, Jo," Gary had said.

"Are you sure it's right for me?"

"I trust you with my patients, and you need a change," Gary had urged gently.

"Do I?"

"Yes. Ever since David died…you sound lost. Hollow."

"I am," she'd whispered, finally admitting it to someone.

"You were such a free spirit. It's what I always loved about you. It's what David loved about you," Gary had said. "You have to learn to live again."

"I'm not sure."

"You want to, though. I know it, and David would want you to as well."

"I do," she'd said, because Gary was right.

"Come to Fogo then. See what I've been raving about. Please say you'll take care of my place?"

Gary had convinced her. He wasn't wrong. So Jo had jumped at the chance to escape her ghosts in Toronto and try to figure out how to live again. She'd been merely existing in a fog for far too long.

She laughed to herself as she thought about that.

Since she'd arrived here she hadn't seen a hair of the place because it had been mostly covered by a fog bank from the rain. Hopefully it would clear up.

"Here you go, miss." The barkeeper slid the glass of wine toward her. "Niagara's finest!"

"You don't have a local wine?" she asked.

"You won't be wanting the local wine," a voice said at the end of the bar.

She glanced over, and her breath caught in her throat at the tall, hunched-over, not-so-scruffy-looking young Viking a few seats down. He had the most brilliant blue eyes that she'd ever seen, under a dark mop of hair.

When his gaze locked on hers, a jolt of familiarity coursed through her, which made her blood heat. It was as though the instant she met his intense regard, it felt like he was a kindred spirit.

Like he could see right through to her inner pain.

Like he knew her.

It had been like that when she'd met David.

Her pulse began to race, and she could feel a blush creeping up her neck to her cheeks. She averted her eyes, trying to calm her nerves, but her gaze immediately tracked back to the large tattoo that started at the base of his left wrist and wound its way up his muscular forearm and disappeared under the sleeve of his fitted cotton T-shirt. That shirt didn't hide any of his well-defined muscles, and a coil of heat unfurled in her belly.

It had been a long time since she'd felt this heat, this kind of attraction for another man.

It was good to feel that jolt of desire again.

There was a half smile just underneath his well-kept beard.

He was nursing a pint of beer, and she couldn't help but smile back at him.

"There be nothing wrong with Nubbin's Harbor wine," the barman said brusquely. "It's just only local folk can handle it."

"Aw, Lloyd, you know that's not it at all," the handsome man said. "It's disgusting, that's why."

Lloyd puffed his chest up. "I save the Niagara stuff for the toffs from Ontario."

Jo smiled. "How did you know I was from Ontario?"

"Your accent is a dead giveaway," Lloyd stated, moving away, and she couldn't help but laugh under her breath. She never really thought of herself as having an accent before, but since she'd landed in the Maritimes and in Newfoundland, she was the one with the accent now.

"Don't mind Lloyd. He's very passionate about anything to do with Fogo Island," the handsome stranger said.

"I can't say that I blame him. It's good to be so fervent about your home."

The Viking nodded. "Aye, and we do have some good things here you should try."

"I wouldn't mind trying some local things. Although, I wouldn't have pegged Fogo Island as a hot spot for a winery. I thought it needed to be a bit warmer and have a bit more soil over the rock?"

The stranger smiled, those blue eyes twinkling, making her swoon again. "Aye, it's a pretty sad sort of wine that Lloyd brews himself. He has a few grape vines in a pathetic ramshackle of a greenhouse, and he fancies himself a vintner. If you're not used to strong stuff or alcohol that tastes like turpentine, I would steer clear of it. And screech too."

"Screech?" she asked, curious.

"Come on, every Canadian knows about screech."

"I guess I've been living under a rock, then. I've never heard of it."

The stranger slid a barstool closer, his eyebrow cocking. "You've seriously never heard of screech?"

"No. Is it like moonshine?" she asked.

His eyes widened, and then he smiled. "No, but maybe it has a similar kick. It's rum—untempered rum. It's from the days we would trade salted fish to Jamaica in exchange for rum. Those who first started drinking it didn't mind its potency."

"I don't mind rum."

There was a mischievous look in his eyes. "I'm thinking that you would be minding this."

Jo had never been one to back down from a challenge, and if she was going to fit in here, she might as well get used to some of the local flair. Not that she was sure that *flair* was the right word, but *untempered rum* sounded a bit reckless, even though in her college days she could drink anyone she wanted to under the table.

At least she wasn't on duty yet.

Maybe tonight was the night she became an honorary screecher.

"I think I can handle it, but first… I'd like to know your name. I don't usually drink with strangers in an unfamiliar bar."

He held out his hand. "Henrik."

She took his large, strong hand in hers.

The simple touch sent a ripple of electric heat through her, a rush of endorphins that were most welcome.

And in that one instant she pictured what it would be like to have those hands on her body.

Touching her.

Waking her up from her fog.

"My name is Josephine." Strangers got the long version of her name. Only those close to her called her Jo.

Henrik turned to the barkeep. "Lloyd, our friend from Toronto wants to try a fine glass of screech!"

The music stopped, and Jo's eyes widened as a bunch of people in the pub turned around in their seats to eye her in fascination and amusement.

Lloyd was grinning as he pulled out a bottle and poured her a glass. "This is the finest I have, miss."

Usually she corrected the person and told them her title was *Doctor*, but tonight she just wanted to be a stranger.

To observe.

The townsfolk would learn soon enough who she was. She didn't want questions tonight. Especially since all eyes were on her, and she was about to guzzle down a shot of untempered rum.

Jo held the shot glass up.

"Wait!" someone shouted. "If she be from the mainland, then she needs to be screeched in."

Henrik was chuckling, and Jo was now getting a bit nervous.

"Pardon?" she asked, clearing her throat. "I need to be what?"

"You need to be screeched in, lass," Lloyd stated. "Does anyone have a cod?"

There were a lot of loud voices and some discussion, and Jo felt bewildered as she looked at Henrik. "Cod?"

He nodded. "You have to kiss a cod and swear an oath. If you're not from here, then it's the rules. I was trying to spare you, but since Lloyd's already announced it, I think you're kind of stuck."

"You can't be serious about kissing a fish?" Jo asked,

laughing nervously as she watched Lloyd digging around in a freezer.

Henrik shrugged. "It's tradition."

"Aha! She ain't fresh, but she'll do!" Lloyd held up a massive frozen bug-eyed whole cod, much to the entertainment of the patrons.

A knot was forming in the pit of Jo's stomach. A shot of alcohol was not worth this.

Henrik, as if sensing her trepidation leaned over and whispered in her ear. "You can't back out now. Would be an insult to do so."

You wanted to fit in, Josephine. This is how you do it.

The last thing she wanted to do was insult potential patients.

It wouldn't hurt to kiss a freaking cod.

Some ceremonious fiddle music was being played in the background as the fish was brought over to the bar.

"She needs to kiss the fish and recite the credo!" someone called out.

Jo was staring at the frozen face, mouth agape, of the ugliest fish she had ever seen. "Seriously?"

Henrik nodded. "There's the piece of paper, with the credo written on it. Go on. Recite it, kiss the fish and down the screech."

Joe took a deep breath, picked up the piece of paper and read from it. "*From the waters of the Avalon to the shores of Labrador, We've always stuck together, with a rant and with a roar. To those who've never been, soon they'll understand, From coast to coast, we raise a toast. We love thee, Newfoundland!*"

There was a loud cheer.

"Now, pucker up," Henrik teased.

Joe glared at him. Gripped the bar with her two hands, closed her eyes and kissed the cold fish on the lips. It was so gross that she instantly grabbed the rum to douse the taste of cod and downed it.

It was rough.

It burned.

It was the worst-tasting, strongest thing she had ever had.

There was a lot more cheering, but she began to cough and held onto the edge of the bar for dear life as that liquor burned a path through her esophageal tract.

"Josephine, are you okay?" Henrik asked, while some of the others in the bar took their turns kissing the fish and dancing.

"I think the local wine might've been better," she managed to get out.

Henrik laughed. "Come on, let's get some air."

Jo gladly went with Henrik. She instinctively knew he was someone she could trust, and she liked how he made her feel. She wanted to get to know him better, even if only for one night, because she wasn't ready for any kind of relationship. She also needed to get away from that cod. She hadn't kissed anyone since her husband had passed. It figured: the first time she managed to get up the courage to be intimate with anyone and it was a dead fish.

Henrik didn't think that the beautiful stranger had it in her.

Usually, when he came across tourists that were alone and female, they weren't really into having a screech-in. Those that participated in the ceremony were usually with a group of friends and were already three sheets to the wind. They would also approach him. Not that anything would ever happen the first night. When he took them to his bed, they were always sober.

Of course, most tourists knew what screech was and didn't have to ask. Although something nagged at him that she wasn't a usual tourist, only because she was on her own. She seemed out of place.

A little lost. He knew that look well. He'd seen it reflected in his own eyes from time to time.

He admired her strength and her determination to take on the challenge, sober.

Henrik didn't often find those qualities in the women that passed through Fogo Island, and they were his specialty. Women who just passed through. Those were his preference because then it was never long-term.

It was always short-term.

It was a fling.

There was no commitment, and that was exactly what Henrik Nielsen wanted.

He had tried to have forever, and that had bitten him squarely on his nose, and he wasn't falling for that again. So he had vacation flings with the women he fancied, and that was all. It was perfect.

Not that he had been planning on meeting anyone tonight.

He usually liked to stick around for a while. At least a week. That's how long women tended to stay, but he couldn't this time. He was headed out of town for a month with the coast guard for training at sea rescue farther up the coast of Labrador.

And he was flying out tomorrow morning. Even by his standards, that wasn't enough time for a fling. He should walk away from her, but he'd discovered he couldn't.

There had been something in her eyes. Almost like he saw himself reflected back in them, and he was incredibly drawn to her. He couldn't quite pin it down, but he just wasn't able to tear himself away. Maybe because she was quiet and reserved, yet spoke her mind, and she seemed to be kind and gentle.

Most women were only with him for one thing, and he was fine with that.

He didn't want a relationship.

Liar.

He shook that voice away.

All he'd planned tonight was a quiet pint at Lloyd's before he shipped out, and then she'd walked into the pub.

Josephine had absolutely taken his breath away.

It was like he had been hit by a bolt of lightning the moment their eyes met across the bar.

She was stunning. And he couldn't remember the last time he'd seen a woman who had taken his breath away like that.

Yes, you can. Melissa.

It had been some time since he'd really let himself think about the woman who had broken his heart. He had been so in love with Melissa. They had grown up together here in Nubbin's Harbor. She'd moved away to Vancouver, but then when she and Henrik were both twenty-two, she'd come back to stay with her grandparents for a bit. He'd fallen head over heels for her.

She had family all over Fogo, and they were Newfoundlanders through and through.

Just like his family.

For him, it was only natural they should get married. They were going to run away together because her family didn't want them to get married right away, and neither did his late grandmother, who'd raised him when his parents had died.

She'd wanted him to make a life for himself first, but he was a fool and had been blinded by love.

Maybe they knew more than he did, because he had been so smitten he couldn't see. He wanted the same kind of love his late parents had had when they'd been alive and it had been the three of them against the world, until that storm had struck, leaving him orphaned.

Henrik had never forgotten the love, though. The feeling

of family. He'd wanted that so badly, and he thought he'd found it with Melissa.

Only, he hadn't.

He'd started his paramedic training, then come back for her so they could marry, but she was already gone. She'd moved back to the West Coast. She'd decided she didn't want to stay on Fogo, and he couldn't leave his gran or his life in Newfoundland.

All that Melissa had left for him was a note saying goodbye.

He'd been heartbroken, embarrassed, humiliated. Love was only an illusion. Melissa had shattered his trust, and Henrik had dealt with enough pain. It was far easier to harden his heart.

As much as he longed for family, he knew the anguish of losing it all and being left alone.

That was something he never wanted to feel again.

So he'd focused on his career as a first responder. That was what he'd always wanted to do. Save lives so others didn't feel pain or loss like he had. He'd worked long days and nights. Work kept him so busy that he didn't think about how badly Melissa had hurt him.

Much.

All he could rely on was Fogo Island and his work.

Those two things never let him down like love had.

Sweeping beautiful strangers off their feet for a week was a distraction. It was safe because he liked being a vacation boyfriend. He knew better than to fall deeply for a woman not from the Rock. Or to ever fall in love. The island didn't change, but people left.

He certainly wasn't ever going to leave.

All his precious memories were here. Fogo was in his blood… It was his roots.

It was home.

If he left, he'd let down the memories of his ancestors.

And since he was the only one who remained, he had to stay so he'd never forget. And so Fogo would never forget his family.

Flings were a nice distraction from loneliness. It was easy, there were no strings and, because he was planning on leaving tomorrow, he hadn't thought of approaching Josephine, the woman with the honey-colored hair and beautiful green eyes who sat a couple seats down at the bar.

Yet, he couldn't help himself. Something about her drew him to her.

And when she'd leaned over, those luscious pink lips puckering up to kiss the cod, for the first time in his almost thirty-one years, he'd envied a fish.

"How was it?" he asked, as they headed outside.

She reached out and gripped his arm as if holding on for dear life. "God-awful."

He laughed. "Aye, well, it is strong."

"No, I wasn't commenting on the screech, though it does have a very antiseptic burn to it."

"Then, what?"

"The cod." Josephine shuddered. "That is a…gross tradition."

Henrik chuckled softly. "Some people like to eat the lips of the cod and the cheeks."

"Are you serious?"

"Have I lied to you yet?" he teased, laughing.

"I would never call you a liar," she said.

"I know, but cod lips and cheeks are quite the delicacy."

"That sounds terrifying." Shivering, she pulled her wrap tighter around her.

Henrik pulled off his sherpa jacket and wrapped it around her.

"Thanks," she whispered, through chattering teeth.

"My pleasure. Anyone who drinks screech like that and

complains about the cod more than the liquor deserves my respect and admiration."

She laughed, and then he smiled. Josephine had a wonderful laugh that warmed his heart. It was a good thing that he was leaving tomorrow. She would be a dangerous woman to get to know: he was feeling things toward her that he'd sworn he would never allow again.

"I should try and find some dinner or something. I haven't eaten a thing since I left St. John's this morning."

"Well, Cherry's Kitchen is just around the corner. She has the best home-cooked food around."

"That sounds good."

She seemed to hesitate, her cheeks flushing pink. "I don't usually do this, but I'm alone, and you seem nice... and you know Fogo."

"Aye, I am, and I do." He grinned, winking.

"Would you like to join me? I could use some company."

Say no. Say no.

"I'd like that." He cursed himself inwardly at not being able to resist her.

He should go home and get some sleep, only he couldn't seem to make himself leave.

Why was he so drawn to her? When they had shaken hands, he'd felt a rush of fire in his veins. A tingle of anticipation as he'd pictured how soft and warm the rest of her was.

Henrik swallowed, his mouth dry and his pulse thundering in his ears.

What harm could one night do?

It might be a pleasant way to pass the time before he left. They made their way around the corner to Cherry's Kitchen.

It was quiet, and they found a table near the back. Josephine took off his coat and handed it back to him as they sat down. He wanted to ask her why she was passing through. He wanted to get to know her better, which was strange. He never did want to know much about a woman he was seeing for such a short time.

And that was maybe because he wasn't planning on doing anything with her.

What was coming over him?

You're lonely.

But he shook that thought away. Loneliness was easier to bear than pain.

Was it, though?

"What's good here?" Josephine asked, interrupting his thoughts.

"Fish?" he teased.

Josephine wrinkled her nose. "I think I'll stick to the salad tonight."

"Because of the fish?" he asked, trying not to smile.

"Are you telling me the salad isn't safe to eat? Is there fish in the salad?"

Henrik laughed and winked. "You're safe. I'm just having a bit of fun with you."

"That's a relief."

Henrik leaned over the table. "You're not going to fare very well here if you dislike fish."

"I don't hate fish… It's just I'm going to have nightmares of fish lips for some time."

"Who wouldn't?" Henrik agreed.

The waitress came over and took their orders and assured Josephine that there was no fish in the beet salad.

"So tell me about Fogo," Josephine said.

"What would you like to know?" he asked.

"If there's anything in particular I should see while I'm here?"

"The Fogo Island Inn is a marvel, and there's lots of little shops, craft stores to visit. You should really buy a Fogo Island quilt. They keep you warm in the winter."

"You're very versed in crafts," she teased.

Henrik grinned. "Well, I am a man of mystery."

Her eyes twinkled, and she tucked back her long hair. He wondered what it would feel like to run his fingers through it. It was probably soft and smelled good.

He wondered where he could kiss her that would make her sigh. Maybe it was her neck that would do it?

"You have quite the tattoo," Josephine remarked.

Henrik glanced down. "It's a tree. My family tree and the sea. It's a part of us all, here."

She reached out and touched it. "It's very beautiful."

Her touch sent heat rushing through him.

"Thank you. Do you have any tattoos?"

"No," she said, her cheeks flushing. "I was never that brave."

"Oh? Is it the needles?"

"Yes. And pain...for myself."

He cocked a teasing eyebrow. "Oh? So you enjoy inflicting pain on others, then? I didn't think you were into that, but I'm game if you are." He'd forgotten himself for a moment. It was so easy to tease her, joke around, and he held his breath hoping he hadn't offended her.

She was smiling, but her blush deepened. "I'm not into that, but it's good to know where you're at."

She was teasing him right back.

Henrik laughed. She was wonderful to talk to. It felt like he didn't have to try so hard with her, as though he'd known her for a long time. It was like talking to one of his old friends.

It was refreshing. He hadn't felt this way in a very long time.

He wanted to get to know her better, but what was the point? He was leaving.

And so was she.

So he didn't ask. Even though he wanted to.

That thought scared him, but not enough to make him leave.

He couldn't.

She was engaging company, and he was hungrier for it than he'd realized.

The waitress brought over their food, and they had a pleasant dinner talking about nothing important, but it still felt nice.

It felt right.

Which was a scary prospect indeed. He wouldn't risk his heart for anything.

The more he talked to her, the more he forgot about all the rules that he'd put into place to keep women like her at bay. He usually compartmentalized his flings. He knew where to put them in his heart so he didn't get attached and it was easy to walk away.

Henrik was not doing that here.

Usually, that was a warning to stay away. He had been burned by love before, but since he wouldn't see her again, it might be worth the risk. He was incredibly attracted to Josephine. She was funny, smart, beautiful.

He wanted to know more about her, which made her dangerous, but his flight out tomorrow meant that it might be okay to live a bit dangerously. Even just for a night.

They paid for their meals and left Cherry's Kitchen as she was closing for the night. They walked down the hill, back to the pub and the only hotel in Nubbin's Harbor. There were a few of the locals hanging about, and there was boisterous fiddle music coming from the pub at the bottom.

"Thanks for walking me back."

"It's not a problem."

"I hope I'm not keeping you from something. Are you local?"

"Yes, but I'm leaving the island tomorrow for work."

A brief look of disappointment crossed her face. It was just a fraction of a moment, and he wasn't completely sure that it was disappointment. Maybe that's what he was feeling and he was projecting it onto her. Josephine was a stranger, after all.

A gorgeous stranger.

"You're not from here, though," Henrik teased, trying to defuse the tension that had settled between them as they stood toe to toe in the cool spring night.

"As we discussed in the bar, I'm the toff from Toronto."

"In Ontario."

"Yes, I was born and raised in Ontario's prettiest town."

"Isn't that Toronto?" he teased. "The way Torontonians talk…"

Josephine laughed. "No. Toronto is great, but it's not the prettiest town in the province."

"Oh?" he asked. "Where is that, then?"

"Goderich. It's on the southeast shore of Lake Huron."

"And what's it known for, besides being the prettiest?" he asked.

"Salt."

He raised his eyebrows. "Really?"

"What's Nubbin's Harbor known for, besides screech, Lloyd's turpentine wine and cod lips?"

He chuckled. "There's a lighthouse."

"That's it?"

"The icebergs will come soon, but the fishing that Nubbin's Harbor was known for is gone. Government restrictions and the like."

Josephine nodded. "I'm sorry."

"Most go to town to work," he sighed. "Not many have stayed."

They stood there in silence, and it began to rain.

"I better go upstairs."

"Aye, well…" He couldn't finish was he was going to

say. Instead he just leaned over and kissed her on the cheek. Her skin was soft, and she smelled sweet, like vanilla. He bet those lips were just as sweet to taste. Henrik stroked her cheek with the back of his knuckles and felt her tremble. He was going to step away, but instead she grabbed him by the lapels and pulled him close.

Pulled him up against her lithe body, and he got to taste those full, soft lips that were so inviting. She deepened the kiss, her tongue entwining with his, and he cupped her silky hair in his hands as he drank her in.

It would be a bad idea, if he wasn't leaving. He was enjoying his brief time with her far too much. He wouldn't mind being hers for a week, but that's all he could give her.

Josephine was a temptation. A complete and utter temptation, and even though he should walk away, he couldn't help himself.

Especially not when she had been the one to pull him close.

She broke off the kiss. "Would you like to come up to my room for another shot of screech?"

Say no.

"Aye. I would like that."

Josephine smiled, her green eyes bewitching as she took him by the hand and led him inside the pub.

He knew he shouldn't, but the appeal was too great.

Josephine was going to be hard to walk away from, but he was certain one night wasn't going to put his heart in danger.

One night wouldn't change anything.

It never did, and Josephine would be gone when he got back.

No one ever stayed.

Only him.

Jo still couldn't quite believe this was happening. The first time she'd met David, she had been a bit rash. She had initiated their first kiss then too. David always teased her that she knew exactly what she wanted, and she'd go for it.

The moment she saw Henrik in the pub, she knew she wanted him.

She was incredibly attracted to him.

While she was with him, she felt like her old self.

And the more she talked to Henrik, the more comfortable she was.

The more she wanted him.

What she wanted was to get out of this funk. She wanted to the rip that bandage off.

Coming to Fogo for the year was to wake her up out of this haze she'd been living in the last three years. How could she move on in her life if she never took another chance? Henrik was going to be leaving soon. He was handsome and kind. She was attracted to him. He'd already mentioned he wasn't into long-term relationships, and she'd told him she wasn't either. So why not indulge?

It had been a long time since she'd felt any kind of pull like that toward another person. This was her new start. A way to find herself again. So she invited Henrik up for a drink. Truth be told, she was a bit lonely.

And scared.

It had been so wonderful to have a conversation with a man again. After David died, she'd thrown herself into her work. It was work, and then home. That was it.

Now she needed a reset to her life.

She was trembling as she pulled out her key card to open the door to her hotel room.

"Are you okay?" Henrik asked, gently.

"I'm fine," Jo said, flicking on the light and hoping her voice didn't shake.

"Look, I don't mind sitting and talking," Henrik said, following her into the room. "I'm not expecting anything, and truth be told, I was enjoying our conversation. I'm definitely not looking for anything ongoing."

Jo smiled and shut the door. "I appreciate you telling me that. I'm not interested in that either."

"I won't lie. I did enjoy the kiss as well as the conversation."

Warmth spread across her cheeks. "I did as well."

Henrik moved closer to her, and her breath caught in her throat, her pulse racing.

"Did you, now?" he asked, softly.

"I-it's been some time…" she stammered nervously.

Henrik reached out and brushed his knuckles gently on her cheek again. Heat flooded her body. All that fear she had been feeling melted away.

She needed this. She wanted to feel something, to live again so that, maybe one day, she wouldn't be so scared if Mr. Right came along again, though she seriously doubted that would happen.

She wasn't that lucky.

Henrik was here, right now, and it had been a long time since she had been so attracted to someone.

She wanted this. She wanted him.

For just one night.

The first step in finding herself again.

"How about that drink?" he asked, his voice deep, husky and full of promise.

"I don't actually have anything," she whispered. Now she was trembling for a whole other reason, and she strengthened her resolve to be with him tonight.

He grinned, his eyes twinkling in the dim light of the room.

"Your lips are good enough for me."

It was a corny line, but she fell for it. The first time she had kissed him she'd felt a jolt of electricity. Now, with him kissing her, her body turned into a live wire. Like she was being woken up after a long sleep.

This is what she needed.

One night of passion.

She didn't need forever. She'd thought she'd had that once, and she was never going to risk her heart for a forever again.

CHAPTER TWO

One month later

JO WAS TRYING to ignore the little stick on the edge of the bathroom sink. It just confirmed her thoughts that doctors do indeed sometimes make the worst patients. All she wanted to do was hurry the test up. She needed the answer right now.

And she was feeling very antsy waiting for that timer to go off.

It couldn't be positive. It just couldn't be.

Jo worried her bottom lip and stared at her watch. Only a minute left.

It had to be a stomach bug. There was a stomach bug that had been going through Nubbin's Harbor, thanks to a tourist who had spread it to the unwitting residents en route to Tilting. For the last couple of weeks Jo had been dealing with a stomach virus that had run rampant through all her patients.

Not much to be done except prescribe fluids and rest.

Everyone seemed to be sick, but Jo thought it had been tapering off; then she'd started to feel nauseated and dizzy at times. Some niggling thought told her it wasn't the virus, and yet she had never been so busy: she was even getting patients in from farther afield because the hospital emergency room was full. It couldn't be pregnancy. It just couldn't be. The only time she'd had sex since David died was a month ago with Henrik.

A warm flush spread though her body at just the thought of Henrik. Her mysterious stranger with the blue, blue eyes and kisses that made her melt.

Even though it had been a one-time only thing, she couldn't stop thinking about him. The way his lips felt on hers, the touch of those skilled hands on her skin.

She tried not to think about him, but every time she walked through Nubbin's Harbor she'd look for him, hoping to see him again, which frustrated her. He'd told her he was leaving. Had she expected him to come back for her?

She wasn't here for romance. She was here to work.

Still, their one night together had been electric, but that didn't mean she was pregnant. They had used protection.

Protection isn't one hundred percent reliable.

Jo cursed under her breath. She had told that to so many others before.

She knew one thing: if she was pregnant, then she was pregnant. It was as simple as that. She'd always wanted children. It was something she and David had always planned for. It was something they had tried for, for over a year, but it turned out that they had unexplained infertility. Every month her heart was broken, and David would remind her that everything was okay. All through the pain from IVF that she'd endured, he had held her hand.

She'd known it would happen for them one day. It was what she'd held on to.

And David had always convinced her of that. When he died, Jo really thought that was it. She would never be a mother now, because she couldn't see herself being with anyone again.

Until that night with Henrik.

Who'd left the next morning.

Jo hadn't regretted that act of impulsivity. It was one

more step toward getting her life back, and that night had been wonderful.

It just tore at her heart that the baby wasn't and couldn't be David's the way she'd hoped for from the moment she'd married him.

The baby she'd mourned when she'd buried her husband.

You're getting ahead of yourself. It's probably just a stomach bug.

The thought of a baby made her stomach flutter with hope and excitement. No, a baby with a stranger wasn't ideal or anything close to what she'd imagined for herself, but she would still be ecstatic if she was pregnant.

A child. Her son or daughter.

Something she'd always wanted yet tried not to wish for too often.

The timer went off, and she picked up the pregnancy test. Her hand was shaking, and it took her a moment to register the fact that there were two pink lines staring up at her, rather than one.

It was definitely not a stomach bug. Although right at this moment a part of her wanted to throw up, there was another, much larger part that was absolutely thrilled that she was going to have a baby.

Before David died, they had used their last embryo, and it hadn't been viable.

They were going to try again, but he'd died before they could, and with his death her dream had sputtered away.

This pregnancy felt like a miracle.

Tears stung her eyes, and she smiled as she stared down at the stick.

She knew when she came to work in Newfoundland for the year that she was looking for a change, she just never expected that it would be this big. Her mind started to whirl about what she was going to do, but she was sure that her mother would come up from Arizona and help her for a bit.

She chuckled softly to herself that her father's dreams about retirement in Arizona might come to a screeching halt with the impending birth of a grandchild.

You're getting ahead of yourself.

Jo took another calming breath and lay the stick down, washing her hands and then splashing some cold water on her face. She was only a month in; something awful could happen. It had happened to her before, when she and David had first started trying...

"Jo?" David had opened the door to the bathroom, and his face had fallen when he'd seen her on the floor.

"I'm sorry," she'd cried.

David had knelt down. "It's okay. I told you, when it happens, you're going to be an excellent mother. I know it."

"I'm not sure about that," she'd sniffed.

David had touched her face, wiping away her tears. "I am."

Jo swallowed the lump in her throat. It was too soon to get her hopes up.

She reached down and gingerly cupped her abdomen.

Stay with me, little one, she begged. Just wanting to hold on to something which still seemed so intangible.

The door chimed as someone walked into the clinic.

"Doc?" they called.

She recognized Lloyd's voice.

She brushed away the tears and straightened her hair. "Coming!"

Jo left the bathroom and smiled at him.

"Lloyd, how can I help you?" she asked.

"It's not me, but there's been an accident in Tilting. A bad one, out at sea, and they're requesting all medical personnel to come as quick as they can. I'm with the volunteer firefighters here, so I can take you."

Jo nodded. "Of course. Just give me five minutes to grab what I need, and I'll meet you outside."

Lloyd nodded grimly and left the clinic.

Jo grabbed all the emergency gear that she had prepared for when the village would be inundated with tourists for iceberg season.

When Gary had talked to her about his practice, he'd mentioned that there were often tourists that would get too close to these massive behemoths of ice and slip. Just trying to get that perfect picture.

And then there were the fishers who were out shrimping and crabbing. Some of the locals even harvested sea cucumbers, and the sea was not always a kind mistress. The sea didn't care what you fished, legally or illegally when it claimed lives.

Gary had told her it was wise to have emergency kits prepared.

So that's exactly what she did.

Fogo had a hospital, but it was always best to be prepared. She'd learned that during her years as a trauma surgeon. She had first learned family medicine, but liked the fast pace of the hospital emergency room more.

Both her experiences would come in handy today.

Jennifer, her receptionist, came into the supply room to help her with the bags.

"I'll cancel the rest of the patients for the day," she said.

"Thanks, Jenn. I appreciate that."

"There weren't that many, really. Most are still out sick with that stomach bug and called in to reschedule."

"I would be lost without you." Which was true. Jennifer was a native to Fogo and had been a huge help in welcoming Jo here.

Jo was thankful for the friend.

Jennifer helped her carry the bags outside.

She shut the door to her clinic as Lloyd took the trauma bags and hefted them into the back of his small truck.

"Will there be paramedics there?" she asked, climbing into the front seat.

"Aye, and the coast guard. When I got the call, I told them that I would be bringing you."

"Do you know what happened?" she asked, as Lloyd drove the short distance to Tilting.

"Aye, pirates."

Normally, if anyone else would've said that to her, she would've given them a look of derision, but Lloyd was stone-cold serious.

And after kissing a cod a month ago, it didn't seem too far-fetched.

"Pirates?" she echoed.

"Well, not real pirates, but boys that were out fishing illegally. *Jigging* we call it. There's a moratorium on who can fish cod here. They're not from Fogo but were going to sell it on the black market. They got into a chase with the coast guard, and their ship exploded."

"Exploded?" she asked, trying to process in her brain how a ship could explode at sea.

"Aye." Lloyd nodded. "The paramedics and the coast guard are a wee bit overwhelmed, pulling the bodies from the water and dealing with the wreckage."

Jo pursed her lips.

A sea faring vessel exploding was not a trauma that she was familiar with, though she had seen her share of combustion injuries. They were probably dealing with drownings, burns and most likely internal or shrapnel injuries.

Going over what she could possibly have to deal with helped her focus on what she had to do. Trying to always think three steps ahead was why she was one of the best trauma surgeons in Toronto, but it was the fast pace that had also threatened to burn her out.

* * *

When they rounded the corner, she could see the smoke rising over the rocky outcrops. She actually gasped out loud the closer they got to the shoreline. The coast guard was out there dealing with the fire, but there was also a stream of smaller boats and divers dealing with the injured and the bodies.

There were several ambulances and makeshift trauma and morgue areas set up. She could see bodies covered in blankets on the beach.

"How big was the boat that exploded?" she asked.

"Large. Such a waste of life. And a waste of cod too," Lloyd grumbled.

Lloyd might lack tact, but since cod fishing had been their way of life for so long and it had been taken away, she could understand his bitterness at the loss of the fish. "Who should I report to?"

"I'll find ma b'y, Rik, who is in charge of this. He'll get you sorted."

Lloyd parked, and they got out of the truck and grabbed the gear. Lloyd started gesticulating and shouted, "Whaddaya at, Rik! I've brought the doc!"

There was a group of coast-guard paramedics on shore. Rik turned to wave back to Lloyd, and that's when her world stopped turning as she stared at the paramedic who was in charge. A lump formed in her throat, and she felt again like she was going to be sick.

At least he looked as shocked as her, as he came closer.

Her one-night stand.

The father of her baby.

Henrik.

The man who'd told her he was leaving the island for work, and she'd assumed he'd meant he was gone for good.

"Rik, this is Doc Jo, as we all call her now, but then

you should know her. You were there the night she came to Nubbin's Harbor."

Henrik's blue eyes settled on hers, and her heart skipped a beat. Her body reacted viscerally to the sight of him, warmth spreading through her as flashes of sensual memories of that night raced through her mind.

It was hard to find any words.

She'd only wanted one night with him, yet standing here now all she wanted to do was leap into his arms and melt.

You can't. That's not why you're here.

"You're Doc Jo?" he asked, interrupting her thoughts with the intense shock in his tone.

"The one and the same," she said, finding her voice.

It looked like he wanted to say more. A lot more. "Good, we need all the help we can get. I'll show you where to start."

"Lead the way…Rik."

There was no time to talk about what had happened a month ago, or how she'd thought he wasn't coming back, or why she hadn't seen him since that night, or how she couldn't stop thinking about him.

None of that mattered now.

She had a job to do.

Henrik was completely floored to discover the doctor he'd heard so much about was not called Joseph, as he'd assumed, but rather Josephine, the woman that he had been thinking about for the entire month he'd been away.

It had bothered him that he couldn't get her out of his head. Usually one-night stands were just that—done and dusted.

It had been some time since he'd been this preoccupied thinking about a woman he had been intimate with. Dreaming about her kisses, the way she'd sighed in his arms, her velvety-soft skin and the scent of her hair.

Even just recalling it again now made his pulse quicken.

He'd planned to throw himself into his work when he arrived back home and forget all about her. He'd thought she was a tourist and would be long gone, and usually work helped to get his mind off his paramours. It always had with the others, even Melissa.

Seeing Josephine, he knew his plan was obviously not going to work. The siren that had been haunting him for weeks while he was at sea was here.

In the flesh.

The new doctor of the community. Someone that he would have to deal with on a regular basis, given that he was a first responder here. Was karma finally getting back at him? His gran always used to say that his recklessness and his hardened heart would bite him in the backside one day. Not that he'd ever been mean or cruel to anyone. His gran had just never approved of his *philandering ways*, as she'd called it.

He'd thought it was just her usual ramblings, but then, his grandmother had never really been wrong.

"The arse is gone out of 'er, my boy, if you keep at this with the come from aways!"

Basically, she was warning him that all was going to go to hell in a handbag if he kept playing around with tourists. He knew that Gran had wanted him to settle down, but after Melissa it was far too hard to even contemplate opening his heart to a woman again. And he certainly was never going to settle down with someone east of the Rock.

His home was here.

This was where he'd been born and raised. Everyone else had left to find work on the mainland, and he wouldn't risk his heart on another person who would leave.

Fogo owned his heart.

Still, Josephine had been in his thoughts, and for one

brief moment he'd even wished that she hadn't been a come from away. He'd wished she was staying.

Now, here she was, staying. She was the new doctor, and part of him was incredibly happy about that, but the loudest part of his soul was telling him to run. To keep away. Josephine was a serious threat to his damaged heart, and he wasn't sure that he could deal with such heartache again.

There was some shouting, and he shook his head, snapping himself out of his thoughts. Josephine was standing in front of him, her finely arched brow cocked, waiting.

Right.

Accident.

"Follow me," he said, gruffly, annoyed at himself for zoning out. That was not something he did in situations like this. He had to get control of himself and his emotions. There was a job to do here, lives on the line.

He made his way down to where they had set up a triage area for those who'd survived the explosion. There had apparently been a crew of twenty onboard, and only ten had been recovered so far, with five of them having perished.

"We're tagging those that need to be taken by ambulance right away." He handed her some tags. "Do what you can, as we only have so many ambulances on the island to take them to hospital. The diving teams are still working on retrieving those in the water."

Josephine paled. "Right."

"You okay? Have you worked trauma before?" he asked.

"I was a trauma surgeon in Toronto," she said stiffly, pulling on her rubber gloves. "I can handle this."

"Are you sure? You looked like you were going to be sick."

Her spine stiffened. "Oh? And you can diagnose that from a glance?"

"Some people can't stand the sight of trauma."

"I'm a physician and a surgeon, and I've seen explosions before in the city. I can deal." Josephine made her way to one of the injured on the ground and started her checks on the survivors. Henrik headed back to the shore as another dinghy came in.

He helped another paramedic as they took a backboard down to the dinghy. The moment he got close he could see the survivor was bleeding out, his femoral artery cut, and the diver was applying pressure to the wound with a towel.

"We have a trauma surgeon triaging," Henrik said, quickly directing the other paramedic to take the man to where Josephine was working. She looked up as they got closer, and he didn't even have to call her over. She could see exactly what the issue was.

"Femoral artery?" she asked, leaning over to check the patient's vitals.

"Yes. If he doesn't stabilize, he won't make it to the hospital," Henrik answered grimly.

"Okay." Josephine pursed her lips. "We're going to do this in the back of an ambulance. I need lots of light, and it'll be more sanitary in there than out here."

Henrik nodded and helped guide the unconscious patient into the back of the ambulance on a stretcher. As the man was secured, Henrik set up a large-bore IV to get fluids into him, while Josephine readied what she needed.

The diver was still applying pressure to the wound, but the towel was soaking through with blood.

Josephine had a clamp ready as they removed the towel.

Henrik leaned over. "Tell me what you need."

"Hold the light still," she directed.

She just nodded in acknowledgment as he did and she clamped the vein to stop the bleeding. "I think that I can suture the artery so that it will hold until he gets to the hospital. Can the Fogo Island Hospital handle a vascular surgery?" she asked.

"He'll be flown to St. John's from there," Henrik stated. "He just needs to make it to the hospital."

"We'll get him there. You have a suture kit?"

Henrik pulled out a kit, and Josephine went to work, getting her tools ready to sew up the artery so that the patient could be transported.

"Start some antibiotics," Josephine said as she cleaned the wound. "If he was in the water, he'll need it, but I'm also concerned about what cut his leg. I don't know what shrapnel from the explosion did this."

"I have cefazolin," Henrik said, going through the medicine that was on hand.

"That'll be fine." Josephine continued her careful work. Cleaning and repairing what she could so the patient had his best shot at survival. Henrik watched in amazement. He had seen trauma surgeons before, but not in the field like this.

Not when there was chaos around them, and doing such a delicate repair in the back of an ambulance. It was like they were in this small bubble of their own in the back of the vehicle, just them working together over the patient.

It took him straight back to the first night they met. When their eyes had locked, he'd almost felt he'd been looking back at the other half of his soul.

And now, here, watching her work, it was calm.

A life was being saved right in front of him.

They shared the same passion. He'd never met anyone quite like her before, which was probably the reason he'd had such a hard time forgetting her. She was a danger to his carefully guarded heart.

"There," Josephine said. "Let's pack this wound and get him off to the hospital."

Henrik handed her what she needed to pack and then cover it. He readied the patient for transport as Josephine disposed of the suture kit and her rubber gloves. She climbed out of the back of the ambulance and called the Fogo Island Hospital.

Telling them exactly what to expect so they could call in the correct surgeon or have the air ambulance ready to whisk him to St. John's.

Henrik helped close the back doors of the ambulance and banged on the back, signaling to the driver that they could leave.

Josephine stepped back as the lights flipped on and the sirens blared.

"That was impressive work," Henrik stated. "I haven't seen a femoral repair in the field."

"It wasn't really a repair. He'll need much more work, and he isn't out of the woods yet. I'm sure the vascular surgeon in charge will cringe at my handiwork. There's a reason we're referred to as the *meatballers* of the surgical world."

"I've always found that distinction quite unjust."

She smiled at him. "Well, let's go check on the others. The divers are still bringing victims in."

Henrik nodded.

He stood there and watched her head back to the triage area, where there were more survivors being loaded into ambulances.

On the other side of the beach, there were far too many bodies, and he was mad that it had come down to this. To this desperation to make money. It cost lives, and he hated it, but the one thing he didn't detest was Josephine being here.

At first, seeing her there, he'd experienced a fleeting moment of panic.

When he'd first met her a month ago, the come-from-away woman he'd spent the night with, he'd thought she was a delicate flower. How wrong he had been. Just watching her throw herself into the fray of this emergency situation had seriously impressed him.

Don't think like that. Don't let her impress you.

He had to be careful.

He had to keep her at a distance.

It was bad enough that he couldn't stop thinking about her for the month he'd been on his training mission.

Now she was close enough to put his heart on the line again, and that was something he wasn't willing to do because she wasn't from here. She'd leave eventually.

Just like Melissa.

Like so many others.

There were no ties for Josephine here, and to protect himself from pain he couldn't offer her any reason to stay.

Even though part of him secretly wanted to.

CHAPTER THREE

HENRIK HAD MANAGED to skirt her for the rest of the time they were at the beach. He'd had to trade off and head out into the water to do retrieval of the victims. It was always the hardest part of the job for him, being in the water.

His parents had been lost at sea.

Their bodies were never recovered. It was difficult not to think about how the water was so dangerous. How fast it could turn and steal a life. There was always a moment of sheer terror when he headed out into the water, but also clarity. Henrik always went into the water thinking he'd do the best job he could. He was beating the sea by working hard to save lives. His own form of revenge. His own way of honoring the memory of his parents.

So that's what he did.

Focusing on that helped him briefly forget about Josephine's presence on shore.

At the end of the day, from a crew of twenty men, there were only twelve survivors and by some kind of miracle they had managed to retrieve all the bodies.

Now the coast guard had to deal with the ramifications of the accident and lay criminal charges on those involved, but that was not part of his job. He was off duty, and all he had to do was head back to his place and put this whole thing out of his mind.

Yeah. Good luck with that.

Henrik threw his gear in the back of his truck, but as he surveyed the area one last time before he left, he saw Josephine standing there, searching for someone. He should just let her be, only he couldn't. She looked a little lost, like that first day he'd met her, just a bit more tired and wrung-out.

"Looking for someone?" he asked. One part of him hoping that it was him and the other, louder part hoping it wasn't.

They'd had a one-night stand. He couldn't give her more. He wouldn't.

"Lloyd brought me here, but he's disappeared."

"Ah, yes… Lloyd is a great volunteer, but sometimes he's the first out of a situation. That and the pub is about to open for the night. I'm sorry he forgot about you."

"He was my ride back to Nubbin's Harbor." She frowned.

"Well, I'm heading back there. I can take you home. Though, I don't know where you're living now."

"I need to go to the clinic. I have some stuff to clean up. And I live above it."

"In Gary's… I mean, Dr. Linwood's place?" Henrik asked.

"Yes. I'm here for the next year, covering for him while he teaches in Munich."

So she wasn't a tourist passing through. That much he had gathered, but there was still an expiry date to her time on Fogo.

Just as he'd thought.

"I had no idea Dr. Linwood had even left."

"Did you know Gary well?"

Henrik frowned and rubbed the back of his neck. "Can't say that I did, to be honest. I mean, we worked together on occasion, but he wasn't one for socializing much with the bayfolk or townies."

"You mean the *locals*?" she asked.

"You're starting to pick up the slang?" he asked, secretly pleased.

Josephine hefted her gear. "How could I not, living here for a month and being the talk of the harbor by kissing a cod on my very first night? That and Jennifer Wells, my receptionist, has been helpful."

Henrik took her bags from her. "Aye, well that would make an impression. I'll try to slow down some for you."

"I would appreciate that, and thanks for offering me the ride. I probably could've walked. It's not that far. Or I could've called Jenn. Just thought of that."

"It's twenty kilometers, and it's getting dark," he said. The thought of being alone with her again was tantalizing, but it was not the smartest thing.

How could he get Josephine out of his mind so they could have a professional relationship if he spent too much time alone with her?

Still, he couldn't abandon her without a ride. He wouldn't.

"It can't be that dangerous. Or not as dangerous as walking up Yonge Street at night." There was a nervous edge to her voice.

"Well, maybe not, but you've only been here a month, and you're still a come from away. You're not local. There's also moose. You don't want to deal with them." He opened the door of the truck for her, and she climbed in.

He closed the door and then climbed into the driver's side. His pulse was thundering between his ears. He just had to focus on the road and make idle chatter.

Just because they'd shared one mind-blowing night of ecstasy didn't mean they couldn't be professional acquaintances.

And back his mind wandered to that night and the taste of her on his tongue...

He needed to get ahold of himself.

"Moose aren't predators," she said, dryly as he started the engine.

"No, but they're seriously big, and they know it. Have you ever seen a car accident involving a moose?"

"No, but I did hear of them. You don't get many moose accidents in Toronto's emergency departments."

He chuckled. "No, I suppose not."

She looked away, and silence fell.

He drove away from the scene of the accident and headed back on the highway. Back through Joe Batt's Arm and toward Nubbin's Harbor. Even though he had to go away from time to time for work, it was always good to be home.

Especially with summer on the horizon.

He liked the late sunsets. The vibrant colors of the houses poised on the rocks.

The blue of the sea.

Nubbin's Harbor was a small community of houses, the pub, the hotel, the diner, the clinic and a handful of shops. The colors alternated between red and white. They were clustered together around a tiny natural harbor that used to have a fishing industry but now was empty.

The old lighthouse was out on the farthest spit of land, and attached to it was a faded yellow house.

His late gran's. Now his.

It was home.

And he'd missed it. He was glad to be back at work. It kept the loneliness away.

He couldn't help but wonder what Josephine thought of Fogo. Most visitors loved the charm, for a short time. Fogo was still fairly isolated. They hadn't even gotten electricity until the midsixties. If they weren't born there, they rarely stayed.

That was his belief.

Even Dr. Linwood left.

He glanced over at her and saw she was wringing her hands nervously. A flush on her face.

He loved the pink on her round cheeks.

"I have to say, I was surprised to see you," he said, breaking the tense silence that had fallen between them. "I thought you were just passing through, as most do."

"I never said that I was, but we didn't talk much about that. Besides, I thought you were leaving the island for work reasons and not coming back."

Another blush tinged her cheeks afresh, and his pulse quickened again. She was so gorgeous, just as beautiful as he remembered. He thought he had built it up in his mind how stunning she was.

He hadn't.

There was something about her that he couldn't quite put his finger on. Something that drew him in, and he didn't like it.

"This is my home. I'm about as local as you can get to Fogo. Generations of my family have lived and worked here."

And he was all that was left here, only he didn't tell her that. There was no need to.

He had to stay.

He couldn't abandon his home. This is where he belonged. Even if it meant being alone for the rest of his life.

"You're a paramedic, so you had a sabbatical? Is that why you were away for a month?" she asked curiously.

"I'm a first responder as well, and I volunteer with sea search and rescue, so I go on training missions with the coast guard. They bring in cadets from all over Canada, maybe even some who didn't grow up by the sea, and put them through training. I assist with that from time to time. I have a lot of experience in dealing with sea ice and rescues in northern waters."

Josephine's eyes widened. "Wow. That's impressive."

Henrik shrugged. "It's my passion. Saving those who are lost at sea."

"They can't be gone, Gran," he'd whispered. "Da knew the sea."

"I know, my b'y. I know." Her hand had been on his shoulder, giving it a squeeze. "Come on, let's go home."

"No. I want to stay here. I promised to wait for them."

"Then, I'll stay with you. Right here."

He knew firsthand the pain of losing family to the sea. The gut-wrenching pain, which felt like your heart was being ripped out of your chest still beating, some days felt raw. Never knowing what had happened, never recovering their bodies.

They were just lost.

He'd been twelve and gone to live with his gran and grandad at the lighthouse, but he still hated the sea sometimes for swallowing up his whole world and shaping his life in such a painful way. It's why he did what he did.

His own form of revenge against the sea, saving as many of those as he could, who might otherwise be lost.

"Well, that explains why you've been away, then," she said softly, and when he glanced over at her, she was wringing her hands and worrying her bottom lip.

"Look, I'm not looking for a relationship...especially with someone I'm working with," he said abruptly. "So if that's what you're worrying about..."

She looked confused. "That's not even close to what I was thinking when I asked where you've been or why you've been away."

"Usually, that's why women ask. I'm not looking for anything long-term. Which I mentioned the night we met."

Her eyes narrowed. "And I believe I said the same thing to you. I'm only here for a year, Henrik. And I've already had my great love. I'm not interested in anything else."

The reference to her loss piqued his interest.

He'd had that great love too. Or so he'd thought. He'd certainly had enough heartache. He knew he had seen something in her eyes the night they'd met.

She'd experienced pain and loss like him.

"Yes. I feel the same," he said, softly.

"Right." There was sympathy in her gaze.

He wondered what had really brought her here and why she'd left Toronto to help out a friend.

"Then…"

"I was getting to know you and…" She trailed off nervously. "There's no easy way to tell you this, Henrik, and honestly if you were a stranger passing through, it would be a moot point anyway. But since you're from here and we'll be seeing each other around… I mean Nubbin's Harbor isn't exactly a metropolis, is it?"

"You're rambling."

"I know." Josephine folded her hands in her lap. It reminded him of every doctor that was about to deliver bad news to a patient. "I'm pregnant, Henrik. And the baby is yours."

His heart stopped beating, and he had to pull over to the side of the road, because if he didn't he was going to crash the truck. His hands gripped the wheel, his knuckles locking as he tried to process exactly what she was saying to him.

Pregnant?

He'd dreamed of having a family once. When he'd thought he and Melissa were going to get married. For that brief moment, he thought he'd get back that happy family he'd lost.

Then Melissa had left.

It reminded him that loving only brought pain. So he'd given up on the dream of ever becoming a father.

He still couldn't believe what Josephine was telling him.

"We used protection," he mumbled. He had one-night stands, but he wasn't a fool.

"And that's not always reliable. You know that."

His tongue felt thick against the roof of his mouth, and it was hard to swallow. It was almost impossible to hear what she was actually saying.

Josephine was pregnant? With his child?

He didn't know what he was going to do.

He didn't know how to react. All he could do was stare out, utterly shocked, through the windshield over Nubbin's Harbor as his gran's words about his sleeping around replayed in his mind.

Yeah, he'd made a right arse of this whole situation.

When she was nervous she rambled. It was a quirk she hated about herself. The last person she had expected to see today was Henrik, but here he was.

And the whole time she'd worked triage on the beach, she was thinking about how she was going to tell him she was pregnant.

So when he'd offered her a ride home, it just came out. Jo was regretting telling him while they were driving, but he was insinuating that she was looking for a relationship with him, and that was the last thing she wanted. When she'd got together with him a month ago, she was just taking a leap into getting her life back.

The last thing she wanted was a relationship with anyone.

Honestly, she hadn't really come to terms with it completely herself since the stick turned positive, right before the boat accident. And the last thing she'd ever have expected was to run into the one man she had had a fling with.

The father of her surprise.

She'd really thought she'd never see Henrik again. Even

though she was terrified at the prospect of being a single mother, she wanted this baby more than anything. It was a dream come true. It was her body and her choice, but she wasn't going to deny Henrik his child. Like it or not, if he chose to be involved with the baby, he was in her life for good.

"Look, trust me, I'm just as taken aback as you, and I really don't expect anything from you. I can take care of this child by myself. A baby was not in my plans for my year here, but I can manage."

Henrik didn't say anything but nodded a couple of times, before he straightened in his seat. "I want to be a part of my child's life."

"Good!"

Henrik nodded again but still seemed to be in some sort of daze.

"Do you need me to drive?" Jo asked.

Henrik chuckled hoarsely. "Nah, I'm fine."

"You're sure?"

"Aye. As fine as I'll ever be." He turned the ignition, and they got back on the road, back down to Nubbin's Harbor. "We need to talk more about this and not on the side of the road."

"Agreed."

It wasn't an ideal location, telling him in his truck, but she really had just wanted to get it out there and let him know what had happened. He had the right to know, and she really couldn't hold it back for long.

"Would you like to have dinner at my place?" he asked. "I have a nice roast in my slow cooker. I usually eat alone, but I think we have a lot to discuss."

"That sounds good."

And she was quite hungry.

Henrik nodded and didn't say much more as they drove through town and down a winding gravel road that made its way out onto a thin spit of rock and land at the edge of the ocean. There was a small, run-down lighthouse that was no longer in operation.

The little cottage attached to it was yellow. It reminded her of a bright sunny day. She'd often wondered who lived in this place.

"You live in the lighthouse?"

"I do. My great-grandad was a lighthouse keeper. When it was decommissioned, my gran bought it. It was her father's place, where she grew up. When Gran died two years ago, it became mine."

"I thought the town would want it as a historical site," Jo said. "The lighthouses in Ontario are like that."

Henrik chuckled. "Not here."

Henrik parked his truck. He got out and opened the passenger-side door for her, taking her hand in his strong one to help her down, treating her like she was some fragile vessel that was about to break.

Although, she really wasn't going to complain. David had treated her a bit like that, in their tender moments together. It was nice that it gave her that memory, but it also reminded her that she was finally getting her family despite it not being David. She had a fleeting thought that maybe she and Henrik could eventually have something more.

You don't know him. He's a stranger.

And that thought sobered her. Henrik wasn't David.

Her husband had been someone incredibly special.

Henrik was just a polite, kind man she'd slept with once. She barely knew him. Just because he had certain similarities to David didn't mean anything in the long run.

Henrik's family home was like all the other clapboard houses that dotted Fogo Island. Its bright yellow paint was different from the reds and blues that she had seen since she'd arrived in Newfoundland, but it was bright and cheerful in the setting late-spring sun.

"Gran liked yellow," Henrik offered. "Everyone always comments on it. It's like a large lemon."

"I wasn't going to say anything," Jo said. "It seems to suit it."

He smiled, those blue eyes twinkling at her just like they had a month ago. "Well, I often get asked why I live in a yellow house. Why I live in a cottage that should be for a little old lady."

"Who says that?" she asked.

"Some of the well-meaning saucy women in town. 'Oh, lover, you should really think about sprucing up your home. 'tis not fit for a man like you.'"

Jo's eyes widened. "The ladies in town call you *lover*?"

Henrik laughed. "No, it doesn't mean the same thing when it's said in a syrupy, condescending tone. It's meant as a form of endearment. Like *dearie*. Not everyone says it, but a few women around Nubbin's Harbor do. Most people refer to others as *ducky*."

"Oh, I was going to ask if you were some kind of Fogo Island playboy," she teased.

"Only with the come from aways. Never the bayfolk." He smiled, that same devious smile that had won her over a month ago. Although, Jo was still adamant that it wasn't his charm but rather the screech that had done it. She chuckled to herself at that thought.

No, she couldn't blame the drink. She had definitely been drawn to him before her screech-in.

He opened the door to his house.

The scent of the roast beef that he had in his slow cooker made her stomach growl the moment she stepped into the mudroom. She was nervous stepping into Henrik's world. It was incredibly intimate.

Even more so than a hotel room.

Henrik took her coat, his fingers brushing her shoulders which sent a thrill down her spine.

"Smells wonderful in here," she said, hoping her voice didn't shake.

"Ta," he said. "I do enjoy cooking."

She was impressed that he could cook. David hadn't been much for cooking, and she was a bit of a disaster in the kitchen herself.

"How is it?" she had asked.

David had smiled, but she'd been able to tell he was overchewing, and the smile hadn't reached his eyes.

"It's good."

"You're lying. It's spaghetti. It's not hard."

"Oh...you're wrong. It's definitely hard."

"What?" she'd asked, horrified.

"*Crunchy* is more like it."

Josephine smiled as the memory faded away.

Henrik slipped off his coat and hung it up with hers, as she kicked off her shoes.

"Make yourself at home. I'm going to start a fire to get some heat going, and dinner should be ready soon." Henrik disappeared around the corner, and she heard the back door shut.

Jo made her way into the tiny parlor that had vintage furniture and crocheted afghans. She could see why the women of Nubbin's Harbor were concerned about him living in his grandparents' home. It certainly didn't scream *bachelor* or *young man*.

Still, it was homey.

And she felt comfortable here. It put her at ease when, inside, she was just a jangle of nerves.

She looked at various family pictures. Black-and-white grainy photographs of the lighthouse when it was functional, and men with catches of fish. It was like a family history, a tapestry, on the faded floral wallpaper that lined the home.

She had family pictures somewhere. In a box, in her storage unit.

Her place in Toronto had been functional and minimalistic.

There was something cozy and eclectic about Henrik's place.

The door in the back opened, and he peered around the corner. "The fire is lit. Are you hungry?"

"Yes."

Jo made her way to the kitchen, which surprised her: it was so modern and updated compared to the rest of the house. This felt more like a successful bachelor's place. All modern and clean.

"I'm renovating," Henrik said, pulling out two plates from the cupboard. "The house is a work in progress, and Gran's kitchen still had a coal stove, so it had to be done first. Just in case you're wondering about the decor elsewhere."

Jo laughed. "I'm sure your work keeps you busy."

"It does." He set down the plates at the table. "Have a seat. Everything is in one pot, as it were. The beef, the potatoes and carrots."

"It smells wonderful. Thank you for inviting me over and sharing your dinner with me."

"It's no problem." Henrik served up the meal. The roast was so tender he didn't even have to cut it. It seemed to fall apart on the serving platter. Once he had everything out of his slow cooker, he set the platter on the table. "I would offer you wine, but I don't think that's wise. I have bottled water."

She nodded. "Water is great."

Henrik got her a bottle from the fridge and one for himself. He served her food first and then took some for himself. Jo couldn't remember the last time she'd sat down at a meal like this. Probably when her own grandparents had been alive.

"You're smiling so dreamily," Henrik said. "Am I that good of a cook?"

"Sorry! Yes, it's delicious, but I was just thinking of my own grandmother and her house. Your living room reminded me a bit of a time capsule."

Henrik smiled. "It is, but I'm having a hard time parting with it. It reminds me so much of my gran. Still, it'll eventually be renovated."

"I can understand that. You had her in your life for a long time."

"When did your grandmother die?" he asked.

"When I was fourteen, and then the year after, we buried my grandfather. I swear he died of a broken heart. I know that's a silly thing to say, but he just gave up."

And then the memory hit her from nowhere.

"Jo, you can't lie here all day. You have work to get back to," her mother had said softly. "David would want you to continue on."

"It's easy enough to say but not to do," she'd murmured.

After his death, she hadn't been able to bring herself to get up out of bed. It had felt like she had a gaping wound in her chest and her life was over. What was there to live for?

"Don't be like my father. Please," her mother had said, her voice catching. "Live. David would want you to live."

Only, she hadn't felt like living at that moment.

She'd wanted to be with David and not live alone with their shattered dreams.

"I could believe dying of a broken heart," Henrik said thoughtfully, continuing on with the conversation and jarring her from her thoughts.

There was that connection between them again. The shared pain as if he knew grief in the same way she did.

"Could you?" she asked, as she swallowed the tears that were threatening to spill.

"Yes. Almost thought my gran would die when my grandad did. She held on, but she was never the same."

She understood that all too well.

It made her uncomfortable to think about the struggle it had been to hold on after David died.

"Well, we're not here to talk about that," she said, trying to steer the conversation away from broken hearts and shattered dreams.

There was a life growing inside her that they had to discuss.

"Right. The baby," Henrik said stiffly.

"Yes. As I said, I can take full responsibility. I kind of sprung this on you, and we didn't make any promises to each other that night. So you can be as involved as you want. It's up to you. I'm not expecting anything."

Henrik frowned. "Aye, but I do take full responsibility. It is my child too."

"Yes." She was glad that he wanted to be in their child's life. She wasn't sure how it was all going to work out when she left Newfoundland and returned to Ontario, but they'd be able to organize some kind of custody arrangement. "Thank you for being so understanding."

Henrik nodded. "So do you think we ought to get married?"

CHAPTER FOUR

Jo ALMOST CHOKED on the mouthful of water she'd just taken. Now it was her turn to be stunned. She coughed and then swallowed the hard lump of panic that was suddenly lodged in her throat.

"You think we should get married?"

Henrik winced. "Isn't that what's expected?"

"Maybe if this was like…fifty years ago. Henrik, I don't want to get married. Do you want to get married?"

He frowned. "No. I don't. It's why I only usually get involved with tourists. I don't want or have time for a relationship."

It sounded a little callous, but she understood: she didn't want a relationship either. Even though her one night with Henrik had been amazing, it wasn't enough to build a permanent future on.

There had to be more than just amazing sex.

"Right." She rolled her eyes. "So you've told me. Look, we can work out raising this child together and not have to marry each other. You should love your partner when you choose to enter into that kind of commitment."

She knew that firsthand.

She had loved David. So much.

Marriage was something she had never really wanted until she'd met David. She'd been so happy with him. Until it all came crashing down. There was a part of her that was nervous about raising this baby on her own and trying to balance a very full career as a trauma surgeon in a Toronto hospital with parenting a child, but she was up to the task. Although she'd always pictured having a traditional family, life clearly had other plans for her.

Her baby would still have two parents.

Henrik was on board with being a part of their baby's life. It was just going to look a little different and span two provinces when her friend came back from Germany and she would have to leave Nubbin's Harbor.

Then a terrible thought crept into her mind. What if Henrik didn't allow her to leave with their child? What if he sued for custody? She hated to think this way about him, but she didn't know him well enough yet.

He was the father of her baby and still really a stranger to her.

You can make it work.

She wanted to be friends with Henrik, and she also had to work with him. She was letting her anxiety get the better of her. They had to make this work.

Of course, the one man she had been attracted to since David died, the one person she decided to have an uncharacteristic one-night stand with was a colleague. Fate was cruel.

"You're right. I wasn't thinking straight. It's just that's what I was always taught to do. I feel very responsible for our child. I want to be involved," he said, earnestly. "It all caught me off guard."

Jo smiled and reached across the table to take his hand in hers. His strong hand clasped hers, and it was reassuring.

Warm.

And she couldn't help but think of his hot hands on her skin a month ago. It made her body tingle at the thought of it.

"I really appreciate it. We'll figure this out."

"I'm glad you told me," he said quietly.

"Why wouldn't I?"

"Why should you? I'm just a stranger."

There was a bitter mistrust to his voice, and she wondered who had hurt him so much.

Hurt she understood.

"Well, when I saw you there, and Lloyd told me you were one of the paramedics in town, I figured it would be kind of hard to hide my condition. It'll be there for everyone to see in a few months."

Henrik smiled and rubbed his thumb over her knuckles. Just that simple act made her skin flush and her heart beat a bit faster. She pulled her hand away, quickly.

It may have been a magical night, but it was just one magical night.

That was it.

It was clear that he didn't really want a relationship, and she certainly didn't want to fall in love again. The prospect of falling in love with someone and being hurt was too great. It was too much of a threat to her heart, and she wasn't willing to take that chance.

There was a furious banging at the door.

Henrik got up and answered the back door.

Lloyd came in, his face red. "It's Marge!"

"Marge?" Jo asked.

Lloyd pushed past Henrik. "Marge, one of the local hookers."

"What?" Jo asked, startled.

"She works at the arts emporium. She crochets blankets for the inn and tourists," Henrik explained. "You know…a hooker."

"Lloyd, what's wrong with Marge?" Jo asked, still confused.

"She's in labor, and she's not going to make it to the

hospital. She's at the clinic! I came for Henrik, but I'm so glad to see you, Doc Jo!"

"Come on," Henrik said. "I'll take you. Tell Marge and her husband we're on the way, Lloyd."

Lloyd nodded and scurried away.

"It's a busy night," Jo remarked, pulling on her sweater and her boots.

"It's not usually like this, but this is Marge's fifth child. It's no wonder that they're making quite the quick entrance," Henrik said.

They both chuckled at that.

It had been a long time since Jo had attended a birth. Usually when they came into the emergency room, Obstetrics was called, but she was pretty sure that she could handle this. But tying off a femoral artery in the back of the ambulance didn't jangle her nerves as much as having to attend an emergency birth in her small clinic without the safety net of the hospital. She hoped it was a smooth birth.

It took all of five minutes for them to make it to the center of town and to her small clinic where Lloyd had unlocked the door with a skeleton key and was guiding Marge and her frantic husband, Scott, inside.

Henrik parked on the street, and Jo dashed inside. Jennifer was there looking flustered.

"Oh, thank the Lord," Jennifer said. "I was trying to call an ambulance."

Jennifer looked at Henrik and then at her. Jo tried not to blush.

"Well, I'm here now. Call the ambulance again in case we need it," Jo told her as she made her way over to Marge.

She looked like she was in major pain and was hunched over, Scott holding her up as she panted heavily.

"Doc, I tried to make it to the hospital, but it's coming something fierce," Scott said.

"Let's get her to the exam table so I can check her," Jo said.

Marge cried out, and her water broke all over the waiting-room floor as Henrik stepped inside and locked the door behind him. Marge was sinking to the ground, screaming.

"I don't think she's going to make it to the table, Doc Jo," Henrik remarked. "What do you need?"

"Blankets, gloves… Everything is labeled and ready in the back. Jenn can help."

"Come along, Lloyd," Henrik said, leading a horrified Lloyd out of the waiting room.

Jo tried to lead Marge away from where her water had broken to a cleaner area. Henrik was back with blankets and helped her spread them out. Jo pulled on the rubber gloves that Henrik had brought her. They removed Marge's undergarments, and Jo was glad that Marge was wearing a nightgown. Then she pulled off Marge's rubber boots.

Scott braced his wife's back, behind her.

"I'm going to look now, okay, Marge?" Jo asked.

Marge was biting her lip and nodding.

As soon as Jo checked she could see the head, and internally she was relieved that this appeared to be a run-of-the-mill birth so far, despite the speed. This she could deal with.

"I called Lisa, the midwife for this side of the island, but she's out near Eastern Tickle dealing with an emergency birth there too," Henrik said. "Jennifer said the ambulance is coming."

Marge cried out.

"Well, this baby isn't going to wait for someone to come back from the… Tickle area." Jo shook her head, because she'd never thought that was something she would say in her life. "Marge, when you feel the next contraction, I want you to push. You're crowning."

Marge nodded. "I feel it."

"Then, push for me," Jo urged.

Marge pushed, the head came through, but then it stopped, and Jo's stomach knotted as she mentally tried to flick through her rotation from ages ago when she had been on the obstetrical floor as an intern.

"Okay, Marge. Breathe, no pushing," Jo said, firmly.

"What's wrong?" Henrik asked very quietly, squatting beside her.

"I think it's shoulder dystocia. I've seen it once, but obstetrics wasn't my strong suit," Jo murmured back. She hadn't dealt with it herself, and she was trying to go through the HELPERR guidelines in her head and hoping that she could remember them.

HELPERR was a mnemonic that was used in case of shoulder dystocia and the steps needed to safely deliver the child.

"I've dealt with a birth like this," Henrik said, pulling on gloves. "We can try the McRoberts's maneuver. Then, we'll have to watch for maternal bleeding. I've called the paramedics on duty, but we should see if that procedure will work first."

"McRoberts's is when we pull her legs up and one of us applies pressure, right?" Jo said, as everything came rushing back to her. She smiled up at Henrik, who was being so wonderfully calm and reassuring. She felt like she was the one who was losing control, and he'd centered her in that moment so she could collect her thoughts.

Henrik nodded. "I'll help her hold her legs, and you apply the pressure to make sure the baby's shoulders rotate."

Jo nodded and then raised her voice so her patient could hear. "Marge, I need you to draw your legs up, way up to your stomach. Henrik and Scott will help."

"What's wrong?" Marge asked, wearily.

"Your baby just needs some help. Their shoulder isn't

in the optimal position. We're going to try this and see if that helps."

Marge nodded.

Henrik and Scott helped Marge pull up her legs, bracing them as Jo placed one hand on Marge's pelvis, waiting for that next contraction. She glanced up to see Henrik. His gaze fixed on her, and she relaxed. He nodded as if to say she had this. A silent encouragement.

Josephine knew what to do.

This baby would live, as would Marge.

"Marge, when the next contraction comes, push for me," Jo said.

Marge nodded. "It's coming."

Jo felt the tightening of her abdomen as the contraction moved across her. Jo pressed on her suprapubic area, and she could feel the rotation happen. The baby's shoulders slipped free. Jo stopped applying pressure as she caught the baby, who started crying right away at the indignity of being abruptly expelled from her warm home.

"It's girl," Jo announced happily as she cleared away everything, and Henrik wrapped the baby, helping place the crying newborn on Marge's chest. Scott and Marge were already doting on their newest child.

Jo smiled and watched them. She could feel the love, and it warmed her heart. She was also relieved that Henrik had been there to help her. She wasn't sure that she would've handled it so well without him.

The placenta was delivered, and Jo cut the cord. There were no signs of extra bleeding, but Marge and the baby should be taken to the hospital so they could be monitored. As Jo cleaned up and got the placenta placed in a biomedical bag for the obstetrical team to examine, the sound of sirens grew louder until they stopped in front of the clinic.

There were flashing lights illuminating the waiting area.

"I'll go get them," Henrik said, peeling off his rubber gloves and disposing of them.

Jo stood as the team came in, and she gave her instructions and information to the head paramedic so that they could tell the hospital staff what had happened and what to watch for. Henrik assisted in getting Marge settled onto the gurney and the baby into an isolette for safe transport.

"Can I ride with her?" Scott asked.

"There won't be room," Henrik stated. "But I'll take you to the hospital, Scott."

"Ta, thanks, Henrik," Scott said, brightly.

Marge grabbed Josephine's hand, smiling at her. "Thank you for helping me, Doc Jo."

"You're most welcome," Jo said, warmly. "Congratulations! I can't wait to see the little miss for her first checkup in a week."

Marge nodded. "Her name is Josephine. After you."

A lump formed in Jo's throat, and tears stung her eyes. "I'm honored."

Marge let go of Jo's hand as the paramedics wheeled her out of the clinic, with Scott following. She turned to Henrik, who was disposing of the mess.

"Thank you for helping me," Jo said. "I couldn't have done it without you."

Henrik grinned. "I can say the same. I'm glad you were here too."

"I'll check on Lloyd and make sure he gets back home," Jo said, trying not to laugh.

"Oh, good. He was a bit shook up. He may be the voluntary fire chief, but Nubbin's Harbor doesn't usually have this much action."

"I don't know if I can take this much excitement nightly."

Henrik chuckled. "I better take Scott with me. Make

sure he gets to the hospital okay. I'll come by tomorrow morning, and we can finish our conversation."

"I think we said all we need to say," Jo said.

"For now." Henrik didn't say anything else and left the clinic.

She didn't know what he meant by that, and she didn't want to overthink it. He was right: they hadn't exactly finished their discussion before Lloyd showed up. She glanced around her waiting room and sighed.

Lloyd peered his head around the corner from her office. "It's safe?"

She smiled. "Yes. You all right to get home?"

Lloyd nodded. "I'll be fine. Tonight calls for a stiff drink. You going to come by and have some more screech?"

Even though tonight did warrant a stiff drink, she was not in a position to indulge, and she didn't feel like explaining the reason to Lloyd. Nubbin's Harbor didn't need to know about her condition quite yet.

"I think I'll pass. I have some cleaning up to do, and I'll have to wait up for a call from the hospital to discuss the birth."

Lloyd quickly ducked his head. "I'll let myself out. Have a good night, Doc Jo."

Lloyd sidestepped the mess and headed out.

Jo breathed a sigh of relief, locked the door to the clinic and then went to look for her cleaning supplies.

Jennifer was filling up a bucket with water. "I thought you'd need this."

"Thanks," Jo said, sighing. "It's been a long day."

"I bet." Jennifer handed her a pair of rubber gloves. "So you've met the Fogo Island heartthrob, eh?"

"Who? Henrik?"

Jennifer grinned. "Aye."

"I met him a month ago."

"And he's the father?"

Jo's eyes widened. "How do you know?"

"I have a kid myself, as well as many sisters, and there's just a look about you."

Jo snorted. "Not the *glow*, surely."

"Also I saw your pregnancy test. You left it on the counter."

Jo groaned. "It's still new. Please don't tell anyone."

"I won't." Jennifer smiled. "I'm happy for you."

Jo shared Jennifer's smile. It was a relief that Jennifer knew, then she wouldn't have to go out of her way to hide it from her. Jennifer was pretty perceptive. "Thanks, Jenn. Now, let's get that waiting room cleaned up!"

Jennifer nodded. "Aye aye, Captain."

Jo took a calming breath. Jennifer had noticed, and she couldn't help but wonder who else in town would. Who knew a one-night stand could get so complicated?

Henrik had had an out-of-body experience last night when he'd had dinner with Josephine. Of course, last night he'd had a couple. The first was when she'd told him that she was pregnant with his child.

The second had been when he'd suggested they get married. He laughed now thinking of it.

After Melissa had left him standing at the proverbial altar, he'd sworn that he was never going to do that again. He was never going to put his heart on the line like that.

Yet, he just couldn't shake Josephine from his mind. When he'd first seen her on the beach today, he'd reminded himself to keep his distance and keep it professional.

All that came crashing down when she'd told him she was pregnant.

Josephine was already firmly entrenched in his life, and it terrified him. He wasn't sure the walls to his heart were strong enough to resist her or able to handle it when she left. Not if, but when.

She was only here for a year.

Nothing was holding her here.

No ghosts were holding her like they were anchoring him to this island.

He was pretty positive that wherever his gran was, she was laughing at him for karma coming to kick him in the backside.

After he made sure that Scott was safe at the hospital and reunited with Marge and the wee baby Josephine, he headed back to Nubbin's Harbor. Instead of going straight home, he drove slowly by the clinic and saw that Josephine was mopping the floor. She had her earbuds in, and she was dancing and singing. Her honey-blond hair was in a high ponytail, and periodically she would stop to bang her head and he couldn't help but wonder what type of rock anthem she was listening to.

It was quite the sight. The mother of his child-to-be.

It made him laugh.

She was so adorable and sexy.

And it took all his resolve not to knock on the door of her clinic and join her in her cleaning. Then he caught sight of Jennifer and thought better of it. Though he knew that he should keep his distance from her, there was a part of him that he'd thought was long buried away. A part of his heart that was bucking over the constraints and rules that he'd set for himself.

Didn't his heart know that it was for his own good?

He drove back to his lonely cottage and tried to get a good night's sleep. He was on duty tomorrow afternoon, and he would be driving an ambulance around the island. His first day back to Fogo had been exhausting, so he should have been out as soon as his head hit the pillow. But no matter how much he tried to sleep, he couldn't.

All he could think about was Josephine.

How kind and smart she was. How she made his blood

heat and his body ache with need. How much he wanted to get to know her and be around her.

She was consuming him.

Then he thought of their baby and remembered that Josephine was only here for a year and then she'd be moving back to Toronto and taking their child with her, and he felt nauseous.

Even the thought of being a father was thrilling. It was something he'd always wanted but never thought he'd have after Melissa left him.

The chance of a family.

It was like a dream, but he was worried of losing it all when Josephine left.

After hours of tossing and turning he gave up, had a shower and got dressed. With a coffee in hand he decided to take a walk out on the beach, which really was just a collection of smooth flat rocks at the edge of the spit that his defunct lighthouse stood on, but he needed to clear his head and wanted to catch the sunrise over the Atlantic.

As he made his way down toward the shore, out of the corner of his eye he caught sight of a massive iceberg not far off. It was the largest he had seen in some time and made his little cottage look like a tiny speck.

"Wow!" he heard someone gasp.

He rounded a tall rock and found Josephine, in running gear, sitting and staring at the iceberg.

"Good morning," he said, surprised.

She turned, and her eyes widened. "Right, I forgot that this isn't the derelict public beach I thought it was for the last month. I'm sorry."

"It's okay," he said. "I don't mind. I just didn't expect to see you out here."

"I like to run out this way first thing, or rather walk, now I'm pregnant. I like to catch the sunrise." She nodded toward the iceberg. "So this is what the start of iceberg season is like?"

"Yes," he sighed. "I did see a stream of traffic heading toward Joe Batt's Arm and mostly likely Fogo Island Inn for just this."

"I can see why it brings in tourists," she said in awe.

"I'll probably be on some search-and-rescue shifts this week," he said, sitting down next to her on the rocky ledge.

She frowned, pulling down her toque. "I hope not."

"It's inevitable. People want to get up close and personal to the icebergs. I mean, what harm could they really do?"

"You tell me," she said, a smile tugging at the corner of her lips. "This is my first experience seeing them up close."

"Well, they're larger below the water than above."

"Ah, *the tip of the iceberg*, as it were."

He grinned and tapped his nose. "They also can tear out the side of a ship. I'm not just talking about the *Titanic*, but the big cargo vessels from Montreal that bring goods up to northern communities in Labrador and Nunavut. You have to be careful. They're beautiful, but they can be deadly, and we've had one too many close calls."

"Wouldn't the ships just avoid them?"

"They can't always be avoided, and as I said, they're deceptive. Something really small on top could be huge and terrifying underneath. Those ones, you usually find out the damage after the fact."

"Well, I will still try and think positively that nothing too bad will happen."

"This is just the start of the tourist season. Be prepared. It's going to be a busy summer."

"It's not even the end of spring yet," she teased. "And I did deal with a nasty stomach flu that ran through town."

"Exactly."

They shared another smile and then sat in silence staring at the behemoth. It was comfortable just sitting here with her. It felt right, and that was a little bit unnerving. The last time he had been this comfortable with someone had been Melissa, and that had ended in disaster.

"Well, I should get back to the clinic," Josephine announced, standing up. "I have a morning full of appointments. I know you mentioned coming by and talking…"

"Right, well, we can talk another time," he said. "Are you free for dinner again?"

"You have leftovers?" she asked hopefully.

He grinned. "No, I'm having them for my lunch today while on duty. I thought you might like to come to Seldom with me. There's a little place down by the water where we can get something to eat and talk, without so many locals from Nubbin's Harbor milling about."

"I'd like that. I'm not quite ready to tell the world that I'm pregnant."

"Agreed."

That's the last thing he wanted, especially when they still really needed to decide how they planned to coparent this child. They walked back up to the main road.

"What time would you like to meet?" she asked.

"I'll come by your place at six, if that's okay?"

"My last appointment is at four. Six is great."

Josephine put her earbuds back in before waving and slowly walking away. Henrik stood there, admiring her back view, remembering how he had run his hands over those round cheeks.

His blood heated, and his mouth went dry.

Get a grip on yourself.

He shook his head and made his way to his truck. He was going to get some breakfast on the road and try to do something out of town before his afternoon shift started. Something away from Nubbin's Harbor, hoping that old saying *Out of sight, out of mind* would prove true.

Of course, who was he kidding?

He would still be thinking about her. He hadn't stopped thinking about her since he met her.

It hadn't worked when he'd been at sea, and it wouldn't work today. It frustrated him that she was invading his thoughts so completely. That he desired her still, and the strength of his need for her was overruling all the safeguards he'd put into place years ago to protect himself.

What was it about her?

This was not the way to keep someone at bay, and Henrik felt with a sense of looming dread that his defenses were coming down.

CHAPTER FIVE

JO HADN'T PLANNED on seeing Henrik. That was the furthest thing from her mind. All night she had tossed and turned thinking about him, so the last thing she wanted to do was run into him.

After getting barely any sleep she'd decided to go for a light jog, or rather a vigorous walk.

It was something she had picked up when David died. There were so many sleepless nights, so much pent-up anxiety that she took to running as a way to calm herself and face the day.

It was how she started most days on Fogo. She loved the way the mist would creep across the rocks. The calmness of the water and the big blue sky.

There were more uneven roads than the parks in Toronto had, but she didn't mind. It was always a moment of tranquility before other residents woke up.

And she always ended up by the lighthouse. Muscle memory had taken her there without her even thinking about it.

She had to remember it was Henrik's place. If she wanted to keep her distance and maintain a friendly relationship not muddied by her annoying attraction to him, she had to steer clear of him as much as she could.

So the lighthouse was out.

Of course, agreeing to go out to dinner with him wasn't the best idea either.

She was nervous about it, but they had to talk about the baby. Fogo wasn't her permanent home. Toronto was.

Why?

Yes, she'd made a home there with David, but he was gone. Was her job there really so important? She could be a trauma surgeon anywhere. All she knew was that Gary would come back to Nubbin's Harbor within the year, and it was too small for two doctors.

Jo unlocked the back door to the clinic. Jennifer was in the back, prepping the charts for the day.

"How was your run, Jo?"

"I ran into Henrik. I somehow forgot the beach by the lighthouse is his."

"He wouldn't mind," Jennifer said.

"I know. He said as much."

"So I'm curious how you two met," Jennifer said, prying.

"At the pub…my first night. Why?"

Jennifer shrugged. "Henrik is a notorious rake, you know."

Jo cocked an eyebrow. "*Rake?* Isn't that term out of a regency novel or something?"

Jennifer chuckled. "Yes! I love reading historical romance."

Jo grinned. "No judgment. I'm just wondering why you think that Henrik Nielsen is a rake?"

"He's always after the come from aways. Never a local girl." Jennifer paused, clutching the patient charts to her chest. "Actually, I'm surprised he went with you, seeing how you were the new doctor in town and all."

Jo worried her bottom lip. "We never actually talked about that."

Jennifer grinned. "Oh, really? Well, then, it just proves my point. He thought you were a tourist, and he's a rake through and through."

Jo laughed and made her way to her apartment above the clinic to freshen up before the day's patients came in.

Henrik as a rake seemed kind of preposterous, but she knew he didn't pursue the locals, just the come from aways.

And she was one of those.

Does it matter?

The truth was, it didn't. She didn't want another relationship. Still, the idea of Henrik being some kind of firm bachelor only interested in flings was silly.

He didn't seem the type.

He was gentle, kind and witty. There was an air of mischief about him, but it was a fun kind of trouble, and she liked that.

Warmth flooded her cheeks, and she smiled thinking about him and those sparkling blue eyes.

Don't think about him like that.

She groaned, frustrated that she couldn't get him out of her head.

All she and Henrik had to figure out was how they were going to raise this baby and keep their working relationship professional.

Of course today had to be quiet. Which was good for the people of Fogo, but it wasn't good for him. It meant that he'd spent all day thinking about Josephine.

Even his partner Hal's stories which were usually entertaining couldn't keep his mind off his dinner with Josephine or the fact that he had made a complete fool of himself asking her to marry him.

What had he been thinking?

His father had told him to treat women with respect. Always.

And he'd seen it all the time growing up, watching his dad with his mother and his granddad with his gran.

Even though he didn't want a relationship, he never treated his flings badly.

Of course, he never thought he would ever be a father, so he'd thought that the most logical thing to do was get married.

Of course, it was silly.

People didn't have to be married to have a child together. All sorts made up families.

She'd agreed marriage wasn't an option.

He was relieved but also slightly disappointed, and that disappointment worried him. What kind of hold did Josephine have on him? It was completely distracting and frustrating.

He could usually get a one-night stand out of his head immediately, but then they were usually gone the next day and didn't turn out to be the new doctor in town.

A new doctor who was talented and kind. Who was smart, funny and not afraid to get her hands dirty.

People around here trusted her; they liked her. That's what he kept hearing.

She was everywhere on Fogo.

After his uneventful shift, he drove back to his place and had a quick shower, cleaned up and made his way over to the clinic. He was running a bit late, which was unusual for him, but he'd lost track of time thinking about her, and he didn't have Josephine's personal phone number to let her know.

She was outside the clinic, waiting for him.

His pulse kicked up a notch when he pulled up. Even though she was dressed casually in jeans and a nice sweater, with her hair tied back, she still looked stunning.

Just like that first night when he'd looked up from his beer to see her sitting at the other end of the bar. So poised and beautiful. Then their eyes had locked, and it was like he knew her.

He wanted to know her.

He wanted to be with her.

Something had told him that approaching her would be a risk to his heart, but he still had, and for one brief flicker as he reached across the seat to unlock the door, he was glad that he hadn't listened to that warning. She was worth all the distraction.

"I was beginning to worry," she said as she climbed up into the truck. "You're thirty minutes late."

"I'm sorry. I didn't have your number to let you know and I wasn't sure if you would answer the clinic phone line. I know it's for business."

"I was worried you'd hit a moose or a caribou or something."

He glanced over at her and saw the mischievous twinkle in her eyes.

Henrik laughed. "No, just lost track of time."

"So we're off to Seldom. That's near the ferry terminal, isn't it?" she asked.

"Everything is about a twenty-minute drive or so—but, yes, Seldom is down on the other side of the island. There's a great little place by the shore that has the best lobster and crab. Or, if you're more adventurous, sea cucumber."

Josephine wrinkled her nose and looked slightly horrified. "Sea cucumbers, aren't they those slimy things?"

"They're echinoderms. Marine invertebrates. Sea urchins are the hard, spiky version, and sea cucumbers are soft."

Why are you talking about marine animals, b'y?

Now he was the one rambling.

"People eat them?"

"Yes. Although, mostly our sea-cucumber harvest is used in pharmaceuticals. Like collagen powder and…other medicines." He cleared his throat, hoping that he wasn't blushing and that she understood what he meant.

"What other medicines?" she asked, carefully.

"Herbal remedies."

"You mean for men?" she asked, cocking an eyebrow. There was a wicked smile on her face.

"Well…"

"Why are you so familiar with the herbal remedies?" she teased.

"I'm informed," he said, pretending his pride was wounded.

"I see. Good to know. Perhaps it's something I can prescribe, since it's all-natural."

Henrik groaned. "I don't want to know. This is a strange conversation."

"You started it."

He chuckled. "I suppose I did."

It was so easy to have a laugh with her. It was so easy to talk to her about the oddities and facts he'd picked up over the years and she wasn't grossed out by the conversation. He could never talk to Melissa like this and certainly not the women that came before Josephine.

"I'm a doctor. I'm familiar with certain medicines. I just didn't know sea cucumbers were involved."

"Well, now you know."

"How about we stick to lobster?" Josephine suggested. "Besides, lobster is safe for me to eat. Echinoderms, probably not."

"Right. I didn't even think of that."

"Lobster is fine," she affirmed.

"Is there anything that's particularly bothering you? I forgot to ask."

"Are you asking if I have morning sickness?" she asked, gently.

He nodded. "I remember your aversion to fish after you kissed the cod."

Josephine laughed, and he liked the way she did it with

her whole body. "Right. Well, maybe I'll pass on the cod too. Only if it's cold and floppy. Maybe if the fishy smell is overpowering it might trigger something, but honestly I haven't had much morning sickness yet. A bit of food aversion and nausea, just sometimes."

"That's good."

An awkward silence fell between them, and he didn't know what else to talk about. He didn't know what to ask her.

He was going to be a father, and he felt absolutely useless.

"I have a dating ultrasound appointment on Monday at the hospital. You're welcome to attend," she said, breaking the silence.

He was surprised. "You want me there?"

"I'm offering you the chance to be there if you want to. You still seem a little bit blindsided about the whole thing."

"I am a bit."

"Didn't you ever want a family?" she asked.

"A long time ago," he said, softly.

"What changed?"

He shrugged, not wanting to talk about his pain or loss. "Just never met the right person."

"So you're okay with this?" she asked, carefully.

He smiled at her. "I am. I just didn't think... I didn't expect this."

"Same," she muttered. "I'm thirty-eight, and this might be my last chance."

He cocked an eyebrow. "You're thirty-eight?"

"Yes," she said, cautiously. "How old are you?"

"Thirty-one. Or I will be next month."

Now it was her turn to be a bit shocked. Her mouth dropped open, and her eyes widened. "I didn't realize you were so much younger than me."

"I thought you were my age or younger, but if you're a

trauma surgeon who's been at it a while, there was a part of me that was wondering if you had been some kind of child prodigy."

Josephine laughed again. "No, not a child prodigy. I always had good grades, but I did it all on the regular timeline."

"I'm surprised you're still single," he said. "A woman like you, so beautiful and warm, you should've been snapped up a long time ago."

Her expression softened. "I wasn't always single. I was married."

"What happened?" he asked, gently.

"He died three years ago."

Jo wasn't exactly expecting to talk about David tonight, but Henrik was the father of her child, and it was important that they get to know each other. When Henrik had just been a one-night stand, their ages hadn't matter. She knew he was over twenty-five by the few errant strands of gray. And it certainly didn't matter about their past romantic history. Henrik hadn't needed to know about David then.

Now it was different, and there was no point in keeping it all secret.

Henrik had the right to know that she had been married once, but he didn't need to know about how much it had damaged her heart and how she still felt raw inside three years later. She didn't have to tell him all that.

That was her pain to bear. Not his.

She didn't like to talk about it. It had been bad enough her friends and family always seemed to want to. So she steered clear of the subject with new people, but Henrik deserved to know.

Even though it hurt.

What she didn't want was secrets from each other.

Not if they were going to make this coparenting thing work.

They had to be friends.

They had to trust each other and be a united, platonic front to raise their baby.

"I'm sorry," Henrik said, gently shaking her from her thoughts. "Grief is...complicated."

And she got the sense that he knew, but she didn't press him.

She understood it was hard to talk about it sometimes.

"It is," she said, wistfully.

"May I ask how?"

"Aneurysm. We went to bed one night after a long shift, and when I woke up the next morning he was gone. He had passed away beside me in the night, in his sleep." She tried to swallow the lump that formed in her throat every time she talked about David.

"Is that why you left Toronto?" he asked.

"No. I told you, I'm helping out a friend."

Liar.

Yes, she was helping out her friend, but she was also running away from the memories. Running away from the hospital where they'd both worked and had been happy. She was running away from the pain, because everywhere she went in that hospital she only saw him.

She felt him.

And if she was going to ever move on with her life, she needed a change, and Fogo was it.

For now.

"Right, I forgot. Well, I'm sorry. I didn't mean to bring up such a touchy subject."

"It's okay. I want you to know. We're going to have a baby together, and I would like us to be friends as we co-parent, if that's what you want?"

"I told you. I'm all in."

Her heart skipped a beat. She was happy he was all in. It gave her hope this could work. "Good. I'm glad."

They drove through the town of Seldom. It reminded her of Nubbin's Harbor, just a bit larger. It had the same kind of brightly colored houses.

Seldom had a bigger wharf area and ships out in the water. This is where they farmed the sea cucumbers, lobster and other marine life in their fishing cooperative. Henrik drove down to a little shanty that was by the shore. It looked busy, and there were a lot of cars full of tourists that were coming off the ferry. She hoped they would be able to get a table. She was starving, and she had her tasters set to a nice lobster dinner with melted butter and potatoes.

Her stomach growled at the thought.

Was this going to be her life now? Letting her stomach rule her thoughts and actions? She smiled to herself. It was a small price to pay to have something she always wanted. When she and David had begun to try for a baby, they'd had such a hard time, and in the end David hadn't wanted her to continue with the treatments.

It still seemed kind of shocking to her that this time, with Henrik, even using contraception she'd conceived.

Almost like a miracle.

She'd heard of pregnancy miracles before. Read about them, tried to figure out how the miracle worked and then never quite believed it.

Until now.

And she was ever so thankful.

"Looks a bit busy tonight," Henrik remarked.

"I hope we can get a table," Jo agreed.

"We will," he said with confidence. "I called ahead."

"That was smart."

"It's the start of iceberg season. I know that Newfoundland doesn't seem like much of a tourist hot spot compared to the rest of the world, but it is. It's a beautiful place, and one I'm happy to call home."

"I don't doubt it," Jo said quietly. "I hope you know I wasn't disparaging your home."

He grinned. "I know, but we're going to have to get used to tourists invading our space soon."

"I think I can deal with that. Toronto was wall-to-wall people on the regular."

They got out of Henrik's truck and headed into the little restaurant. It was busy, but there was a table waiting for them by the big bay window that looked out over the harbor of Seldom.

The waitress approached them with menus. "Our specials tonight are cod and rock lobster."

Jo cringed at the thought of cod, and when she glanced up at Henrik he was smirking, his blue eyes twinkling at her.

"I think we'll both have the rock lobster," Henrik said. "I'll have an iced tea."

The waitress nodded and wrote it down and then she looked at Jo. "And what will you have, ducky?"

"Iced tea sounds great, and maybe a glass of water."

The waitress smiled and took their menus, before scurrying off.

"I will never get used to that term of endearment."

Henrik chuckled. "It does take some getting used to. Is there any other slang you're not used to? Something I can clear up?"

"Hmm, well I've been referred to as *saucy*, and I didn't think that I was being sarcastic at the time."

A dimple popped in his cheek. "Let me guess. Lloyd?"

"Yes. He said, 'She's some saucy, b'y.' And I'm not sure that I should take that as a compliment."

"You can in Lloyd's case," Henrik said. "He means you're clever. You're quick on your feet. Lloyd likes you. I mean you did kiss the cod on your first night in Nubbin's

Harbor. You didn't shy away from it. You've got gumption, and Lloyd likes that."

Josephine wrinkled her nose thinking about the cod again. "And that's why I'm having lobster tonight instead of cod."

They both laughed at that.

"So about the baby…" Henrik said.

"Yes. We have to figure out a way to do this."

"Agreed. We're going to have to work together."

"Right. I want to keep things professional," Josephine said, firmly.

"As do I. We're both adults. We can do this."

"Yes. We can."

Jo had to make this work. She didn't want to deny Henrik his child, but she also didn't want to fall in love with someone again, and certainly not someone who had no interest in a relationship. Although, the more she got to know Henrik, the more she could see herself being with a man like him.

He's off-limits.

Still, it was hard not to think of him like that. Not when he made her pulse race and she recalled his delicious kisses.

She wanted to be around him, but it was hard to keep up the protective walls around her heart when she was. "So are there any other questions?" Henrik asked. "About Fogo, that is."

She grinned. "Maybe some more language stuff."

"Shoot," Henrik said, confidently.

"Okay, so bayfolk are people who live around the bay, and townies are those from St. John's, and come from aways are tourists."

"Yes, b'y!" He winked.

"Nar bit?"

"Nothing left," Henrik stated.

"Well, I think by the year's end, I should have it all down pat."

"I've heard there's some discussion about pronunciation of the word *Toronto*."

"Well, if you're from Toronto, and indeed a certain part of Toronto, you pronounce it as *Tahrahna* rather than *Toerontoe*."

Henrik's eyebrows rose. "Interesting."

"People in different parts of Ontario have different accents too."

"I'll have to go to Ontario one time. Maybe."

"You've never been?" Josephine asked.

"Never been much of anywhere," Henrik said, offhandedly. "I did some schooling in Halifax, but I've never left the Maritimes…other than going north to Nunavut."

"Well, I hope you can get to see more of the world one day."

His spine stiffened. "I'm not one for traveling. Why would I? This is my home."

It was the way he said that this was his home, like she had insulted him or something. And she couldn't help but wonder what had got his back up. She knew there were people who were so attached to their homes and didn't want to travel far from the place of their birth, but he did seem to have a curiosity about other places. So why did he become closed off when she mentioned traveling?

Don't worry about it. It's not your problem.

Only, it was her problem. She wasn't going to settle here in Newfoundland; at least, that wasn't the plan, and if he wanted to be in their child's life, then he was going to have to travel to Ontario to spend time with their kid. She couldn't always be coming to Newfoundland.

And she couldn't stay.

Even if she was really starting to enjoy her life here.

Gary would come home from Germany, and she wouldn't have a job.

Her sabbatical from the hospital was only a year, and she couldn't see herself giving up her life, her work as a trauma surgeon in Toronto, for anything.

Couldn't you?

Toronto had been a place she'd loved as a child and the city she and David had made their home, but other than her job, there were no ties there. David was gone; her grandparents were gone. Her parents weren't there. Toronto was familiar, but nothing was holding her there.

She could work anywhere, and she had a feeling her mother would want her to come to Arizona, but she had no desire to leave Canada.

Still, how could she leave Toronto and the memories there?

She wasn't sure that she could or that it would be right. It felt a bit like a betrayal.

David would want you to be happy.

Yet, there was a part of her that told her Fogo could become home, even if she was scared to admit it.

Henrik didn't mean to close himself off to her when she'd suggested that he travel. It was just a bit of a defense mechanism that he couldn't seem to stop. Melissa had always talked about leaving Newfoundland and moving back out west. She'd been obsessed with the West, and he'd always told her that he didn't want to go. Melissa told him it was okay and that she loved him, and he'd foolishly believed that. He'd believed he was enough.

Until she'd left him for the West, and he just couldn't follow.

This was his home.

It was the place his parents lived, and they were who knit him. Family who lived here for generations, and he wasn't about to leave. He couldn't leave: this place was in his blood.

"Remember where you're from," his dad had told him as they walked along the beach.

"I will, Da," Henrik had said. "I wish I could come with you and Mum."

His da had smiled down at him, squatting next to him to look him in the eyes.

"Not this time. You can stay with Gran and your mum, and I will be back before you know it. You can watch for us from here in two days."

"Promise?" Henrik had asked.

"Aye. No worry... We'll come back. Just wait for us."

And that's what he'd done. Fogo was the place his family loved.

The place he loved. He couldn't have betrayed his family or left his gran all alone like that.

Of course, he'd thought it was in Melissa's blood too, but it wasn't, and it wasn't in Josephine's blood either, and it probably wouldn't be in his child's unless he could convince Josephine that Newfoundland and Fogo Island was a great place to call home and raise a child.

He had always been happy here, even after losing his parents.

So even though marriage was off the table for him and Josephine, he could work hard to convince her to stay put so they could raise their child together. Couldn't he?

He at least wanted to try. He just had to show her the very best of it, which in his opinion wouldn't be that hard at all.

The waitress brought their dinners.

"Here you are, duckies," the waitress said, cheerily. "Enjoy! And I just got word there's swiles out in the harbor!"

"Ta," Henrik said as the waitress left.

Josephine cocked a finely arched brow. *"Swiles?"*

"Seals."

"Oh, really?" she asked, excitedly.

"Most likely. Have you never seen a seal in the wild before?"

"No, never. There are no wild seals in southern Ontario."

"Well, we'll take a walk down and see if we can spy them."

"I would like that."

Henrik passed her the butter, without her having to ask. "What do you think of Fogo and Newfoundland so far?"

He wanted to know, so he could figure out what he needed to do to show her the very best of it all.

"I like it," she said, taking the butter from him. "I haven't seen much, though. When I landed in St. John's, it was sunny and beautiful. Driving here was rainy and foggy..."

"Mauzey," he suggested, winking.

"I feel like I'm learning another language here," she teased.

"Sorry, go on," he urged.

"It was rainy and *mauzey*. I was tired and had just got into a car that I had bought online before I landed and headed here. I didn't see much, although I did see some caribou."

"Where?" he asked.

"Swimming alongside the ferry!"

Henrik chuckled. "That's not uncommon."

"It really feels like I'm at the very edge of the known world here."

"But do you like it so far?"

She cocked her head to one side. "So many questions."

"Usually the women I meet are passing through and are here to see specific things, so I'm curious what brings a big-city girl like you here."

A blush tinged her cheeks. "A change, but I am enjoying

it here. I would like to see more before I leave. I would like to really get to know Newfoundland before I head back to Ontario."

"We can arrange that."

And he smiled to himself as they ate their dinner. She wanted to know Newfoundland before she returned home, but his plan was that she would get to know Newfoundland so well she wouldn't want to go back to Ontario.

And then she'd become a bayman or townie after all.

CHAPTER SIX

AFTER DINNER THEY made their way down to the shore so that Josephine could see the seals in the water. He was hoping they would still be there when they got down to the pier, and sure enough, they were.

They were barking and swimming in the water.

"This is amazing," Josephine whispered.

"Aye. It is," he admitted. He didn't often take the time to admire the seals. It was just something he took for granted as a local. Josephine took a step but teetered on the uneven path. He reached out and steadied her.

"Thanks," she said. "I keep forgetting how rocky some of these paths are here."

Henrik held her close for a moment. She felt so small, so warm in his arms. He could catch the scent of vanilla in her hair.

And he remembered running his hands through her silken tresses.

Henrik took a step back quickly.

Josephine had a flush to her cheeks.

"You're welcome. If you think this is bad, check out the fjords near Gros Morne on the main island."

"I would like to see them one day," she said, a nervous lilt to her voice.

"I think we can make that work."

He hadn't wanted to let her go, but what reason did he

have to hold onto her? Josephine headed down the path in front of him so she could take some pictures of the seals.

Josephine snapped a couple, and they continued walking along the water until he spied a shed that was all lit up, with fiddle music wafting out. It was a public party that had just started up.

Shed parties were fun and full of island life and friendliness.

If he wanted to get Josephine to fall in love with Fogo, this was a great start.

"Come on," he said, taking her delicate hand in his.

"Where are we going?" she asked, following him.

"To a shed party."

She stopped. "Are we invited?"

Henrik chuckled. "It's not like that. This is a public one. It's put on for tourists, and even though you're technically not one, you're still not from here, and I think that everyone should experience a proper shed party once in their life."

Josephine worried her bottom lip. "As long as I don't have to kiss anything."

"I promise, no kissing cod or anything else." Although, in that moment, holding her hand along the shore he didn't really want to make that promise to her. Not when kissing her was something he wanted to do badly. Even though he couldn't. They'd both agreed to keep their relationship platonic and professional.

Thinking about kissing her was wrong. Remembering the softness of her lips was bad.

He shouldn't think like that because he couldn't have her. He couldn't kiss her.

He wanted to.

He could still remember the way her lips had felt under his.

Vividly.

It made his blood heat, and it was taking all his willpower

not to do that. If he was romancing a tourist, this would be a perfect moment.

Only, Josephine was not a regular hookup.

She was far more dangerous to his heart.

They climbed the rocky path up to the shed. The music was loud, and there was singing and laughter through the open windows.

The man at the entrance was selling tickets. "Yes, b'y, I can sell you two tickets. The money is going back into the township to fund grants for the arts."

"Let me buy the tickets," Josephine said, pulling out a ten-dollar bill. "You paid for dinner, Henrik. It's the least I can do."

The man smiled and handed over the ticket stubs. "There will be a raffle later on."

Henrik nodded, and they walked into the crowded shed. The plywood walls were lined with pictures and postcards. There was a map drawn on the wall full of colored thumbtacks that marked where the come from aways were from.

"You have to mark your hometown," Henrik said, fishing out a pink pin.

Josephine smiled and took the tack from him and marked Goderich, Ontario. The first pin in that location.

"Hey," a voice that sounded vaguely familiar said behind them. "I worked for a spell in London, Ontario, and did some work in Goderich!"

Henrik and Jo turned around, and his eyes flew open wide as his gaze landed on someone he hadn't seen in close to five years.

"George Aklavik!"

"Rik!" George opened his arms, and they embraced. "I knew you were from Fogo, but I honestly didn't think I would run into you. This was a last-minute trip, and I thought you'd be out with the coast guard or too busy for me."

Henrik grinned. "G'wan with cha, b'y. Never too busy for the likes of you."

They hugged again, and then he turned to Josephine who was smiling but looked a bit stunned at their greeting.

"Dr. Josephine York, this is one of my oldest friends, George Aklavik, from Cape Recluse in Nunavut."

Josephine's eyes widened. "Cape Recluse? How did you two meet?"

George was grinning that big smile that endeared him to everyone who knew him. "Henrik did some training missions up there. Our doctor, Dr. James, insisted on it when I was starting out as an air paramedic, and he was just a brand-new coast guard and first responder doing ice rescues."

"It was bloody cold," Henrik recalled.

"It still is!" They all laughed at that.

"I never thought I would see you in Fogo," Henrik said as they found a small corner to sit down together.

"I was flying bush planes in Northern Ontario for a few years with my wife, Samantha. Then we moved to Iqaluit to work and bring up our kids."

"You're married?" Henrik asked, surprised.

"Yep. For a few years now. She's a pilot paramedic as well."

"I'm happy for you," Henrik said.

"What about you?" George asked.

"No, not married."

George glanced at Josephine. "I'm sorry for hogging the conversation. So you're from Goderich, Ontario? What brought you to Fogo?"

"Work," Josephine said. "Covering for a friend. I'm a trauma surgeon in Toronto."

George looked impressed. "A trauma surgeon. Impressive. If you're looking for work after your time is up in Fogo, we're always looking for surgeons in Iqaluit. My brother-in-law is a neonatal surgeon there."

"Now I'm impressed," Josephine said, with awe. "You have a neonatal surgeon up there?"

"My sister was too much of a pull for him," George teased, winking.

"How long are you in Fogo for?" Henrik asked.

"For a couple of days, then I head back up north. My wife is due with our third child, and she'll be very angry if I miss it." George finished off his ale. "I'll be back in a moment," he said and made his way through the crowd.

"He seems friendly," Josephine said. "It almost makes me want to check out Iqaluit to work, if I didn't loathe winter so much."

"You're Canadian, ducky. You're supposed to be used to winter," Henrik teased.

"I'm used to it. Doesn't mean I like it," she murmured.

George came back with three pints of ale, which Henrik knew that Josephine couldn't drink, but it was very generous of George.

"Sorry, if you don't like the brew, I can get you something else," George said.

"I like it," Josephine said, quickly. "I just can't drink it at the moment."

There was a deep blush in her cheeks, and it took George about three seconds to put it all together.

"Oh! Would you like an iced tea or a pop instead?" George asked.

"I'll get it," Henrik said, clapping George on the back.

He disappeared into the crowd, looking back once to see that Josephine and George were leaning over the table to talk. The fiddle music was getting louder, and someone brought out a drum.

It was at that moment that a reel began. Henrik was stuck

on one side of the shed and Josephine was on the other, but he wasn't worried about George saying anything that he wouldn't want Josephine to know. George didn't know about Melissa.

The only people that knew were the original folks of Nubbin's Harbor. The ones that knew he had been stood up when Melissa had left the island to go back to Vancouver. Even then, they kept that to themselves and didn't trouble him with it.

There was a part of him that wanted to tell Josephine about Melissa, but he also didn't want to burden her with problems that were private. Although, perhaps it would be best if he told her. She had told him about her late husband. Josephine understood grief. She understood pain and a broken heart.

If anyone was a safe person to talk to it would be her, but he just couldn't at the moment.

"You're too closed off, Henrik," Melissa had said over the phone.

"What're you talking about?" he'd said.

"You never tell me anything. You keep everything close to your chest. You don't want to talk about our future, you just want to stay in one place and raise kids. That's all I know. Do you even feel anything? You're so stoic and serious."

"I have laughs."

"That's not what I mean, and you know it. What're you afraid of, Henrik?"

He shook it away. He didn't need those memories to invade his head. They should be gone, buried. Just like his heart.

Just like his parents.

Of course, they were just empty graves in the Nubbin's Harbor cemetery. Only the sea knew where his parents really were. How many days had he waited out there on the beach, the last place he had seen them?

Yet they were still lost.

He took a deep breath and headed outside of the shed to get some fresh air. It was all suddenly a little stifling. He walked a few paces away from the party and the light and stared up at the clear sky. There was no moon, but the inky black of the sky was painted full of stars that reflected onto the rippling, churning waters of the Atlantic.

He could never leave this place.

This was the only thing that held his heart. However, he knew deep down that despite all his efforts to persuade her to stay, Josephine would leave with their baby. Fogo wasn't her home.

She didn't have ghosts or tragic memories holding her back.

Why let them hold you back, then?

"Hey," Josephine said, coming up behind him. "You left."

"I needed some air, and the dancing was a little much." Henrik reached down, without thinking and took Josephine's hand. Even though he knew he shouldn't, he wanted that moment of human contact. Even if only for a moment. It felt so right to hold her hand. It scared him. He swallowed down his emotions. "Come on. I promised you an iced tea."

Jo had never been one to enjoy herself at parties. David had liked them, because he was definitely more social that she was. And even though she spent her time in very loud and crowded emergency rooms, it was the quiet of the operating room that calmed her.

She was an introvert at heart and didn't mind sticking to David like glue when they were out, so this was a new experience, this shed party in Seldom. Another way to break out of her shell. When David died she'd isolated herself so much.

It was loud, and there was music and dancing, lots of laughing and a great mix of bayfolk, townies and come from aways, as the locals put it, but this was the first time in a long time that she was enjoying herself.

And she actually liked being a part of it all. It made her feel like she wasn't completely alone.

She felt like she belonged.

Henrik's friend George and some of the locals had made her so welcome. They were friendly, and she didn't feel awkward or like she had to make a lot of banal small talk that would frustrate her to no end.

She wasn't that square peg trying to fit in a round hole like she thought she'd be when she first came here.

It was like she fit in perfectly with the people of Fogo.

Henrik had been drafted to take over for the resident fiddler, and she had been shocked when he took the instrument and placed it under his chin and began to play a sea shanty with ease. She couldn't help but tap her foot and clap her hands in time with the music.

He looked over the bow and fiddle and winked at her, his eyes lit up, and she could feel warmth flood her cheeks, her heart beating a bit faster as their gaze locked over the crowd of people.

You're supposed to be keeping your distance with him. You're supposed to be platonic.

She'd agreed to come to dinner tonight because she thought they were going to talk about the baby and their plans about coparenting, except they'd barely talked about that at all. They'd fallen into other conversations, and what was a bit unnerving was that it was so easy to do that with Henrik Nielsen.

So easy.

It was comfortable. Just like when he reached out and took her hand, and she didn't pull away because it felt so good. It felt right.

It calmed her.

And the last time this had happened to her was when she'd met David. The fact that Henrik was making her feel like this made her nervous. She was trying to convince herself that she was falling into this trap too easily, because Henrik himself had admitted that he'd often sleep with women that were just passing through.

Only, she wasn't passing through. She was living here.

For now, a little voice reminded her.

Suddenly, she didn't feel as comfortable in this crowd of people, and she told George that she needed a breath of fresh air. Her stomach was churning. Maybe morning sickness was starting to kick in.

Right now she felt dizzy and out of sorts, and it felt like the walls of the shed were closing in on her. She found her way outside and stood there, taking in deep breaths of air. The music stopped, and there was cheering and some talking.

She turned as more people filtered outside, and she saw Henrik come outside, his hands in his pockets.

"You didn't have to stop," she said. "I just needed some fresh air. I was feeling a bit nauseous."

"I hope it wasn't my fiddle playing?" he teased.

She laughed. "No, it's being crammed in with a lot of people, and it was getting a bit stuffy in there."

Plus she was worried about her end date on Fogo. She was worried about the baby and Henrik being separated for long periods of time. The only thing she was certain of was that the baby wasn't a mistake.

They could make it work for the baby.

Couldn't they?

"The shed party is ending. I said goodnight to George.

I'll see him tomorrow before he flies off in the evening," Henrik said. "How about I get you back home?"

"Yes. I think I've had enough excitement tonight. Lobster, swiles and a shed party."

"And that's just the tip of the iceberg!"

Jo rolled her eyes. "That's such a bad pun."

Henrik grinned and took her hand. Though she should pull away, she didn't. The path was rocky back to where his truck was parked, and she really didn't want to trip in the darkness.

"Sorry we didn't get to talking about the baby much," he said, reading her mind. "That was my original intention, I swear."

"Mine too. We still have to talk about that. We have to make plans other than our agreement to be professional."

"I know. And I mean what I say. I want to be involved with the baby and your pregnancy. I'll do whatever I can." He reached down and touched her face, his knuckles brushing gently against her cheeks.

It made her week in the knees, his touch sending a rush through her, making it harder to breathe.

She looked up at him. "I really appreciate that."

"I care about you."

"You only just met me," she said, softly.

"There are some people you meet and you just know. It's easy."

She understood that too well. She had felt that way with David, and she felt that way with Henrik too. It was usually so hard for her to be intimate or close to anyone unless she felt some kind of connection that was difficult to put into words.

Her skin heated, and she was glad that it was dark and he couldn't see her blushing, but she shivered and Henrik pulled her closer.

"I understand that," she whispered, her voice breaking as she leaned in to the warmth of his body.

"I think… I think I'm going to make a big mistake," he murmured against her ear.

"Oh?"

"Aye." He leaned down and kissed her. The moment his lips touched her, all those internal arguments she was having with herself seemed to melt away into a big puddle of goo. Jo became lost in the sensation of his lips, the touch of his hands cupping her face and the heat of his body pressed against hers.

Henrik made her feel alive.

He made her feel safe too, something she hadn't felt in a long time.

This was bad.

This was not what she wanted, even though there was a part of her that really did and was enjoying it. It was what she had been thinking about for the last month. His mouth on her again. She wanted to be in his arms, melting into him. But wasn't that what had got her into her current predicament?

Pregnant.

She broke off the kiss, even though she didn't want to do that. It was for the best, for her heart's sake. "I can't."

Henrik swallowed. "I'm sorry."

"It's okay. I wanted it too, but…we agreed on a professional relationship."

"I know." He cleared his throat and took a step back from her. "Come on, let's get you home."

Jo nodded.

They headed back to his truck. Not saying much, and the awkward tension was more than she could bear. What she needed was a couple of days away from him to process what was happening, and then maybe they could talk about the baby and set some boundaries.

Boundaries were very important.

There was a time frame to her life here on Fogo Island, and because of that, there could be nothing between them.

Except their child.

CHAPTER SEVEN

AFTER HENRIK HAD dropped Josephine off, he went home, where he tossed and turned all night again. He was unable to get that kiss out of his mind. He wasn't sure what had come over him in that moment.

Especially after they'd agreed to be platonic.

That had lasted all of—what?—five minutes?

He had watched her when he'd been playing music. Actually, he couldn't take his eyes off her all night. She was enchanting, glowing as she smiled and laughed with George and the other locals as well as the other come from aways that had stopped in for the charity shed party.

He loved the way she laughed, the way her eyes lit up and her kindness shone for everyone around her to see. It was like she belonged here.

It was like she was a part of Fogo already, and she'd only been here for a little over a month.

It strengthened his resolve to convince her to stay, so the baby could be in his life on a regular basis. He didn't relish being parted by a long distance from his child.

He was tired of everyone leaving him.

So when he'd found her outside because she needed some air, he couldn't help himself, holding her so close she overwhelmed his senses, and he was pulled inexorably into kissing her again. He was very familiar with the taste of her kisses and the softness of her lips.

It was even better than he remembered.

When she pushed him away, he came to his senses. He didn't want to fall in love. Having her remain on Fogo or in Newfoundland was one thing so he could see his child, but falling in love with Josephine was not acceptable.

His heart was in danger.

After giving up on sleep, he had a cold shower and headed out for his shift, and then he was going to see George at the hotel where those on the training course were staying. It was better that he didn't see Josephine for the next couple of days.

Even driving past her clinic on the main road toward the hospital made his pulse kick up a notch and his palms sweaty.

Suddenly he felt like a young man with his first crush, and he didn't like that feeling at all. He had worked so hard to protect his heart, he didn't expect to feel this out of control.

He changed in the locker rooms into his paramedic uniform and met his partner outside.

"Should be a quiet day," Hal said cheerily. "Although, it's a bit mauzey out."

"Oh, me nerves, b'y. You know you've just jinxed us," Henrik teased.

Hal was fairly new, and he cocked an eyebrow. "How do you mean?"

"It's foggy and you never, ever say it's going to be a quiet day," Henrik stated.

"G'wan with cha. This is the best kind of day!" Hal scoffed.

"How do you figure that?" Henrik asked.

"No one is going to be driving out in mauzey weather," Hal insisted.

"And why do you assume that?"

"Think, man!" Hal tapped his head. "Would you be out sightseeing on a day like this?"

"No, I can't say that I would."

"See. Should be quiet," Hal said, beaming.

Henrik just chuckled. "You better hope so."

Henrik sat down on the bumper of the ambulance and sipped his strong coffee slowly. He was tired and felt groggy. This was not how he liked to start a day. He took his work very seriously. He usually ate healthily and went to bed early.

All that had changed since he'd got back and had found that the new doctor in town was the most tempting woman he'd seen in a long time.

Henrik shook his head, trying not to groan out loud.

"Hey!"

Henrik looked up to see George heading over to him, grinning.

"What're you doing here?" Henrik asked.

"Training got canceled for the day. The instructor is stuck in Farewell. Too foggy out for a ferry run. So I thought I'd come and lend a hand with you today. I got the okay from Health Services."

"You mean it's too mauzey out," Hal corrected, winking.

George laughed, and Henrik just sighed. "Ignore him. Well, I'll be glad to have your help, but it's not all that exciting."

"It's more exciting than walking around town. Which I have done," George said. "Twice."

"I wouldn't count on excitement," Henrik said, and the moment he said that, Hal got a call on the radio.

"Accident near Tilting. Multiple cars. Lots of casualties," Hal stated, grimly.

Henrik looked at George. "Let's go."

George nodded, and they climbed into the rig. Hal

hopped into the driver's seat and flicked on the siren and flashing lights.

They crossed the island in record time, not that it took too long to cross it normally. The closer they got to Tilting, the foggier it was, and soon he could see the caution lights from the RCMP on the road and emergency crew.

The RCMP directed the ambulance through the road-closure signs to where there were about six cars that had collided with a truck.

"The most wounded is with the doctor who was on call. Most of the other injuries are superficial, according to the doctor," the police officer said.

Hal pulled the ambulance over to where the doctor was kneeling on the ground by a patient. A totaled car was nearby.

George helped Henrik get the stretcher down, and they wheeled it over to where the doctor was. As they got closer, he saw it was Josephine. She was in scrubs.

She glanced over her shoulder, and her eyes widened only for a moment when she saw him. "I suspect the patient has a broken clavicle and possibly a broken neck. We're going to need a backboard and a halo."

"A broken neck?" Henrik asked, in shock.

Josephine's lips pressed together in a firm line. "The air ambulance can't get through the fog, but if we can stabilize him and get him to the hospital, then hopefully it will give this fog time to clear."

George nodded. "I'll take a first-aid kit and tend to the other wounded."

"Thanks, George," Josephine said, turning back to the patient.

Hal retrieved a halo, and Henrik knelt down on the other side of the patient. He was surprised at how alert the man was.

"This is silly," the man groaned. "I'm just here to see the icebergs."

"What's your name?" Henrik asked, trying to keep the man occupied as Josephine continued her examination of him.

"Saul," the injured man replied. "I'm from Edmonton."

"Edmonton is a distance," Henrik commented as he got ready to set up an intravenous line so they could administer pain meds and antibiotics. Placing someone in a halo brace in the field wasn't exactly the most pleasant thing in the world.

"Yeah, I lived there my whole life, and I never seen the ocean. Never traveled... This was supposed to be a once-in-a-lifetime trip." Saul snorted. "Some trip."

"Saul," Josephine said, interrupting. "We're going to be attaching a halo to keep your neck from moving so we can transport you. It's very important you stay still."

Saul looked nervous.

Josephine took the halo from Hal, who sat at Saul's head. The three of them worked together to make sure that there was no undue movement to the patient. A broken neck could go bad fast, and they needed to make sure that everything was secure so they could get him to the hospital.

Henrik had placed halos before.

Usually, though, the patients weren't this alert.

Saul seemed calm, and Henrik wondered if the patient could move at all or if the spinal cord been severed.

Josephine was calm as she got the halo on.

"Okay, we're going to slowly get you on the backboard and then take you to the hospital," she said.

An RCMP officer came over. "All air transport has been suspended, but the ferry is cleared."

"This man needs to get to a trauma center," she stated.

"We can take the ambulance," Henrik said. "St. John's

is three hours going at the speed limit. So we'll get there faster, especially with an escort."

"I can escort you," the officer said.

Josephine nodded. "And I'll go, but I need someone to stay behind here to be with the wounded."

"I'll stay," George said, coming over. "As long as one of these officers can take me back to Fogo proper later on. I can treat everyone else."

The RCMP officer nodded. "No worries, someone will take care of you."

"Then, that's what we'll do," Josephine said, firmly. "Saul, were you alone or was someone traveling with you?"

"My wife is at the Fogo Island Inn," Saul said.

"I'll make sure she's notified, and one of my officers will bring her to St. John's," the RCMP officer said before walking off to speak to the other Mounties.

They finished securing Saul, then Henrik and Hal raised the gurney and Josephine carried the IV bag as they made their way to the back of the ambulance. They loaded Saul in and secured him. Josephine secured the IV line and then sat down in the back.

Hal got into the driver's seat, and Henrik climbed into the back to assist Josephine.

The RCMP officer that was escorting them got into his cruiser and turned on his lights, while others directed traffic. Hal flicked on his lights, not needing his siren until they were away from the accident.

The Mounties were calling ahead to hold the ferry, which had just docked after a delay in crossing, so that the ambulance would get priority boarding and be the first off the boat in Farewell.

"Hold on tight," Henrik said.

Josephine smiled. "I'm used to it."

She might have been used to it, but her knuckles looked white as she gripped the handle in the side of the wall.

As they cleared the road closure and moved away from the accident, the Mountie and the ambulance both flicked on their sirens. They sped across the island to the ferry. Usually a good twenty-minute drive, they were there in a flash.

Josephine closed her eyes as the ambulance rocked back and forth around the winding roads, and Henrik hoped that the baby wasn't giving her morning sickness. She kept her eyes closed, and he could tell her body was tense.

The ferry was waiting, and the ambulance was ushered onboard with the officer's cruiser. They didn't allow anyone else to board because it would take too long. Once the ambulance was secure, they closed the ferry to civilian traffic, and she slipped from her moorings, heading as fast as she could to Farewell.

Their main focus during the lightning-fast trip to St. John's was to make sure that their patient was stable. Anything could cause the injury to shift and either paralyze or kill him. Henrik had done an emergency trip like this before, but it was rare. Usually, they could get the air ambulance into Fogo.

The hospital was prepared for them as the traffic in St. John's seemed to work in their favor, and they rolled up to the trauma-bay doors with lights flashing. The trauma team was waiting as Henrik opened the doors, and Josephine helped him off-load the gurney with Hal.

"Patient was in a motor-vehicle collision. Blood pressure is seventy over sixty, and he was alert in the field. There is a broken clavicle and suspected fracture of the spine between C3 and T1. Halo was placed in the field." Josephine rattled off data as the trauma doctor took notes, not quite keeping up with how fast she was giving information.

"Are you a trauma surgeon?" the emergency doctor asked, bewildered.

"I am," Josephine stated. "And you're a resident. You'll learn, but right now we have to move."

Henrik and Hal took him into the trauma pod, where Saul was carefully taken off their gurney and placed onto a hospital one.

The doctors cleared Henrik and Hal to leave, and Josephine signed off as the doctor who was on scene.

There was a part of her that wanted to go in after Saul. It didn't feel right to just hand him off. She should be in there, in the emergency room. It's what she was used to, and she was starting to miss the rush of the action.

They left the hospital, and Josephine kept looking over her shoulder with uncertainty as the two paramedics loaded their up gurney.

"Josephine?" Henrik asked as Hal climbed up into the ambulance.

"Huh?" she asked, distracted.

"Are you okay?"

"I am." She laughed to herself softly. "This is the first time in my career where I just handed off a patient to another trauma team. Usually, I'm the one in there dealing with the incoming patient. It felt a bit weird to be rendered useless."

"I would hardly say *useless*," Henrik said, smiling. "It was a good thing you were so close to the accident and that you were able to help and assess his injuries so quickly. Your quick thinking most likely saved his life."

"I know, it's just…different. I'm so used to the rush and the urgency of an ER. It's been an adjustment getting used to the slower-paced life of a small-town physician."

Henrik helped her up into the ambulance front seat. "Hal, how about you rest, and I drive back to Fogo? I'm afraid we can't use the lights, and we'll have to wait for the ferry."

Hal nodded. "Fine by me."

Henrik took the driver's seat, and Hal climbed into the back to sit on the bench and secured himself in as they pulled away from the hospital to head back to Fogo. Thank goodness they weren't the only ambulance on Fogo.

It was going to take three hours to get back to the island from the main island of Newfoundland.

Josephine gazed out the window. "The fog is clearing up, and the sun is coming out. When I drove to Fogo it was raining, and I was so worried about my new job that I didn't really get to appreciate the drive."

"Well, now you can." Henrik was pleased.

The more she fell in love with Newfoundland, the more likely she would stay, and that made him happy indeed.

"Where is L'Anse aux Meadows?" Josephine suddenly asked, interrupting his thoughts.

"The Viking site?" Henrik asked.

"Yes."

"Past Farewell."

"I figured it was past Farewell, but is it far to drive in a day?"

"Yes. It's about eight hours one way, past Gros Morne National Park. Why? Do you want to go there?"

"I do. I might have to do just that on one of my weekends off. Like a mini vacation or something."

"I'll take you," Henrik offered.

"Really?" she asked, surprised. "You don't have to. I am a big girl, and I can get there myself."

"It would be my pleasure. I've been there before, and I wouldn't mind showing you around."

"I don't know if it's wise…" she whispered.

"We said platonic and professional, but how about friends? We can be that."

Josephine smiled, warmly. "Friends would be good."

"So what do you say?"

* * *

She should turn him down. She didn't want to take any more of his time, especially when this wasn't going anywhere, but truth be told it might be nice to not be alone for a while. Not that she was completely alone.

Jenn had become a good friend, but she had a kid and a husband. It would be nice to go with someone to L'Anse aux Meadows. Still, it would be a whole weekend, not just a simple day trip.

"It's a two-day trip," she pointed out.

He shrugged. "I could use a break too. Let me take you. I don't mind. I'll drive, you book the hotel rooms."

Jo did enjoy his company, and they were having a baby together. Maybe this would be a good way for them to bond.

They could be friends. Even if they had shared that illicit kiss that neither of them had been expecting.

That kiss was anything but friendly.

And just thinking about it now made her skin heat, and she hoped she wasn't blushing too brightly, but Henrik's eyes were on the road so she was safe. At least he did mention that they should get two hotel rooms and not share, which was a slight disappointment on one hand, but a big relief on the other.

"You don't have to come," she said again.

"No. I'll take you," Henrik said, firmly. "It's a done deal. No more arguments."

"Fine. It sounds great."

And it did.

Since David had died, she'd isolated herself from a lot of people, and it was nice to have someone to spend time with. It was nice to talk to someone. She wanted Henrik to be her friend and nothing more.

Really?

Jo shook that thought away.

It didn't matter that the night after their kiss she hadn't got a wink of restful sleep, that every time she closed her eyes all she could feel was his arms around her. The way his gentle touch had made her body quiver and her heart race.

And when he kissed her, she had melted.

Just like that first time he had kissed her. Of course, a month ago she'd thought it was a harmless one-night stand. She had been so wrong about that.

It would be just easier to keep her distance from him, push him away, but she couldn't do that. For the sake of her child, their child, she had to try and make an effort to have Henrik in her life, and being friends was the easiest way.

Even though that way was risky for her heart.

They hadn't said much more on their trip back to Fogo. It was kind of hard to talk about the baby when Hal was in the back. Even though Jo was only a new Fogo Island resident, she knew very well that Hal and Lloyd were hardly discreet. If there was any mention about the baby, then the whole island—and maybe beyond—would know Doc Jo was pregnant.

And she didn't want that.

It would become apparent soon enough: by then she would be out of the dangerous first trimester and could deal with the questions.

Can you?

Henrik dropped her back off at the clinic.

She'd lost a whole day to that accident, but she didn't have many appointments that were urgent and all the urgent patients had gone to the hospital for the day.

Jenn had left her messages and a note inviting her to dinner, but Jo was too tired. She would have to make it up to Jenn and take her out to lunch at Cherry's Kitchen.

Right now, she just needed to decompress, so she headed

back to her apartment to make some dinner and veg out in front of the television.

What she had to do was avoid Henrik for a couple of days to get a hold of her erratic emotions, so they could deal with this baby situation as platonically as possible.

At least she would be off emergency duty this coming week.

Which meant that she wouldn't have nearly as many run-ins with Henrik, and that was fine by her. She could get her bearings.

There was a knock at the clinic door, and she groaned inwardly. She made her way to the door and glanced out the window. It was George. She unlocked the door.

"George!" She stepped aside and let him into the clinic. "Come in."

George grinned as she shut the door behind him. "I thought I would come say goodbye. I'm flying back to Nunavut tomorrow morning."

"Thank you for all your help today."

George shrugged. "It's what I do."

"Still, you were here for training, and you didn't have to come."

"I was with Henrik when the call came in, and I didn't have anything else to do."

"Well, I'm glad we got to meet. It's not often I meet air paramedics from Nunavut."

George grinned. "I'm glad we met too. You know, Henrik is a good guy."

Josephine's heart skipped a beat. "Oh?"

"I see the way he looks at you, but he's too stubborn to tell you, and I know all about being too stubborn to see what's right in front of you sometimes."

"Well, we're friends. I'm only here for a year, and Henrik doesn't seem to want to leave Fogo. But I have to go back to Toronto."

"Okay, just thought I'd put it out there. Don't let his prickly outer shell put you off." George turned and opened the door. "I better see if I can track him down."

"He had to take the ambulance and Hal back to the hospital," Jo said.

"Have you heard the status of the tourist?" George asked.

"Not yet. I hope I do. I want Saul to make a full recovery."

George nodded. "I hope to see you again, Dr. York—Doc Jo."

He stepped out into the night and headed off toward Henrik's.

Jo locked her door and headed for bed. Henrik wasn't the only with a prickly outer shell to protect himself. She had one in her own way, and even though she liked Henrik a lot, she had to be careful of her heart.

And his.

CHAPTER EIGHT

THERE WAS A knock at his door, and Henrik went to answer it. George was standing outside.

"Finally, you're home," George exclaimed.

"Come on in," Henrik offered. "Can I get you a drink?"

"Labrador tea, if you have it," George said, following Henrik into the kitchen.

"I do," Henrik said, pulling down two mugs and a tin. "I thought you'd be back at your hotel trying to catch up on sleep."

"There's time to sleep," George remarked sitting down. "How often do I see you?"

Henrik chuckled. "Not often. When are you flying back to Nunavut?"

"Tomorrow morning, and Samantha is happy."

"How long have you two been married?" Henrik asked, flipping on the kettle.

"Seven years." George pulled out a photo. "Most recent picture of the wife and kids."

Henrik smiled. "Gorgeous. But how do you have a preteen kid?"

George chuckled. "Samantha was a widow and had a son."

"Josephine's a widow." He regretted those words the moment they slipped out of his mouth, and he cursed under his breath as the kettle whistled. He poured the tea, bringing

George a mug. He didn't like talking about personal stuff with friends.

With anyone.

No one needed to know.

That was his and Josephine's business.

George was smirking. "Oh, really? Is that so?"

Henrik rolled his eyes. "Drink your tea."

"When are you going to get over whoever hurt your heart?"

"How do you know someone hurt my heart?" he asked. "I never told you that."

"You looked pretty lost when I first met you. Believe me, I know heartache and pain when I see it. I watched my sister Charlotte go through it."

Henrik sighed. "Her name was Melissa, and it was a long time ago."

"So you're over it?" George asked, but Henrik could tell George didn't quite believe him.

"I am," he replied stiffly. It was true, he was over her; what he wasn't over was the way she'd hurt him. That was something he never wanted to experience again.

"Hmm," George murmured. "It's obvious you and Jo have some kind of connection, and it's also obvious you've been together."

"How is that obvious?" Henrik asked.

"She wasn't drinking, remember? Doc Jo is so pregnant. Are you the father?"

Henrik fiddled with the handle of his mug. "Yes, but it was meant to be a one-night stand."

George laughed. "That's awesome."

"No, it's not awesome. It makes everything completely complicated," Henrik muttered.

"No, it doesn't."

"She's headed back to Toronto in a year. She's not here permanently."

"And you're trying to hatch a plan to keep her here, I bet."

Henrik frowned. "It's annoying how you can read minds."

George winked. "I'm sorry. I just know you, and I also know how it was with Samantha and me. All that denial and trying to fight our feelings."

"Josephine and I are not you and Samantha. Our situations are different."

George cocked an eyebrow. "Are they?"

Henrik stood up and took his empty mug to the sink. "Yes."

"Okay." George stood and brought his mug over. "I just want to see you happy, my friend."

"I am happy," Henrik stated.

What wasn't there to be happy about? He lived where he grew up, in a family home. He loved his work and everything to do with his life on Fogo. There was a lot to be thankful for.

Is there?

Henrik shook that niggling voice away. The one that reminded him that he didn't have family left. That he was alone.

That he was often lonely, but it was better this way. It was better for his heart. He was tired of losing people.

Yet, the time he'd already spent with Josephine and the thought of their baby made him realize that maybe being alone wasn't all that it was cracked up to be.

But it's too risky. You'll be hurt.

And the pain of losing everyone he loved was fresh in his heart and mind again. It frightened him.

"Well, I'd better get back to the hotel." George sent a message to his cab driver. "I'm flying out early. Hopefully it won't be mauzey."

Henrik chuckled and gave him a half hug. "Or foggy."

George grinned. "It was good to see you. If you ever come back up to Nunavut for training, let me know. I'll fly you up to Cape Recluse so you can see my childhood home."

"I promise."

George shook his hand. "Take it easy, bro."

Henrik opened the door and watched as George got into his cab. He sighed and went back to the kitchen to wash the dishes.

He'd forgotten how perceptive George could be, and Henrik couldn't help but wonder if others were noticing a connection between him and Josephine. Had any of the locals guessed her condition?

He smiled, thinking about Jo and remembering the taste of her kisses and how she'd felt in his arms.

Stop thinking about her. Friends only, remember!

The best thing he could do was avoid Josephine. He was working a lot, and he knew from checking the rosters that she was no longer on emergency duty this week, which should mean fewer surprise run-ins. Except that he had promised to take her to L'Anse aux Meadows in his ploy to get her to stay. A trip to Newfoundland's most northern tip was a long way to go, but it was still worth it to convince Josephine she loved it here, which was what he wanted, wasn't it?

Still, he had to be careful. And as he flipped through his calendar, he groaned when he saw that tomorrow, bright and early, he was supposed to meet Josephine at the hospital because she was having her first ultrasound.

He rolled his eyes. Most of the staff at the hospital used discretion and wouldn't divulge personal information. As long as Lloyd or Hal didn't see him making his way to Ultrasound with Josephine.

There was a part of him that told him not to go.

To avoid the situation. Only that was cowardly, and he

was anything but. This was his child, and he intended to be there.

Every step of the way, as long as Josephine let him.

Henrik was at the hospital early. Josephine had managed to get an appointment first thing for her ultrasound because she had patients to see, and he was glad of that. It meant that he got there before Hal, and he wouldn't have to take time off his shift.

Josephine was in the waiting room of Radiology when he got there.

She was calm and flipping through a magazine on crochet. Her hair was done up in a bun, and she looked put together, like she was heading to a fancy business lunch in Toronto. The only thing off was the crochet magazine. It was a quirk.

A smile tugged at the corner of his lips. "Learning about hooking?"

Her eyes widened, and then she smiled, a pink blush rising in her cheeks as she set down the magazine. "I'm never going to get used to that."

"I'm teasing."

"As a matter of fact, I am learning how to crochet. Baby Jo's mother is teaching me," Josephine said proudly. "I figure I'll crochet a baby blanket."

Henrik cocked an eyebrow. "How is that keeping a low profile if you're having a local teach you to crochet baby blankets?"

"She thinks it's for a friend," Josephine said, slyly.

"Sure." Henrik wasn't convinced as he sat down in the chair across from her and nerves had him tapping his foot. Josephine watched him.

"You nervous?" she asked.

"Well, you wanted to keep this situation quiet, until after the first trimester."

"I do, but no one is going to notice anything here. We have an early-morning appointment, and the technician won't say anything to anyone. That breaks all kind of patient-confidentiality rules." She reached across and placed a hand on his knee. It was comforting.

"I'm sorry. I've never been in this situation. I'm not that good with babies."

"No siblings?"

He shook his head. "Nope. I'm an only child. My parents died when I was young, and my mother was my gran's only child. I've held friends' babies and helped in emergency situations involving children, but this is different."

"Yes."

"You have any nieces or nephews?" he asked.

She shook her head. "No, I don't. Only child too. And my late husband was as well. As for friends' babies...well I was always working and didn't see them or their kids much, but it'll be fine."

"Right."

"Dr. York?" a technician called out, reading her clipboard.

"Here," Josephine said, tucking her crochet magazine into her bag.

The technician smiled and then recognized Henrik. "Henrik...do you have an appointment?"

"No, Sally. I'm here with Dr. York," he said, clearing his throat.

Sally nodded. "Sure. No problem. Follow me."

Henrik followed Josephine and Sally into the ultrasound room and stood there awkwardly as Sally helped Josephine lie down.

Sally turned to Henrik, her cheeks a little red. "You might want to wait in the hall. Dr. York is not that far along, and we have to do a transvaginal ultrasound, with a probe. I'll let you know when it's okay to come back in."

Henrik nodded. "No problem."

Somewhat relieved, he stepped out into the hallway.

Jo was a doctor, and she should've remembered that a first ultrasound this early on would involve a very delicate situation that Henrik might not be comfortable with, but when she'd booked this test, she didn't know that she would be working so closely with him.

And she really didn't think when she'd invited him to come. To her, inviting him to attend was the right thing to do.

Which it was, but right now she felt kind of silly about the whole thing.

Sally made extra sure that she was draped properly before turning on the screen.

"Can I call Henrik back in now, Dr. York?" Sally asked, carefully.

"Yes. It's okay."

Sally went to the door and motioned for Henrik to join them. Henrik looked uneasy and was keeping his eyes averted, which Jo was grateful for. He took a seat on the other side of the monitor in the small, dimly lit ultrasound room.

"We won't see much, as you're only about seven weeks now," Sally said, checking the file. "But your obstetrician, Dr. Marks, wanted this dating ultrasound."

"Sounds good," Jo said, nervously.

The last time she had been on a table undergoing an ultrasound like this was when they were trying to check her ovaries for follicles, to see if she had eggs to harvest after her first round of in vitro fertilization medication.

She had been so hopeful, only to find out that there was nothing for the fertility doctors to use. Jo had been so crushed in that moment, but David had been with her there, holding her hand.

Jo swallowed the lump that formed in her throat as that memory faded from her mind. She was now feeling terrified that something happened to this baby. That the pregnancy test and the blood work she had done since then were lies.

"You won't usually be able to hear a heartbeat this early," Sally said as she brought up the image on her monitor. "But we certainly can see it!"

Jo craned her head and saw the tiny embryo. It was too early to even be considered a fetus yet, but it was there. The beating of its little heart.

She gasped, and a tear slipped from her eye. "That's it."

Sally smiled. "Yes. Looks good. It's not extrauterine, and everything is looking healthy. Dr. Marks will want another ultrasound at around sixteen weeks, but when you next see the doctor, which will be at about eleven or twelve weeks, you'll be able to hear the heartbeat on the Doppler by then."

Jo wiped tears from her eyes and then felt a warm hand slip into hers. She looked over to see Henrik smiling broadly at the screen. It made her heart skip a beat, and she squeezed his hand back, acknowledging him.

"It's wonderful," Henrik said, softly. "It's a clever-looking embryo."

She laughed. "Clever already?"

Henrik grinned. "Big and good-looking."

Sally was laughing too. "Best kind."

"Yes, b'y," Henrik agreed.

Jo chuckled. "As long as it's not too large when I go to deliver it."

"I was ten pounds," Henrik announced proudly.

Josephine groaned. "G'wan with cha."

Henrik laughed out loud. "That's not bad."

Sally finished taking her images and then printed out a picture. "Here you go. A nice first picture."

And indeed it was. Her heart was so happy she felt like

she was going to burst. Henrik leaned over, and his blue eyes were sparkling, a smile on his face.

"Beautiful," he whispered.

"It is, isn't it," she said.

Henrik squeezed her shoulder. "Family."

The word caught her off guard, and she felt a little dizzy as she gazed up at him. They were a family, in a certain way.

"I'll just remove the probe, and you can leave when you're ready, Dr. York," Sally said.

Henrik turned away as the probe was withdrawn, instead of stepping out of the room. Sally cleaned up and then left.

"How are you feeling?" Jo asked.

"It wasn't what I was expecting."

"Me neither."

"I have an hour before my shift. Would you like to get a coffee?" Henrik asked. "It's a fine sunny day. We can sit outside."

"I'd like that if you can just let me get dressed first."

Henrik flushed. "Right. Sorry."

He slipped out of the room, and Jo cleaned herself up and got dressed. She headed out into the hallway where Henrik was waiting.

"Where are we getting this coffee?" she asked.

"The cafeteria. Then we can head outside."

"Lead the way."

They made their way to the hospital cafeteria and Henrik ordered himself a large black coffee with a shot of espresso and a decaf London Fog for Jo. She was craving espresso and a really strong hit of caffeine, but it wasn't good for the baby.

They made their way outside and found a bench. They could see the village of Fogo spread out on the rocks. Fogo Island used to be separated by little towns and still had their names, but the whole island was Fogo. All the little spread-out, colorful houses made her happy.

There was a warmth to the sun, and Jo was glad about the summer weather coming. They sat side by side in silence staring out over the water, but it wasn't awkward. It was comfortable, just like it had been every time she'd been with him.

What was it about him, this man she hardly knew? She didn't know, but there was a part of her that wanted to find out.

"That was amazing," Henrik said, breaking the silence between them. "I mean, I knew you were pregnant, but it was still a sort of nebulous idea in my head, the idea of a baby."

"I know what you mean. Before my husband died, we had gone through IVF in our efforts to have a baby, but we had no luck. To be honest, when I was on that table waiting for the ultrasound, I was having a bit of anxiety about the whole thing."

"Oh?" he asked, gently. "You seemed so calm."

"I was still worried."

"You were?" he said.

Jo nodded. It was hard to talk about with him, because it was something she didn't talk about with anyone. Only David, but even then she hadn't really shared all her feelings, her worries about it.

How she'd felt like such a failure most of the time, which was silly, but that was how she'd felt.

"I was really worried that nothing was going to be there, that the baby was gone because I haven't had a lot of symptoms, like the whole puking thing."

Henrik laughed. "I'd think you'd be okay with not having that symptom."

She grinned. "It's true, but that symptom would also be a

sign that it's real. That I'm really pregnant. I never thought it would happen."

Henrik reached out and gently placed his hand on her abdomen. "You are, though."

Warmth spread to her cheeks, and his simple touch meant so much to her that she placed a hand over his. Their gazes met, and she could see the tenderness in his eyes.

"George said you're a grump," Jo teased.

Henrik frowned. "What? When were you talking to George?"

"He came to say goodbye to me."

"Did he, now?" Henrik shook his head. "He's a meddler."

"A kind one."

Henrik snorted. "Yes. I suppose."

Jo glanced at her watch. "Oh, I better get back to the clinic. I have a patient in about forty minutes."

Henrik nodded, and they stood up. They walked back to the parking lot together.

"So when are we going to go sightseeing?" Henrik asked.

"You tell me when you want to go."

"I have this weekend off, which is kind of a miracle," Henrik remarked. "Would you like to go on Saturday and we can come back late Sunday night? See the Viking site early Sunday morning, since by the time we get there it'll be closed on the Saturday. Kind of a whirlwind trip, but what do you say?"

"Sure."

She still wasn't sure this was the smartest idea, but she wanted to be friends with Henrik, and he was offering.

They shared a child.

Like it or not, their lives were connected forever. And that wasn't such a bad thing, was it? She wouldn't mind being with Henrik.

The thought unsettled her.

This wasn't part of the plan, but maybe it could be. Maybe she could open her heart again, even if she was scared to.

"It's better to go before June hits and more tourists invade. It might still be somewhat quiet, and you'll be able to enjoy it."

"Maybe I'll pack a lunch."

Henrik grinned. "I'd like that. Thank you for including me in this moment."

"Of course. I'm glad you were able to come."

Henrik leaned over and kissed her cheek. "I'll message you later."

Jo watched him walk back to the ambulance bay, and she took a deep breath. She was glad that he wanted to be so involved; she only hoped that he would want to continue to be when she headed back to Toronto.

Even though she was falling in love with Fogo Island and Newfoundland, she had to go back to Ontario.

Jo sighed. Toronto was her home. Except, the more time she spent here, the more attached to it she got, and she was starting to get worried about what next year would bring, when she would have to say goodbye.

CHAPTER NINE

Jo DIDN'T SEE much of Henrik that week. He was busy working and there weren't many emergency situations where she was needed to work with him, now that she wasn't on call.

Her practice, or rather Gary's practice, was busy.

As more tourists came into town to watch the icebergs go by, a common cold seemed to rip through Nubbin's Harbor, and Josephine just hoped she didn't catch it, so she took extra vitamin C in an effort to avoid it.

She didn't want to be sick for her trip to the main island and a chance to see L'Anse aux Meadows. It would be her first real touristy thing, besides kissing a cod, that she'd done since she'd arrived in Newfoundland. And it was a place she had always wanted to see.

It might be nice to go on a mini vacation. She couldn't remember the last time she went somewhere, and it would be nice to have friendly company. Someone to chat to. She'd missed talking to someone.

You mean you miss Henrik.

It was true. She missed his company. She had gotten so used to being alone these last three years. It was easier to shut people out rather than to feel.

Especially the emptiness and loneliness that had saturated most of her life. It was easier to ignore it by keeping people away.

Now Henrik was in her life for better or for worse.

Since he'd arrived back in the village, she had gotten used to him being around, even if they didn't get to chat much.

It was good to connect. She didn't feel so lost, so alone in the world. It was exciting to have a friend and someone to look out for her.

This week the only thing she had heard from him was a message to say they were on for Saturday and he'd pick her up at seven in the morning. Sharp.

As much as Jo wanted to sleep in, she was ready at seven and waiting outside the clinic with their picnic lunch, her small suitcase and a thermos full of coffee.

Decaf coffee.

Henrik's truck came around the corner and pulled up. Henrik got out. He was grinning, and that friendly charming smile made her heart skip a beat.

"You have a proper picnic basket and all!" Henrik remarked.

"I went to Cherry's Kitchen, and she put together a picnic for me. Something she does during tourist season."

"Smart. I didn't know she did that," Henrik remarked.

"Isn't Cherry's Kitchen your go-to place for dates?"

Henrik raised an eyebrow and saw she was smirking. "Where would you be hearing that?"

"Lloyd."

Henrik rolled his eyes. "Of course. Yes, I've taken other women there. Are you jealous?" he teased.

"Nope, I'm just surprised you didn't know about her picnic lunches." She winked, and he laughed as she folded up the blanket she'd brought.

Although, there was a bubble of jealousy at the thought of him with other women. It surprised her. She wasn't a jealous person by nature.

Don't think about it.

He was her friend and nothing more, even if secretly she would like a little bit more. Warmth crept up her neck, and she looked away, hoping he didn't notice her blush.

Again.

He took the basket and blanket and placed them in the back seat. Then he took her overnight bag and set it next to his.

"I also brought coffee. It's decaf, though," she said.

He wrinkled his nose. "Well, that's thoughtful of you."

"I need to limit my caffeine."

"I know, but decaf coffee is like drinking American beer. Weak." He chuckled at his joke.

Jo rolled her eyes. "Don't let any Americans hear that."

"An American told me that when he was up here working with the coast guard," Henrik said, winking again. "He couldn't handle the screech at all. You at least kissed the cod. He passed out with it."

Jo laughed as he opened her door and helped her up into the passenger seat. She buckled up, and Henrik climbed in and pulled away from the clinic. She opened the thermos and poured him a cup of coffee in one of the paper cups she had brought.

"Ta," he said, sipping it, making a face. "Awful. Awful."

"You suck, you know that," she said, chuckling. It was so easy to tease him, to joke with him. She liked that about him. Everyone might think he was a bit aloof or grumpy at times, and she'd heard the term *loner* tossed about by other town folk, but that wasn't the person she saw when she was with him.

When she was with Henrik, he was easy-going and friendly, like most of the residents here.

"Are you ready to see my Viking ancestors?" he asked, grinning as they made their way from Nubbin's Harbor to the ferry.

"Your Viking ancestors?" she asked.

"My dad's family is Norwegian, and my mother's family were original Newfoundlanders that descended from Irish immigrants, ages ago."

"I was wondering about your name, Henrik Nielsen. It's a bit different from others around here."

He nodded. "My mother was a Power."

"I've heard that name."

"My gran only had my mother, but Gran had a couple of brothers, and most of their family, third cousins and the like, have moved away. Moved west."

"It seems like a lot of people move west," she remarked.

He nodded, his lips pressed together firmly. "Aye. I was engaged to a girl, and that's what she wanted too."

Jo could tell by the furrow of his brow and the stiffness of his spine it weighed heavily on him.

The jovial mood had melted away.

"Tell me about it," she said, gently.

"There's not much to tell."

Jo reached over and slipped her hand over his. He smiled sweetly, and she saw pain in his blue eyes that were usually full of mirth.

The same pain of loss she knew all too well.

"Tell me anyway."

He sighed. "We were going to get married, and I thought we were going to settle here. Make a life, like our ancestors did, but she left me the night we were going to run away together. So in a way, she left me standing at the altar, not in the literal sense. She headed out back to British Columbia. She didn't want to live with me here."

"And you didn't follow?"

His back straightened, and he frowned. "Fogo is my home. I won't leave. Other people leave, but not me. Not that I blame them. There was no work when the fisheries died down, but we're working hard to build back up, and people are gradually coming home again."

"Home is important."

"The most. So that's why it ended."

Jo wasn't sure she had a home anymore. It had been some time since she'd felt that inexplicable draw to a place where she had roots. She didn't know what else to say, so instead she tried to introduce another side of leaving home.

"Where I come from it's just too expensive. If you leave some communities in Ontario, you might not be able to buy back in, and then farmland is getting swallowed up by the urban sprawl."

Henrik shuddered. "That's terrible. The idea of urban sprawl."

She smiled. "It's a different kind of life compared to this one."

"And which one do you prefer so far?"

Jo chuckled softly to herself. "I like both."

"We'll work on that."

They pulled up to the ferry and got in the line. The ferry was off-loading the first run of passengers. It wasn't too long until they were boarding. Once Henrik's truck was secured in the hold, they got out and headed out to the passenger deck for the voyage across. As they were leaning over the rail she saw antlers in the water, which caught her off guard.

"Henrik," she exclaimed, gripping his arm. "Antlers."

He chuckled. "And there be caribou attached to those antlers."

"I still can't believe they swim across the channel. I know I've seen it before, but it's still amazing."

"Yep." Henrik nodded, like it was the most normal thing in the world to see a herd of caribou swim by, but Jo supposed, for him, it was. She watched in awe as the caribou made it to the shoreline and clambered up out of the water, shaking as they pranced away over the rock into some brush.

The ferry sounded its horn and slipped its moorings. The ferry jolted, and Henrik's arms came around her to steady her. It was comforting to have his arms around her. It felt right, and she didn't push him away. Instead she relished the feeling of being held again.

It had been a long time.

It felt wonderful.

Henrik didn't mean to reach out to wrap his arms around her, but when the ferry jerked, she fell back against his chest and so he steadied her, but Josephine didn't move away, and he didn't want to push her away.

It was lovely having her in his arms again. Her sweet scent of vanilla surrounded him, and he knew firsthand that she tasted just as sweet. It was taking all his self-control not to caress her and kiss her, like he longed to do.

Just like he'd wanted to do when he saw their baby on the ultrasound. Not that there had been much to see. It was just this little blob, but it was a little blob with a heartbeat, and it was his child. One day it would be a person, with their own personality, and he was both scared and thrilled about that.

He had been so overcome with emotion, and he saw that Josephine was holding back tears, then she'd opened her heart and told him why.

Which is why he'd finally decided to share his pain about Melissa. Even then it took him some time to tell her. He'd wanted to tell her then but hadn't been able to put it into words until just now.

Josephine understood his pain, and he understood hers.

It was easier to keep himself closed off usually. He didn't like to talk about his feelings, but she had opened up this piece of her heart to him, and he couldn't help himself from reciprocating. When he was around her, it felt right.

Henrik was still scared and fearful for his battered heart,

but he wanted Josephine to stay, to be in his life, and if she left Fogo he would miss her company. So he held her close during the whole ferry ride to Farewell.

It was just an hour, such a short time, but it was worth it.

He wasn't sure that she was going to stay yet, and he wanted to savor every moment that he could with her.

The thin sliver of land of Newfoundland grew on the horizon, and he reluctantly let go of Josephine, and they headed back down to his truck to prepare to disembark. There were a couple more jolts, and the ferry moored on the other side.

Josephine settled in the passenger seat and he climbed up, waiting until the bay door opened and he could start his truck.

It was only a few minutes before the traffic from the ferry began to slowly make its way off and onto the highway. He navigated his way inland on the island to the other coast to take the highway that ran to L'Anse aux Meadows at the very tip.

"Would you like to stop for lunch at Gros Morne?" Henrik asked. They had been driving for a few hours, and it was almost noon.

"Sure. Wherever you like."

"It's a beautiful spot, but we'll have to come back another day to see it properly. Maybe take a trip up the fjords."

"Fjords?" she asked.

"I told you," he teased. "This is Viking land."

"Fitting, the inn you booked our rooms at is called the Valhalla Lodge Motel."

They approached the park gates, and Josephine stared in wonder at the steep mountain cliffs and the water. Gros Morne Mountain loomed as they made their way into the park to find one of the many picnic sites that overlooked the ocean vista.

"You can camp here?" she asked.

"Yes, and you can hike up the mountain, but I wouldn't suggest you do that in your condition."

"No, but maybe one day," she said, offhandedly staring out the window.

His heart skipped a beat.

Maybe she was giving up on her idea of leaving, and his plan was working to get her to stay here in Newfoundland, where they could be a family.

Don't get ahead of yourself, a little voice warned.

Henrik didn't say anything as he found a fairly level picnic site with a view of the mountain and the water. Something that Josephine could manage easily. He parked the car, and they got out. She grabbed the blanket out of the back, and he took the picnic basket.

She didn't go for one of the tables but headed out into the tall grasses that were gently blowing in the sunny June wind and spread it out. It was a patchwork quilt.

"Is that one of Gary's?" Henrik asked. "I only ask because it looks like one of the ones that are done by the ladies in Nubbin's Harbor."

"Yes. It was the largest one and looked the most comfortable."

"They are comfy, and they're very warm." He set the basket down on one corner so the blanket wouldn't blow away. Josephine sat down and began to unpack the basket. There was sparkling cider and sandwiches, both cheese and meats.

It was brilliant.

"It looks like it's turkey. I hope you like turkey." Josephine held out the sandwich.

"I do." He took it from her and unwrapped it, taking a bite of it before leaning back against the quilt.

"What's that mountain called?" Josephine asked. "The one you don't want me hiking yet."

He grinned. "Very difficult name."

"Oh?"

"Gros Morne Mountain," he said.

She smiled. "That is certainly complicated. So have you ever hiked up there?"

He nodded. "When I was doing a training session a few years back. It's steep, lots of sharp rocks and wildlife, but I think the most challenging training that I've ever done has been on northern Labrador and up into Nunavut."

"Seen a polar bear?" she asked.

He nodded. "One got a little too close to me once, but George was with me and scared it off. They're beautiful, but they are predators."

"I wouldn't mind seeing a wild one, but from a distance," she said.

"Distance is good. If you go into northern Labrador you can see them. Sometimes they wander down this way, but usually that's when they're on some sea ice."

"Poor things," Josephine remarked.

"What about me?" he asked, joking.

"Why should I feel sympathy for you?" she asked, her eyes twinkling.

"No reason. I just wanted all the attention on me." He winked and finished his sandwich, enjoying the scenery from their picnic site. It had been a long time since he'd been here for leisure. He'd seen some beautiful sites when he did travel from Fogo, but it was always for work, and he always returned to the place he called home.

"When we get to our hotel, we should stop for some great fish and chips near there. There's a little tavern near Hay Cove. If it's still there."

"I could go for some traditional fish and chips. As long as I don't have to kiss anything and it's not a sea cucumber."

Henrik cocked an eyebrow. "You're getting over your

aversion to fish. Maybe you'll become a native Newfoundlander after all."

One could only hope.

They finished their lunch, packed up their garbage and headed out of the national park and back to the highway. It was still another four hours or so from Gros Morne to just outside L'Anse aux Meadows.

Josephine drifted off to sleep and slept most of the way with her head pressed against the side of the truck as they drove to the Valhalla Lodge Motel, which was off the main highway not far from the national site. It was made of logs and really embraced the Viking flair, and there was a longhouse restaurant called Thor's Place that was attached. Since the place he wanted to take Josephine was actually closed, he thought that Thor's Place looked interesting.

Josephine checked them in. She came out of the office holding two keys. "They're adjoining, but seriously, don't be pestering me all night."

"I wouldn't do that." He grinned and took the key.

"So where is this place that you wanted to have dinner?" she asked.

"It's closed. We passed it when you were drooling on the side of my window."

Pink tinged her cheeks. "Oh, no. I wasn't snoring, was I?"

"No." He grinned. "There's a restaurant attached to the motel. How about we meet there in twenty minutes? Gives us a chance to stretch and freshen up."

"That sounds good. I'll meet you there in twenty." She picked up her overnight bag and made her way to her room. Henrik couldn't help but admire her as she walked away. He couldn't believe how much he was enjoying himself. Usually his life was mostly work, barely any play unless a tourist he fancied was in town, but he never went on trips just for pleasure like this.

Not in a long time.

Josephine seemed to drag out all the bits of him that he'd thought were locked away. There was a glimmer of light in his life again. It made him smile. He was very thankful that they had separate rooms, because he wanted to take her in his arms again and not let her go.

He wanted her to be his, and that thought scared him straight to his core.

Jo took her time freshening up. She changed out of her jeans and sweater, slipping on a sweater dress and some nice shoes. She put her hair up and changed her jewelry, then put on some more makeup. She wasn't sure how fancy Thor's Place was, but she had a feeling it wasn't a five-star wear-a-suit-or-get-out kind of place.

When she got there, Henrik was already seated. He waved and then stood up. Heat rushed to her face, realizing he had changed into different clothes too: well-fitted jeans and a fisherman's sweater that hugged his wide shoulders perfectly. It also brought out the color of his eyes and his dark hair.

He was incredibly handsome, and she could see some of the other women in the restaurant admiring him. Not that she could blame them. She had been extremely attracted to him the first time he'd spoken to her at Lloyd's bar.

Had been? That little voiced questioned her, teasing her.

Had been was not the right tense. She was still extremely attracted to him, which was part of the problem with having him in her life. Their eyes locked across the room, and a flutter in her stomach made her catch her breath.

She could get lost in those eyes. She had before.

It was so hard to remain friends with someone who you knew could make your blood sing with just a simple touch.

And right now, she wanted that touch again.

"You look beautiful," he said, as she slid into the booth opposite him. He sat down when she was settled. Their booth was tucked in the corner and overlooked the ocean.

"I love your sweater," she said, trying to be vague, but her cheeks were heating again, and she was blushing. She knew she was.

"Thanks. My gran knitted it for me a year before she died."

"She was talented," Josephine remarked.

He smiled, nodding. "Yes. She was."

The waitress came over, handing them their menus. "Can I get you something to drink, ducky?"

"Iced tea is fine," Josephine answered.

"And you, ducky?" the waitress asked, addressing Henrik.

"Brewis would be the best kind."

The waitress nodded. "Back soon, and I'll take your order."

Josephine opened the menu and saw that Thor's Place did have fish and chips but also caribou steaks.

"What're you going to have?" Henrik asked.

"I'll stick with the fish and chips. I was looking forward to it. What're you going to have?"

"Caribou," he said.

"Seriously?"

He shrugged. "I've had it before. Mind you, George's auntie cooked it up, but I'll see how this place manages it."

"Maybe I can steal a bite?" she asked, not sure if she was going to or not, but she was curious just the same.

"Perhaps," he said, slyly.

The waitress returned with their drinks and then took their orders, and it was just the two of them again. She knew that she would eventually have to bring up the subject of their baby. She knew that he wanted to be involved, but she was having a hard time picturing what that would look like in a year, when she would head back to Ontario. Yet, if she stayed she'd have to fund her own practice. Trauma surgeons weren't in high demand on Fogo.

At the very least she'd have to go to Newfoundland proper to work, and so she and the baby would still be separated from Henrik.

She flinched.

She didn't want to deprive her child of their father.

It was hard to contemplate or rationalize in her that this one-night stand, the first one she had ever had in her life, was not just for one night. He was completely part of her life from now on.

"Something seems to be gnawing at you," Henrik asked, cautiously.

"Something is." She swallowed the lump of dread that had been lodged in her throat. "You want to be involved with the baby?"

"I do. You know that I do."

"What happens after the year is up?"

Henrik frowned, only for a moment. "We'll figure it out."

"I know, being a trauma surgeon, I can usually think three steps ahead of a situation, but when I think ahead about this, I see lots of plane fares and…"

Henrik reached across the table and took her hands in his. It was reassuring and comforting. He looked into her eyes, and all that trepidation melted away.

"Josephine, I plan to be in my child's life. I promise you this. For now, let's focus on getting to know one another better, working on our friendship so we can give our baby the best possible chance of a stable childhood."

"I'd like that."

And it was true.

She wanted to be his friend. At the very least, even if her heart was telling her that she wanted more. She was just too scared to have it.

CHAPTER TEN

JO'S MEAL WAS quite good, and in the end she did try just a bite of well-done caribou meat, as anything that wasn't cooked through was a no-no. It was okay, and she would have it again if she had the chance.

After a filling dinner, they both retreated to their separate rooms as they had to get up early for when L'Anse aux Meadows opened. They were going to spend a couple hours there before heading back to Farewell in time to catch the last ferry to Fogo Island.

They checked out of their motel, Henrik grabbed coffee with a quick joke about not having to be subjected to decaf again, and they drove to the historic site as it opened for visitors.

There was a crispness in the late-spring air. The sun was rising but hadn't burned off the low-lying mists that clung to the mounds and hollows of the ancient Viking settlement hugging the coast of the ocean. Long grasses blew in the gentle breeze.

It was green, and the sky was as blue as the water. There were white caps on the waves, signaling that it was slightly windy out there.

The edge of Canada.

It certainly had that look, and she couldn't help but wonder what the indigenous people had thought of Viking invaders.

"Amazing," Jo whispered, as they parked.

Henrik nodded. "It's indeed impressive. Let's take a walk."

They got out of his truck and paid the admission fees so they could walk around the site and the museum that housed artifacts and information about the settlement.

"People only think the Vikings traveled to Europe and Iceland, but really their migration was much farther," Henrik remarked.

"I read once that there were artifacts found in places like Northern Manitoba and Baffin Island."

Henrik nodded. "History is one of the things I like. Especially ancient history and seafaring."

She grinned. "Maybe you should dive for treasure?"

"Well, I used to want to, but honestly I have a huge respect for the ocean. My parents lost their lives to it." There was a sadness to his voice, and his gaze focused out on the blue ocean. "They went out on my dad's fishing trawler, and a storm crept up, hard and furious. They were lost."

Her heart ached for him. "How old were you?"

"Twelve."

She couldn't even begin to imagine the pain of losing her parents at that age. Instinctively she reached down to her abdomen, cradling their child.

"I'm sorry."

"I respect the ocean, and I love it, but I also hate it." His spine stiffened. "Still, it's in my blood."

"I get that. Home, where your roots are, is important."

A strange expression crossed his face. "Aye. You haven't said much about your parents. Are they still in—"

"Goderich? No, they retired to Arizona."

"Arizona? That seems random."

"They don't like the winter, and they don't like humidity, so they opted for Arizona over Florida. I really don't want to leave Canada either."

"I have no desire to leave Canada, but my unadventurous attitude has cost me much."

And she knew he was talking about his former fiancée then. "I think you're pretty adventurous."

Henrik cocked an eyebrow. "How so?"

"You say you hate the ocean and are unadventurous, yet you work with the coast guard and head up to the far north. You were out there, during that boating accident, helping to save victims. You're fixing up an old lighthouse, and you're willing to take a chance on a stranger."

Henrik grinned softly and caressed her face. "You're not a stranger anymore, Jo."

"Aren't I?" she asked, her voice catching in her throat, her body trembling in anticipation of another kiss.

"No." And he took a step closer.

Her heart was racing. She was going to say something more when there was a commotion down by the shore, and a couple of the park rangers went rushing by them.

"What's wrong?" Henrik asked, one of the rangers dashing by.

"Tourist fell into the ocean, hit their head," the ranger said.

"I'm a doctor," Jo said. "He's a paramedic. Can we help?"

The ranger looked relieved. "Yes, please follow me, but be careful the path is a bit rocky where he climbed down."

Henrik took her hand, and they followed the ranger down the path, to an out-of-bounds area where tourists weren't supposed to be.

"This has never happened. These come from aways sometimes are a bit bold," the ranger murmured.

On the beach a couple other park rangers had managed to retrieve the man from the water, and Jo could see the blood on his head. Once she had her footing, she made her way to the rangers.

"I'm Dr. York. I can help," she said. "I need you to be careful in case there's trauma to the spine."

The rangers nodded as Henrik was helping the other ranger lay out a tarp and gather supplies until the summoned paramedics could get there. The man's wife was crying.

"He was with our daughter. She's not here," the woman screamed.

"There's someone else in the water?" Henrik asked.

The hysterical woman nodded. "She's only eighteen."

Henrik was peeling off his leather jacket, his shoes, socks and jeans.

"What're you doing?" Jo asked.

"Going in after her. The water is calm here. I'll find her," Henrik stated. He pulled off his flannel shirt, holding it between his teeth as he swam out. She knew he was going use it as a sling to hold the girl.

Jo's heart was racing, worrying about him. The water was calm, but she knew there were things like undertows and sea life.

He's done this before. He said so himself.

Only, she had a hard time calming that inner dialogue. The one that kept thinking about how she'd lost David and she couldn't lose Henrik. Not when she was just getting to know him. Their baby needed him.

So do you.

Josephine shook those anxieties away, as the park rangers laid out the patient, and ignored the fact that Henrik was swimming out to find a missing girl. What she had to do was check on the girl's father. She pulled on gloves from the first-aid kit that the park rangers had.

He was bleeding badly.

Jo knelt down beside him and assessed his airway,

breathing and consciousness. There was an open wound at the base of his skull and bruising under his eyes. He had hit his head hard, on what Jo could only assume was rocks.

She checked his eyes, and there was no pupillary reaction from his right eye, which meant there was trauma and bleeding in the brain.

His Glasgow Coma Scale rating was a three, at best, which was severe. He was breathing, for now.

What he needed was pressure relieved.

"Do you have a drill? For maintenance work perhaps?" Jo asked.

The park ranger who'd guided them to the shore frowned. "Yes. In the ATV. What do you need it for?"

"How long until the ambulance gets here?"

"An hour," the ranger said.

Jo worried her bottom lip. "We need to make sure his cervical spine is stabilized, and I may need that drill to make burr holes and relieve pressure or he won't make it to the hospital."

"I'll get it." The ranger disappeared and returned with the drill.

Jo pulled out the antiseptic and began to clean the drill bit and the patient's head.

There was a shout, and she turned to see Henrik carrying the girl out of the water. The other two rangers went to help him.

"How is she?" Jo called over her shoulder.

"Starting CPR," Henrik shouted back.

She turned to the ranger that was still with her, one that looked a bit nervous now. "You going to be okay to help me?"

He nodded. "I'm just doing this for the summer. I'm saving up for medical school."

"Good. As I just said, we're going to do some burr holes to relieve pressure. It'll allow the pooling blood to drain.

What I need you to do is hold the head still. Think you can do that for me?"

"Yes, Dr. York. I can."

Jo was relieved as she started the drill. She could hear the ambulance coming, but this man needed the emergency field surgery if he was going to make it to the airfield to be airlifted to St. John's.

It had been some time since she'd done burr holes. Usually, in the hospital, a neurosurgeon would be on hand to do it, but at least she had done it before. She took a deep breath, made an incision and then made her first hole.

She repeated the process a couple more times. The last hole was created, and the man groaned.

Which was a good sign.

The paramedics came rushing over.

"Patient was pulled from the water. Unconscious with a Glasgow Coma Scale of three. Cranial pressure was building so I made four burr holes to relieve the pressure. If you have mannitol, I suggest dosing him with that before you airlift him to St. John's. There is an open wound to the base of the skull, so add in some antibiotics. I don't know how long he was in the water."

The paramedic nodded. "Thank you, Doctor."

Jo stepped back as the paramedics secured the patient to a backboard and inserted an IV. She cleaned off the drill and handed it back to the ranger.

"Thank you," Josephine said, "for the steady hands."

"Thank you, Dr. York," the ranger said. "We're so glad you were visiting today."

Jo turned to see Henrik wrapped in a blanket and the girl being loaded onto a gurney. She was coughing still, but she was alive. Jo made her way over to Henrik, who was shivering.

"We need to get you warm," Jo said, gently.

"I would like that."

"I think we'll reserve the rooms for another night and go back to Fogo tomorrow. I'll make the calls, and I'll drive us back."

Henrik nodded and scooped up his clothes. "I just need a couple hours to get warm."

"I think we've had enough excitement for today. We'll go back, have some warm soup for lunch and relax. Besides, the RCMP will be coming by to see us for a report, I'm sure."

She would drive to Farewell herself, but she was feeling pretty tired. This was not how she'd pictured her morning going.

Back at the motel, the only room left was the honeymoon suite, but she didn't care. Henrik needed to have a hot shower and curl up in bed.

She could handle one night with him in the same room.

She was positive.

Henrik was still shivering. He had worn jeans and couldn't pull them back on wet, and he had lost his shirt out in the water. Like he had been taught when he'd first started learning about sea rescues, you took your shirt for a drowning victim to grasp at a bit of distance, instead of them scratching or punching you or pulling you underwater in panic.

It might seem foolish to take off clothes and run into a bitterly cold ocean, but his jeans and jacket would've weighed him down.

When they got back to the motel, he was taken aback when Jo told him there was only one room left. He would have argued, but he was just too cold, and he needed to get warm again.

He just followed her into the room and when she flicked on the lights, he rolled his eyes at the gaudy, Viking-themed honeymoon suite they had been landed with for the night. Including the heart-shaped bed and Jacuzzi in the corner.

"Oh, dear," she said, her voice laced with trepidation. "I had no idea."

"It's a warm, clean room," he said. "It's what we need."

"Right." She shut the door. "I'll go to the front desk and ask for more blankets. You have a warm shower, and I'll be right back."

Henrik nodded as he made his way to the bathroom.

He wanted to wash the ocean off him.

More like he wanted to scrub it away. It was a battle every time, but it was one he willingly faced to save lives.

Still, washing it off him was a way to put his worries behind him for that particular day.

Rescuing someone from the ocean was common for him during tourist season and with his training. When his instinct to save lives kicked in, he could drown out that fear, the anger at the ocean for taking away his parents. He could lock away the trauma he felt and just get the job done.

A way to conquer his fear head-on.

So when he'd found that girl floating in the water, he'd done his work. Wrapped his shirt around her and brought her to shore. He'd ignored the sharp, numbing pain of the frigid water.

All that mattered was saving the life.

Adrenaline kicked in to help bring her back to shore and pump the water out of her lungs. He'd felt a smug satisfaction of winning when she'd coughed up the water and gasped for breath. After she was okay, that's when he'd realized that he had become hypothermic, and all that stuff he usually locked away came rushing back.

He wasn't even sure who'd wrapped the blanket around him, because after the paramedics came to assist him and he had the blanket, he took a look at Jo. He saw the drill and he knew what she was doing on that beach.

And he was amazed by it all.

Amazed at her skill and ability and calm confidence.

She was beautiful, smart and kind. She was basically everything that he'd always dreamed of when it came to getting married and starting a family. It was what he thought he'd had when he was in love with Melissa, but that was a long time ago now.

He'd changed.

Have you?

Henrik turned off the shower and wrapped himself up in a towel. He crept out of the bathroom and as much as he wanted to put his clothes on, he was still shivering and suffering from some effects of hypothermia.

Clothes wouldn't help.

He clambered into the bed and pulled up the blanket. Jo entered the hotel room, and he was glad to see she had extra blankets with her.

"The soup is being brought to us," she told him.

"Great."

Jo spread out the blankets for him and leaned over. He caught the scent of her hair. She glanced at him.

"You're grinning, but your lips are still kind of blue."

"You know what the best way to heat up someone is?" He waggled his eyebrows, which made her chuckle.

"I will climb into bed with you, but I'm keeping my clothes on."

"It's a heart-shaped bed," he teased.

"It was the only room available," she said dryly as she slid in next to him, grabbing the remote from the nightstand.

"You're going to watch television?"

"Yes. I didn't bring a book, and I don't have my crochet, so we're going to veg and watch some mystery shows."

"Mystery?"

"Yes." She scrolled through the channels. "I know a

certain show is on at this time—reruns—but they're fun. It's a historical detective series. He's quirky and smart."

She found the show that she wanted to watch, and he lay back as she snuggled against him. He had no real interest in the show that was on, but he was happy to be here, with her in bed with him.

"I'd heat up even faster if you were naked," he murmured, as he playfully ran his thumb in a circle on her shoulder.

Jo sat up and glared at him, with a smile tugging at the corner of her lips. "I'm not getting naked."

He chuckled. "Shame."

"If we were in the wilderness, then, yes, I would, but we're in a warm room. You've had a hot shower and there are blankets. You'll be fine"

"I'm naked."

Jo snorted. "What?"

"I was only following basic safety protocols in situations like this."

She laughed. "It's a good thing I trust you."

It warmed his heart. "You do?"

"Of course." She smiled gently. "I can't think of why at this moment, though…"

Then she sighed, pulling off her damp jeans but leaving her oversize sweater on. He let his gaze drift over her shapely long legs, and his blood heated.

Jo snuggled up against him. "Hmm, you are still cold."

"See? I told you."

She leaned her head against his shoulder, and he drank in the scent of her, reveling in this moment of her tucked up against him. It felt right.

There was a knock at the door. She got up and hastily pulled on a pair of sweatpants before she answered it, taking the bag from a waiter who'd delivered their lunch from Thor's Place. She tipped the man and shut the door.

"Soup," she announced.

"Soup in a bag?" he teased, but he really didn't want soup. He'd rather she came back to bed instead, but this was less tempting and therefore better in the long run, he supposed.

"They're in cups with lids."

"What kind?" he asked, propping himself up on his elbow.

"Clam chowder for you. Not for me, though. I just got plain chicken noodle and some crackers." Josephine set down the bag at the little dinette table that was in the room.

"Toss me my overnight bag, and I'll get dressed," he said.

She grabbed his bag and threw it to him before turning her back to him. Henrik pulled on his clothes and made his way over to the table.

"Feeling warmer?" Jo asked.

"Much. All kidding aside, thanks for helping me back there."

"Anytime. You were amazing diving in and saving that girl." She handed him a spoon.

"You were awesome with that girl's father. Was it my eyes playing tricks, or were you actually doing brain surgery on that beach?"

"Burr holes. Hardly brain surgery."

"Burr holes is neurosurgery. That's impressive."

"It's not like I was clipping an aneurysm or something," she said.

"You took a drill and put holes in a man's head. On a beach. I think that's something worth celebrating. It probably saved his life."

Jo blushed, that pink tingeing her beautiful cheeks. "I'm sorry we're here for another night."

"I'm sorry too, but thank you again for taking care of me and getting the room sorted."

"You're welcome."

After their soup they sat back on the bed and watched television. Not saying anything. Jo curled up next to him and fell asleep on his arm so it was pinned down, but he didn't mind at all.

He should mind. This was not somewhere he thought he'd be again, feeling vulnerable and cozy with a woman, but it felt so right. It felt good and easy with Jo. And he couldn't recall feeling like this with Melissa.

Ever.

What was so different about Jo?

Whatever it was, he didn't care in this moment, but he was worried for his heart when she finally left him.

He was worried about the inevitable and how much it would sting.

CHAPTER ELEVEN

IT HAD BEEN two weeks since Henrik had taken Jo to L'Anse aux Meadows, and she hadn't seen much of him since they got back to Nubbin's Harbor. The trip back to catch the ferry had been quiet. He hadn't said much, and she hadn't known how to draw him into a conversation.

She was feeling a bit awkward about their night together.

She was worried that she'd done something or that he was bothered by the fact that she'd woken up plastered to his chest.

It was embarrassing.

She'd apologized for hogging the bed and snuggling with him all night.

If she'd been aware of it, she wouldn't have done it. She was mad at herself for letting her guard down with him and sleeping so soundly practically on top of him. Henrik was her friend, not her lover.

It wouldn't take much to make him your lover, though.

Jo ignored that voice and just tried to focus on her work, which wasn't difficult to do. Or so she thought, because as hard as she tried, all she thought about was him. Something would remind her of the way he smiled, or she could almost feel the touch of his skin.

Throughout the day she would think of funny things and couldn't wait to tell him. Except, he wasn't there to talk to.

She missed him.

When they were apart, she worried so much about her feelings for him, but when she was with him, she didn't let those little anxieties creep in.

It just felt so right.

"You seem distracted," Jennifer said, interrupting her thoughts.

"What?"

Jennifer grinned, knowingly. "I'm heading for lunch. Marge called, and she's on her way."

Jo nodded. "Oh, good."

"Want me to bring you a sandwich?" Jennifer asked.

"Sure, that would be great. Thanks, Jenn."

The receptionist waved and left.

The bell over the door chimed, and Marge came in carrying a car seat with baby Jo and looking a little bit flustered.

"Hi, Dr. York," Marge said, brightly and a bit out of breath. "Sorry I'm late. I got stopped by Lloyd, and he can chatter something fierce."

"No worries," Jo said. "What's up with Lloyd?"

"Oh. Nothing," Marge said nervously, flushing. She wasn't looking her in the eye.

"What?" Jo pressed.

"Lloyd is such a gossip," Marge stated, as she followed Jo into an exam room.

"So I've heard," Jo answered dryly, as Marge lifted baby Jo out of her carrier and handed her over. Jo cradled her little namesake happily.

"Lloyd says you and Henrik are an item!" Marge blurted out.

Jo's heart skipped a beat, and she tried to keep a straight face. "What?"

Marge chuckled. "I know. Lloyd sometimes sees things that aren't always there."

"What is he seeing?" Jo wondered out loud.

"Just that you're spending a lot of time with Henrik."

"We're friends, and we work together."

"I know that."

"So why is Lloyd speculating?" Jo asked, rocking little Jo back and forth.

"No one spends time with Henrik. He's kind of a loner... Been that way since his parents died. And then when his fiancée left him."

"Melissa?" Josephine said, cursing herself for continuing this thread of discussion.

"Yes. He was crushed when she left him. We all thought Melissa would cure his grief of losing his parents, but she only made it worse, and he retreated into himself. But it's like he's been a different person lately."

"Jenn calls him a rake," Jo murmured.

Marge chuckled. "Perhaps. I can see that."

Jo's pulse was thundering in her ears, and she was sure that she was breaking out in a sweat. She didn't want to hurt him, and she didn't want to lead him on. He didn't want to leave the island. Henrik had made that perfectly clear to her, but when Gary came back from Munich, she had to go back to Toronto. Fogo Island Hospital was much too small. They didn't have openings for a trauma surgeon, and with a baby on the way there was no time for her to set up her own practice.

Why?

Jo ignored that annoying, pushy voice in her head again.

"Well—" she cleared her throat "—we're friends."

"That's good. I'm glad Henrik has a friend, and you as well, Dr. York." Marge grinned.

"Well, let's check on this little gal, shall we?" Jo said brightly, even though her gut was churning and it felt like a big knot was trying to escape from there.

Maybe Henrik was keeping his distance because he'd heard the gossip about them too.

Jo finished her exam of baby Jo and sent Marge on her way.

As Marge was leaving, Henrik entered the clinic and Jo gripped the counter, hoping that Marge didn't say anything. His coming into the clinic was just a coincidence.

"Hey, Henrik," Marge said, walking quickly past him.

"See you, Marge." Henrik turned back to her. "Hey, Jo."

"Hey, yourself. Are you my next appointment?" she asked, fumbling to pull up her appointments on her phone.

"Yep. Need a tetanus booster." Henrik held up his hand, which was bandaged.

"What happened?" Jo asked anxiously.

"I was working on my house and caught my hand on a rusty nail."

She winced, and her stomach turned slightly, which was odd. She'd seen worse stuff working in the trauma center in Toronto. "That sounds nasty."

"It didn't feel good, let me tell you," Henrik said with a grimace.

"Well, come on in, and I'll take a look at it."

"I just need the shot," he said.

Jo crossed her arms. "I'm sure, but I'm going to examine it, nonetheless."

He followed her into an exam room. She got out the tetanus vaccine as Henrik removed the bandage.

Jo leaned over to inspect it and began to sweat, but ignored it. "You did a good job of cleaning it up."

"Well, I do have some experience with wounds." He grinned and winked.

She smiled at him and did a little more cleaning, replacing the bandage and trying to ignore the churning of her stomach.

"You have a light touch," he remarked.

Her cheeks flushed with heat. "Careful how you compliment me."

Henrik cocked an eyebrow. "What do you mean?"

"The town is talking…or rather, Lloyd is talking to everyone."

"Oh, aye?" he asked, carefully.

"He's been telling everyone we're an item, and I'm sure he's been talking about our weekend away."

She prepared the needle as Henrik rolled up the sleeve of his shirt. She wiped his arm with alcohol.

"Are you serious?" he said.

"About the needle or the gossip?" she teased.

"The gossip."

"I'm afraid so." She gave him the shot and applied pressure against his arm with the cotton ball. "Apply pressure."

Henrik took over, their fingers brushing as she removed her hand. He was frowning, and she didn't blame him. The whole thing was making her upset. All she wanted to do was lie down.

"Well, I suppose people will really start speculating about it when you begin to show, so we won't have peace for much longer," he groused.

"I'm aware," she said, dryly.

She disposed of the used needle and bandages. As she put other items away, her stomach turned again and her head felt weird. She gripped the edge of the counter as the world around her started to sway.

"Jo?"

"Hm?" she asked, but she couldn't turn around to face him. She wanted to throw up, and her head was becoming clouded. She heard him move toward her, the paper on the exam table crinkling as he got up. His hands were on her shoulder, steadying her, only it didn't seem to work as the room tilted.

A sudden wave of dizziness was overtaking her. She

tried to tell him that she was going to faint but couldn't form the words. Her pulse was thundering between her ears.

"Jo?"

She let go of the counter, slipping into blackness.

Henrik called for the ambulance because after he'd caught her and safely laid her on the floor, he'd had a hard time bringing her out of her faint. It was terrifying him.

"Jo, come on," he said, loudly as he cradled her. "Come on, sweetheart."

"Where you at, b'y?" Lloyd called out.

Henrik groaned inwardly. "In the back. Jo's fainted. Is the ambulance here?"

Lloyd came rushing back with a first-aid kit and knelt down. "Aye. Hal and Johanna are unloading the gurney. Why did she faint?"

"I don't know."

Henrik didn't know for certain, and he was worried about all sorts of things at the moment. He'd dealt with others fainting, but never someone he really cared about. The impact of it hit him like a ton of bricks.

Try as he might, he was falling for Dr. Josephine York, and he was angry at himself.

And now they were the talk of Nubbin's Harbor, apparently.

Still, when she fainted and wouldn't rouse, he worried. What if something was wrong with the baby? Fate seemed determined to take away his family whenever he left his guard down.

First his parents, his grandad, Melissa and then his beloved gran. He couldn't lose the baby as well. It would be too much for one heart to bear.

Johanna and Hal came into the room. Jo was moaning, but then her eyes would roll into the back of her head, and she'd faint again. It could be anything from low blood sugar to internal bleeding.

"What happened?" Johanna asked, as she helped Hal and Henrik get the doctor onto the gurney.

"She fainted five minutes ago. She can't seem to stay conscious," Henrik stated. "She'll need fluids."

"Aye, she could be dehydrated," Lloyd speculated. "She's been sick with that stomach flu, I suspect."

Henrik shook his head. "It's not the flu."

"How can you be sure?" Lloyd asked. "It's been going around the harbor for nigh on a month now."

"I'm certain." Henrik took a deep breath. Jo would probably clobber him, but Hal and Johanna needed to know so they could inform the doctors at the hospital about her condition. And honestly, it was only a matter of time before the whole of Nubbin's Harbor knew it all anyway.

She was here for ten more months. The baby would arrive before she left, and people would put two and two together.

"She's pregnant," Henrik stated.

"And how would you be knowing that?" Lloyd asked.

"Because I'm the father."

"Lord almighty," Lloyd exclaimed. "Well, let's get her to the hospital."

"I'll follow in my truck." Henrik wanted to go with her in the ambulance, but he knew once Jo was discharged she'd need a ride home and someone to take care of her, and that person was going to be him.

Hal nodded. "We'll see you there."

Lloyd still looked shocked as he left the clinic and started dispersing the small crowd that had gathered around outside.

Henrik made sure Jo was safely loaded. Jenn the receptionist had just arrived, and he let her know what was going on so she could send all urgent patients to Joe Batt's Arm.

After everything was settled, he got into his truck.

He was driving so fast he was hoping there weren't any RCMP on the road to give him a ticket for speeding. All he could think about was getting to her and making sure she was all right.

By the time he'd parked and made his way into the hospital, he found Jo conscious in an ER bed. She still looked pale and had an intravenous. At least she was alert now.

"Henrik?" she asked, as she poked his head around the curtain.

"Hey, I got here as fast as I could," he said.

"What happened? The last thing I remember is getting your tetanus shot ready. Oh, no, I didn't faint during the vaccination, did I?"

"No. I got it, and then you fainted," Henrik said, gently.

"And you called an ambulance?" Jo asked, stunned.

"You wouldn't rally. You were unconscious for a while. I was worried."

She groaned. "Oh. Now I remember feeling off."

He pulled up a chair and sat down beside her, taking her hand in his. "What has the doctor said? Is the baby okay?"

"The baby is fine," Josephine said with a tiny smile. "They're running tests."

Relief washed through him. "I'm glad. You scared me."

"Yeah, they knew I was…" Jo's eyes widened as she realized that he'd told the paramedics. "Oh, no."

"I had to tell Hal, Johanna…and Lloyd."

She groaned again. "So I guess the cat is out of the bag for good now."

"I'm afraid so. I just wanted to make sure that you and the baby were safe."

"I get it." Jo sighed. "I don't know what happened."

"You fainted, or have you forgotten?" he teased.

"I know that. It just came out of the blue."

"Dr. York?"

Henrik turned as the emergency-room doctor, Dr. Cranbook, peeked his head around the curtain.

"Dr. Cranbook," Henrik greeted him, standing up.

"Mr. Nielsen," Dr. Cranbook said, surprised.

"He's the baby's father," Jo offered. "You can tell him anything."

Dr. Cranbook nodded. "Well, we ran your blood work, and you had a drop in blood sugar. I'm going to order a requisition to test you for a fasting glucose test tomorrow so we can test for gestational diabetes."

"Okay, but the baby is all right?" Henrik asked, needing to hear it from another doctor who was not the mother.

"Yes," Dr. Cranbook said. "The heartbeat is strong, but I would like you to rest for a couple of days, at the very least, until your results for the glucose test come in."

"I can do that," Jo said.

"I'll get to work on your discharge." Dr. Cranbook left.

Jo sighed again. "I'm going to have to make sure the doctor in Joe Batt's Arm can handle my patients. So now they'll all know."

Henrik rubbed her shoulder. "Lloyd will have already told them."

She chuckled. "So then, all of Fogo knows by now."

"Yes, b'y." Henrik grinned. "As soon as you're discharged I'll take you home and look after you. I'm off work because of my hand."

"You don't have to take—"

"I do," he said, firmly cutting her off. "I don't want you fainting and being alone. So until we're sure you're going to be okay, I'll be your roommate."

"I guess I can't really argue with that."

"No. You can't."

"I'm sorry the whole town knows this soon," Jo said. "That was not my intention."

"I know. It's fine. Let's just focus on you getting stabilized."

"Thank you," Jo said, softly.

"It's the least I could do for you since you took such good care of me when I nearly succumbed to hypothermia."

She smiled at his exaggeration. "I'm a doctor. It's my job."

"And I'm a paramedic. It's also my job."

She grinned, her eyes sparkling. "I guess we have no choice, then."

It was another hour before Jo was discharged. Henrik pulled his truck to the front entrance of the hospital, and once she was loaded in, drove her straight back to her apartment over the clinic.

"I guess I get to see your place," he said.

"You mean Gary's place." She flicked on the light, and he followed her in. There was nothing cozy about it. It was white, modern and minimalistic. The furniture was sparse and didn't look comfortable at all. It just didn't seem like Jo belonged there. When he first met her, he would've pictured her as a modernist; now, not so much.

The couch was white leather and narrow. He was already regretting his decision. That couch would be like sleeping on rocks. Actually, rocks would probably be more comfortable.

Jo curled up on the couch, tucking her feet under her and hugging a white shaggy pillow that looked like a puppet had been murdered.

"I'm going to grab my stuff. I'll be back. You okay?" he asked.

"I'm fine. Really, you don't need to stay with me."

"Are you trying to get rid of me?" he asked.

"No. I wouldn't mind the company, but this couch sucks."

He chuckled. "I'm staying."

"You don't need—"

"Yes. I do. I won't take no for answer," he said, firmly.

"Fine." She threw up her hands. "No more argument from me."

She leaned back, her face pale. Henrik's heart skipped a beat, and he sat down next to her.

"I thought you were going to get your stuff?" she asked.

"Later," he said, softly. "I think you need to go to bed."

"I'm not that tired."

Henrik shook his head. "You're going to bed."

He helped her up and led her to the large king bed that was covered with quilts and got her settled. He sat next to her.

"Is there anything I can get for you?"

"No. Maybe just keep me company for a bit."

"Of course. What should we talk about? Maybe you can tell me what Marge said about me, or Jenn for that matter!"

Her eyes widened. "Who said Marge said anything about you?"

"I figure she's the one who told you about Lloyd."

Jo laughed. "All she said was that you're a loner."

"It's easier that way."

"I understand."

"And what did Jenn say?" he asked.

Jo smiled. "She called you a rake."

He chuckled. "Hardly."

"I agree. More of a rogue than a rake."

Their gazes met, and his heart skipped a beat as he looked into her eyes. What was happening to him? His loneliness had never bothered him before, but when he'd kept his distance from her since they returned from L'Anse aux Meadows, he had missed her so much.

He was lonely.

"What do your parents think of you moving here to Newfoundland...even for just a short time?" he asked.

"They think I should move to Arizona."

Henrik smiled wryly. "I'm sure it's warmer in the winter."

"Tell me about your parents," she said, softly.

"They were wonderful, loving. We had happiness and laughter."

"I'm sorry you lost them."

"I'm sorry you lost your husband," he said quietly.

Josephine squeezed his hand. "I think I'll try to sleep."

"Okay. I'll go and get my things. You rest."

Jo nodded and rolled over. Henrik slipped out of her apartment. He knew he really shouldn't stay with her. It was too much temptation.

The trouble was, he wanted to.

The problem was, he was falling for her.

Jo still felt exhausted, but she couldn't sleep. The apartment was silent, and she could hear the waves rolling outside her open window. Usually that sound calmed her, but she was on edge because Henrik was sleeping on the couch.

She could hear him tossing and turning and she knew that couch wasn't very comfortable.

She got up and made her way into the living room.

"Jo?" Henrik asked, sitting up.

"You can't sleep on the couch," she stated.

"Neither can you, if you're thinking of switching."

She crossed her arms. "We shared a bed at that motel."

"Yes. I remember. The heart-shaped one."

Jo chuckled. "It was smaller than my bed here. I think we can share for a couple of nights."

"I would argue, but Gary's couch is ridiculously awful."

"I know." She turned back and climbed into bed.

Henrik came into the room, stepping into a pool of moonlight. He was only wearing a pair of athletic shorts, and the shadows and moonlight illuminated the broad expanse of his bare chest.

Her blood heated, and she tried not to stare at him. He pulled back the covers and slid next to her.

"This is better," he murmured, closing his eyes.

He was so warm, and she liked being snuggled up against him with his arm around her. She just wanted to be held, and it was hard to sleep knowing he was so close. So instead she watched him.

Then he opened one eye and stared at her. "You're watching me. Why?"

"I can't sleep."

Which was true. What she didn't tell him was that she couldn't sleep because she was aroused by him.

That she wanted him.

"Try," he said, closing his eyes again.

"Sorry, I'm wide awake," she said.

Henrik rolled over and propped himself up on one elbow. "Would you like a bedtime story?"

"Only if it's a spooky one," she teased.

"This isn't a glorified slumber party," he muttered.

"Oh, come on. You're telling me there are no ghost stories about Fogo, or even Newfoundland for that matter?"

He scrubbed a hand over his face. "Oh, me nerves! Ye got me drove! Fine. I can tell you about the forlorn widow who walks the beach howling."

She grinned. "That sounds creepy."

"Aye, it is."

"I'm all ears."

His eyes twinkled in the dark. "You sound way too excited for this. Somehow, I don't think it will put you to sleep."

"Just tell it," Jo said, curling up on her side, watching him in the moonlight.

"Fine. Well, there's this beautiful widow, right?"

"Right."

"And she's dead," Henrik said with emphasis.

"Okay."

"And she walks along the beach. She's howling," he whispered in her ear, sending a shiver of delight through her.

"And?"

"And what? She walks along the beach howling. Now, go to sleep."

He rolled over on his side.

"That sucked," Jo huffed.

Henrik was laughing silently. "You asked for a story. I didn't say I was any good at storytelling."

"Well, that's a disappointment. I guess I'm going to have to tell the stories to our kid."

"You're not telling our kid ghost stories at night," Henrik said, flatly.

"No, but I'm a better storyteller than you. If they asked you for a fairy tale you'd be like, *There's a giant and a knight with a sword. And they're dead. The end.*"

Henrik chuckled. "Yeah, it's probably for the best that you tell the stories."

Jo sighed. "This is not how I pictured my life."

"Well, at least you're not walking along the beach howling," he said jokingly.

She grabbed a pillow and whacked him with it before jamming it back behind her head. "You know what I mean."

"Yes, I do. This is not how I pictured my life either."

"And how did you picture it? I mean, when you were young and innocent."

Henrik sighed in the darkness. "I thought I'd be a fisherman, if I'm honest. Have a wife and kids by now."

"Why aren't you a fisherman?"

"Because of the moratorium on cod fishing."

"You could harvest sea cucumbers!"

"I suppose, but after the sea took my parents, I just…

I wanted to help others. I wanted to save lives. And what about you? How did you picture your life before, when you were young and undamaged?"

"I wanted to be a doctor for as long as I can remember. I thought by now I would have kids and own a nice house… next to my late grandparents because I loved that area of Toronto, but now…"

"Now?" he asked, gently.

She didn't know.

Jo hadn't been here long, but Fogo was starting to feel like home. The way that Goderich used to feel and the way that Toronto had never seemed to.

Henrik was starting to feel like home.

"I guess I could move out to the suburbs to raise a family now, instead of a place in the city." It wasn't a lie, but it was a deflection. She didn't want to give him false hope when she was uncertain what tomorrow would hold.

CHAPTER TWELVE

JO WAS CLEARED to go back to work when her glucose-tolerance test came back clear. She didn't have gestational diabetes, but the doctors warned her to take it easy. She'd had a simple spell of syncope. It was, hopefully, a one-off. Her obstetrician also wanted her to rest and make sure she ate regularly.

Henrik was taking the doctor's words to heart. He hadn't moved out of her place and brought her lunch almost every day. Even though it was okay for him to go back home, she was finding herself not wanting him to leave.

She liked the company.

When David had died, she didn't want anyone around. She just wanted to be alone.

She'd thought it was better.

Like she could still feel his presence if it was just her there. It was foolish to think, but it got her through some lonely moments. She'd forgotten how it was not to be alone.

She had missed companionship.

Friendship.

Before, she'd been worried about what the town thought, but now everyone knew she was expecting and Henrik was the father, so it didn't matter anymore, and it didn't seem to bother Henrik at all.

They just settled into this pattern of living together for the last few days, and it was nice. They'd get up and go to work, and at night they'd share dinner and talk about their day.

It was so comfortable and easy, and she looked forward to it every day.

The more time she spent with Henrik, the more she wanted him again.

And not just as her friend.

The more they laughed and talked, the more she remembered their night of passion. She craved his touch, his kisses, but he had made it clear he didn't want a relationship, and she wouldn't push him.

"Well, I think it's great!" Lloyd said, interrupting her out of her thoughts, and she continued checking over a bump he had gotten on the head during a boisterous shed party with some tourists.

"The bump?" Jo teased.

"You and Henrik and the baby!" Lloyd exclaimed.

"Oh, that." Jo cleaned up the wound and bandaged it.

"Melissa was never good for him. Even his gran said so. That girl wanted to explore the world, and so she did. So I'm glad he has you, especially now that she's back."

Jo's breath caught in her throat. She wasn't exactly sure that she had Henrik. "She's back?"

"Aye. To visit her grandparents. She said she's thinking of moving back. It's good when the kids of Fogo eventually find their way home."

"I'm sure it is." Jo didn't know what else to say.

She knew Henrik had loved Melissa. If she was back, Jo wouldn't get in their way. Still, that green-eyed monster of jealousy rose up in her.

Melissa had left Henrik. Why was she back to stay? Jo was worried her return would interrupt Henrik's and her happy little existence.

She grew frustrated with herself for feeling that pettiness again.

She had no right to feel this way. Henrik wasn't hers. They weren't in a relationship. There were no promises between them.

Just a baby.

And, if the situations were reversed and David somehow could come back, she'd be with him. The only difference was that David was dead and Melissa was alive. If Henrik wanted a life with Melissa, she couldn't interfere. Even though she was doing what she'd said she never would do, and that was falling for Henrik.

"There's a terrible storm coming," Lloyd said, changing the subject. "It's out of season. Be sure to have your groceries and emergency supplies tucked away."

"Thanks for the tip. You're all done, Lloyd."

"Ta." He got up. "I'm off to prepare."

"Remember to take it easy," Jo warned, but she seriously doubted he would listen to her.

Jo walked Lloyd out to lock the door, as he was the last patient.

Henrik snuck in, in his paramedic's uniform. He was frowning, and she wondered if he had seen Melissa.

"Do you have emergency supplies?" he asked.

"You're the second person to mention that," Jo said.

"Well, there's a bad storm moving up the eastern seaboard."

"I'll have to see what I have."

"I'll take you shopping. I'll be on duty when it hits," Henrik said, firmly. "Grab your purse, and we'll go stock up."

There was no point in arguing. She had sent Jenn home early because the school had called her to come get her daughter Missy ahead of the storm. Jo had never been in a storm that warranted emergency supplies. She'd never been in a hurricane or any kind of ocean-based storm. The worst had been the odd snowstorm. The best thing to do was listen to Henrik, and if he wanted to take her for supplies, she would gladly follow.

"What should I be getting?" she asked.

"Water, canned goods, storm chips."

"Storm chips?" Jo asked.

He grinned. "Just tradition, but everyone gets some chips to pass the time. I'll show you. Does Gary have candles?"

"Yes."

"Good. The power will probably go out."

Jo climbed up into his truck, and they drove off.

"Do you have supplies?" Jo asked.

"I do. Not that I will need them, being on duty. Hopefully the storm will just sideswipe us."

"Lloyd said it's not usual for this kind of storm at this time of year."

"He's right. I'm hoping for a quiet weekend."

"Oh, no. Don't say that," she said, feeling dread rise within her.

"Why?" he asked, perplexed.

"Superstition in the emergency room. It's like, as an ER doctor or nurse or other frontline worker, you never walk through the main emergency doors to start your shift. Everything will go completely wrong."

"Seriously?" Henrik asked.

"Have you never heard this?" she asked.

"No. Of course, I never did talk to the ER doctors, besides giving information about the patients. I never realized you were all so neurotic."

Jo laughed as Henrik winked. They pulled up in front of the co-op. It was busy, but not as bad as Jo thought it might be given the situation.

She grabbed a cart, and they headed inside.

"I'll get you bottled water and some batteries for your flashlight," Henrik stated.

"Okay," she agreed.

"Henrik?" a female voice behind them called out.

Jo didn't need to turn around to know it was Melissa because the look on Henrik's face said it all. His eyes were wide, and he looked like he was in shock.

Another pang of jealousy stabbed her. She turned and got her first good look at the woman who had broken Henrik's heart all those years ago.

Melissa had strawberry-blond hair and green eyes with a spattering of freckles across her nose. She was also younger than her.

She was very beautiful, and Jo could see why Henrik had been in love with her.

"Melissa, what're you doing here?" he asked.

"Thinking about moving back." Melissa's eyes darted between Jo and Henrik.

"This is Dr. Josephine York," Henrik replied, stiffly.

"It's a pleasure to meet you," Jo said. "I think I'll just go round and get the rest of my supplies. Excuse me."

She walked away from Henrik and his ex. He needed space to talk to Melissa, and she couldn't blame him.

"It's great to see you," Melissa said.

At least that's what he thought she said. He was still having a hard time believing that she was there. "It's good to see you too. It's been a while."

"It has."

He didn't know what else to say.

Truth be told, he was angry that she was back.

"You completed your training as a paramedic, then," she said, looking appreciatively at him in his uniform.

"I did, and I'm just about to go on shift, so I'd better go."

"Henrik, can we have a coffee sometime?" Melissa asked.

"Why?" he asked stiffly.

"To catch up?" she offered.

"We'll see. I'll see you around."

Henrik stormed off and found Jo getting ready to check out. When he saw her, instantly his anger melted away, and he saw that she had chips in her cart. She looked over at him and smiled, that sweet smile he already adored.

Of course, Melissa had smiled at him sweetly too, and he'd been thoroughly duped by her back then.

Don't let Melissa ruin this for you.

"You got your storm chips?" he asked, trying to calm himself down.

"I did. You okay?" she asked with concern. "Your face is like thunder. Very cloudy, very tense."

"I do feel a bit tense, but I'm okay. I just want to get you home before this storm hits."

"Hopefully it'll blow over," Jo said.

He knew she wanted to ask him about Melissa, but he didn't want to talk about it, and he appreciated that she didn't pry. That's what he liked about Jo. She didn't push him to open up. Although, she was the one person he'd confided in the most.

Seeing Melissa had annoyed him, but it didn't hurt the way it had when she'd left or the way that he'd thought it would if she ever came back.

Right now, he was just confused. All he wanted to do was focus on work and forget that Melissa was back in Nubbin's Harbor.

He didn't want to talk to her or about her.

After Josephine paid for her supplies, he dropped her off at her apartment, carrying up her water and making sure she was settled as the dark storm clouds could be seen over the ocean.

"How long are you on duty for?" Jo asked, staring out the windows toward the sea.

"Forty-eight hours straight," Henrik said. "I have to

make up for that hand injury. Just in time for the storm, apparently."

"If you need help, please come get me, or let me know where to go. I'm willing to pitch in."

"You need to rest," Henrik said, firmly.

"I'm fine. I've been resting, but if there's an emergency situation… I'm a trauma surgeon, after all. I mean, I was pregnant when I tied that man's artery in the field, and I did burr holes on a beach pregnant."

Henrik smiled. "Yes, I know. I remember."

"If I'm needed, I'm here." She took his large hand in her delicate one. Usually he liked to be touched by her, but he was still bothered by Melissa's return, so he instinctively pulled his hand away.

"I'll keep that in mind. Be safe and rest."

He left the apartment. He was confused and hurt, and he just needed the distraction of work.

Just like he had when Melissa left him all those years ago and like he suspected he'd need to do when Josephine left him too.

The storm hit within twenty-four hours. It was eerily quiet. He and Hal were parked, and he just stared in the direction of the churning ocean, not that he could see much through the rain, but he knew it was there and what it looked like.

It was a cyclone. It had been a hurricane farther south, but by the time it got here it was downgraded to a cyclone, but it was strong, nonetheless.

He hadn't seen a storm like this since his parents had died. Henrik just continued to stare out the window, with the rolling waves and the wind howling and the rain coming at him sideways.

Hal had been out getting them a coffee and jumped into the passenger seat, drenched.

"It's a doozy out there, my b'y," Hal stated, handing Henrik his coffee.

"It is indeed." Henrik gripped the coffee cup and took a sip, not really tasting it, because it wasn't just the storm that was eating away at him, and neither was it Melissa. He was mad at himself for pulling his hand away from Jo's like he had, especially when she was just offering comfort.

What was he so scared of?

She understood him like no one had ever done before.

He was just so terrified of getting hurt again because if Josephine left him too, he knew it would hurt him so much more.

It would shatter his already-badly damaged heart.

The radio crackled.

"Capsized wharf in Tilting. Mass casualties. All medical personnel able to attend are requested."

Henrik set his coffee cup down and flipped on the lights and sirens. They made their way to Tilting. Henrik had seen collapsed wharves during storms, but he had a feeling this was the hotel that was built on the wharf.

He was unfortunately right, but he was not expecting to also see homes that were being washed into the ocean by hungry, angry waves.

"My God," Hal whispered in horror.

"We need Josephine and any other person with first-aid experience," Henrik said, thinking about all the casualties.

"I'll get on the horn and call in all the volunteers I can," Hal said, texting.

All Henrik could think about as he stared at the disaster laid out before him was his parents. The storm that took away his family. He couldn't think straight for a moment.

He felt like he was going to crack.

Usually he could hold it all back, but for some reason he was feeling that bite of loss particularly keenly right now.

* * *

Perhaps it was the storm that triggered him.

The one on the outside and the one raging on the inside. A storm that wanted Jo, wanted a life with her, one that wanted to take a chance on them.

One he was trying desperately to hold in because he was terrified.

As he stared down at the destruction, he vowed that everyone would be found.

No one would not know what happened to a loved one or feel the same rage he'd felt all these years.

Jo had never been in a cyclone before. It was terrifying, but when she got the call about the wharf collapsing, she knew she had to be there. So she was downstairs and ready when Lloyd swung by to get her because all emergency personnel had been called to Tilting.

The wind was tossing her around, and her yellow rain jacket's hood was plastered to the side of her face.

Lloyd grabbed the bags of emergency supplies and fastened them into the back of his truck. They didn't say anything on the short ride to Tilting. She wasn't sure what to expect when they got there, but the first thing she saw through the rain was the flashing lights from the ambulances.

Then she saw the destruction. The crumbling rock, the shattered homes and the wild sea.

"Lord have mercy," Lloyd whispered.

"I need the bags taken to that tent. That's obviously the triage area."

Jo got out of the truck. She drowned out the howling of the wind and the cries of the injured and the scared. She had to compartmentalize all of the horror that was going on around her so she could focus on the task at hand.

She could see Henrik in the fray, tending to the wounded

and helping the search-and-rescue teams pull people from the rubble.

Dr. Cranbook was there with a small team from the hospital. He took one look at her and relief washed over his face.

"Dr. York, I'm so glad you're here," he said. "I could use another good trauma surgeon."

"Glad to be here, or rather, glad to be of help."

She went straight to the first patient and got to work checking vital signs and going through her mental check list of the ABCs of trauma. Airway, breathing and consciousness.

There were fractures and lacerations, and then there were people coming in from the sea with water in their lungs.

Exposure patients.

Hypothermia.

The whole gamut.

"Jo," Henrik called, waving at her frantically.

She came over to where he was crouched protectively over a small child he had pulled out of the wreckage.

"I think he might have a collapsed lung. He has a chest-wall injury," Henrik said.

"Let me listen." Jo leaned over, and she heard the air constriction and inspected the wound.

"Well?" Henrik asked.

"We're going to have to place a drain until this boy can get to the hospital, or he won't make it there."

"I'll get what you need," he said, quickly moving to gather supplies.

Jo prepped the area, cutting away the child's shirt. She had to perform a stat tube thoracostomy on a kid. She hated doing it, but it would be the only way he'd survive the trip.

"I have a large-bore needle and an IV catheter," Henrik stated.

"I need an antibiotic," Jo said. "Is there any cefazolin?"

"Here." He handed it to her.

Jo prepped everything. She didn't have to instruct Henrik further as they worked together to get the boy ready for the chest tube. It was like he knew what she was thinking, and it made the whole procedure that much easier.

Jo took the scalpel and made a transverse incision. She inserted the clamp on the pleura, and a rush of air came out, which made her smile in satisfaction. She had found the right spot. She inserted the tube catheter and sutured it into place.

The boy started to breathe easier, and he moaned.

Henrik grinned at her. "Good job, Doc."

"Good job recognizing it. He'll need to be taken right away to the hospital."

"I'll take him." Henrik motioned to Hal, and they loaded the boy into their ambulance.

Jo made her way through the crowds. She looked back to see Henrik smiling anxiously at her, and a rush of pleasure washed through her.

She knew what he was thinking.

"I'll be careful," she shouted. "Go."

It was nice that someone cared about her again.

Henrik nodded and climbed into the back of the ambulance. She watched it leave. The wind was howling, and it was dangerous out there. She hoped Henrik would be okay too.

He'll be fine.

And that little reassuring voice calmed her. She took a deep breath and continued on with her work as the storm raged on, glad to see it was starting to die down.

Jo kept working until all the injured were dealt with. After six hours on her feet she was finally able to go home.

Dr. Cranbook dropped her off on his way through, and

she intended to head straight for her shower and then her bed. She'd worked longer shifts, but this had wiped her out completely, and as she glanced at the clock she realized that it had been thirty hours since Henrik had taken her to get groceries.

She tried to turn on a light, but it when it didn't come on, she remembered that the power went off just before she'd left and hadn't been restored yet. She had her quick shower in the light of a flashlight, then got into her comfiest lounge wear to climb into bed.

Before she could settle, there was a knock at the door.

Jo sighed and made her way there, answering it to see Henrik standing there. He had dark circles under his eyes.

"Henrik?"

"I wanted to make sure you were okay."

"I'm tired, but I'm fine." Jo stepped to the side. "Do you want to come in?"

"Yes, please." He stepped inside, and she closed the door. Instantly she noticed he looked agitated.

"Are you okay?" she asked, gently.

"No." He scrubbed a hand over his face. "A lot has been happening."

"I noticed. Do you want to sit down?"

"No." Henrik paced.

"Okay, you pace. I'll sit." She settled in her chair, watching him closely. "Is it Melissa?"

Henrik stopped. "Partly."

"I can only imagine," she said, softly.

David hadn't chosen to leave her, so her heart had been broken a different way from Henrik's. Then, the more time she'd spent with Henrik, the more she'd discovered it had healed, which made her sad because she felt like she was betraying David. Only, she knew she wasn't.

Even since she'd got pregnant, she'd been feeling this

guilt and fighting feelings for Henrik. Regretful that she
and David had never had this chance, yet at the same time
she was so thrilled to be pregnant, to become a mother.
Henrik didn't know why Melissa had left him, and a
stranger was carrying his child, so it was no wonder he
was struggling too.

Are you two strangers, though?

No, they weren't. They'd become friends. They'd
become close.

You've become more than friends, and you know it.

She considered that carefully. David would want her to
be happy. She knew that absolutely. There was no reason
to feel guilty about Henrik or the baby.

"It was today, or rather when the wharf collapsed, the
storm...all of it." Henrik ran his hand through his hair.

And then she knew. "It was a storm just like this that
killed your parents, wasn't it?"

He nodded. "I've assisted search and rescue before,
countless times and in other storms but...we didn't recover
some of the people today."

"I know."

"The sea took them, and I'm so mad I can hardly speak."

She could see his heart was breaking. She got up and
didn't say a word, just pulled him into an embrace, holding him as tight as she could. At first Henrik was stiff, but
then his arms came around her too.

Holding her. She could feel his heartbeat against her
chest, the warmth of his body, the comfort he offered her,
and she melted against him.

He touched her face, his fingers brushing her skin,
making her body tremble with anticipation.

"I'd very much like to kiss you," he whispered against
her ear.

This time she wouldn't try to stop it. This time she

wanted to feel. She wanted to heal. She wanted this moment with him.

Here and now. Try as she might to resist, she was falling for him.

"I'd very much like you to kiss me now too," she murmured, her heart racing. She'd been fighting this for so long, telling herself she didn't need this and that one night was enough. She hadn't come here for love, but it was finding her, nevertheless.

Henrik smiled, and her pulse thundered in her ears as his lips hovered over hers. Her mouth going dry, her body trembling in anticipation. Her lips remembered his kisses. Her body longed for his.

This is where she wanted to be, in his arms, melting for him.

Vulnerable to him.

She didn't want it to end.

She wanted to savor this moment, to take it with her when she had to go back to Toronto and leave him behind.

You could stay.

She flicked that thought away. Now was not the time to think. Now was the time to feel.

"Jo, I want you so much. It's hard to stop kissing you, touching you."

"So then, don't stop." She kissed him again, nibbling on his lower lip.

The kiss deepened, his tongue melding with hers. His hands ran up her back into her damp hair.

"I need you, Jo," he whispered.

All she wanted was for them to be skin to skin.

Henrik scooped her up in his arms and carried her off to bed. Her body was thrumming with excitement, longing and need. She was still a little afraid but also tired of living alone.

Like a ghost.

Tonight she could feel alive again, even if it was for a short time. Henrik set her down, brushing her cheeks.

"Don't be nervous," he said.

"I'm not."

"You're trembling."

"I know. It's because I want you, Henrik. So much."

He closed the little bit of distance between them and put his arms around her again. She could feel the hardness of his chest.

"I've tried to fight this, but I can't any longer. I've wanted you so badly too." Henrik tipped her chin and kissed her again. She swooned.

"Henrik, please."

"I know."

They moved to the bed. She wanted to feel every part of him again, to remember this moment. Her body craved it and demanded no less. She wanted to bury all the ghosts that haunted her and held her back so she could move on.

His kisses trailed from her mouth down her neck.

"You're wearing far too many clothes," he whispered, huskily, pulling her sweatshirt off.

"So are you," she teased, unbuttoning his shirt, tossing it behind her. She ran her hands over his gorgeous chest. He snatched her hand and kissed her fingertips.

"That's not where I want your kisses," she said, her voice catching in her throat.

"Oh?" he asked, smiling. He kissed lower, cupping her breasts. "And where would you like my lips, then?"

He removed her bra, and then his tongue swirled around her nipples, sending a zing of electricity through her. Henrik knelt in front of her, untying the drawstrings of her pajama bottoms and pushing them down over her hips.

Her nipples hardened as his mouth kissed her hips, the slight swell of her belly.

"Oh, God," she moaned, each press of his lips heating her blood.

Henrik picked her up and laid her down on the bed, removing his pants so she could drink in the sight of him. He leaned over her and slipped his hand under her lace underwear, stroking her and touching her.

Teasing her, making her wet and inciting her to want him all the more.

"Don't torture me," she gasped. "I want you. You know that."

He grinned, and she parted her thighs, eagerly awaiting him. He settled between them, where she could feel the hard swell of his erection at her opening, teasing her, and all she wanted was for him to be inside her.

To claim her.

To be a part of her.

She urged him to enter her, as the head of his shaft slipped into her warmth.

He moaned. "Jo… Oh, God…"

He thrust forward, filling her.

She rocked her hips, wanting him to take her harder.

Faster.

"You're so tight. You feel so good," Henrik murmured against her neck. "So good."

She ran her hands over his shoulders, holding onto him.

Not wanting to let go.

Henrik's hands skimmed her hips, controlling her movements, guiding her to an exquisite release that washed through her body like a cleansing wave. She arched her back, crying out as she came. Henrik soon followed, his thrusts coming faster and shallower until he groaned with the strength of his own release.

Henrik kissed her again tenderly and carefully withdrew.

She curled up against him, not saying anything. She

just listened to the sound of his reassuring heartbeat as he held her.

It calmed her.

He was alive, and for the first time in a long time she felt alive too.

Henrik watched Jo sleep next to him, reveling in the feeling of her soft skin and the fact that she wanted to be with him in that moment when he'd been feeling so out of control and vulnerable.

He didn't like being that way in front of anyone, but he'd felt like maybe he could be with her. He couldn't recall ever feeling comfortable enough to let go with Melissa. That scarred side of him, those memories that were triggered sometimes, no one saw that side of him ever.

He'd kept it locked away, but Jo saw him.

And he saw her.

She was so beautiful.

He had been dreaming of making love to her since the first time they were together.

All during the accident, he'd struggled with emotions from the past, but then he would catch Josephine working.

He would watch her saving lives and healing.

She was an oasis of calm among the chaos and the sea.

When she was with him it felt right. He forgot about everything else.

Including his pain.

His loneliness.

This is what he wanted, even though he was still afraid to reach out and take it.

Even though it was right here in front of him.

There was a knock at the door. Jo stirred, and he rolled over, giving her a kiss on her bare shoulder.

"Stay here, I'll get it." Henrik got up and quickly dressed.

He opened the front door.

"Dr. Linwood... Gary!"

Gary looked surprised. "Henrik!"

Henrik stepped aside as Gary came in.

"I thought you were in Munich," Henrik said.

"I was, but I came back." Gary set down his bag. "Is Jo around?"

"Gary?" Jo was dressed and came out of the bedroom.

"Hi, Jo! Sorry for not calling. It was sort of a last-minute decision, and then you guys had a storm," Gary said.

"It's okay," Jo said.

"Can we talk?" Gary asked.

"Sure." Jo looked at Henrik, and he took that as his cue to leave.

"I'll head out." Henrik got his coat and left, with a knot forming in the pit of his stomach. Why was Gary back so early?

He was supposed to be gone for another ten months. That would have given Henrik time to convince Jo to stay. How would he be able to convince her now? By the looks of it, there was going to be no time left.

For one wild moment, he thought maybe that them being together last night would change her mind, but it was only for a fleeting moment.

Just because they'd made love didn't mean anything. There had been no promises between them. No declarations.

Just their baby.

He wandered around Nubbin's Harbor. The power was still out, and everything was closed. It was quiet and a good time for him to think. He made his way down to the water, picking his way over driftwood and other debris that had washed ashore.

He looked up to see an iceberg slowly making its way by.

It calmed him.

It gave him the clarity he was searching for, like it always did.

As he scanned the shoreline he caught sight of someone else walking among the rocks. It was Melissa.

For so many years he had wanted her back. He'd dreamed about Melissa returning, but then it had never happened, and he'd just grown angry.

Bitter. Cold. Hard.

He'd given up all hope.

Now here she was, and even though he didn't like that she'd hurt him, he also found he didn't really care. And with that came a sense of freedom.

Instead, he was mildly annoyed she was back and wanted to talk to him, to infiltrate his life again. She turned and looked up at him. She was smiling, but it wasn't a warm, beautiful smile like Jo had. It wasn't a smile that made his heart beat faster.

"That was some storm, eh?" she asked.

"Indeed. Is your family okay, then?"

"Yes. Grandad has a generator up and running."

"Good."

"You don't sound so okay yourself. I heard what happened in Tilting. What a tragedy," she said.

"I'm fine. Tired, but fine."

"Are you?" she asked.

"Why did you come back?" Henrik asked abruptly.

"What?" Melissa asked hesitantly.

"You didn't want to be here. You didn't want to live here."

"You're right," Melissa said. "I was young, and I didn't want to be here, but people can change."

"I didn't change," Henrik stated.

Melissa half-smiled. Like she was pitying him. "I know."

Henrik watched as she turned around and walked away. It didn't bother him watching Melissa go. What was eating away at him was that Josephine could leave soon, taking his baby with her.

Would leave.

You can still convince her to stay.

But he couldn't figure out how he was going to do that. There was nothing he could offer her. His heart was too broken. He couldn't open it up again to a killing blow, and so to protect himself he had to let Jo go.

You could go with her.

Only he couldn't do that either. It terrified him to leave. Yet it terrified him to lose Jo and the baby. He hated himself in that moment.

Hated that he was too scared to take the leap.

He loathed himself.

Fogo was in his blood. He'd promised his parents he'd wait.

It was where he was born, and it was where he'd die.

Alone.

CHAPTER THIRTEEN

JO HAD LOTS to process. Gary didn't particularly like his work in Munich and missed Fogo. He wanted to come home. He wasn't permanently back yet. He had just flown in to talk to her face-to-face. He still had to give Munich a month's notice, and then he'd be back to take over his practice.

She had a month left on Fogo Island. That was it. In thirty days she would be returning to Toronto and to her empty house and the crowded city where she felt alone.

You don't have to.

Except that she did.

Gary was taking back his practice. It wasn't hers. There was nothing left for her here.

What about Henrik?

She had just spent a glorious night with Henrik, yes, but that wasn't a basis to stay forever. Their baby was, but she and Henrik had made no promises to each other. She knew Melissa had once meant so much to him and probably still did.

Melissa was his first love.

That she understood.

And she wasn't sure that her heart could take staying on Fogo and watching Henrik build a life with someone else.

Gary was heading to the local inn, and Jo went for a walk. She had a lot to process. Things that she'd never thought she would have to think about when she first decided to come here, because she'd been so certain that she'd never feel that way again about someone.

Yet here she was.

She was terrified of losing her heart to Henrik when his most likely belonged to another. Her whole point of being alone these last three years was so she would never have to feel that pain of loss again.

Now, she was setting herself up for that by falling for someone who'd made it clear he didn't want a relationship with her.

Someone who had a real chance to make it work with their first love. Was she really the kind of person to stand in the way of that?

No.

She wasn't. Even if part of her wanted to.

She made her way down to the shoreline. Maybe walking by the water would give her some clarity. When she needed to clear her head she often went down to the beaches in Toronto and walked along the shore of Lake Ontario.

But at the waterfront she saw Henrik.

He was standing with his hands in his pockets, staring out over the water.

"Hey," she said, softly. "I was wondering where you went when Gary showed up."

He turned, and a shiver ran down her spine. His expression was clouded. The walls surrounding him were up again. Just like they had been when he'd come to her place after the storm. His face softened slightly when he saw her.

"Hey, yourself. Is Gary gone now?" he asked.

"Yes. He's going to the inn. He's only here for a few days."

Relief washed over his face, and his body relaxed. "Oh, I thought he was coming back early to stay."

Jo worried her bottom lip. "He is."

"What?" Henrik exclaimed.

"He's coming back in a month. Things didn't work out in Munich. So he was super apologetic but thanked me for covering his practice."

"He can't just come back," Henrik snapped.

"Yes, he can, and he is. He owns the practice."

"Didn't you sign a contract?" he asked.

"No."

"No?" Henrik growled.

"No, because he's a friend of mine. Why are you so concerned about that?"

"I guess I'm just surprised at your irresponsibility coming all this way with no contract."

Jo crossed her arms. "I was already on a sabbatical from the hospital in Toronto. I don't actually need to work while I'm on it. Taking this position without a contract didn't hurt me in any way. I have a home, a life that's waiting for me back in Ontario."

Henrik's expression hardened. "Oh, aye, I'm sure you do."

"I do."

"So you're just going to leave?" he asked.

"Gary's coming back. Why wouldn't I go? It was never my intention to stay." She regretted the words the instant they came out of her mouth, but it was the truth. Still, the look on his face was like she had slapped him.

"I see," he said, quietly.

"My time on Fogo Island was always temporary," she said, trying to soften the truth, trying to convince herself that leaving was the right thing, even though it didn't feel like it.

"I was hoping you'd change your mind."

"Why?" she asked, hoping her voice didn't crack. Hoping he'd say he cared for her, he wanted her.

"You're carrying my child. I would like to be in its life."

"And you can't be in it if I'm in Toronto? Is that it?" she asked, trying to swallow the lump of emotion that was forming in her throat.

Henrik said nothing at first. "It's not fair."

"No. It isn't, but life isn't fair. I'm very well aware of that," she said.

"So you were just always planning to leave, then?"

"Yes. My time here was limited. I told you this."

It was the whole truth. Fogo was never permanent. No matter how much she was falling for the place. Falling for the people and the way of life.

Falling for Henrik.

"What do you have left in Toronto? What do you have in Ontario that you don't have here?"

"My home, my job…"

"Your husband's dead," he said bluntly.

That hurt.

It really stung.

She was keenly aware that David was gone and had been for some time. The house in Toronto was empty. His side of the bed was cold. He was never coming back.

"I don't understand your point," she said.

"He's not coming back. Why are you waiting for a ghost?"

"Why are you?" she asked, hotly. "Why can't you leave Fogo?"

His eyes narrowed. "I'm not waiting for anyone. Fogo is my home."

"Then, why can't you come to Ontario?"

"Fogo is my home," he repeated again, stiffly.

"What's holding you here?" she asked, turning it around on him.

"My whole life!" he replied.

"But my life…my home means nothing? I'm supposed

to give it all up? For what, Henrik? What am I giving it up for?"

He didn't answer.

She knew then that this was futile. He didn't say she was supposed to give it all up for him. He'd made it clear in the words he didn't say that he didn't want her in that way.

"I can't leave. I have to stay."

"Now who's waiting for ghosts who are never coming back? Your parents aren't coming back, are they?"

She knew his reluctance wasn't about Melissa. It was his fear about leaving. Deep down he was still that frightened boy waiting for endless, hopeless days on the beach for his parents to come home. After all this time, he was still grieving. He was still holding on to that trauma.

Aren't you holding on to yours too?

"I think we're done talking," he said, brusquely. "I have to go to St. John's."

"Why?" she asked.

"My job. The coast guard needs me. It's what I can do to help my home."

"You didn't mention this to me before. It feels like you're running away from this conversation, Henrik."

"What is there left to talk about?" he asked, loudly. "You're leaving, and I'm staying, and our baby will be schlepped between us until you decide that you don't want to do that anymore, and I'll be cut out of their life."

"I would never do that to you," she said, quietly.

He didn't seem to believe her. His face was like stone. "You say that now."

"Why do I have to be the only one to change, Henrik?"

"I never wanted to be a father like this. You didn't ask me."

"You think this is how I wanted things? We used protection. It failed. And don't pretend I'm the only one at fault here. You admitted to just being with women you thought were passing through, because you're so afraid of falling in love and having someone leave you again. Well, it takes two to tango, my friend. This is not how I wanted to be a mother either. I wanted a child with my late husband. Not some stranger in a bar!"

The tears came freely, and she was shaking. She hated saying that and instantly wanted to take it back, but she was just so angry that he was trying to lay all the blame on her.

"And that's it. The root of the problem. We are strangers." Henrik walked away then, leaving her there angry, hurt.

She watched him climb into his truck and drive away.

Stop him.

Only she couldn't move. She was so afraid. She had laid it out, asked him to give her a reason to stay, and he couldn't. When she'd come here, she hadn't wanted her heart broken again, but here she was, with her heart in pieces for the second time.

She did love him.

It terrified her how quickly she'd fallen in love with a man she barely knew.

Henrik didn't love her, though.

Not the way she loved him.

You didn't tell him you loved him either.

She was kicking herself for not telling him. It was clear to her that his reluctance to leave here had nothing to do with his ex being back and everything to do with fear, and there was nothing she could do about that until he came to that realization himself.

You could stay.

Jo wiped away the tears and made her way back to her place. Or rather, Gary's place. People were starting to wake up, ready to begin their day. There was laughter and happiness. The storm was over, and Nubbin's Harbor had weathered it. It made her love this place even more. They were tough and resilient Canadians.

Could she stay?

If she was honest, her life in Toronto was hollow and empty.

Here, her baby would have access to their father and the support of a tight-knit community.

She took a deep breath. She could call Fogo home, because this place, the people, Henrik made her feel alive again.

There was nothing left for her in Toronto. She saw that now.

Henrik might not want her, but Fogo did, and that's what she wanted again.

A place to call home.

A week later

He'd been a right arse.

As soon as the ferry docked in Farewell and he drove off, he realized what an idiot he was. If he didn't have work and a duty to the coast guard, he would've turned around and got on the next ferry back home.

Only, he was bound by duty and also realized he'd left his phone at home.

He had none of his numbers and no time to call Lloyd to track down Jo. Although, he really didn't want Lloyd knowing what an idiot he'd been.

He was positive that he'd messed everything up and she wouldn't answer even if he did manage to phone her. He knew the only way to make amends was to do it face-to-face.

So for the entire week he fretted.

Jo had been right.

All these years he wouldn't leave Fogo because he was waiting for people to return who never would. He was the one who was clinging to the ghosts of the past, not Jo.

Melissa had come back, but she wasn't the same, and he didn't even care that she was there.

What he cared about was Jo. From the first moment he'd seen her, he'd been drawn to her. Every moment with her since had felt like coming home. He was blind not to see it, to be scared to reach out for what he wanted.

To be home.

It wasn't a place. It was her. She was his home.

But he was pretty sure he'd blown his chance with her when he'd left her on that beach. When he called the clinic before he got back onto the ferry, he got the voice mail, over and over again. He was worried that she'd already left.

It didn't matter. He'd go to Toronto to find her. He couldn't let her go. He didn't want her to leave without knowing how he really felt.

He had to win her back.

No matter what it took. And he'd live wherever, just to be with her. He couldn't let Jo go.

Once he got back to Fogo he went straight to the clinic, and his heart sank when he saw a notice to say it was closed until Gary returned.

There was a sign directing people to the hospital in Joe Batt's Arm and a message that Gary would be taking over the practice again.

His heart hit the soles of his feet, and his mind raced, formulating a way to get to Toronto as fast as he possibly could.

"She's gone, my b'y," Lloyd said, walking by.

"I know."

"Dr. Linwood is coming back."

"Yes, so I've heard," Henrik said mechanically.

"I never did congratulate you on your baby with Dr. York. What a lucky twillick you'll have there, being knit by two such intelligent, well-suited people," Lloyd offered.

"Thanks," Henrik said numbly.

But Lloyd was right. He was incredibly lucky that Jo was his child's mother, and he wanted them to be a family, no matter where that was.

"I've got to run, Lloyd. I'll talk to you later," Henrik said.

Henrik needed to get to the hospital and take a vacation from his paramedic duties. He headed straight there and made his way through the ambulance bay to talk to his chief.

He glanced into the quiet emergency room and did a double take when he recognized a familiar figure going through the charts at the nurses' station.

"Jo?" he asked.

She looked up, but didn't smile the way she usually did when she looked at him. The twinkle in her eyes was gone.

And he knew it was because of him.

"Henrik! You're back."

"I am… What're you doing here?" he asked, taking a step closer to her.

"Working," she said crisply.

"I can see that, but the clinic…"

Jo crossed her arms. "What's up, Henrik?"

"I thought you'd be back in Toronto."

"I'm flying out tomorrow."

His stomach heaved.

Well, what did you expect?

"Jo…"

"Don't try to convince me to stay, because I know you don't want me—"

"I want you, Jo, and to prove it, I'll go to Toronto with you."

Her eyes widened. "I was going to say—but you cut me off—that I'm staying because this feels like home, and if you want to be with Melissa, that's okay. You love her. I get it."

"I don't love her, Jo. I love you."

* * *

Jo wasn't sure that she was hearing Henrik right, at first.

"Pardon?" she asked, finally finding her voice.

"I said, I love you." Henrik took another step closer. "And if you're going to Toronto, then so am I, if you'll have me. I want to marry you, Jo. Doesn't matter where we live. As long as we're together."

"I told you…we don't have to marry because of the baby."

"I don't want to marry you because of the baby. I want to marry you because I love you, Jo."

A lump formed in her throat. "I don't understand. A week ago you refused to leave… I put myself out there, and you didn't want me."

"I was a fool, and I was scared. Scared of losing you, and in that fear I almost pushed you away."

"You didn't push me away," she whispered.

"I didn't?" he asked.

"No, I love you too." Tears stung her eyes, and Henrik took her hands in his. "But I wasn't going to keep you from Melissa or your life here."

"The only way that you'll keep me from my life is to leave it."

Jo brushed away the tears. "I love you too. I didn't think I would ever fall in love again, but… I did. And I'm scared."

Henrik smiled and pulled her in his arms, holding her. "Me too. I've never, ever contemplated leaving home before."

"Leaving?" Josephine asked, confused.

"Toronto. Gary is coming back so…" He cocked an eyebrow. "You said you were flying out to Toronto tomorrow."

"I am. I need to sell my home. I have some logistical things to work out to make my move here permanent."

"You don't need to give up your life there," Henrik said tenderly. "I told you I'd go with you."

Jo smiled. "I know, but I already told you, this place is my home. It's where I came alive again. But I have to sell my house in Toronto so I can buy one here."

"And your practice?" Henrik asked.

"I work here now. Dr. Cranbook offered me a job when he learned Gary was returning, and I took it."

"Really?" he asked, stunned.

"Yes."

Henrik cupped her face and kissed her, making her melt. "You don't need to buy a place. Your place is with me. If you'll have me, that is."

Jo's heart felt full. Fuller than it had in years.

"Yes. I'd like that very much."

Henrik kissed her again and held her close. "I love you so much, Jo. I knew you were trouble when I spied you at the bar."

"I love you too." Jo kissed him back. "I didn't think that I would ever love again. I was wrong."

"So was I." Henrik kissed her gently, one more time. "Welcome home, Jo."

And she was home.

For the first time in years, they both were finally home.

EPILOGUE

One year later

JO WAS EXHAUSTED after her first twenty-four-hour shift since she'd returned to work after maternity leave. Not that it had been an overly eventful night, but she had learned how much she valued her sleep since having her daughter, Willa.

Willa was easy during the day and difficult at night.

She thought she'd be fine, having worked in one of the busiest emergency rooms in Toronto for many years, but there was nothing more exhausting than the earsplitting scream of a colicky baby.

Not that she would trade it for anything in the world.

Jo stifled a yawn and headed outside. Henrik was waiting for her, with a cup of coffee and a baby asleep in her car seat. One thing that always settled Willa was a nice, long car ride.

Jo gladly took the coffee from her husband.

Something she'd never thought she would ever have again. A husband. Someone to love and who loved her.

She'd come to Fogo for a change and she'd got one.

"This is great," she said, appreciatively.

"What? No *I missed you*? No throwing yourself in my arms?" Henrik teased.

Jo leaned over and kissed him. "Sorry. I did miss you."

"Good."

She peered in at the sleeping dark-haired blue-eyed little cherub she was blessed with. She was so much like her father. Henrik referred to Willa being saucy like her, and yet Jo didn't see it. She only saw Henrik's stubbornness.

"She was pretty good," Henrik said as they leaned against the side of the truck to enjoy their moment of silence and the beautiful May morning. An iceberg was meandering by out on the calm water.

"Iceberg season is beginning again," Jo said.

"Bit late this year," Henrik remarked. "It's been busy with tourists already, though. Let's just hope no storms or burr holes or…what else happened last season?"

Jo grinned. "Don't jinx yourself. Remember I'm superstitious."

Henrik chuckled softly. "Of course. How could I forget?"

Jo smiled. "Thanks for picking me up and bringing me coffee."

Henrik kissed her nose. "You know our anniversary is coming up."

"I know."

"Well, tomorrow the first part of your present is coming." She was intrigued. "Oh?"

"Your mother."

She choked. "That's hardly romantic, but nice."

Henrik laughed. "Well, someone needs to watch Willa for the week."

"The week?" Jo asked curiously.

"We didn't go on a honeymoon, remember?"

"I can't leave on a vacation too far away from her," Jo argued. "She's still too young."

"I know. I talked to Dr. Cranbook. You're off for the week, and we're headed to L'Anse aux Meadows and the tacky, heart-shaped honeymoon suite for a couple of nights, and then a glamping experience in Gros Morne before we come back home."

Jo's heart raced. "Are you serious?"

Henrik nodded. "I am. I know it's not the most exciting trip—"

"It's perfect."

"Good. The last time we were there we couldn't do much, and this time I plan to make full use of that bed and Jacuzzi."

"Ooh, I like the sound of that." She set down her coffee cup and slipped her arms around Henrik's neck. "Have I told you lately that I love you?"

He grinned. "Yes, but I could do with hearing it again."

Josephine kissed him. "Well, I'll gladly accept your anniversary gift. What should I get you in return?"

Henrik cocked an eyebrow. "I can think of a few things. I'm patient. I'll wait until we leave for our trip."

"Why wait? Willa is asleep, and we have that great big bed at home."

"Saucy," Henrik teased. "Well, get in so we can get home."

Jo got in the truck. Willa was still sound asleep, and she couldn't believe how lucky she was. How glad she was that she'd taken the risk and come here.

"Yes. Let's go home," she said, softly.

As she looked at her daughter and at her loving husband, she realized she really didn't need to go anywhere else.

Where they were, she'd always be home.

* * * * *